MOLT

MOLT

a novel

by

R. Tim Morris

EMPIRE STAMP

Empire Stamp trade paperback edition: April 2019
ISBN 978-1-7750598-6-8 [eBook]
ISBN 978-1-9990728-0-3 [Paperback]
ISBN 978-1-7750598-7-5 [Hardcover]

In Memory of Cody

*"All your life, you were only waiting
for this moment to arise."*

—Paul McCartney, Blackbird

I Blame Mrs. Wyatt

HE TOLD ME I'd be safe in here.

He told me this was the one place in the city I could be if I wanted to stay the way I was.

This was my only hope for a last chance.

He called it my last chance at death.

Whatever it was I thought he meant at the time, I'm sure I'd seen it the other way around. But as the air slowly diminishes and the darkness seems to turn back to light, I'm beginning to rethink my original point of view.

I feel around me again just to make sure there's no crease of a door I've missed. Or an overlooked latch. A loose floorboard to crawl under and make my escape. Maybe even an emergency axe or a doorknob.

But still I find nothing.

There's a chill in the air that feels colder with every frightened breath. My left arm is killing me. There's a pain in my lower back I didn't feel before. I want to check for a bruise, but I know it wouldn't matter even if I could see anything.

This can't be where I'm going to die.

I haven't lived all this life of mine only to have it come to a sudden, shadowy end.

Life? That's a funny word for it, now that I think about it. An odd choice, since I feel as though I've barely even lived yet.

My memory skips back to the time when the old fortune teller told me I would die one day. That wrinkly French woman had asked me if I'd like to know the details; if I'd like to know how my end would come. Who wouldn't? So, like any curious and anxious teenager would say in the same situation, I was stupid and I told her yes. I said, "Yes, tell me everything." And the old woman proceeded to explain how I would die somewhere up higher than I'd ever think was possible. Higher than any mountain I'd ever know. So high I may as well have been in Heaven. I would be able to see the clouds below me.

Really.

There were no crystal balls, tarot decks, tealeaves, or lifelines. I was instructed to stand on the obituary section of the "Ville Constance Weekend Edition" beneath the blue-and-gold track lighting as the gypsy ran her thin, shriveled finger along a crack in the wall of her small apartment. I thought it was all a bit strange, but my best friend in high school, Cindey Fellowes, had recommended her to me. As I stood there, shaky and sweating and contemplating my ultimate demise, the fortune teller told me not to worry about it because, more than anything else, my death would be something important.

"Aren't they all important?" I asked, as one of her twenty-seven cats started to claw at my leg warmers.

She just winked and held out her wrinkled hand. I gave her a ten and didn't think much at all about that entire experience until now.

Now it's sixteen years later and I'm trapped inside this airless deathtrap. Part of me is thankful I'm not high up in the mountains right now, while another part is wondering what possessed me to ever wear those leg warmers.

 I slump back down to the floor. I can't hear a thing outside of these heavy walls. I can only hear what's inside: my heartbeat trying to give up on me.

But I won't let it. Not when there's still a chance.

I've seen this vault before, but from the outside, so I know there's a door here somewhere. The trouble is, I have no idea which direction I'm facing, and I'm certain the complete lack of light will make it far easier for me to find myself going bonkers in here long before I ever find a way out. I don't even know how long I've been inside this thing; I've been conscious for what seems like twenty minutes, but it could just as easily be an hour or more. As I worry about how much time I might have left, I'm still finding myself a bit envious of how much space is in this vault. Considering the size of my one-bedroom apartment, that is.

"Forty-five hundred cubic feet would allow for about five-and-a-half hours of air," is what he told me when I had first inquired about this metal box. But did he mean five-and-a-half hours for the *both* of us, or just one? I hate myself for even worrying about details I don't understand. I find myself hoping an end might come sooner, rather than later.

How will I know when the end is coming? I guess my ability to form coherent thoughts will be a good basis. The less of this perverse tale I can recollect, the closer I'll be to not having to worry about it anymore.

I stop myself for a second and wonder, is this a good thing?

The last I can remember, I was trying to prevent a disaster. The details of which are still a little unclear to me, but I know for sure this wasn't some "spill the grape juice on Mom's new sofa" kind of disaster. This was an "end of the world as we know it and I don't feel particularly great about it" kind of disaster. Those ones don't usually go over too well with anybody, and I'm positive this would be no different.

I feel the cold metal floor once again with the sweaty palm of my hand. It's hard to explain, but some strange appreciation for this floor comes over me. Like something that's been taken for granted?

The sharp pain in my back stings as I take a seat on the hard surface. But it's too much to take, so I stand up again. I stretch my back and pace the room, trying not to walk face-first into any unseen walls.

So, what exactly has happened out there since I've been unconscious? One of two things I imagine. Either, A) nothing. Or, B) I'm the last person in this godforsaken city who can still appreciate cold metal floors. What I mean by that is fairly easy to comprehend if your mind can shut off its ability to use any sort of reasonable logic. My mind was finally starting to, and that's why I'm in here now. Of course, at the time it didn't seem as though I would be getting in quite as deep as I've gotten, but that's how trouble usually comes about: when it's the last thing you're expecting.

If I hadn't believed his lies.

I reach my arm out to get a sense of where the wall is, and that's when I feel it: the slight crease of a well-sealed door. I wonder how I had ever missed it before as I run my fingernail along the indentation. The nail breaks off, yet I barely even notice because of how much pain I'm already in. I use another finger only to break another nail. I stretch up as high as I can, but I can't feel where the top of the door might be. Almost entirely beyond my reach is some kind of control panel, perhaps an emergency lock. It's too high to feel any buttons, if there are any. Frustrated, I bang on the wall with my fist, and I try my best to curse the man responsible for all of this. That no-good twit.

As aggravated as I am about this whole rotten situation, that someone so awful could ever do something so unbelievably selfish and immoral, I'm more annoyed by the fact I just referred to him as a "twit." He would often laugh at me whenever I attempted to insult someone, claiming my choice of words were always "charmingly derogative." Well, I can't help the fact I was raised properly. He even asked me one time to make my last words the most appalling words I could think of at the moment, and to scream these profanities as loud as I could the instant before I died.

"I'll try to remember that when it happens," was what I told him. It's a good thing I thought of that just now, since I might get my big break before long.

If I hadn't been so lonely.

I jump up a few times and stab at the panel with my hand, but I can't feel anything within my reach.

I've been told a number of times throughout my life that I'm a really bad jumper. A bad jumper? How can anyone be a bad jumper? Mrs. Wyatt, my high school gym teacher, was all too happy to inform me I was the worst jumper she'd ever seen. I was the only girl to ever be rejected from the basketball team. I wasn't even cut; I was flat-out rejected. She insisted I wasn't too short, but that I simply couldn't jump.

"I guess my feet don't like leaving the ground very much," is what I told her.

It's strange how many times an excuse as ambiguous as that can occur in one lifetime; I think I said it again just a few days ago.

I use up what feels like the remainder of my strength to bang on the door, generating barely even an echo. But I can't tell if it's simply because my hearing is off; if this ringing in my head is making the whole world seem smaller than it is. What the stink is going on out there?

My left arm is really hurting now. I think I might have done some serious damage.

I crash back to the floor, this time lying on my side. I want to blame someone other than myself for being stuck where I am now. So, I blame Mrs. Wyatt. This is what I always do; it's kind of my thing. I link chains of events in my life to one another in order to find exactly where the critical point lies. Let me explain: I wouldn't be here now if I hadn't been hit by that car. I wouldn't have been hit by that car if I hadn't come back to Boston. I wouldn't have returned to Boston if I hadn't ever slept with one of my students. I wouldn't have met this particular student if I wasn't teaching at the university. I wouldn't hold my position at Hawthorne University if I hadn't been involved with Professor Nickwelter. I never would have met Nickwelter if I hadn't been accepted to Hawthorne. I wouldn't have been at Hawthorne if I hadn't joined the high school science club. I wouldn't have joined the science club if I had never met Cindey Fellowes. And I doubt I would have ever met Cindey Fellowes if Mrs. Wyatt had just let me join the basketball team in the first place.

And that's how I can blame Mrs. Wyatt for my being here right now.

With one ear to the floor, I listen carefully for any signs of life.

Nothing.

There isn't anything I want more right now than to get out of this deathtrap. But even if I *could* snap my fingers and appear on the other side of the door, I don't know if I'd actually want to see what's out there. What *is* out there, I wonder?

Maybe nothing.

Maybe everything.

Am I willing to take that chance? Am I willing to face him again? The only alternative here is starting to sound reasonable: death over life. It's a much harder decision to make when you're actually given the ability to make it.

But did I already make the choice?

Or am I still waiting for one final opportunity?

Litter of Angels

MY NAME IS Isabelle Donhelle. I prefer to go by "Bella," but the truth is I've always hated any version of it. I know what you're thinking though: *"Why doesn't she just change her name?"* Well, that's just what the issue here is, isn't it?

Change, that is. It's always been a problem for me.

My parents adore my name and pretty much everything else about me. They've always been proud of me, and I was almost proud of myself too until about a week ago. It's funny how self-esteem can take a nosedive so quickly when given the right opportunities. And even though things have gone about as downhill as they can, I'll bet my parents would still be proud of me right now. From the outside, most people would probably call it unconditional love. From where I've been standing most of my life, I'd just call them nuts. The kind of nuts you want to avoid like an allergic reaction.

If my parents had been telling this story, instead of me, they'd probably be proud of it too.

~~~

The Donhelles live in the small town of Ville Constance. That's in northern Quebec. Canada, if you're still unsure. Ville Constance's origins are believed to have been tied to Saint Constantina, but all indications point to its literal meaning — "Constant City" — as being a far more accurate interpretation of its history. Because nothing ever seemed to change much in Ville Constance.

My father worked at the local paper mill, along with most of the other fathers in town. He worked hard and tirelessly to put food on our table. Mom
~~~

didn't work; she cleaned the house and cooked all day. *Every* day. I'm willing to bet our house was the cleanest in all of Quebec, maybe even in all of Canada. There was always the aroma of food in our home, but the smell of warm pastries, soups, and meatloaf was vastly overpowered by the smell of cleaning products. When Mom took another pie out of the oven, no one could tell if it was apple, blueberry, lemon, rose, or pine.

She was never diagnosed, but my mother was an obvious OCD. One of the most traumatic events I can remember from my childhood was the day I placed my glass of orange juice on the coffee table without setting the cork coaster down first. She totally freaked out. To this day, I cannot bring myself to put anything on any table of any sort for fear of something ruining the finish. I don't remember losing my first tooth, or getting my first *A* in school, but I certainly remember The Great Coaster Incident.

They might sound a touch cliché, but those were my parents. The stern, burly father who works assiduously in the factory sixty hours a week, and comes home to find his pipe, slippers, and daily sports page waiting for him beside his favorite chair. The happy little homemaker who makes her kid tuna fish sandwiches for school lunches, takes all the drapes down three times a month for a thorough cleaning, and is never seen in the kitchen without her trademark pink apron on. The one with the word "MOM" stitched right on the front. I certainly didn't notice any of their faults when I was a kid; I loved them no matter what. And I still love them today, but those annoying habits and eccentricities which went unnoticed when I was twelve have flared up to near-horrific proportions. We're talking Mothra-like magnitude.

It's as though I could stick my hand into a hat filled with quirks, foibles, and idiosyncrasies, and Mom and Dad could match any one I drew. Here we go: Dad, you get *incessant throat-clearing, involuntary use of the speaking voice while reading,* and *complete unawareness of anyone within twenty feet of you during a hockey game.* And Mom, you get *washing the floors at three AM, spying on the neighbors at night from the second floor with the lights off,* and *the ability to refer to anybody as "Sweetheart."* Anybody at all. The paperboy. Her gynecologist. Even the Prime Minister when she met him once. And here, you two can fight over *unnatural flatulence.* Enjoy.

As far as brothers and sisters went, I could never keep track. You see, there was a small orphanage just down the street from us, and they were constantly running out of space for the children. I don't know what it was about Northern Quebec and kids without parents, but there must have been some kind of connection there. So, the orphanage struck a deal with my parents, and Mom and Dad took one or two of the kids off their hands for days or weeks at a time. And just so the children didn't get the feeling they had it better than any of the others, the orphanage took them back in, and gave us another one. This exchange happened every week or so. I imagine it couldn't have been too good for the well-being of the kids, but they seemed to like coming to the Donhelle home, even if it was only for a day or two. And nobody else asked any questions or ever showed much concern over the entire situation. In the time that I lived at home, I must have seen three hundred different children sleeping in the spare room next to mine. Three hundred different siblings sitting across from me at the dinner table. Three hundred different brothers and sisters stinking up the bathroom in the morning before I left for school.

For a while I thought that maybe I was just another orphan myself, the one kid the orphanage *didn't* want back. I presumed that my parents kept up the whole "child intern" cover in order to make me feel special. Of course, whenever I thought of this scenario, it only ever made me feel worse about myself. Was I really an only child, or was I just one more from the litter of angels?

If I hadn't been an only child.

I managed to form some close bonds with a small number of the kids we looked after. And I did what I could to find families for them. I put up posters on telephone poles and at school on the wanted board. I made flyers that I delivered to random houses, apartment buildings, and local businesses, hoping someone out there would consider something they might not have otherwise thought about. Yeah, I was a sweet kid, wasn't I? I even included hand-drawn pictures and biographies of some of my favorites to help ensure they might be chosen. However, some of them unintentionally started to sound like ads for used cars:

Annie. A radiant little six-year old who loves pancakes and soda crackers. She'll warm your home and melt your heart. Just passed her check-up.

Daniel. Nine years of age. Sporty. Enjoys bedtime stories and baseball. Speaks with fluent Sir's and Maam's. Claustrophobic. Has a small scar on his forehead, but no serious damage.

Looking for a new owner: Monique. Dark-skin with green eyes. Eight years old, and still runs like new. Very quiet, clean, reliable. Pigtails are optional.

Daniel and Annie had subsequently been snatched up by brand-new loving parents, but poor Monique was still there when I left home for university. Honestly, I don't know which kids were happier though: the ones who eventually left the orphanage or the ones who stayed there. And I don't know which ones I was happier for.

The one kid in particular I can still remember quite clearly is Antonia: the chubby little girl who had nowhere else in the world she'd rather be than at the Donhelle house. She was actually taken in by my parents dozens of times, which was unusual since I only saw any of my siblings two or three times in my life.

I'll never forget this one time when Antonia had come upstairs to unload her bag in the spare bedroom. She was crying, which was the usual routine with her. There was always some kind of problem with Antonia. But this time was different. There'd been a change.

If Antonia had been telling this story, she'd only have cried about it.

I asked her, "What's wrong now Antonia?"

"Ostrich," she said to me.

"Pardon?"

"They call me Ostrich at the orphanage." She sat on the bed and wiped the tears from her mouth so she could speak without slurring. "Everyone gets a nickname they said, so I'm Ostrich."

I sat down next to her. We'd had these kinds of talks before. The last time she cried was because Tommy Hamil told her that food had gone missing from the orphanage. My brother Tommy accused my sister Antonia of stealing the food and hiding it in her pillowcase for a late-night snack.

"Ostrich isn't so bad," I told her.

"Michel Bourdon said the ostrich is the fattest of all birds. That's why it can't fly. Just like me."

Michel Bourdon? He was here just last week, sleeping in this very bed, I remember thinking to myself. A line of drool dripped from the crease of her mouth onto the bed sheet. My mental countdown had started; I knew Mom would have the sheets changed and put into the wash in less than ten minutes. "Have you ever seen Michel Bourdon fly, Antonia?" I asked her.

"No." She looked up at me, wide-eyed, as if just realizing something important. Antonia had a habit of always believing every line anyone said to her. So, I fed her another one.

"What's *his* nickname?" I asked.

A bubble of saliva popped from her lips. "Pipes."

Seriously? *Pipes*? Was this an orphanage or the mafia? "Well, you just tell Michel that a pipe can't do anything but sit and rust, okay?" That probably wasn't the best line I could've fed her, but it was quite likely she'd just forget it anyway. "Okay, Antonia?"

"Yeah, okay," she said, her eyes lighting up with delight. Running to leave the room, Antonia turned back to me in order to double check her facts. "Pipes can't fly either, right?"

"I've never seen one fly," I told her.

She giggled a little to herself, and dashed out into the hallway and down the stairs. It took me a few minutes before I could pull myself off that bed. I wondered how many lies Antonia must have had to believe to get through just one day at that orphanage. And how many lies I would have to tell her just to keep her there. To keep her as far away as possible from the world outside; a world I knew she wouldn't ever be able to handle on her own. To keep her inside the safest nest I could find. There couldn't possibly be a better place for her than that.

Antonia would never be willing to change. I knew that. As much as I would have liked her to, I realized then the truth is some people are willing to change, and some people aren't. It's as simple as that. I never told Antonia how I really felt, because I knew deep down she really just wanted to belong. And what kind of big sister would I have been if I had ever denied her of those dreams?

The Strangest Feeling

THURSDAY, OCTOBER SECOND. I'm riding the bus, which is a terrible place to begin a story, but I suppose it's as good a place as any other I can think of.

Boston, Massachusetts. One month ago. It's my twenty-ninth birthday, and I'm sitting on the cold, orange plastic seat of bus #3031, probably the oldest bus the MBTA owns. This thing seems to be running on time that's already run out. Every bump in the road causes every part of it to shake violently. Some things shake when I'm certain they shouldn't. I can feel parts of myself shaking which shouldn't be. The floor seems to move independently from the rest of the bus, which definitely has to be a safety hazard.

On the seat next to me is an old, ragged newspaper. The date is smudged, but it appears to read November 2, 1982. That can't be right, can it? One of the banner ads above me has a picture of a Spine-Tailed Swift (*Hirundapus caudacutus*) on it, the second-fastest bird in the world. I think it's an advertisement for an ink-jet printer, but I'm really not sure.

Professor Nickwelter and a few more of the teaching staff at Hawthorne University decided to throw an intimate birthday dinner for me tonight, and after calling it an evening, I decided to treat myself to this spectacular bus ride. Happy birthday, me.

There's something about turning twenty-nine that seems to instantly make you feel older than thirty. I can't explain it, but I can certainly feel it tonight.

I remember when I was a little girl, growing up in Ville Constance and dreaming of this day. Well, let me make it clear: not this day as it's *turned out* to be, but this day as I *thought* it would be. An imaginary life: the perfect husband, fresh flowers beside my bed, and a walk-in closet bursting with wide-brimmed sun hats. My personal opinion is, until girls turn sixteen they shouldn't have even the slightest concept of marriage explained to them. It's a dangerous idea to have in your head when you're an eight-year-old girl. Like carrying around a loaded gun, not that I would have any idea what to do with it. So many dreams are forged at that age; dreams which seem realistically attainable, it's hard to face the inevitable and disappointing reality of it all.

I do own one wide-brimmed sun hat though, but it's been folded up, and living inside an unmarked box for a decade now.

So now I'm twenty-nine years old. I'm allergic to flowers and about as close to being married as I was twenty-one years ago. Actually, it seems as though I might have been closer back then, because that's when I still had some hope.

Thinking about all of this, I start to zone out. My thoughts are somewhere else entirely, but my eyes are focused squarely on a metal pole before me. I'm paying specific attention to a tiny screw in the center, attaching the pole to the seat in front of me. One of those screws with the X-shaped hole in the middle. I know buried somewhere deep within that empty black cross lies the answers to whatever it is I'm asking myself. I'm looking, but not seeing. The mind and the eyes are so closely related, it's impossible to imagine just how far apart mine must be at this moment. Like they're two Snow Buntings (*Plectrophenax nivalis*) on opposing mountain peaks. Or like the American Rhea (*Rhea americana*) and the African Ostrich (*Struthio camelus*), who so obviously share a common ancestor, but haven't had contact with one another since before the continents divided. The entire world is flying by me right outside that yellowed bus window at a steady pace of fifteen miles per hour. But I remain completely unaware of it.

I know in my bones it all comes down to my being single. Yes, there's been a couple of turbulent, distasteful, and wildly forgettable relationships along the way, but mostly, I'd say I feel like I'm speeding inevitably toward the sad, spinster, cat lady life. Only replace the cats with birds.

I need to turn my own personal bus around, because I know for a fact I do not want the spinster bird-lady life. I've seen it, and it looks really sad.

In my peripheral, my reflection in the window seems to independently nod a confirmation at me.

I almost seem to be getting somewhere when my senses come crashing back together. A hand grips the pole in front of me; a little dirty, but a perfectly flawless hand nonetheless. It covers up the screw and seemingly all of the answers buried within it, and it's enough to bring me back down to Earth.

There's a man here; he seemed to appear out of nowhere. He steals a couple of short glances my way, but I try to avoid eye contact. Dark brown eyes will forever my weakness. Instead, I adjust my thoughts back to the dinner party I'm escaping from.

Okay. Concentrate. It's Thursday night. I was just downtown at Café d'Averno with the four of them: there was Professor Nickwelter, former head of the Ornithology Department, now my assistant at Hawthorne University; Professor James, head of genetics; Professor Claus, our zoology expert; and Jerry Humphries, who runs the school's bird sanctuary and laboratories. I don't know whose idea it was to invite Humphries, as no one seems to be able to stand the despicable man. Especially myself.

We would have an unscheduled long weekend due to a small fire this morning in the university's south laboratory. A blown fuse box I was told, but more likely it was a student horsing around. Quite a dangerous place for a fire, but I was told no serious damage was inflicted. And so, in order to make sure the rest of the school was safe, we were given Friday off.

Café d'Averno, as far as I know, is named after a famous lake in Southern Italy: Lake Avernus. The ancient Romans considered the lake to be a gateway to Hell, and that its volcanic fumes which filled the air were deadly enough to kill any bird that flew in its vicinity. The word for Hell, *Averno*, literally means "a place without birds." And maybe I'm just biased, but I personally believe this to be a correct statement.

At the center of Averno's, there is a fountain surrounded by eight Muscovy Ducks (*Cairina moschata*) meticulously carved into the marble base. The French crossbred Muscovy ducks and mallards for cooking to obtain Barbary ducks, which have a milder taste. A popular belief is that Muscovy ducks had gotten their name from the musky odor of their flesh.

Yes, I'm a bird nerd.

There's something about birds that I find extraordinarily soothing. Whenever I'm feeling uncomfortable, or if I simply need to calm myself down, I have a habit of looking around for birds wherever I am. They're everywhere, whether real or not. You'd be surprised if you really focused on it. Anyway, the duck carvings on the fountain were just enough to put me at ease again. That is, until I turned back to the dinner party. Or more specifically, toward Professor Nickwelter.

Nickwelter and I had a history together of which everyone here knew about, and it only served to make the meal even more uncomfortable. For me, at least. But everyone at Hawthorne has always done their best to try not to bring up any off-handed mention of our shaky past. It's been two years since our relationship — let me put that in quotations: "relationship" — ended, and I'm still awkward about the entire situation.

If I hadn't slept with Professor Nickwelter.

After hors d'oeuvres, we ordered dinner. Nickwelter, James, and Humphries all had the roasted duck, which is remarkable, for three grown men who have made the studying and caring for birds into their chosen career. Professor Claus (who is affectionately known as "Mrs. Claus" by the faculty and students at Hawthorne) had the tofu spinach burger with cabbage. I ordered the spaghetti and meatballs, and was met with cheers from my surrounding company. They had actually made a bet earlier as to what I would order; three of them said spaghetti. Humphries guessed pork chops. Pork chops? I've always hated pork chops, not that he would know that. I'm almost certain pork chops weren't even on the menu, but apparently, he had his reasons. The pretentious twit. Although, now that I think about it, I hadn't noticed whether or not I've ever eaten such an exorbitant amount of spaghetti, with meatballs or otherwise, that people would take such active notice either.

I tried to change the subject, to talk about something other than myself. But once dinner was served, the conversation had quickly been forced back toward myself, and it was definitely the figurative arrow I did not want pointing my way. It went something like this:

PROFESSOR NICKWELTER: "You look magnificent tonight Isabelle. Is that a new wristwatch? Whatever happened to the last one?"

PROFESSOR JAMES: "I hope you don't consider yourself old for being on the brink of thirty. You're still a spring chicken, Donhelle! By the way, do you know the origins of the term 'spring chicken?' Remind me to tell you later. It really is quite an amusing anecdote."

MRS. CLAUS: "Isabelle, why don't you come by my place after dinner for some non-fat organic birthday cake? I have a family recipe that's to die for."

JERRY HUMPHRIES: "You need a ride home tonight, Bella?"

And my answer was the same for all of them:
ME: "I think the spaghetti was bad. Excuse me while I go use the ladies' room."

We hadn't been at the restaurant any longer than an hour, and I had already made two trips to the ladies' room. It seemed to be the only the place I could go to get some air. Engraved in many of the tiles on the bathroom wall were images of Sandhill Cranes (*Grus canadensis*) standing one-legged in pools of water. When roosting, cranes will tuck one leg up under their feathers to keep it warm while standing on the other. In the Middle Ages, it was believed that a sentry crane held a stone within his hidden foot, and would drop it if he fell asleep or if his attention was diverted, thereby waking his companions. In heraldry, a crane is often shown holding a stone, as a reminder of alertness.

If only I had been paying attention that night.

To make this exhaustively boring story just a bit shorter, I decided to simply leave Café d'Averno early. I honestly don't know if spaghetti has the capability of going bad, but they let me go on my own without too much of a struggle, even though I had gotten a lift to the restaurant with Mrs. Claus. Humphries still had the ride home offer on the table, and I still declined. That smug little weasel. For some reason, the idea of riding public transit seemed to appeal to me much more tonight than it ever has before in my life.

If I hadn't decided to take the bus home.

Had all the talk of me being another year older, another year closer to thirty, been getting to me? Maybe a little bit. The truth is, I've never dealt with change very well. I am from Ville Constance, after all. The Constant City.

But do I avoid change because I'm really just itching to turn it around? Do I keep my life stagnant because I'm aching to do something completely unexpected? Was I staring so intensely into the void of the screw in front of me because I'm really just afraid to be a part of the changing world around me? Is the world changing without me?

I turn back to this man on the bus, his eyes still flickering my way. He does sort of remind me of someone; I can't place it though. Like a lost piece from my youth? As much as I can in this seat, I turn myself away from him. In my head, I count down from ten before looking back up…

…Three…Two…One…Zero.

And he's still here. He smiles at me. It's not a so bad of a smile really, it's just not the kind of thing that happens to me often enough to not make me feel a tiny bit uncomfortable.

I almost say something, but I don't. I think of my mother instead. My mother always told me to never talk to strangers, but when exactly comes the point in one's life that Mom's advice can be disregarded? When can I make my own decisions without having to hear the echo of her voice nattering away inside my head?

He blinks, in what seems like slow motion, before turning away from me.

Still, I use this moment to separate myself from this stranger: I pull the bus dinger as if it was a parachute's ripcord and I'm perilously close to hitting the ground. The driver slows to a stop and I exit out the back of the bus, jumping off into the darkness of the city. I turn back to make sure the man — whoever he is, and whatever his intentions might be — didn't follow me.

He didn't.

Bus #3031 speeds off to where, just one minute ago, I thought I was going.

Taking a look around me, I discover a part of Boston I don't recognize. It's dirty. It's smelly. It's making me uncomfortable. Maybe I should have thought about this a bit more before extricating myself from the bus. But I think *not* knowing where I am is exactly where I want to be. Directly behind me, nestled in between two of the vilest triple-X establishments I've ever seen, is The Strangest Feeling, a little diner with yellow, smoke-stained windows. Beneath the alternating green lights flashing from one pornography shop to the orange lights flashing from the other, The Strangest Feeling seems strangely welcoming. Strangely comforting. And strangely, just what I need right now. If for no other reason than it should give me some time to myself right now.

So I go in.

If I hadn't walked inside The Strangest Feeling.

Inside, it appears to be one of those retro eateries that make you feel as though you're sitting right in the middle of the 1940's. I sit up at the front counter on a stool with a worn, plastic cushion, even worse than the seat on the bus.

I slowly take in everything behind the counter; malt vinegar bottles, pancake syrup, plastic bears filled with honey, jars and boxes stuffed with dozens of different types of tea bags, and an old-fashioned pop bottle with a faded image of Marilyn Monroe on it.

The night waitress enters from the kitchen. She grabs the menu, wedged between the sugar dispenser and the ketchup bottle, and she tosses it in front of me. Before I can even open the oversized laminated menu, she speaks up.

"What'll it be, sweetheart?" she asks, instantly reminding me of my mother. She smacks her bubble gum as though she really doesn't care what my answer will be.

I'm almost too overwhelmed by the sight of this girl to give an immediate response. Her nametag says "Kitty" for one thing, and her lips are this sort of neon green color. The kind of color that should strictly be reserved for tacky electric signs on steak houses. Or maybe they were just reflecting the flashing green of the porno shop signage outside. Feeling pressured to make some kind of decision, I simply ask, "What's your special?"

"Tonight's special is pea soup with our homemade cheese bread." She smacks her lips a couple more times before finishing her response. "I highly recommend it."

I'm not exactly full from my earlier meal at Averno's. I mean, since my dinner guests kept bombarding me with ridiculous questions, I didn't get a chance to eat my meal while it was still hot. It really wasn't fair; four mouths shooting off questions and only one mouth left to answer them. They all took turns talking and eating, while I was too polite to speak with my mouth full, so I opted to not even try.

"How bad could it be then?" I ask, mostly to myself.

Kitty answers anyway. "No worse than tomorrow's special, I suppose," she says with a smirk. "Is that all then?"

Behind the counter I spot a varied selection of tiny cereal boxes, three ceramic dancing Hawaiian hula girls with ukuleles, and a large coffee maker with five pots of coffee brewing. I don't know if it's because there are five full pots of coffee and I'm the only customer in here, but I think about having some. To tell the truth, I've never had a cup of coffee in my life before. Honest. I think it's partly because my father once told me caffeine was a drug, and I'd be good to stay away from drugs. I take a moment to consider how much of a lame-O I must be, and then I ask Kitty for a cup of coffee.

"You sure about that?" she asks, as if seeing right through me.

"Maybe just a tea then," I say, taking it back. But I stop Kitty before she can walk away. "No. Sorry," I say, the words stumbling out of my mouth. "I think I *will* have that cup of coffee." It's subtle, but I know she's rolling her eyes at me a little.

If I hadn't asked for that one cup of coffee.

"Thanks," I confirm.

"You got it." She writes my order down in her head, and saunters back into the kitchen. I slide the menu back into its resting place and consider just how bad tomorrow's special might be. I also wonder when neon green lipstick was ever in style.

I take notice of the large Jones Cola machine, a breadbox which may or may not contain bread, a coffee bean grinder, and an old-fashioned metal fan with a wire grate covering the blade. An unplugged cord is loosely tied around the base. Above the order window to the kitchen are about a dozen black and white photographs, which appear to be both employees and patrons of The Strangest Feeling. On one of the walls, there is a poorly painted mural of a sunrise; the colors are cracked and bubbled, showing years of neglect. On the ceiling are matching painted clouds.

But in this entire diner, I can't seem to find a single image of a bird anywhere. It makes me feel a little uneasy; as though I'm way too far out of my element.

It really is the strangest feeling.

An early October Boston chill creeps inside the diner.

Kitty comes back out and pours some coffee from one of the pots into a generous-sized ceramic mug, then places the mug and a spoon onto a tiny plate in front of me. The spoon has a design on the end of it which I can't quite make out. I imagine if I held it at just the right angle under the diner's dim lights, it might be charitable enough to resemble an African Penguin (*Spheniscus demersus*). Maybe I'm trying too hard to look for a comforting sign, but maybe the unknown is better right now. Maybe I need to feel out of my element tonight.

If I hadn't been out of my element.

Kitty tosses some plastic cups of cream onto the table, smacking her gum all the while. I can smell that pink, sugary stuff with every bite she takes. If smell can be described as pink, this is definitely it.

Can I play make-believe in this caffeine-induced society? Can I pretend to belong here? Tearing the lids off of two cups of cream — tearing? Actually, it's more like picking away at the slippery paper seal until I can get a grip on it with my teeth, then pulling it off slowly enough so as not to spill the contents all over myself — I pour it in with a dash of sugar. That's right, a dash. It sounds like the correct amount. I think from a stranger's perspective, I must appear pretty experienced for someone who's never had a cup of coffee in her life.

I take a sip.

And it's really not very good. I pour in what must be the equivalent of three or four packs of sugar into my cup.

Another tentative sip.

It's tolerable now. Who knows, maybe it'll grow on me by the end of the night?

Five minutes later, I'm hoping the pea soup and cheese bread might grow on me as well. I'm also hoping there really *are* peas in here somewhere, because I can't tell for sure. At least the bread is decent enough, though I can't seem to decipher the crust from the actual bread. There are a few reasons running through my head as to why this diner is called The Strangest Feeling. Still, I feel more content here all by myself than I did at Café d'Averno earlier tonight with my incessant co-workers. And I certainly feel safer than I did on the bus.

That is, until ringing bells indicate the door to The Strangest Feeling has swung open. A lone man enters, and he sits right beside me at the counter, even though there are plenty of other empty seats in here.

"What can I get you, sugar?" Kitty asks him, smacking her bubble gum between those crayon-colored lips.

I catch his reflection in the mirrored mini fridge behind the counter. It's the same guy from the bus; the one I specifically came in here to avoid. How the fudge did he follow me in here so quickly? I'm certain he didn't exit the bus when I did. Just a coincidence, I suppose?

I can see his reflection motion toward mine as he replies to the waitress, "I'll have what she's having."

"And a coffee?" she asks.

In the reflection, I see him glance down into my coffee cup to check its contents. "Yep."

Kitty walks off, and I continue to stare at him from the mini fridge. The surface of the fridge is a little warped, and his reflection is sort of crooked; like what I'm seeing isn't real. Like I'm making him up. Then his eyes turn to mine in the glass. Those same dark brown eyes from the bus; there's something odd and enigmatic about them. "You recommend the pea soup and cheese bread?" he calmly asks my mirror image.

I'm feeling something crawl under my skin; like a grub or worm in the dirt and I'm not hungry but I need to dig it out with my beak. Common sense tells me I don't need to answer him, but I'm feeling a bit irrational. "Not really," I say to him. "I just wanted to try something new tonight."

If I hadn't answered him.

Our reflections don't break away from each other, and I get a much better look at his features now: those beautiful brown eyes beneath a thick, messy head of hair; a strong jaw and that overly confident smile breaking through cracked lips; his skin has a certain hardness to it — well-tanned, but with just the faintest trace of dirt or soot on his face. Probably from the same source as the grime on his knuckles I captured earlier.

"You get that feeling often?" he asks, reaching into his coat to scratch his armpit. "That you want to try something new?"

"To tell the truth, I get that feeling all the time," I say. "But tonight's the first time I've ever acted on it."

He peers into the kitchen now, as though he's already growing impatient for his meal. With his elbows, he pushes himself up to take a better look. He's not paying attention to me, but still asks, "Is that a French accent?"

"Uh—yeah." I say. "French-*Canadian*."

With a quick motion, he reaches over the counter and grabs a spoon from behind the bar. I don't know why he does it, but he sits right down again and turns back to face my reflection. "What's that?" he asks, as if just realizing I had answered him.

"I said I'm French-Canadian."

"Is there such a thing?"

I can't tell if he's joking or not. He's not blinking. He simply stares through the mini-fridge, and into my eyes like he's waiting for me to go on. I wonder if my reflection is as contorted as his own. He rattles the spoon between his teeth.

Before I can utter another word, Kitty makes her timely return. She sets down an empty cup, pours some coffee for him and then refills mine. She's still smacking her gum as she tosses some more plastic cups of cream onto the countertop.

I dump in some more cream and sugar, pick up my spoon, and stir the coffee around. He does the same. Our metal spoons clinking with the rims of our ceramic cups in perfect harmony. He places his spoon back down, just as I do.

Upon closer inspection, I notice the t-shirt he's wearing underneath his buttoned-up weathered coat has an image ironed on the front. It appears to be the feathery cap of a Brown-Headed Nuthatch (*Sitta pusilla*). At least, that's what it looks like from this angle. It's enough to make me smile a little, whether I mean to or not.

He holds out his hand. "My name's Templeton Rate."

I don't move an inch. Templeton Rate, I think. Sounds made up to me.

"I know it sounds made up, but that's really my name," he says, as if taking the words right out of my head. Actually, the words were still in my head, so I guess it's more like he got in, made a Xerox copy of my words, and then got back out again before saying it. Well, whatever. You get the idea.

This man is not wholly auspicious, but I do think, at the very least, I am finding the slightest bit of comfort from the head of the nuthatch peeking out from Templeton Rate's coat.

He tells me, "You know, I used to be afraid of trying new things. All the time. It was crippling, really. But it's not such a terrible thing, once you start making an effort. You get used to it."

It was at that precise moment I made the mistake; the one mistake that led this story to end it the way it does. I could've gotten up right then and there, but instead, I stayed.

If I hadn't had that first cup of coffee; if I hadn't entered The Strangest Feeling; if I hadn't gotten on that bus; if I hadn't lied to my co-workers about the spaghetti; if I hadn't been cut from the Doneau High basketball team.

That's right Mrs. Wyatt; this is all your fault.

Templeton repeats his last comment, since it probably seems as though I didn't hear him. "You get used to it," he says. His hand is still held out, waiting for me.

"I don't know," I finally squeak out. "The bread's a little stale. And the soup is mostly water."

That's what I chose to say to him. Stale bread and watery soup. I just couldn't leave well enough alone.

And whatever it was he was telling me, I just believed him.

If I hadn't believed a word he said.

His hand is still held out in front of me, so I lift mine into his. It's the warmest hand I think I've ever felt. "Isabelle," I say to him. "Isabelle Donhelle."

He pauses for a moment, thinking about this. "You know, that name sounds more made up than mine."

"Well, I'm telling you the truth," I say defensively.

"Really?"

"Why wouldn't I be?"

If I hadn't told him the truth.

He stares back into my eyes. It feels like he knows I'm lying, even though I know I'm not. "That's funny..." he starts, as he raises the coffee cup to his mouth. He takes a loud slurp. It's almost loud enough that one would assume he's doing it intentionally, or for whatever reasons men seem to do anything. But it's just loud enough that I can tell he simply has no manners. Basically, he's a pig. Still, it seems as though he's at least trying his best to be a gentleman.

He swallows the coffee, but before he can finish what it was he had started to say, he squirms uncontrollably in his seat, as though he just had a sip of vinegar instead. He turns back to me accusingly, "Damn," he says. "I put way too much sugar in this coffee."

I laugh at him a little. "Me too. Though I've never had a cup of coffee before now, so I didn't know any better."

"Not once?"

"Not once. I guess I'm really spreading my wings today, aren't I?"

"Of course you are." He places his cup back down in front of him, though he continues to feel the handle with his fingers. Not wanting to let go. "But just be careful when spreading your wings that you have a safe place to land."

I look down to the floor, but I can't tell if I'm looking for a safe place, or if I'm looking for the right thing to say instead.

It doesn't matter though, as the moment is ruined anyway. Templeton's hand tips his coffee cup over. Steaming, sugary coffee spills onto the countertop and drips down onto the checkerboard-tiled floor. Immediately, I reach for some napkins and attempt to soak up some of the mess. I can't tell for certain if this was intentional or not, since he doesn't seem the least bit surprised or embarrassed. The waitress runs over to help clean it up. I tell her "Sorry," since Templeton clearly isn't going to. In fact, he doesn't even acknowledge her. She says it's all right and asks Templeton if he wants a refill, but he continues to ignore her, keeping his attention focused entirely on me.

"So, are you new in town? I haven't seen you around Boston before, Isabelle Donhelle."

I try my best to forget about the coffee too. "It's a big city, Templeton Rate."

"Hey, I'm from Schenectady. I know big cities. This is nothing."

Schenectady? I don't know whether to laugh or just agree with him. He sure seems serious. A few years back, I took part in a bird count in Schenectady, New York, and that town had, like, thirty people in it. Maybe I'm just thinking of another Schenectady? Also, did he really just use the "*Are you new in town*" line?

"Well," I say. "The truth is, I really don't get out all that much."

The waitress comes back with Templeton's soup, bread, and a fresh cup of coffee.

"So, tell me something," he says to me, and then waits for a response. Although I'm not quite sure what it is he might be looking for.

"Pardon?" I ask.

He reaches for the salt and pepper, and shakes some into the hot soup as he clarifies. "I want to know something about you that I couldn't have pieced together just by sitting here at this counter for the last ten minutes. Like what do you do for a living? Have you ever mixed your whites with your colors? When I say French impressionist, do you think painter or comedian? Have you ever seen the sun set from underwater?"

"Can one *see* a sunset from underwater?"

"I don't know. I'm just asking."

"I can answer the first one for you."

"Go ahead."

"I'm a teacher. Well, university professor, actually."

"And the rest?"

"I either have no idea what you're talking about, or it's simply none of your business."

He takes a package of saltine crackers, crushes it inside his palm, and sprinkles the contents into his soup. "Well, teaching is a good start," he says, satisfied for now with the amount of information I've awarded him with. "I'm a student. But I also work part-time as a doorman."

"I see. What is it you're studying, exactly?"

He takes some more packages of saltines from the counter, and crushes them in his hand too. "I guess that depends on what it is you're *teaching*." Is this flirting? Is that what's going on here? He smiles an already-patented Templeton Rate Smile.

"It does, does it? I don't think you'd ever find your way into *my* class Templeton. You kind of need to know something first."

Pouring more cracker dust into his soup, he tries his best to impress me. "I know the human heart creates enough pressure to shoot blood thirty feet. I know the circumference of our planet would never be exactly the same, no matter how many times you measure it. I know why it is that vertical stripes look better on fat people than they do on skinny people. What makes you think I don't have what it takes?" There's a mountain of crumbled crackers on his soup now.

"Maybe you just seem like the type of guy who copies the answers from the person next to you."

"I don't copy answers. There's no need to copy anything when there aren't any right answers in the first place."

"For nothing at all? What about your vertical stripe paradox?"

"Listen to me, Isabella. The number of things in this world we *don't* know so greatly outnumbers the things we *do*, that I don't think any 'answer' can ever be one-hundred percent correct. Does that make any sense?"

"If you've been paying attention, my name's *Isabelle*. Not Isabella."

He ignores me completely, and takes a big bite out of the bread. "There's a difference between having the right answer and knowing the truth." *The Templeton Rate Guide to Etiquette* obviously doesn't say anything about talking with a mouth full of food.

"That's profound. I don't know how you could ever top that." I don't mean to sound like I'm challenging him, but that's how it comes out.

He forces the bread down his throat without much gratification. "Fuck. This cheese bread really is terrible. I've got to take a shit." I don't know how or where exactly this conversation went from mild flirtation to whatever it is that's happening here, but something's definitely shifted in this man. Templeton gets up to use the bathroom, but turns back to me before exiting. "I want to buy you another cup of coffee though. What do you say?"

"I honestly don't think so," I tell him bluntly.

He leans in closer to me, closer than what I'm comfortable with. I can see a tiny piece of bread still lodged between two of his front teeth. "I know you," he says, inching toward me a little more. The smell of cheese and coffee coating his breath. "I can tell you're wanting to break out. You're itching to do something completely unexpected, aren't you? You want to become someone you've never had the chance to be before. And you want me to help you get there, don't you?" Even closer now. There's a disregarded nose hair that's grown longer than the rest, and I can see it fanning back and forth with his every breath. "What do you say, Isabella?" His faults are just obvious enough that I can tell he's the most realistic person I've ever met. And there's the familiar little brown-headed nuthatch poking its head out from under Templeton's coat.

"It's *Isabelle*," is what I say, correcting him once again.

He doesn't respond with anything more than turning around and walking toward the washrooms. As he exits, I replay the whole encounter in my mind. What does Templeton Rate want from me? It's very likely even he doesn't know what it is.

Though maybe not.

Maybe.

Then a sensation comes over me, a feeling I'd been trying to place since I'd first seen Templeton on the bus. Like he was reminding me of someone I'd known only momentarily so long ago. But I just can't place it.

"I know you," he said.

It's enough to give me pause, but my senses soon come back to me.

I'm quick to finish off my meal, hoping I can be done and gone before Templeton returns, and I discover the bread and soup are really not so bad now. Why is that? Why is it that when you start to focus on something else, when you sense a particular feeling in your heart, all of your other senses take a temporary vacation?

The steam from our coffee has vanished. It's cold, but I swallow the rest of mine with determination. Beside me, the soggy mess of cracker crumbs sink ever-deeper into Templeton's untouched soup.

I pay up with Kitty — she tosses two complementary pieces of pink gum my way — and exit The Strangest Feeling without having to see Templeton Rate ever again.

Two Months of Kissing Claude

I WAS IN grade ten when I first met Claude. He had transferred to Doneau High in Ville Constance from a smaller high school in a smaller town even farther north. Cindey Fellowes told me this new kid was eyeing me up in the hall as we came out of biology class one morning. I saw him too, but pretended not to notice. It seemed so much easier to simply appear interested in classes rather than boys, but fourteen-year-old urges have to give way sooner or later.

Claude was a natural beauty. Hidden under long, disheveled, dirty brown hair and thick eyebrows were dark brown eyes that seemed to never look any farther than my own. In fact, I don't recall ever seeing him blink; his attention was unyielding. He strode through the halls of Doneau High every day in the same fur-trimmed brown coat with an assured confidence which never seemed to waver. Even when he'd bump his shoulder into the wall as we sneaked glances at one another.

Our insecure peeking soon became timid smiling, which then turned into the odd "Hi" and "Hey there" greetings. It seemed a strange coincidence, but each morning when I came to school through those big red double doors, I would see Claude. We would say hello and then proceed with our daily schedules, sometimes without seeing one another for the rest of the day. Those mornings alone quickly became the only reason I went to class each day.

~~~

So, I figured it out. It came to me in a dream the very same night I got home from my first visit to The Strangest Feeling. The conversation with Templeton
~~~

Rate was still playing in my head. In my dream, I was leaving the diner just as I really had only hours before, but instead of walking out onto the sidewalk, I was entering the halls of Doneau High.

They were both waiting for me at my locker: Templeton and Claude. And I knew immediately they were the same. I was so aware, it hit me so hard, I woke from my dream. They were the same exactly. Certainly not the same person in reality, but identical in my dream.

Coincidences like that just don't happen in the real world.

But the lucidity of the dream did get me wondering. And for three straight nights now, I've imagined the yellowed glass doors of The Strangest Feeling were actually the big red wooden doors of Doneau High, and that Templeton would be waiting outside for me just as Claude once did.

Why would I need him to, though? I think I just wanted to talk to him again. To make sure.

His words still ring in my head: *"I know you,"* he muttered.

Maybe there is some doubt, or else I wouldn't be here. Maybe I've gone too long without someone who could challenge a change within me. But like all dreams, this one has now been interrupted by some egregious reality.

It's now Sunday, October 5. I'm sitting in the exact same seat I was in last night. And the night before. And the night before that: the night I met Templeton Rate.

If I hadn't returned to The Strangest Feeling.

On Friday night, I stuck my face to the cigarette-stained window, hoping to find him in the diner, waiting to buy me that cup of coffee he promised. He wasn't there, but I went in anyway. I ordered a coffee, and waited for him to follow me in again. I didn't really have a plan for what I might say to him, but it doesn't seem at this point like it's going to matter much.

Three days and thirteen cups of coffee later, I've realized Templeton Rate probably isn't going to show. I've also realized I have a caffeine addiction.

Seriously, what made me think some rude, insincere guy with filthy hands and a penchant for ambiguity would plan to show up looking for me? What made me feel as though I even wanted to see this peculiar individual again? I guess the longer I dwelled upon it, the more I started wondering what it was I had been waiting twenty-nine years for.

Kitty's not working tonight, but that's fine by me because I'm not here to see Kitty. Although I must admit, I do miss her cheery smile a little.

"I don't think he's going to show, honey," I hear from behind the counter. Her name tag says 'Sylvie,' and she pours me another cup of coffee. Which brings my running total to fourteen now.

"Excuse me?" I mumble.

"You're waiting for some guy, aren't you?" she asks, with her thick Boston accent. "Kitty told me there'd be a pretty young blonde in here tonight who'd be waiting for some guy who wasn't going to show. I'm assuming she meant you."

I barely spoke two sentences to Kitty the previous three nights, but I guess she knew what was really going on. I'm sure she could sense my desperation. Maybe Sylvie can too. "Is it *that* obvious?" I ask. "Am *I* that obvious?"

Sylvie is a heavy-set woman, probably in her late forties, and looks as though she's been here most of her life. There's something about overweight people that makes me want to place my trust in them. She puts the coffee back on the machine behind her, and then leans in toward me, her giant breasts getting some much-needed support. She has a sparkling hairpin that catches my eye as it pokes out of from under her hairnet; it has what appears to be a Painted Stork (*Mycteria leucocephala*) design on the end of it.

"You French?" she asks, picking up on the fading accent of mine, just as Templeton had.

"French-Canadian actually."

"What the hell are you doing waiting for some loser out here then? You're a pretty girl. You can definitely do better than this, can't you?"

"I'm not sure if I can." I'm not sure if I have the strength to try and do better than this. Simply being here now seemed like a giant step forward for me. The questions crashing around inside my head and the just-now-resurfacing memories of the boyfriend from my youth could have something to do with it too. "I just needed a change, I think."

"Listen to me, honey. All I'm saying is that I don't want to see you sitting here in the same seat thirty years from now, waiting for the same guy that's never going to show."

"I appreciate that," I tell her, even though I really don't.

~~~

I came to school late one Wednesday. My twelve-year-old sister Madeleine, that pernickety princess, was holed up in the bathroom all morning. Thankfully, she was on her way back to the orphanage that day. Although, I think she presumed she was off to some fantasy world where the other kids actually cared about what she looked like. I could smell the hairspray through the door. I knew I was going to be late, but I still didn't want to miss seeing Claude that morning.

I banged abrasively on the door. "I need my bathroom, Madeleine!"

"It's still my bathroom too, bitch," she growled back at me in her usual pleasant demeanor. She had the charming trait of referring to me as "bitch" in just about any situation, claiming it was actually a term of endearment. I knew better than this of course, but I've never been very good at telling someone they're wrong.
~~~

Late as I was, my mother had the nerve to inform me that she simply must get some of her gardening done. Something about new bulbs that needed to be planted, and according to her gardening bible, it was recommended they be planted midweek before nine AM for the best results. Because of this vital agricultural predicament, I had to walk Madeleine back to the orphanage that morning on my way to school. I tried to explain how important it was that I didn't miss my first period gym class, but Mom told me she'd write me a note. Of course, a note for Mrs. Wyatt certainly wouldn't make up for any missed chance encounter with Claude. This boy had a hold over me that I couldn't resist. Even at fourteen, I wondered if it was healthy to need someone this way.

I put my mother's note into my pocket, and headed out the door with Madeleine. It started raining after only a block or so, but I had no intention of going back to get an umbrella and being even more late than I already was. We had never really talked to one another in the short time that I'd known her, but Madeleine nonchalantly asked me questions as though we were the best of friends.

"Do you have a boyfriend?"

I told her no.

"Have you ever kissed a boy before?"

Again, I told her no. And unfortunately, it was the embarrassing truth.

The rain was really starting to come down, but it couldn't put a stop to Madeleine's relentless, one-sided conversation. "I have a boyfriend at the orphanage," she said. "His name's Leo, and we're going to get married."

Leo? My brother Leo? Is it okay for my non-literal sister to marry my non-literal brother? I felt really sorry for Leo at that moment.

I wanted to ask her if Leo even knew about this pre-arranged matrimony, but decided not to. Instead, I asked her, "But what if Leo gets adopted Madeleine? What if the two of you never see each other again?"

"It doesn't matter, because we're in love. Maybe we'll leave the orphanage together one day, and go to some deserted island to spend the rest of our lives. That's how love works."

My sympathy for everyone but Madeleine seemed to change right then and there. I looked at this twelve-year-old girl all soaking wet from the morning's sudden storm, and I started to feel incredibly sad for her. I realized then that Madeleine and all those poor kids at the orphanage didn't know the first thing about how love really worked. I certainly wasn't the expert on boyfriends and kissing, but I knew I had the love of my family, and that would never change. My siblings had next to nothing at that moment in their lives that would still be there in fifteen years. They had to keep those make-believe stories going in their heads just to get through the day. It didn't seem fair to me. Not for Antonia the Ostrich. Not for Leo. Not even for Madeleine.

If Madeleine had been telling this story, she would have dreamed up a much different, much more positive ending.

We arrived at the orphanage, and I walked Madeleine to the front door where Mr. Martin was waiting for her. He said, "Hello," and I waved back politely.

I remember placing a wet hand on Madeleine's shoulder, and I said, "Obviously I don't know anything at all about how love actually works. I don't know if I ever will. But I think that might be the point."

Both Madeleine and Mr. Martin looked at me with some concern.

"I mean, what's the harm in dreaming about how you want things to turn out, right?"

Madeleine hesitated before walking to the door. She turned her body back to me, without making eye contact. "Well, thanks for the talk." It was the first time she'd ever thanked me for anything, not that I had done much to deserve such gratitude. She didn't call me "Bitch" though, so there's that, at least. Then she ran in through the front door to rejoin the litter of angels inside.

That was the last time I ever saw Madeleine. Some family from New Brunswick adopted her the following week, and I doubt she ever saw Leo again either.

~~~

First period gym was almost over by the time I neared the school. I was completely soaked from the rain, which had since passed, but I hoped to at least catch a glimpse of Claude in the halls between classes. Yet, as I approached the big red doors of Doneau High, impossible as it seemed, I saw him. He was at the flagpole, smoking a cigarette and looking a little misplaced. I walked up to him with a courage I never knew I had, trying to dry myself off as best I could. When he saw me coming he dropped his cigarette and instinctively extinguished it under his boot, even though the puddle beneath him had already done the job.

"Hey," he said to me.

"What are you doing out here?" I asked. Instantly, it had occurred to me that this was the first non-greeting I'd ever spoken to him.

"Waiting for you," he said timidly, avoiding direct eye contact. He leaned up against the flagpole. "You're late. Have you got a note from your mother?"

I smiled at him, and produced the folded paper from my pocket. He took it from me and briefly examined it before handing it back. "Your name's Bella, right?"

"Isabelle," I replied, but I didn't want Claude to think I was correcting him. "Or Bella. Sometimes people call me Bella."
~~~

"Listen Bella, these stupid days here just seem a lot easier to take when I see you every morning. I like it when you say hi to me. That's why I wait for you out here every day. I wait until I see you coming, and then I make it seem as though I'm just arriving too. I know it sounds stupid, but I was wondering if you'd like to meet me after school."

I couldn't believe this conversation was happening. My heart was fluttering so fast I thought it was going to burst. I couldn't wait to tell Cindey.

"So, what do you say?" he asked.

And all I could manage to respond with was, "You smoke?"

~~~

I pull my eyes out from inside the dried-up, empty coffee cup. "It's strange, you know?" I say to Sylvie.

"How's that?" she asks as she wipes the counter in front of me.

"He told me he wanted to buy me another cup of coffee. Then he went to the bathroom and I just got up and left."

Sylvie looks at me with some concern, and with some mental note-taking, the way any social worker might eye up their newest project. "What're you sayin'?"

"Was I right? I mean, is it okay for someone to simply ditch someone else without warning?"

"If the guy's a mega-creep, sure."

"I guess what I'm wondering is, why would I ever treat someone as though they didn't exist?"

"Maybe he didn't," she says ominously.

"Excuse me?"

"I mean, maybe he was a spirit. Like a ghost or an angel or something."
~~~

An angel? I remember when I was younger I heard one of my siblings praying through the wall in my bedroom. He was saying things to angels, but I didn't know what an angel was. The next morning, I asked my father.

"Angels are just like you and me and your mother," he told me. *"They're regular people who just want to help one another out."*

Was Templeton Rate even there at all, or was he just one more from the litter of angels?

"If you believe in those kinds of things, that is," Sylvie continues. She finishes wiping the countertop and goes back into the kitchen, leaving me alone to think about it.

If Sylvie had been telling this story, she'd probably have a refreshingly different perspective.

"I don't know," I say, shouting over the counter and into the kitchen. "He told me he worked part-time as a doorman. But if he was actually an angel, and not a hotel doorman, why would he come to see me?"

She comes back out with a fresh pot of coffee. "There must be a reason, honey. Damned if I knew all the secrets of the universe. But angels are supposed to help sort peoples' lives out, right? Has your life changed at all since then?"

I watch the coffee as it pours into my cup. The color is fantastic and the hot steam rises slowly between us. This brings my total to fifteen. "I'm drinking coffee now. Do you think it's possible an angel visited me in order to make me start drinking coffee?"

"We all need a vice, honey." Sylvie pours a cup for herself now too. She clinks her cup against my own, even though mine only sits on the tabletop, and takes a sip.

"I don't know what it is though. He was rude, intolerable, and self-centered, but I feel inexplicably drawn to him." I remember exactly how

Claude had once made me feel. "Like he has some strange, undefined hold over me."

"Wow," Sylvie seems to say with a little remorse. "I'd love to feel inexplicably drawn to somebody."

"It's not as magical as you might think," I tell her.

~~~

Claude and I met that same day after school. I waited for him at the yellow electrical box behind the gym, just as I promised I would. Of course, we really didn't know each other very well yet. Our two-minute conversation that morning was the only one we'd ever had up until that point, and thinking about it now, it feels like it was the last one we ever had too.

He came stumbling around the corner, not the least bit surprised that I was really there waiting for him. The nervousness that only two teenagers in just such a scenario can feel was shared between us, and we figured the best way to overcome it was by making out every day after school on that yellow electrical box. A part of me was disgusted by the cigarette taste of his mouth when we kissed, while another part of me just told myself to take what I could get. I still had no idea how all of this had really come to be anyway. It seemed impossible to me then how something like that could ever happen twice in one lifetime. What are the chances?

It was on a Monday, the fourth afternoon behind the gym, when Claude sat still for a moment after parking himself beside me. His hair was cut a little shorter that day. I wondered if his mother still went to the barber's with him to get his haircut, or if she did it for him herself. I waited for him to move closer, to kiss me, or to say something. Anything. But maybe he was just waiting for the same from me.
~~~

"I like your hair," I told him, but my words seemed to have little effect. He appeared very nervous, as if trying to find the strength to say whatever it was that was on his mind.

"I need to ask you a question, Bella," he said quietly.

"What is it?" I asked, knowing full well he must want to ask me to go steady with him. I wanted so badly for Claude to be my first boyfriend, and I was sure he felt the same about me being his girlfriend. He'd probably spent all weekend preparing himself for this moment. All he had to do was ask.

"I need to ask you a question," he reiterated nervously. "But not now." He moved in closer to give me a kiss, and I made no effort to hold back. I desperately wanted to hear him ask me what it was I surely had an answer for already, but instead I gave in to those beautiful, pouty lips of his.

"I guess he could always ask me tomorrow," I thought to myself, with his tongue in my mouth.

~~~

"So, what was it he wanted to ask you?" Cindey Fellowes prodded as we made our way through the hordes of students crowding the halls of Doneau High. This was about two weeks into my relationship with Claude, and he still had yet to ask me the question, which had come to be known officially as The Question between Cindey and I. "Maybe he had a math problem or something he wanted you to help him with," she suggested. "I mean, it's kinda weird that he would bring it up and never actually follow through with asking you, isn't it?"

It did seem a little weird. Claude and I were still making out behind the gym every day, so I guess I just assumed he felt we were already an item.
~~~

Forget such technicalities as actually having to ask me. My only problem with the whole arrangement was that we never did anything else. He had never taken me to a movie, or out for dinner like normal boyfriends did in normal relationships. I had never seen where he lived or met his parents, nor had I ever been offered a ride in his car. And he hadn't yet been absorbed into my life outside of grade ten either.

I made the mistake of telling my parents I met a nice boy at school named Claude, and that I really liked him. I was even dumb enough to tell them about The Question. Dad assumed he was dealing drugs and wanted to sell me something illegal, while Mom guessed that he wanted to sell me something religious. Both of them, of course, wanted to meet Claude as soon as possible. But that just wasn't conceivable since I couldn't seem to get him anywhere farther than the yellow electrical box behind the gymnasium.

"What do you kids do every day after school, sweetheart?" Mom would ask, trying not to sound as though she was really asking if I knew what STD's were.

"I don't know," I would tell her. "We just hang out. We study at the library sometimes, and other times we study in the cafeteria."

"That's a lot of studying," Dad would say ambiguously in his best, non-ambiguous tone. "I never did that much studying when I was your age."

I wanted to say "And look where it got *you*, Dad," but seeing as how my after-school activities could very possibly lead to eventually working at the paper mill myself, I decided silence was a much better alternative.

"Well, as long as you can keep those grades up, sweetheart, there shouldn't be a problem with you seeing this boy," Mom concluded reassuringly. Only to throw in the not-so-subtle "But we do want to meet him," hint.

My parents always tried to find some sneaky way to get the answers for all of their overbearing questions, but they weren't going to crack my secret code on this one. They may have found out where the missing mixing bowl went when I was seven, or what exactly had happened to the severed gardening hose, or that Cindey Fellowes and I were actually watching the Learning Channel's "History of Sex" unsupervised on her thirteenth birthday and not The Breakfast Club, but they weren't going to get anything from me this time.

So they went to him instead.

Two months of kissing Claude had culminated in my parents showing up completely unannounced after school, and at my locker of all places. They were even devious enough to come by on Valentine's Day, a day when I was sure to be seeing Claude after school. Dad had signed up on the graveyard shift at work that week in preparation for the day's big event.

How perfect.

I was at my locker, unsuspectingly showing Cindey Fellowes the hickey I got from Claude the day before, when her attention suddenly turned to someone behind me. I didn't even notice Cindey sneak away as I rolled up my turtleneck sweater and turned to see my parents standing there.

"Is that a rash you've got there?" Mom asked me. "Because I've got some ointment in my purse that would clear that right up."

I couldn't answer; I was too freaked out at the sight of my parents silhouetted by the Doneau High Valentine's Dance poster on the bulletin board behind them.

"Your father will go back to the car and get it, sweetheart. It's no problem." She moved in to try and get a closer look with her fingers, but I was too angry to let her. I smacked her hand away.

"What are you guys doing here? There's no parent/teacher conference today, is there?" I don't even know how they knew where my locker was.

"Your mother and I were in the neighborhood," Dad started. "And we thought we'd give you a ride home."

How utterly convenient.

I looked at my Degrassi High watch; I had to meet Claude in five minutes! "We practically live in the neighborhood," I tell him. "I can walk home, you know. It's not a problem. Not in the least conceivable way at all."

"We're not trying to make a problem sweetheart," she said. "We just—"

And that's when Claude made his unexpected and oh-so-untimely appearance. He tapped me on the shoulder, as though we had a big game to prepare for. "Five more minutes, Bella," was all he said before stopping to notice it wasn't teachers I was talking to. My mother, my father, and Claude all took a few long seconds to look each other over. Like the Common Kestrel's (*Falco tinnunculus*) piercing stare as it circles the vole before swooping down for the inevitable kill. No one wanted to make the first move.

"Mom. Dad. This is my friend, Claude," I said nervously, beating them all to the punch.

They did their best impression of a mature greeting.

"'Allo," said Dad.

"Hey," said Claude.

"Well hi there, sweetheart," said Mom predictably.

The silence continued for what felt like another minute, as uncomfortable glances and uneasy hand gestures were exchanged. From somewhere around the corner, I could hear a locker door close. It seemed like the only sound in the world right then: the creaking hinge, the metal latch connecting back into place, and the slow, reverberating footsteps walking away and fading into silence.

I thought I heard the sound of water dripping slowly from a tap in the girls' washroom: tiny droplets hitting the pool at the bottom of the sink one after the other, in a perfect rhythm of loneliness.

I blinked once or twice nervously, and I could actually hear my wet eyelids as they slapped together.

All of this until Claude bravely spoke up, "So five minutes, okay?" Then he left, walking away from us, yet still keeping an uncertain gaze on my parents for a moment before turning his head away too.

Dad tried his best to take something positive from this painfully impassive assembly. "He seems very—punctual. How are his grades?"

Mom, however, only had vague warnings to deliver: "That boy will break your heart if you're not careful, Isabelle. He's far too good-looking to take your relationship seriously." I could tell she was genuinely concerned because she referred to me as "Isabelle" and not her usual "sweetheart." Of course, I knew better though because I was in love. And isn't that how it's supposed to work?

That's certainly how Madeleine would have perceived it.

Sometimes I felt I wanted Claude for no other reason than for making out behind the gym. I also just liked the way the word "boyfriend" sounded. My parents left the whole thing alone from that point on, and we never spoke of Claude again.

~~~

And then, one day after school on the yellow electrical box, my relationship with Claude ended. We pulled our lips apart for a second, and he said, "It's my birthday today, you know?"

I had already made sure that we'd established when each other's birthdays were at the beginning of our relationship in proper teenage girlfriend fashion. "Yeah, I know," I said to him. I knew that day was his birthday, and I'd made
~~~

him a card the night before out of flimsy construction paper which had said in haiku:

> A birthday itself
> Is not so very special,
> Not special at all
>
> It can only be
> As special as you are then,
> As you are to me

I'm not entirely sure what the words I wrote meant, but it had the right number of syllables and I was proud of the effort I had put into it. I slipped the card into his locker first thing in the morning, before Claude even got to school. He didn't meet me outside at the flagpole anymore.

"So—?" he asked me, as if waiting for something more.

"So, what?" was all I could give him.

"So, what do you say?"

I thought about this for a moment. What do I say? I wasn't entirely sure what he wanted to hear from me. So, I gave it my best effort. "Um, good for you—?"

"No. That's not it."

"Way to go?"

Still nothing.

"What do you want me to say, Claude?"

"You're supposed to say *happy birthday*."

"I made you a card. I slipped it into your locker this morning. Didn't you get it?"

"Yeah, I got it. But it didn't say *happy birthday* on it."

"Well, happy birthday then."

"Thank you."

He leaned back into position to continue where we left off, but I wasn't going to leave it at that. He seemed so self-righteous listening to me say exactly what he had wanted to hear. "How old are you?" I asked him.

"Sixteen." he replied, followed by another attempt to make lip contact.

"No. I mean in terms of maturity. That's a pretty immature thing to say to me, Claude."

"I would say happy birthday to you on your birthday, Bella. I can't believe you'd be so selfish."

"Selfish?"

He got up, turned to me, and said it: "I don't think I want to see you anymore."

If Claude had been telling this story, he wouldn't have put much thought into it.

Then Claude walked away. He dumped me right then and there, behind the gym, and on his birthday no less. Maybe the worst thing about it all was the fact that I'd never learned what it was he was going to ask me. Not only had The Question remained unanswered, it had remained unasked.

~~~

"Claude was a foolish kid," I say to Sylvie, after telling her all about that embarrassing relationship. "But I've heard it said the jerks are harder to get over than the good ones." The bottom of my coffee is nothing more than a mound of sugar. "I'm still waiting for the other half of the equation to find out if that's true or not, but it certainly has taken me a long time to forget about him. As embarrassing as that sounds."

She looks at me the way my mother used to look at me right before saying something profound. "The ones that are easily forgotten are the ones that aren't worth remembering." I didn't notice until now, but Sylvie has already
~~~

locked the door and turned the outside lights off. The Strangest Feeling was closing up for the night. She gives the counter in front of me one final wipe, and motions to the empty cup still in my hands. "Did you want to pay for that now, honey, or should I put it on your tab for tomorrow?"

I give her a ten for a night's worth of coffee, and insist she keep the change. "Actually, I don't think I'll be showing up here tomorrow," I say, removing my coat from the stool beside me and slipping it on. I wrap my scarf around my neck, take my purse, and then I thank Sylvie for the company tonight before heading out the door.

"My name's Maria," Sylvie replies.

"What? But your nametag—?"

"Is still at home on my kitchen counter. I borrowed Sylvie's nametag. Besides, what does a name matter anyway when all I'm doing is standing behind a counter?"

I tell her she's probably right, and I unlock the door to let myself out.

Sylvie disappears back into the kitchen as I leave The Strangest Feeling with the feeling that I would be all right.

My Nest Away from Nest

MONDAY, OCTOBER SIXTH. Hawthorne University of Applied Sciences is located in Boston, Massachusetts. The school is just off of Huntington Avenue, on Parker Street. It was founded in 1932 by Nelson Hatch, who had also been an esteemed member of the National Audubon Society. The school has always had a strong connection to the Audubon Society (Anton Frye, the university's current Dean of the Faculty, is also an Audubon member) and the ornithology program is the only reason students even attend Hawthorne as it is widely regarded as one of the best in the world. Greater Boston has over thirty-five university campuses, and the likes of Harvard, UMass, and MIT leave Hawthorne and its bird program in some rather large educational shadows. But if you know birds, you've heard of Hawthorne University, and if you never studied there you wished you did.

It's Monday morning and I find myself getting back to my nauseatingly monotonous routine. Or is it monotonously nauseating? I won't bore you with the mundane details of the route delays on my way to work, but I still somehow managed to arrive earlier than usual. It seemed unusually usual: there was something so very not right with the way the morning felt, that it didn't seem to worry me in the least.

The radio this morning informs me the six swan boats from the lagoon in Boston's Public Garden were stolen last night. The famous boats had been moored to the dock waiting for the return of spring, but somehow someone managed to bird-nap all six of the giant fiberglass Mute Swans (*Cygnus olor*). It's one of the strangest crimes I've ever heard of, and there are no leads as of yet. Sometimes the reasons for why so many people do so many ridiculous and cruel things can really baffle me.

I pull into the university staff parking lot and turn the engine off. It's bitter cold, but my gloved hands are wrapped around the giant-sized cup of Brazilian Copacabana Beach Bourbon blend. I learned from the coffee menu board that the Copacabana Bourbon is "a nutty blend with subtle cocoa notes. A mild and pleasing complexity." Who knew how fascinatingly diverse a cup of coffee could be?

I remain in my car for a few more minutes in an attempt to mentally plan out my day. I do this sometimes; I try to decide how the day will unfold before it actually happens. I recall one time being pretty dead on, but that was a single positive note out of who knows how many miserable days I've had here.

Okay, fine. I'll admit it's maybe not as bad here as I make it out to be, but this is how you subconsciously see your world when there's a giant void that needs filling: you hope it might be filled as soon as possible, so that you can simply get on with your life. You imagine everything else just falling into place after that.

I look up from my seat, and I notice Professor Nickwelter's car directly in front of mine, facing me. I stare at the car for a minute, remembering a time when I was all too familiar with the sight of it: a black Honda of some sort with the same long, twisted crack in the windshield. If I was in the passenger's seat and I looked through the splintered window at just the right angle, I could see two cars in front of me when there should only have been one. Maybe two shining Hancock Towers instead of one. Perhaps two Willets (*Tringa semipalmata*) flying above the traffic in front of me. The long, stout bill and distinctive black and white underwing pattern easily identify a willet. Or I might have been lucky enough to see two setting suns, turning the Massachusetts skies into an amazing concoction of brilliant reds, oranges, and blues. The most beautiful of these colors would seem trapped right there between that crack. I always tried to keep my head in just the right position, so as to make the most out of my travels with the conversationally-challenged Professor Nickwelter.

I decide to get out of my car and take a closer look at his, telling myself this is purely for old time's sake. Sentimental stuff. I sling my bag over my shoulder, and with books and coffee in hand I walk closer to the scratch on the hood from when I tossed him the set of keys he'd forgotten from my apartment window. There must have been thirty or so keys on that one big metal ring, like he was some Medieval dungeon keeper. I never had a clue as to what they were all for.

There's the dented hubcap from when he tried to make a point about how reliable his Honda was. *"See, you can knock it as hard as you want and the car can take it,"* he said, giving it a good, hard kick. The hubcap flew right off, and we had to hammer out the indent from the toe of his shoe to fit it back on again. His designer shoe from Italy, of course. Much like his car, for some reason Professor Nickwelter never liked anything that was made in America. Which is why I think he was also attracted to me in the first place.

I peer in through the front passenger's window, my fingertips press gently upon the glass. I imagine sitting beside him again. Those seats were almost unbearable, not because of the make of the car, but because Nickwelter's wife sat in this car more often than I ever did. Beth Nickwelter has a much larger frame than I do, so this seat had conformed to her shape much better than mine. I was swimming in the seat of my boyfriend's wife.

It was on a class field trip a few years ago when Nickwelter first made his intentions clear. I was the student and he was the teacher. Myself and a few other students accompanied Professor Nickwelter to Cape Cod to take part in the Christmas Bird Count, an annual count of bird life taken primarily during the Christmas week. Groups of birders from the U.S. and Canada are assigned a day and an area fifteen miles in diameter, and they make a list of all wild birds they see on that day. The twenty-seven of us reported one hundred and thirty-three species that day, the majority being the 4,474 Herring Gulls (*Larus argentatus*) and the 4,051 Dunlins (*Calidris alpina*). Unusual species we had spotted were the Least Sandpiper (*Calidris minutilla*) and the Blue-Gray Gnatcatcher (*Polioptila caerulea*), of which we saw two of each. I almost missed the one Northern Saw-Whet Owl (*Aegolius acadicus*) entirely when the professor and I were making out in the woods.

I felt horrible about having a relationship with a married man; it was without a doubt the worst thing I'd ever done. But Professor Nickwelter loved me much more than he ever loved his wife, even though he never told me so. Those three little words every girl waits to hear were never spoken. At least not to me anyway. I'm twenty-nine now and I'm still waiting for someone to tell me they love me.

If I hadn't slept with Professor Nickwelter.

I run my hand along the edge of the roof as I try to remember everything I can about this car. But then suddenly, I feel my stomach jump into my mouth as I spot someone in the backseat. I jump back awkwardly, tripping over my own feet. The coffee spills on the ground and one of my textbooks hits the back door as it flies from my grasp. Did this person see me? Was he watching me the entire time? I only hope I can retrieve my book and get out of sight before some vagabond in the back of Nickwelter's car jumps out and grabs me.

I try to reach for my book without getting too close to the car, but then the window rolls down and Nickwelter himself sticks his head out. "Isabelle?" he asks, without really asking a question.

"Professor?" I put my hand over my heart, in an attempt to calm myself down. Considering how close my relationship to Professor Nickwelter once was, it does seem a little strange that this is what I choose to call him. Professor. The truth is, I don't even think about his first name anymore. Call it an experiment, or maybe I'm just fooling myself, but perhaps I can will myself to forget it. Everyone else around here calls him Professor Nickwelter, so why shouldn't I? Besides, what better way to forget a memory then to start with a name? "You scared me," I tell him.

"What are you doing here?" he continues, probably already aware I never call him by his first name anymore. So aware, it doesn't even bother him.

"I just dropped my book, and now I'm picking it up," is the best I can come up with.

And the best he can come up with is, "Oh. I see." I think he's outdone me in the crummy response challenge.

I take the textbook into my hand and notice him watching me. It's not so much that he's watching me, but more like he's staring blankly in my direction. Almost exactly how I was staring into the void of the screw on the bus four nights ago. I wipe the coffee off of the wet side of my book.

"What are you doing in the back of your car? Were you sleeping in there?"

"Hmm?" he asks. I seem to snap him right out of the peculiar state he's in. "Oh, why yes. Yes, I was."

I've tried my best for the last two years to not give Professor Nickwelter too much of a thought. I mean, that part of my life was over, right? It was temporary at best. The silly crushes and, as much as I loathe the word, affairs have to end eventually. So why do I choose this moment to approach the man who's given me nothing more than misery, heartache, and a birthday dinner?

I suspect it's because these feelings of loneliness, inadequacy, and rejection have been piling up since the moment he broke it off with me two years ago. I think it's the fact that I need to feel safe *somewhere.* With someone. Maybe anyone. So I ask him, "Do you mind if I sit with you for a moment?"

"You know you don't need to ask such a question, Isabelle," he replies with a reactionary flick to unlock the door. I get in, but leave the door open behind me.

We sit side by side quite uncomfortably and with words unspoken for some time. It must have been a few minutes, but I can't be certain. Our eyes glance off one another's, back and forth. Something desperately needs to be said here in order to break this silence, but I'm sure as sugar not going to budge. I don't even know what I'm doing in the backseat of this haunted car anyway. It smells funny; not like how this car used to smell, but a new kind of scent. One that doesn't bring any memories at all to the surface, like smells are renowned for.

"Beth and I had a fight last night," he starts. "Again. She didn't kick me out, but it wouldn't have been long before she did. I always did have to make the first move with her."

"I'm sorry," is the most obvious I can do. I hate how I seem to want to apologize for other people's mistakes.

"It's not your fault," he says calmly.

Of course it wasn't. But I still feel at least partially guilty. Whether he wants me to feel this way or not, it's there. "Well, in a way," I admit, "it kind of *is* my fault. Don't you think?"

"Nonsense. Not at all. It's *my* fault for being this way."

I'm not sure in what way exactly he's intimating at, for I know Professor Nickwelter in many ways. He's kind, yet selfish. Warm, yet isolated. Handsome, yet unattainable.

He stares down at his folded hands. His tired eyes are distant, and seem focused on something that's been forever out of his reach. His skin is leathery from years of smoking, but those years are now far behind him. In fact, I wouldn't have known he'd smoked at all if his face hadn't shown it. But there's no denying that he is still an attractive man. My mother once told me when I was a little girl that men were most attractive in their forties. I didn't believe her when I was younger, but I know now that she was right. Even though Professor Nickwelter must be at least fifty. I don't know for sure because he's done a remarkable job at dodging my date-of-birth inquiries over the years.

I notice his eyes are tearing up. I get the feeling he really has no idea where his life is going anymore. If indeed he ever had any idea.

"It's *always* been my fault, Isabelle," he continues.

But what about me? Do I really have an idea as to where it is I'm heading? I turn my head and look out the open door to my right. I see Jerry Humphries parking his ugly brown car a few of spots over. I close the door quickly so that obnoxious little slime won't see me. I see him take a large, empty birdcage from out of the trunk, and he walks from his car to the faculty entrance.

Just as I turn back to Nickwelter, he wipes some tears from his eyes. I put one hand on his knee and move a little closer to him. Maybe it's just that I've been feeling more than a little undersexed lately, but I can't seem to help myself. Desire and emotion can only be bottled up for so long before they simply find the easiest possible release.

If only Templeton had returned to The Strangest Feeling to find me there.
If Claude had simply asked me The Question I was waiting for.

He stops weeping, just long enough for me to timidly inch my words a little closer to his ear. "Do you still love me?" I ask. Even as I'm saying the words, I don't really know why they're being said. By the time I realize I'm still in control, it's too late. The words are already out there. Although a part of me is actually still hoping he might say yes.

"I already sent my signals, Isabelle," he turns and says quietly. "Do you really have to ask me that?"

Yes, he'd sent his signals. Just like the Australian Superb Fairy-Wren (*Malurus cyaneus*). A courting male will pluck a bright yellow flower and show it off against his own cobalt-blue plumage. Nickwelter is also similar to the fairy-wren in that they are socially monogamous, yet sexually promiscuous birds: pairs will bond for a long time, but they will mate with many other individuals during that time.

And if you're keeping score, the percentage of bird species that are explicitly monogamous is ninety. The percentage of mammal species? Three.

"Unfortunately, my marriage is a little shaky right now. I can't risk losing Beth."

Now he thinks of his wife? It seems as though those two are always arguing about one thing or another. I pull back a little and ask him, "What are you saying? That if your marriage was going just fine, you'd say yes?"

"Yes. I probably would."

"That's sickening! Here I am, looking for something, for anything! All I'm feeling right now is that I've spent my entire life being rejected. And you're just worried about yourself, and some fat wife who would never love you another day of your life if she ever found out about your affair. With one of your students, no less!"

"You are talking about yourself, are you not?"

"Of course I am. Why, are you sleeping with another one of these kids?" I know I'm mad at the man, but I'm not sure what's made me fly off the handle like this. I consider it's perhaps all the coffee I've consumed over the last few days.

Nickwelter notices too. He knows I'm usually more in control of my emotions. "Isabelle. Bella. We all make silly, stupid mistakes that we regret for the rest of our lives. It's terribly normal in a depressing sort of way. What went on in this car a minute ago — all I'm asking is for you to try and forget about that, and everything else that's ever happened between the two of us. Please? Can't you do that for me?"

I've got to give the man at least some credit for almost making it sound easy.

"Believe me, Professor. I will certainly try." I get out of the car, and slam the door behind me. I hate myself for a moment when I think of the words I just said to this man. A man who, for better or worse, is still a good friend of mine. But how could he say those things to me? I mean, to think that I was still hung up on him. Really? It was only a moment of weakness on my part, wasn't it? I suppose that's how it all started back in Cape Cod years ago.

And I suppose that's how things like this always start: in moments of weakness.

I walk angrily toward the ornithology department's faculty entrance, but I stop when I see Jerry Humphries coming back outside. I freeze for a moment, and wonder if I should head back to Nickwelter's car to apologize, if only to simply avoid this oncoming weasel. Another moment of weakness. I can't believe I don't find myself in more awful situations than I do, seeing how often my mind wants to run back to its familiar comfort zones.

But I don't turn back. I walk right by Humphries. Sure, he might have smiled perversely and said a greasy "Good morning". And yes, I might have caught his reflection in the school doors, observing me from behind as we passed one another. I do my best to put both of these men out of my thoughts for now. All I need to do now is hope I can hide myself away for the rest of the day. Away from Humphries. Away from Nickwelter. And away from those feelings I should never have let loose in the parking lot.

I watch out the window a minute longer as Humphries takes another large cage out from the deep trunk of his car. There must be a shipment of birds coming in this morning. I should have double-checked my calendar.

~~~

I toss my textbooks and bag onto the desk in my office. My own office. As much as I enjoyed sharing an office with Mrs. Claus for the last two years, it's nice to actually have my own space outside of my own home. I call it my nest away from nest.

Mrs. Claus is a fine woman, but we really don't have all that much in common, aside from how much she can sometimes remind me of my mother. That being said, the amount we don't have in common is far more tolerable than the amount we do. The most ironic thing about Mrs. Claus is at Christmastime she has the tendency to overdo it with the office decorations. It's a little too much for me to handle, but I'm not about to say anything to her. I mean, she is Mrs. Claus, after all.

If Mrs. Claus had been telling this story, it would be much more festive, and it would probably reek of gingerbread and peppermint.

I have just enough time to sit down before there's a knock on my door. Professor James enters the office, placing a notepad onto my desk. "Your mother called for you last night, Donhelle. She said she tried calling your place, but you weren't home. Out tearing up the streets at all hours on a Sunday night?"

"Something like that," I smile at him. Steffen James is maybe the most likable person I know, even with the annoying habit of calling everyone at the university by their last names. Just their last names. Even the students. At
~~~

five foot three, he stands about an inch taller than me, which I'm sure is a welcome relief for his ego. He has the upward-curving nose of the Pied Avocet (*Recurvirostra avosetta*), the red cheeks of the European Goldfinch (*Carduelis carduelis*), and a short-trimmed beard, which has always reminded me of the look of the Short-Toed Eagle (*Circaetus gallicus*).

Men with beards are a big issue for me. My father had a beard when I was growing up, and then decided to shave it off one day. Just like that. I barely recognized him. My own father. I kept looking at him when we were at the dinner table, watching his jaws clench and cheeks expand like I'd never seen them do before. That was probably around the same time I started to lose respect for my father. He wasn't the same man who had raised his little girl. He was someone new to me now, and I couldn't help but feel uncomfortable.

Professor James once told me he was thinking of shaving *his* beard off, but I kind of freaked out and begged him not to. That was a year and a half ago, and he hasn't mentioned it since. I do still imagine what he would look like without it, but all I see is my father, so I usually try and distract myself with something else instead.

I read the note he handed me. All it says is "MOM" in Steffen's bold, confident printing.

"Quite the detailed note," I say, as I tear it from the notepad and drop it into my wastepaper basket. "Thanks, Steffen." I figure I must have been at The Strangest Feeling last night when my mother tried to call, though I wonder why she didn't leave a message on my answering machine at home? Maybe it's time I break down and get myself a cell phone.

So why was Professor James at the school answering phones anyway? I ask, "What about *you* then? What were you doing here on a Sunday night?"

Steffen holds up a stack of textbooks and papers under his arm. "Just getting my paperwork ready for today's classes. I've got Nickwelter's

Comparative Anatomy class this semester, and it's kicking my tail feathers." I can tell the instant he mentioned Professor Nickwelter, he wished he hadn't. Steffen James knows all about my history at this school. He taught me when I was a student here, and now he helps me out a great deal with my responsibilities as head of Hawthorne's ornithology program. He's seen me at my best and worst, and he knows when something will rattle my nerves. Something as stupid as mentioning a name. He tries his best to change the subject. "Anyway, my C.A. was cancelled on Friday due to the fire, so I've got twice as much to cover today in order to stay on track. Hey, did you hear about the swan boats being stolen last night?"

Back it up a little Steffen. We're not moving on just yet. "I had a talk with him this morning you know? Professor Nickwelter. Outside in the parking lot. Beth kicked him out again, although he wouldn't admit it."

"I really don't think we should be talking about this, Donhelle," is Steffen's response. "Poor Nickwelter must've had another rough weekend."

"You can't say it's not his fault though, right Steffen?"

He studies my eyes for a moment, knowing this is exactly the type of subject that could unravel my entire day. He thinks about it, and I can tell he almost says something else, but he resigns to his old trusted standby: "I really don't think we should be talking about this." As kind as Steffen James is, his only character flaw is that his home life was perfect, and he really doesn't like to get involved in lives that aren't as perfect as his. He gets downright awkward about it, actually.

If Steffen James had been telling this story, he'd definitely leave out all of the bad parts.

"Genetics is easy," he says. "There's a logical reason and a purpose for everything. Like the Atlantic puffin's bright orange bill plates that grow in spring for their courtship rituals, and then shed after breeding. Or the spruce grouse's digestive sacs that increase in size in the winter to support the bird's seasonal diet of conifer needles. You know all of this too, of course. But relationships are a whole other entity, outside the realm of science. It's an unanswerable question which requires constant calculations and deductions. It's the formulae we know we'll never deduce, but we also know we can never stop trying."

He sits down on the small chair across from me, thinking about the gibberish he just churned out. After a moment of thought, he comes up with something new to say. Something safe that won't allow me to dwell on past mistakes. "Hey, did that spaghetti do a number on your stomach this weekend?"

"I'm fine, thank you," I say, my mind still trying to piece together what Steffen had said.

"I would have given you a ride home, but you flew out of the restaurant like a peregrine falcon."

Falco peregrinus, I think to myself. "It's all right, Steffen. I took the bus home."

"That's good. The last time I rode the bus the driver got lost. We ended up in Brookline Village! Do you believe that?"

"Well, I got home safe and sound. It was pretty uneventful." I take a stack of papers from my bag, and holding them upright, I tap them onto the desktop so the edges are flush. It's the illusion of looking busy.

I notice Humphries as he walks past my office, another large cage in his hands. He sneaks a peek at me on his way by. There's a look in his eyes that doesn't even care if I ignored him on my way in this morning. He's just being himself. I think that bothers me more than if he actually was upset with me.

Without moving my head, I scan the office with my eyes, taking in the few pieces of my past I have on display. There's my Hawthorne University ornithology diploma. After six years of studying genetics, statistics, comparative anatomy, physiology, ecology, quantitative analysis, taxonomy, and avian science, it was my greatest achievement to finish top of my class. Five years ago seems like a lifetime now.

Next to the diploma is a small, handmade box, given to me by the Dias family, who lived across the hall from me during my first few years in Boston. The ornate wooden box is sealed, and according to South American superstition, bad luck would follow should I ever view its contents.

Above that is a painting given to me by Luis Dias. Luis was only three years old when I first met him, but we grew very close, and when I accepted my current job as head of Hawthorne's ornithology program two years ago, he had given me this painting as a gift. He said it was a portrait of me and that he had painted it with his bare hands. I accepted it graciously, even though all I could see was just a mess of color, somewhat in the shape of a child's hand. The Diaz family moved out of the building last year, and now there's a mean old Romanian man with a glass eye living alone across from me.

There's a bottle of Brazilian Pinot Noir, given to me by the ornithology staff for my birthday last week.

My shelf that's bursting with textbooks and field journals.

My Massachusetts teaching certificate.

And Steffen James. He's still waiting for me to say something more, since it seems he's exhausted himself of any more thoughts.

We're all just waiting though, aren't we? The state bird of Massachusetts is the Black-Capped Chickadee (*Poecile atricapillus*). I moved to Boston almost twelve years ago, and I'm still waiting to see my first black-capped chickadee.

I take the stack of papers from in front of me, and tap the edges flush once more. Part of me wonders why I'm still trying so hard to look busy, while another part wonders why I can't just move on. "You're right," I say to Professor James.

"About what exactly?"

I realize I'm simply answering my own question. "I do need to move on. This whole ridiculous situation with myself and Professor Nickwelter has gone on long enough, don't you think?" A little unsure of what kind of answer I'm looking for, Steffen nods cautiously in agreement. "It's not healthy for me to be in a relationship like that, right? Even if both of us did want it."

"I really don't think we should be talking about this, Donhelle."

I push the stack of papers aside. "And I really do think you're right, Steffen. Thank you again for the phone message."

With textbooks still under his arm, Steffen rises from his seat and turns to exit my office, but he reaches back for the notepad on my desk before he goes. "I'd better put this back before Humphries realizes I stole his notepad. Have a good day, Donhelle."

Steffen James closes the door behind him, leaving me alone with my thoughts.

~~~

I remember the last conversation I had with Professor Nickwelter before our relationship ended. This was two years ago. We were walking through Boston Common, and he told me how it couldn't go on anymore. I let go of his hand for the last time. His hands always felt horribly cold to me.
~~~

"I'm not feeling what I think I should be feeling in this relation-ship, Isabelle." Thinking back on this moment now, I know he and Beth must have been having another fight at the time. "It's not your fault though," he continued. "It's just chemistry."

Chemistry? I don't know how I ever swallowed that road apple. "What's the feeling?" I asked him.

"Hmm?"

"You said you're not feeling something. What's the feeling supposed to be?"

"It's just that; a feeling. It's not something that can be explained with words, it's just sort of a sensation more than anything." I looked up at the Great Elm, and considered the irony that in the Eighteenth Century its very branches were used for public hangings. "That's all I can tell you, Isabelle."

We stood gazing at one another for a few minutes more, each of us not knowing what else could be said at that point. Not knowing what else could possibly make anything better or worse. The six swan boats in the lagoon bobbed up and down, waiting for someone to say something. After much deliberation, Professor Nickwelter thought of the perfect words: "You can keep the wristwatch I gave you though. It seems to keep good time."

Just go ahead and hang me. Those branches have been begging for this for centuries.

<div style="text-align:center">~~~</div>

I snap out of my semi-sentimental flashback to find I've scribbled something onto my Avian Structure and Function textbook. I sit back, almost in disbelief of what I've written. It's the question I should've asked under the Great Elm two years ago:

So why the hell did you fuck me?

Embarrassed by my own thoughts, I pull some tape over the words. I gather my books, and leave for my Avian Field Study class. And I try not to think about the watch I had thrown into the Charles River that very same day two years ago.

Unnecessary E's

I HAVE NO idea who Phil Ferguson is, but I know he's smarter than this. I could never pick Pat Vargas out from a crowd, but I can tell you where Pat will be this time next year. I have no emotional attachments in any way to Caren Kessler, but I'm the one who's going to help decide her future, aren't I?

I can't help it if they all seem the same to me though.

All birds are called "birds." There are so many families of birds, so many different phylums, classes, and orders, that it's nearly impossible to learn every one of them. They have to first be broken down into more basic categories. Field identification teaches us to use locomotion (walking, hopping, swimming, and flight patterns) and habitat (birds of a sea coast, shorebirds, wire and fencepost sitters, deciduous forest birds, and marsh birds) as useful starting points for identification. Noting the silhouettes of flying birds is useful too; the shape of the wings, whether pointed or rounded, narrow or broad, slotted or unslotted; the length of the neck and tail in proportion to body length; the position of the feet, and whether they extend beyond the body and tail while in flight, or if they're tucked in close to the body.

By comparison, all students are simply "students" to me. So many come and go — from year to year, from class to class — there's no way I can possibly identify them all. All I have to go by are the reports I mark, and the grades I assign to them.

This is what I'm doing tonight. After what happened between Professor Nickwelter and I this morning, I almost dragged myself to The Strangest Feeling again, but by now I figure Templeton Rate is probably busy chasing some other naïve girl around Boston anyway. It's just as well, I suppose. I told myself earlier today that it was time for me to move on, so here I am marking papers and trying to imagine who exactly these students really are.

But I'm not quite "moving on," am I? Since I'm doing precisely what I was doing this time a week ago.

On a Monday night, in my humble, one-bedroom apartment conveniently located above the Starbucks on Newbury Street, I sit alone at my desk with my Tanzanian Ol Doinyo Lengai blend: full-bodied, with hints of herbal, peppery notes. Marking my students' papers, I systematically use a blue checkmark for every correct notation, and a red circle for every wrong one. The desktop background on my computer is the same Indian Blue Peafowl's (*Pavo cristatus*) tail feather design that's been there for the last eighteen months.

Sometimes when I'm feeling wild, I use a green marker for the checkmarks instead of blue. If this isn't screaming lonely, I don't think I could be trying any harder.

Phil Ferguson is correct when he says one can identify the Eastern Meadowlark (*Sturnella magna*) as alternating its flight pattern between sailing with the wings spread and flying with rapid wing-beats. However, he's wrong when he states the Eastern Kingbird (*Tyrannus tyrannus*) has an undulating flight pattern. The kingbird flies in a straight line, with continuously quivering wing action. Red circle. I'm thinking Phil is the kid who is always trying hard to get noticed; trying so hard that he ends up being right only half the time.

Caren Kessler made the mistake of claiming a particular bird spotted on a telephone wire outside her Inman Square apartment was a Scarlet Tanager (*Piranga olivacea*), which is a deciduous forest bird. I'm sure what she described must have actually been a Barn Swallow (*Hirundo rustica*), which she would have recognized had she noted the obvious forked tail. Red circle. I'll bet she's the kid with the inch-thick glasses who can never see my projection screen. The one with undiagnosed ADHD which won't allow her to go an entire class without running out of the lecture hall for some reason or another.

But Pat Vargas is dead on when he says the European Starling (*Sturnus vulgaris*) can be identified in the winter by their speckled plumage, while after the season it is more of a glossy black. Blue checkmark. Could this be that quiet kid in the back, who always dresses in a different camouflage pattern for each day of the week? With his knowledge of wildlife, I'll bet he's done some hunting in his free time too.

Of course, Pat could just as easily be a girl. It's all just insufficient data at this point.

I know everything there is to know about birds because I have to know everything there is to know. I also know it all because I've always had this innate ability to catalogue such information. Call it a gift or call it a curse, but all I know is that, academically speaking, I've breezed through my entire life at the top of my grade curve.

I take a deep breath, a sip of my coffee, and a long look around me at this nest I've built for myself. The nest crafted from the sticks and leaves and mud of my past. Nestled quietly on one of my bookshelves is a tiny black-and-white picture of my family: Mom, Dad, and me. No brothers or sisters shared this moment with us. It was the last year I lived in Ville Constance. I believe the picture was from a holiday dinner at the orphanage, and I think one of the kids must have taken it, since the angle is a little off. But I really can't remember.

I don't know if I've ever spoken with Tyler Izen, but he's tried to convince me in his reports that the Barn Owl (*Tyto alba*) uses sonar to find its prey in complete darkness. Of course, the truth is that barn owls utilize echolocation to catch prey in the dark, where their facial discs form receptors that bounce sound between their ears. Their two ears are of different heights, which helps them to localize sounds and pinpoint the precise location of movement and its direction, so they can catch prey in darkness or scuttling underneath leaves and snow. I know this because I have to. If I don't know it, then Tyler Izen never will. But who the stink is Tyler Izen anyway? Red circle.

I started collecting all of this information back in high school. Yes, that's right; it was about the same time that Mrs. Wyatt wouldn't let me play for the basketball team.

I wouldn't be here now if I didn't score perfect on my biology finals; if I didn't join the Doneau High science club; if I had never met Cindey Fellowes; if I wasn't rejected from the basketball team.

Rejection after disappointment after misery. That's all your life adds up to, especially when you pick the worst possible moment to look back on it all.

~~~

Cindey Fellowes was the kind of girl who wanted so desperately to be noticed, that nobody knew exactly who she really was. I was looking over the list of girls who had been cut from the basketball team, and I was upset when I read my name on the initial list. Right there at the top, although it wasn't even alphabetical. Cindey was looking over a similar list next to me when she found out she had been cut from the Doneau High volleyball team, and after only one tryout. She told me how she'd been cut from pretty much everything at the school, so she was planning on joining the science club instead. Mostly just to feel as though she was a part of something, and partly because no one
~~~

could ever get cut from the science club. I think it was after only a minute of talking to this girl, I had felt as though I needed to be a part of something too.

If I wasn't rejected from the basketball team.

That was part of the charm of Cindey Fellowes: she despised herself so much she made others hate themselves too. Charm? That's not quite the right word, but it's close enough I suppose.

If Cindey Fellowes had been telling this story, she'd make you think it was all your fault.

~~~

Jonah Mitcherson has three full pages of blue checkmarks, but when he turns the page to see the giant red circle around his descriptive and informative writings on the Rufous Hornero (*Furnarius rufus*), he's going to regret he had Professor Donhelle checking his facts for him. At least I assume he was talking about the rufous hornero, since he continued to refer to it as an Ovenbird (*Seiurus aurocapillus*), which is actually a warbler. Jonah's confusion no doubt lies in the fact that the rufous hornero is a member of the genus *Furnarius*, and that the horneros family are also known as ovenbirds.

I know the bird in question is actually the rufous hornero since he described it as building mud nests that resemble old wood-fired ovens. I know this because I have to know this. It can be easy to accidentally mix up genus and species, but this is one of the most careless mistakes I've come across this semester. I'll wager Mr. Mitcherson did some rushed and heedless internet searches to write this paper, without actually cross-checking whether or not his information was correct before heading out to the pub to get liquored up with his booze-head pals. And yet, I'm somehow finding myself envying his social life.
~~~

~~~

The Doneau High yearbook labeled us "The Science Club," but we were really just a bunch of kids with different science-related academic interests thrown together in a room after school because we had no other place we could fit in. I guess that was the truth behind most clubs, actually. I was even more pathetic, since I didn't even have a science-related interest at the time; I was just there because Cindey told me she'd be there.

As much time as Cindey and I spent together in school, we never saw much of one another outside the halls of Doneau High. Her family lived on a farm, just outside of town. The school bus would pick her up every morning, and take her home every afternoon, but I had never actually seen where she lived. Cindey claimed her home life was normal, but I always wondered about the details of this self-professed "normal" existence. As boring as Ville Constance was, I didn't think anybody here could ever be categorized as normal. We would see each other every morning before class, we would eat lunch together, and then spend another ten or fifteen minutes after school together. Interrupted by two months of Claude, that is. And just like Claude and I had our own special place on the yellow electrical box behind the gymnasium, Cindey and I had the science clubhouse, known more affectionately to the rest of the school as "Room 210."

I know what you're thinking though: aside from sitting around reading Power of Science textbooks and quizzing each other on anything and everything from genealogy to protists, just how did Cindey Fellowes have such a profound effect on the direction my future would take? As far as Cindey herself goes? Not much, really. Friends in high school are friends due to circumstance much more so than because of compatibility.
~~~

To be honest, those unnecessary E's in her name really drove me bananas. The reason I bring up Cindey so much goes back to one of our after-school science club cramming sessions.

Thinking back to that particular afternoon, I can remember myself, Cindey Fellowes, Darlene Turcotte, and Sonia Desjardins. Of our regular group, only Julie-Anne Loucette wasn't there. She told us she was getting her eyes checked that afternoon, but we all knew she was secretly seeing Marc Courchaine after school instead. We were quizzing one another on every subject imaginable, when suddenly, and seemingly out of nowhere, something came crashing through the second-floor window of Room 210. It startled every one of us; in fact, I think Sonia might have even soiled herself, since she left the room before we even realized what had happened. I don't think Sonia ever came back to the science club after that day, now that I think of it.

Because I had befriended Cindey Fellowes, I was now sitting at a desk in Room 210 after school with blood-covered shards of glass in front of me.

If I hadn't joined the Doneau High Science Club.

It was a raven that had flown through the window at that moment, and it was dying right there in front of me, bleeding on my textbook. Cindey and I carefully examined the poor bird, which was still alive, but suffering tremendously. Darlene soon fled the classroom as well, off to retrieve someone at the school who had some kind of authority in matters concerning wildlife flying through windows.

I looked at Cindey, with eyes so wide as if to say, "This is the most important, most significant moment of our lives." Cindey, however, was simply grossed out by the entire event. While her heart was persuading her to wrap the unfortunate animal up in loose-leaf paper and toss it back out the window, my heart was letting me know I didn't have any use for Cindey

Fellowes from that moment on. But I needed her to get me to that day with the bleeding raven on my desk. It's all connected. It's all important.

If I hadn't met Cindey Fellowes.

That's all it took for me to pursue my ornithological interests. The events from that afternoon led to me enrolling at Hawthorne University of Applied Sciences in Boston, Massachusetts. I left my dysfunctional parents, Antonia the Ostrich, the litter of orphan angels, my best friend Cindey Fellowes, my non-boyfriend Claude, the Doneau High basketball team, my bloodied science textbook, and the whole godforsaken town of Ville Constance behind me for good.

~~~

I'm reading a report written by some kid named David Lee. Some idiot kid who has no idea there's a difference between the Laurel Pigeon (*Columba junoniae*) and the Bolle's Pigeon (*Columba bolli*). Obviously, brown, rather than dark gray plumage, and the lack of dark bands on the gray tail distinguish the laurel pigeon from its popular Canary Island relative. I know this because I have to know this. I can't believe they think they're impressing me with any of this information. Red circle.

I stop for a moment, and look at the phone across the room. I take a second to think about calling my mother back. My twenty-ninth birthday was four days ago, and what, she calls me last night? Three days late? I stay put at my desk, send her a quick and emotionless thank-you email and leave it at that.

Skimming through Lester Coolidge's paper, I notice he's catalogued, or attempted to catalogue, the calls of woodpeckers around the world. Sorry Lester, wrong on pretty much every account. But please, let me correct these for you: The Red-Headed Woodpecker (*Melanerpes erythrocephalus*),
~~~

deciduous of southern Canada and eastern/central United States, produces a *tchur-tchur* sound, while the Gila Woodpecker (*Melanerpes uropygialis*), found in desert regions of south-western United States, has a similar, but more rolling *churr* call. And finally, the Grey Woodpecker (*Dendropicos goertae*), common in much of equatorial Africa, has a very distinctive loud and fast *peet-peet-peet-peet* call. I know this because I have to know this. I'd say *A* for effort, but it doesn't seem as though there was much effort put forth. Red circle. My red marker is drying up fast.

I turn my eyes toward the wall clock as it silently ticks to 11:28. It's just about time for the nightly arrival of the delivery truck downstairs. Exactly one minute later, I hear my blown-glass Atlantic puffin trinket rattle against the window overlooking Public Alley 434. Every night this truck pulls into the alley behind my apartment with all of the next day's frappuccino, cappuccino, and macchiato supplies. Not to mention the boxes full of metal thermoses, corrugated cardboard coffee cup sleeves, and wooden stir sticks. All of this used to bother me to no end, until four days ago that is: last Thursday night at The Strangest Feeling, when my caffeine addiction was first conceived. Now I'm sitting here with a cold coffee on my desk and wondering just how much they can fit into the back of that delivery truck.

I have only one thing of extreme importance in my apartment. Sure, I do have the same horrible habit as most people for keeping small, sentimental, yet ultimately insignificant items around me. Like the letter from my sister Antonia which sits folded inside its original envelope, and rests safely between some books on my shelf. She wrote to me when I first moved to Boston and promised to write again as soon as she was adopted. I never heard from Antonia again. I've kept a pink plastic lighter that fell out of Claude's pocket fifteen years ago, and now sits at the bottom of the drawer of my bedside table. I found it sitting in the rocks around the yellow electrical box the day after he dumped me, and for reasons that will probably become clear on a psychiatrist's sofa one day, I decided to keep it for myself. There's the two pieces of rock-hard gum from The Strangest Feeling that lay inside a tiny wicker basket on my kitchen counter. I wonder if I'll ever tear open the paper wrap and read the sugar-stained cartoons inside. Probably one day, when I really need a good laugh.

But the only item of real importance within my nest is my parrot, a Blue-and-Gold Macaw (*Ara ararauna*), who I have sympathetically named Claude. Don't judge me. I suppose some names are impossible to forget, aren't they? I can feel you judging me.

There are two families of parrots: the true parrots (*Psittacidae*) and the cockatoos (*Cacatuidae*). Cockatoos are quite distinct, having a movable head crest, different arrangement of the carotid arteries, a gall bladder, and a lack of the Dyck texture feathers that produce the vibrant blue and green colors found in true parrots. This coloration is due to a texture effect in microscopic portions of the feather itself that scatters light. The spectacular red feathers of certain parrots owe their vibrancy to a rare set of pigments found nowhere else in nature.

Claude was rescued by Professor Nickwelter while on a university birding expedition in Brazil five years ago, and was brought back to the school for the purposes of rehabilitation and study. The poor bird had fallen victim to a horrible device common in that part of the world: a claw-like metal spring trap set in the trees, which clamps onto its prey and drops to the ground for capture. Most of these traps are set to capture rare birds, to keep as pets or to sell overseas, but sometimes they are simply nothing more than cruel torture devices. The poor bird must have been clawing for life for maybe a day or two before Professor Nickwelter came along, his left wing almost completely severed. Suggesting amputation of the wing and rehabilitation for the bird was the best thing to do, Nickwelter brought it back to Boston with him.

The parrot remained nameless for a couple of months, until Professor Nickwelter proposed that I pick a suitable name. Just one of the perks of dating your superior, I suppose. I decided "Claude" would be the best fit for him. If the raven that flew through the window of Room 210 and landed on my textbook had actually lived, I probably would have named him Claude too.

Please stop judging me.

Macaws are monogamous and mate for life, but in captivity, an unmated macaw will bond primarily with one just person: their keeper. Since I had named him and spent more time with Claude than anyone else, he picked me. I formed such a unique bond with Claude, it was also suggested I bring him home with me.

I hear him rattling his beak along the bars, so I walk over to Claude's modest, one-bedroom cage. He may be lacking the ability to fly anymore, but I still have to keep his cage locked tight, or else he'd chew up anything he could get his beak on. I toss in a new doggie chew-toy once a week to give him something other than metal bars to gnaw at.

Turning from his spectacular third-story view of Public Alley 434, Claude looks at me. "Poop," he says, indicating dinnertime. When I tried to teach Claude how to ask to be fed, I was getting frustrated and used the word "poop" as one of my famous curse word substitutes. He doesn't know why I said it of course, but that's now our codeword for food.

I grab a measuring cup and a bag of mixed sunflower seeds, pumpkin seeds, pine nuts, almonds, dates, and dried apple from the kitchen. There are some foods that are toxic to parrots, and to most birds in general. Cherry pits, avocados, chocolate, and caffeine should be absolutely avoided. I wonder if he's at all envious as I take another sip of my Tanzanian Ol Doinyo Lengai.

Claude's solitary wing is not his only identifiable characteristic. He has a butterscotch-colored underbelly, where most macaws will be golden or orange. There's also a thin, gray, fork-shaped line — it almost looks like a scar — running along the right side of his lower jaw. But everything about Claude is special to me. The look he gives me when he wants something isn't greed. It's not using me to get his way. It's not selfish Happy birthdays or affairs. It's not men.

It's love. And I think that's why I named him Claude in the first place. I suppose since I never got the chance to have that meaningful relationship with the Claude from my youth, I can just come home and not worry about who's loving who the most.

The most curious thing about Claude is that I taught him how to count to ten, and he understands how to use the numbers one through ten, but he doesn't understand eight. If I hold out five jellybeans, he can identify them as five. If I hold out ten, he knows there are ten. But if I have eight of anything, he's stumped. He simply skips the number eight when counting. It's strange, but love is about acceptance and compromise, isn't it?

If Claude had been telling this story, he'd skip chapter eight.

"How many scoops, Claude?" I ask, holding out the bag of food and the measuring cup.

"Two scoops," he replies. It's always two scoops. Macaws thrive on frequent interaction, and their high intelligence requires constant intellectual stimulation to satisfy their curiosity. Plus, it just makes him happy to answer my questions.

Now, after all that I know about macaws, Leonard Gillespie has the audacity to sneak into his report that a parrot's feet are heterodactylic. He obviously was not paying any attention at all when I covered dactyly last week.

Anisodactyly is the commonest arrangement of the digits, with three toes forward and one back. You'll find this in perching birds and hunting birds. Parrots and other climbing birds are zygodactylic, with two toes in the front and two in the back, with the outside toes being longer than the inside toes. This is also found in cuckoos and roadrunners. Heterodactyly is similar to zygodactyly, except for the foot's two long toes being arranged in the front, while the two short toes are situated in the back. I know this because I have to know this. Another sloppy mistake calls for another faded red circle.

Even Claude clucks his tongue in disappointment.

Reading through this last paper, it's apparent I may have to switch my marker colors; the red simply isn't going to make it through to the end of this one. I'm not even sure what it is I'm reading here. There are eleven pages of random, uneducated gobbledygook, all written in what appears to be charcoal:

CHICKENS CAN'T SWALLOW WHILE THEY ARE UPSIDE DOWN. AND THEY CAN'T SPIT WHILE THEY'RE RIGHT-SIDE UP

NORTH AMERICAN GEESE CANNOT COMMUNICATE WITH EUROPEAN GEESE BECAUSE OF THE LANGUAGE BARRIER

DONALD DUCK'S MIDDLE NAME IS FAUNTLEROY

I say the words out loud, mostly to check if it sounds as dumb spoken as it does on paper. "Donald *Fauntleroy* Duck?" If any of this is actually true, maybe I don't know everything there is to know about birds after all.

The report is complete trash. I'm not even sure why I flip back to the cover page to check the name, since I won't know who this person is anyway. Since every kid in that lecture hall is just a name to me, and nothing more.

But I check anyway.

My jaw drops.

How can this be?

"Templeton Rate?"

The First Day of Snow

TUESDAY, OCTOBER SEVENTH. It's a bitter cold morning as I pull into the university parking lot. I lock my door just as the first snowflake of the season lands on my eyelid. It's not the sudden chill of the ice on my face that sends a shiver down my spine; it's the sudden knowledge of what this day is: this is the first day of snow.

Over the years, I have not had the best of success on the first days of snow.

The first day of snow was the day my grandmother died. The first day of snow was the first time I got my period. Last year was a double whammy: I had my wisdom teeth removed on the first day of snow, and when I returned home from an afternoon of dental surgery, I opened my door to find my apartment had been broken into. Claude was untouched, but the rest of the place was a mess. I remember yelling at the snow from my open window that night. Even though the pain from oral surgery was unbearable, I had to let the snow know how I felt once and for all. But with fluffy words like "dang" and "hula-hoop" of course. I can't recall the context in which I used the word hula-hoop exactly, but I'm sure it had applied.

The snowflake has already melted from my eyelid and I fool myself with the hope that maybe it's just a false alarm. I turn to the front doors of the school, I think about the report in my bag with the name Templeton Rate on it, and I wonder just what might be in store for me behind those doors today.

On this day, the first day of snow.

~~~

I'm sorting papers as I sit at my desk in the lecture hall, waiting for my Avian Science class to begin. If any of these students would stop texting long enough to actually notice me, they'd probably notice I'm doing a very poor job at
~~~

looking like I'm sorting papers.

Last night, I was imagining what I'd say to this man who I ditched at the diner last week. This man who I had myself believing didn't actually exist. An angel is what Sylvie had suggested he was.

Just one more from the litter of angels.

Last night, I wanted to ask him whether he followed me into The Strangest Feeling on purpose or if it was merely a coincidence.

Last night, I wanted to ask him why he said he knew me, and if that really meant anything at all.

Last night, I wanted him to apologize for being rude, even if I was the one who disappeared on him.

Last night, I wanted to know how the paper with his name on it fell into my hands.

But that was last night. Right now, I just want to see him again.

If I hadn't wanted to see him again.

As I contemplate all of this, I zone out a little. The stack of over-shuffled papers in my hand almost falls to the floor. I need to focus, and get things started here. I don't know how many students should be in this class, but most of them appear to be here, so I rise from my desk and get on with it.

"Who here can tell me the step-by-step process by which a bird will molt?" A hand is raised, and I'm sure I've never seen this girl before. "Yes? Go ahead."

"Molting is cyclical, right? Birds shed older feathers, which are replaced by pin feathers. Once the pin feathers become full, the older ones will shed again."

Blue checkmark. A molt will occur at least once a year for adult birds, and in some species, up to as many as four times. Because feathers take up anywhere from five to fourteen percent of a bird's total body weight, molting requires an enormous amount of its energy. I know this because I have to know this.

"That's good. Thank you, um, Tanya."

"Haley."

Whatever. I take a sip of my coffee. This morning's selection is a French vanilla latté. Non-fat. No whip cream. The barista who made it wrote "N-V-L" on the side of the cup. Sadly, I'm starting to recognize the handwriting of the various employees.

"Can anyone specify the proper order in which feathers will molt?" Four hands go up, and I make my selection. "John?"

"Jack."

Come on. That was close enough.

"Generally," Jack continues, "a molt begins from the bird's head, progressing downward to its wings and torso, and finishing with the tail feathers. Is that correct?"

He's absolutely right. Blue checkmark. Many birds' feathers are molted progressively in waves, beginning on the head, face, and throat, then extending backward toward the tail. Usually, there is a symmetrical loss of feathers from both sides of the body, which balances feather loss, so the bird can maintain its energy levels and function normally. I know this because I have to know this.

"I'll accept that. Are there any examples of a molt that can take place outside of a bird's standard molting period?"

No hands are raised. But after a few moments to think it over, one student takes the plunge. I gesture an open palm toward him, giving him the go-ahead to share his thoughts. I'm not going to waste time in attempting to identify this student.

"How about a frightmolt?" he asks.

"Go on," I urge him.

"Well, a frightmolt is sometimes activated through fright or fear. In a frightmolt, the rectrices are shed most frequently, as are the smaller feathers of the breast and the dorsal tracts. In this type of molt, the bird usually retains the feathers from its head and wings."

This kid's been studying, whoever he is. Blue checkmark. In a frightmolt — a peculiar molt unique to only a few types of birds such as Passenger Pigeons (*Ectopistes migratorius*), Mourning Doves (*Zenaida macroura*), and some upland game birds — feathers are simply expelled or dropped. The slightest contact or pressure will relax the muscles of the feather follicle, and the quill is set free. I know this because I have to know this.

"Can anyone think of other biological examples of molting? Not just in birds?"

And then I hear a voice from the hall. Everyone hears it. Rows of heads turn in unison to take a look toward the door.

And I knew it wouldn't be long.

"I thought this was ornithology?"

I take in that glorious mop of hair over those hauntingly dark eyes. Some dirt still marks his face. It's Templeton Rate all right, leaning on the frame of the open door.

"That's correct," I say. I won't let him shake me. "This is Avian Science."

"Well let's get back to the birds then, huh?" He moves deftly up the steps to find an empty seat next to some skinny brunette I instantly dislike.

If that skinny brunette had been telling this story, I certainly wouldn't read it.

He's snuck up on me again. I feel totally unprepared for what's happening here. But I'm a professional. I will not be put in my place. Not in my class. "Not quite yet, *Fauntleroy*."

"It's Templeton, actually."

"Pardon me. My point was, sometimes it's important to be aware of how other animals evolve in order to find the exact answers you're looking for."

"Do tell, Professor Donhelle," he quips sharply. Some of the other students snicker a little at his abrasiveness. I can feel him trying to turn my class against me.

But I am undaunted. "Of course, the most obvious example would be in reptiles, where a snake will shed its skin. Or how about in mammals, when old hairs fall out, only to be replaced again? And molting is known as ecdysis in arthropods, such as when a crayfish sheds its exoskeleton."

"Simply fascinating," he says, in his most un-fascinated tone. "Let me ask you *this* though: can't molting be a psychological process as well as a physical one?"

Red circle.

"You mean in the figurative sense?"

"To molt is to change, correct? It's a transformation into someone or something else. Psychologically or physically. Temporarily or permanently."

Another red circle. If this were any other student on any other day, I probably would have excused them from the lecture hall for being so antagonistic. I'm not the kind to simply put up with unjustified hostility in my class. And yet, Templeton Rate has a sneaky way of getting me to listen to his every word.

"Don't you agree?" he asks me. Without another response from me, Templeton looks around him for some endorsement. "Do any of you agree?" I catch some nervous eyes as they dart around the room. The students are starting to wonder where this conversation is headed, and whether or not it might hold any relevance to what will be on their next exam. "Aren't any of you paying attention in this class?" And truthfully, I'm starting to wonder if I should be taking notes myself.

"Change is *one* thing, Templeton," I finally say. "It's a small shift in behavior. It's taking the bus home instead of an offered ride. It's drinking your first coffee, or smoking your first cigarette. But evolution dictates another thing entirely."

"Not to me it doesn't."

"Well, that being said, fact will always win out over opinion."

"Is that a fact?" The brunette beside him shifts away from Templeton, just a little closer toward the wall. Maybe my dislike for her was not quite as justified as I had first thought.

"Yes, it is."

Lacking any better answer, all I get from Templeton is, "Well, that's just your opinion, Professor."

Again, red circle.

~~~

Just over an hour later, my class is finished. Not soon enough though. Templeton Rate kept to himself for pretty much the remainder of the lecture, scribbling something down on a piece of paper the entire time. I couldn't avoid being a little bit distracted by his presence. And I don't work well with distractions. It was as though my class was the Power of Science, and Templeton was that smelly, bloodied raven.

The students begin to file out, on to live the rest of their lives. Templeton coolly walks to the front of the lecture hall, picks up my empty coffee cup and
~~~

tosses it into the recycling bin. He sits in its place on the edge of my desk as I try to piece all of this together.

"How have you been, beautiful?" he asks.

I take a peek at the coffee cup in the garbage, and I wonder if there might have been at least one more cold drop left. "I've been a lot less wired," I say to him. "I think I've had too much coffee lately."

"So, where did you disappear to on Thursday night?" he has the nerve to ask me.

But I don't have the nerve to answer him.

"I came back from the can, and you were gone. That horrible cheese bread made me shit like a goose." As unimpressed as I am by his language, I'm more than a little astonished by his on-the-spot avian simile. Geese spend most of their waking hours consuming mass amounts of vegetation, but their digestion is rapid and inefficient. As such, they excrete feces almost nonstop.

"So, what's the deal?" he continues, "I thought I still owed you another cup of coffee? How's tonight sound?"

"I don't think so, Templeton. I've got more papers to mark. And if they're as bad as last night's bunch, I won't be going anywhere tomorrow night either." I start collecting my materials, hoping this problem will disappear soon.

But he's already generating some new problems for me. "I've got another paper for you to look at. I wrote it right now, during class."

I try my best to downplay any interest. "Wonderful. I'm sure it's another brilliant opus." I wish my façade were the truth, and I wasn't really interested. That would make things so much easier. But how do I change the subject? And do I really want to? "You wrote a full paper in the last hour?" I ask him, hoping the end to this conversation might be getting a tiny bit closer. "How is that possible?"

"Well, I don't know what constitutes a full paper, but it is two pages."

"I'd say more than two pages."

"Actually, it's more like one-and-a-half. And double-spaced. And I did some of it last night while I was working."

"The doorman thing, right?"

"Yeah, that's right. It's nice to know you were paying attention to the details." He unfolds two pieces of paper from inside his coat pocket, and holds them out for me. I notice his hands are covered with tiny scrapes and scratches, all in various states of healing. "I had to borrow some paper from that babe next to me though."

"I knew you were the kind of guy who copied answers."

"I don't know if that would help me much in this class. Everyone here seems a little tardy."

"Tardy means late."

Templeton presses, and waves the papers in his hand. "Well, are you going to take a look at it or what?"

As I scan all one-and-a-half double-spaced pages, I'm careful to not get any of the dirt from the paper on my fingers. Like the report I read through last night, this one is also written in charcoal. All things considered though, his penmanship is still quite reasonable. The content, however, is anything but. It's just more of the same unsubstantiated randomness as Templeton's previous paper. Actually, it's even worse, as if on purpose. I mean, someone would really have to be trying pretty hard to get his facts any more wrong than this, but he's managed to pull it off.

Red circle.

I'm almost too distracted by what's going on around me to remember what the most important issue here really is. "Why exactly are you giving me these papers anyway? As far as I knew, you're not enrolled at Hawthorne."

"Who said I am? I never told you I was."

"Well? Are you, or aren't you?"

"Why *wouldn't* I be?" he replies defensively. "I'd have to be pretty fucking bored with my life to have nothing better to do than hang out with a bunch of bird-watchers in my free time."

I hand the papers back to him. "You're a very perplexing individual, Templeton Rate."

"So that's what you like about me. I was wondering what it would be exactly." Templeton re-folds his masterpiece and slips it back into his pocket. "Listen, the reason I'm here is to learn. And the reason *you're* here, in case you didn't know, is to teach people like me."

"People like you?"

"It's all very simple, Professor Donhelle."

He's got me right where he wants me. And something inside me simply doesn't want to fight it anymore. So, I get up on the figurative diving board and take the figurative plunge.

"I suppose if you're free later tonight, I'd be willing to meet you in the library for some extra help. How would six o'clock work for you?"

Templeton leans right in my face. And am I mistaken, or is that cheese bread still wedged between his two front teeth? "Really?" he asks, almost surprised by my offer.

"You're right. It is my job. I would be doing a disservice to this school if I didn't offer you my help. You could obviously use it."

If I didn't offer him that extra help.

"Look at you," he says with a victorious smile. "You are molting. Right before my eyes."

He turns away from me and exits the lecture hall, his last words trailing from beyond the door. "Let's make it six-thirty. I've got another class this afternoon. See you then. And don't go vanishing on me this time."

I look back in the trash at the empty cup of coffee, and I wonder if I have just made a big mistake. On this day: the first day of snow.

Hedge Interlude

SAINT FRANCIS ELEMENTARY in Ville Constance, Quebec is where I attended school from kindergarten to grade seven. All along the contour of the school ran a thick hedge. There was about a foot of space between the hedge and the outside of the school through which many of the kids would run. Due to potential damage caused to the shrubbery, and the possibility of medical issues such as skin rashes and allergies, the school made it clear that no kids were allowed to run behind the hedge. But of course, they all did. Except for predictably-boring Isabelle Donhelle. I always wanted to, since my friends all did and it seemed like it would be fun, but I obediently followed every single rule which was clearly laid out before me. It's some sort of inborn anomaly of mine. I always wondered what it would feel like though, charging through the brush, avoiding other kids coming from the opposite direction. I imagined what else might be found back there: wonderful treasures and hidden clubhouses with secret passwords and handshakes. I also considered the possibility of there being scary animals back there too, and poorly trained kids using that prohibited area as a makeshift bathroom.

So I did what I was told to do. I lived the life I was instructed to live. I played by all of the rules that no one else would. I remained safe and sheltered.

I went back to Saint Francis on my way home from high school one day, during my first week at Doneau High. There was no one around. Without a thought, I put my backpack down on the ground and I ran behind the hedge. I followed it all around the outside wall of the school, running the entire way. I tried to be careful, but the branches scratched my face and I bruised my shoulder and knee along the solid, red brick wall. Some of the branches had thorns, and one snagged my shirt, tearing a hole in it. I even muddied my favorite shoes.

I emerged right where I began, and stood in place for a few minutes, catching my breath. I checked my forehead for blood and removed the knots and leaves from my hair. Picking up my backpack, I limped home alone and embarrassed. My mother made me remove my dirty clothes on the porch in the freezing cold before I could come inside. And I wondered why I had ever made such an impulsive decision in the first place.

~~~

As silly as that story may seem, it's had a significant impact on how I would choose to deal with change in my life from that point on. It was a very simple decision: I would avoid it.
~~~

In the Lek

From the field journal of Professor I. Donhelle:
The process in which the male Black-Headed Grosbeak (*Pheucticus melanocephalus*) will attract a potential female partner is through determination. With its wings and tail feathers spread wide, he sings his song as he flutters from one large tree branch to the next. From his vantage points, the black-headed grosbeak instantly knows if there are any intruding male competitors that need to be chased away. Eventually, an interested female will answer his call, and the two will nest monogamously for the one breeding season. After which, they will part ways forever.

MEETING TEMPLETON RATE in the library at six-thirty that evening was not so much a mistake as it was just me doing my job. Why then did it feel as though I was making a big mistake? After all, it was me who had suggested this rendezvous. I actually pushed to help Templeton. He probably would never have even asked me. I was just doing my job, wasn't I?

At least, that was what I thought at the time.

If I hadn't suggested helping him in the library that evening.

So, although the arrangements were made, and even though he had confirmed the meeting with the last words spoken, it's now eight o'clock; I've been sitting here alone in a darkened corner of the university library for an hour-and-a-half. I've been marking papers the entire time, but I have yet to find any that are anywhere near as compelling as the one with Templeton's name scratched on it. I contemplate leaving right now, but that all-too-familiar sad-sack part of Isabelle Donhelle opts to give it another half hour.

The old librarian, Mr. Giacomin, comes over to my desk with a cup of black coffee from the cafeteria. "I don't think he's going to show," he says to me, bringing back memories of Sunday night at The Strangest Feeling. Along with a package of sugar, he sets the coffee down on the desk beside the stack of unopened textbooks. This cafeteria sludge will certainly pale in comparison to, let's say the versatile and complex Venetian blend: full and creamy, with a sweet finish. One pack of sugar is definitely not going to cut it here, but I don't want to sound ungrateful.

"I thought there was no food or drink allowed in the library?" I ask him.

"What makes a life worth living if you're going to play by all of the rules all of the time?" he asks with a twinkle in his eye. "Besides, it's *my* library, so I make all of the rules. All of the time. Just make sure nobody else sees it, okay?"

"You got it, Mr. Giacomin." As he walks away, I take a few more packets of sugar from my purse; I've gotten into the habit of carrying extra, just in case. I pour all of the sugar into the coffee and stir it with a pencil, telling myself I'll give Templeton only until the coffee is gone.

From the field journal of Professor I. Donhelle:
The process in which the male Greater Prairie-Chicken (*Tympanuchus cupido*) attracts a prospective female mate is by displaying his best assets. With his head bent forward, his ear tufts raised, his throat pouch expanded, his wings held close to the ground, and his tail broadly fanned, the bird parades around the display grounds, known as the lek, snapping his tail and filling the air sacs located on either side of his head. Forcing out the air, the greater prairie-chicken produces a resonant, booming love song.

Females peruse the lek and they choose their mate on the basis of this display. The one or two most dominant males will undertake roughly ninety-percent of the mating in one lek. The birds mate quickly, before any rival males can disrupt them, and then the female leaves to nest elsewhere. In this brief encounter no real pair bond is formed, and the male has absolutely no participation in raising the young.

With those memories of Sunday night flooding my head, I can feel myself falling into this newly created — and incredibly feeble — self-destructive pattern. That being said, this first day of snow was shaping up to be not so terrible after all. Through the library window, I see the thinly blanketed parking lot glowing under the streetlight. In some areas, it's already melted away to nothing. Sure, I may be disappointed by how this evening's scheduled tutoring has turned out, but I convince myself I had already gotten over Templeton Rate anyway. All I was waiting for here was a struggling student who never really wanted my help in the first place.

I hear footsteps approaching, and I realize Templeton Rate is far more complicated than I had first thought. There's much more going on here to warrant my concern.

Because, after all, this was the first day of snow, was it not?

"You're not supposed to have coffee in the library," the voice behind me states confidently.

I slide the cup out of view behind my textbooks. "You weren't supposed to see that."

"Ah, but I did." Templeton pulls out a chair from the table beside us, even though there's one here already, and he sits next to me. "You can't change that."

I notice he hasn't brought study materials of any kind with him. That is, unless he has some more pieces of scrap paper and a stick of charcoal in his coat pocket. Pushing the stack of texts between us, I try to get down to business. "Seeing as how you've wasted most of my evening already, I'd like to get right to it. Where do you want to start? Avian bone structure? Respiratory systems? Migration patterns?"

"How about we start with *this*," Templeton reaches across me, and takes the coffee cup into his hand. "Why is it you want to help me so badly, anyway?" He takes a loud slurp of my coffee, deliberately getting the attention of some students to our left. They politely shush us.

I whisper back, "Honestly? I'm not really sure." I search for some generic answer I can give him. I don't want him to think there are any feelings I'm holding back, and I certainly don't want him to know I was at The Strangest Feeling four nights in a row waiting for him like some schoolgirl with a pathetic crush. But I'm over that now, aren't I? "I think what it is, Templeton, is I can see *potential* in you. Potential I don't want to see going wasted."

Templeton calls it perfectly. "That is such a load of generic bullshit." He braces himself before opening his mouth again, "Can I tell you a little story about wasted potential?"

"All right," I say, and I brace myself for whatever might be coming.

"I once read an article about a shipment of myna birds that was coming from China to America. I think they were on their way to the New York Zoo, or somewhere like that. It doesn't matter though, because they never got to the zoo. The shipment arrived in New York, but a cage in one of the crates had broken open during the flight. When the crate was inspected at the airport, there must have been twenty or thirty myna birds that flew out and escaped into the city." He takes another greedy sip of coffee before continuing. "Here's the amusing part: those birds had been trained to mimic speech. And when they began nesting in Manhattan, they would fly by hot dog stands and office towers. They would buzz around Central Park, and you could hear them screaming things like, *'Good morning! What's your name? Which way is the airport?'* All in Mandarin, of course." Templeton doesn't care if he yells out in the library. He's shushed again from across the room, but he ignores the students and continues his bizarre story. "But do you know what I thought when I read this article? All I could think of was how much of a wasted idea this was. Those birds could have been trained to mimic car horns. Or crying babies. Or the theme song from Tetris. How awesome would that be? But all they could do was say things in Mandarin."

"Is there a point to telling me this story?"

His dark eyes are intense. They study the pile of textbooks, figuring out how to challenge me next. "You really don't think I know the first thing about anything in these textbooks, do you?"

I have to be completely honest with him. "That's exactly what I think. You can't give me information like 'birds prefer sex outside of their own species,' and expect me to assume you know what you're talking about, can you? That's incredibly presumptuous."

"What? That's not true then? Boy, I'm going to need a lot of help here, aren't I?"

If I hadn't waited for him in the library for an hour-and-a-half.

From the field journal of Professor I. Donhelle:

The process in which a Southern Royal Albatross (Diomedea epomophora) will attract a mate is through dance. A non-breeding male will spend many years practicing, learning, and perfecting his own personalized elaborate breeding dance. His repertoire will involve such actions as preening, pointing, calling, bill clacking, and many combinations of such behaviors. He will dance with many different partners during multiple returns to the same breeding colony. But after a number of years, he will interact with fewer and fewer females, until eventually one partner is chosen and a pair bond is formed. This pair bond will last their entire lifetime since the albatross is completely monogamous. As such, the specific dance which was so carefully refined over so many years is forgotten, and it will never be displayed again.

"Can I ask you something personal?" Templeton prods.

"I think that depends on what it is you plan on asking me."

Of course, he asks anyway. "What's with all the tension between you and that Nickwelter guy?"

"I'm afraid that's too personal."

"You fucked him, didn't you?"

"Please, Templeton! That's really inappropriate." I can't help it, but I raise my voice just a little, only to get shushed myself.

"But you did, didn't you? Like a Fischer's lovebird wanting to fuck a dirty old turkey vulture. Isn't that right?"

Again, one part of me is disgusted by the language Templeton throws around so callously, while another part is impressed by his knowledge of the genus. I reach out in an attempt to re-collect my textbooks without him noticing. "I suppose you're more within my genus? Is that what you're implying?"

"That's not what I'm saying at all, Professor." Pulling the textbooks back into his dirty hands, Templeton moves them out of my reach. "Listen, why don't we just cut out all of this ornithological foreplay and get down to the real business at hand?"

I don't mean to turn away from him, but I do. From the library window, and against the darkening night sky, I see a flock of Snow Geese (*Chen caerulescens*) flying against the wind. They flap their wings, but stay glued to that same piece of sky. I know they'll stay right there for as long as it takes the wind to back off, as their migratory route will not be affected by something as insignificant as the weather.

I get a sudden flashback of that first snowflake on my eyelash this morning. It's still cold enough to give me a chill. I turn back to Templeton. With my eyes, I ask him a million questions at once without saying even a single word. And he gives me absolutely zero answers in return.

From the field journal of Professor I. Donhelle:

The process in which the Indian Peafowl (*Pavo cristatus*) attracts a mate is through sheer beauty. The male utilizes the eyespots on his tail feathers to attract peahens. This is sometimes referred to as the food-courtship theory, where over time, a male's plumage will genetically evolve to have patterns and colors that appeal to the diet of prospective female mates. The peafowl's eyespots bear a striking resemblance to blueberries, a common diet of the peahen. The males with the most eyespots on their tail will have the greatest mating success. No singing or dancing talents are required, this is merely a show where beauty is the main attraction.

"What were you saying earlier, when you said you could see me molting?" I ask him. "What was that all about?"

Templeton folds his hands together and puts them behind his head. "I know you probably don't deal with a lot of metaphors in your line of work, but that's all I was getting at. You were *changing.* Even right now. You still are. These thoughts and feelings inside you at this moment, they're not the same as the ones you had last week. Those are gone. And these new ones? They're still feelings, still raw emotions, but now they're entirely different. You're still *you* though; you've just become better adapted to deal with your current environment."

I hate myself for it, but what he's saying is actually starting to make sense, in a Templeton-kind-of way. "You've been working on this for a while, haven't you?" I ask him.

"The metaphoric molting speech? Nah, I only came up with that just now." He takes another mouthful of coffee, and slides the cup back in front of me, disgusted. "You know, you really need to stop putting so much sugar in your coffee, Professor Donhelle. It's going to be the death of you."

No it's not, Templeton Rate. You are.

If I hadn't stayed there believing his lies.

I take a gulp of coffee myself, before committing to any further moves.

From the field journal of Professor I. Donhelle:
The process in which Pacific Gulls (Larus pacificus) will attract a mate is through regurgitation. A male will bring food to the nest site in an island colony, and regurgitate a half-digested mixture of fish, krill, and squid at the feet of the female, who eagerly accepts the

gift and slurps it up.

Sometimes it's not romantic. It's simply about what a girl is
looking for in a guy.

Through the window, I notice the snow geese have persevered, and they
continue along their predetermined migratory path.

"Do you wish that was *you* up there?" Templeton asks the moment the
geese disappear from sight.

I only need a second to answer him. "I think it's unavoidable in this line
of work. Imagine if we knew what it felt like to fly like that." I drop my empty
coffee cup into the garbage beside our table, before embellishing my desires.
"You know the Prudential Tower? I see it every morning as I leave my
apartment. Sometimes I see ring-billed gulls perched at the top of the
building, just waiting for me to come around the corner, fifty-two floors below
them. At least, that's what I imagine they're waiting for. Then they'll jump off
the edge and freefall for a moment. For just one short moment they're stuck
in the air, attached to nothing but that piece sky. And I know those gulls are
making sure I can see them, because they know that's the moment I wish I
could have. *That's* the moment I'm most jealous of."

His dark brown eyes finally pierce right through my moment of weakness.

From the field journal of Professor I. Donhelle:
The process in which Templeton Rate attracts his mate is simply
through a few days of clever planning. First, he will follow her. It's
not any specific pattern; maybe he'll stand beside her on a bus.
Maybe sit next to her in a sordid diner or a university library. Once
proper conversation has been initiated, and adequate interest has

been piqued, he will temporarily disappear from sight, and slowly begin invading her personal life. He'll plant traces himself, in her paperwork for example. He'll appear in her classroom. Making a fool of himself is not out of the question, but the end result will most assuredly involve those dark brown eyes and their ability to exploit any possible weakness in his potential mate, whereupon sexual collapse is inevitable.

Again, I suppose it's all about what a girl is looking for in a guy.

And that's exactly how I succumbed to Templeton Rate. I couldn't resist it any longer. It was almost unfair in a way. I suppose that's why mating rituals work so well though; it's always going to be a lopsided victory for one side.

If I actually carried pepper spray in my purse, I probably would have blinded him that first night on the bus. But because I didn't have pepper spray — because I've never considered myself vulnerable and defenseless — any portent of fear had passed me by unnoticed, and left me with nothing but the ache of desire.

In retrospect, I suppose it would have been more prudent and a much smarter move, both personally and professionally, to at least wait until we had left the building. I tackled him right there in a dark corner of the Hawthorne University library. Locking my fingers into his hair. Digging my nails into his skull. Between chewing on his lips and striking his teeth with mine, my tongue was finding its way shockingly far down his throat. I didn't want to ruin the mood with ridiculous thoughts, although I felt I must have looked like a youngling feeding from the mouth of its regurgitating mother.

The sexuality was flowing from somewhere I never knew existed. Thanks to the cigarette taste of Templeton's kisses, I was reminded of Claude. It's not pleasant, but it's a deeply personal memory that supersedes any temporary disgust. A part of me was thankful Nickwelter had quit smoking long before

I'd ever kissed him, while another part of me had secretly hoped he'd pick up another cigarette one day. The feeling was still there yesterday morning, when I'd made those embarrassing moves on him in the back of his car. But where Nickwelter resisted, Templeton was only encouraging me.

I didn't realize it at the time, but I recall now the shushing from across the study area had quickly turned into roaring applause.

Formally and informally, my class was officially over.

Of the Ambiguous and the Once-Amphibious

WEDNESDAY, OCTOBER EIGHTH. I wake up and it's staring right at me with empty, dried-up sockets. Wanting to lick its zippered lips. It wants to leap on me from hollow legs.

Templeton Rate's aftertaste stings like poison and it's left my body inert. It hurts underneath my fingernails. My jaw is sore; my hair in knots, my taste buds flared. And for some reason, one of my big toes is in an incredible amount of throbbing pain. It all adds up to being a most invigorating feeling; one I wish I hadn't gone so long without.

Still, all isn't quite right, is it? My clothes are not on the floor where I'd left them. Instead, they're on the bed and above the covers, as though tossed to the bed from the floor, rather than the other way around. As I gather them up, I do so routinely, but certainly this is embarrassingly far from routine for Isabelle Donhelle. Slowly and awkwardly, much like my performance last night, I put my clothes back on while still under the covers, just in case Templeton enters as I'm dressing. Even though he's unfortunately seen it all, I'd still rather save myself as much embarrassment as I possibly can.

When I see my socks on the floor, I instantly realize that, although I put my socks on left foot first and then right every day without thought, today I would be pausing to think about it. Because this isn't my modest one-bedroom apartment on Newbury Street. Because I'm used to mornings where the first sound I hear is Claude rattling his beak along metal bars. Because I always wake to the smell of coffee lazily drifting in through my open window, and to the ultra-hygienic taste of mouthwash still on my tongue from my habitual 3 AM trip to the bathroom. Instead, I've got the sound of this crooked ceiling fan whirring hazardously above me, the smell of these horribly-faded pink bed sheets and this long-forgotten lingering taste of sex and cigarettes.

I don't even have a clue as to where I am. Or where Templeton is for that matter. I only pray I'm still in Boston.

On the floor just beyond my socks and shoes, lies a pair of women's underwear: a tiny blood-red mound of string and mesh fabric. They're certainly not mine, and yet I can't help but stare at them. I wonder who the last girl was to wrap herself in these sheets just as I'm doing now. I also think about how desperately I need that 3 AM oral cleansing right now.

What am I doing here? What exactly brings a girl like me to a place like this, and into pink sheets that smell like spoiled milk? What takes me from helping a struggling student after hours in the library to this? How does this happen? What is it that attracts a girl like me to a misfit like Templeton Rate in the first place?

If he hadn't offered to pay for the cab ride last night; if he hadn't suggested a return to The Strangest Feeling for coffee and dessert; if he hadn't made out with me at the university library; if only that report hadn't been so horrible and appeared so suddenly on my desk at home two nights ago in the first place.

It all culminated in the first sex I've had in the last two years. I'm ashamed to admit it, but I feel as though I'm much more intimate with the sexual devices of the avian world than I am with my own inner-workings. In birds, there is not usually a true penis-vagina copulation; instead, most males impregnate the female by what is known as a cloacal kiss, where the male mounts the female and presses his cloaca, or anal opening, against that of the female's cloacal opening, into which he deposits his sperm. This will take anywhere between one to fifteen seconds. Embarrassingly, the whole process

I've just described borders closely on the level of romance I experienced with Templeton last night.

I snap out of it and look again into the dried-up eyes of this thing in front of me. This leathery, green-brown horror staring at me from the foot of the bed is a dead frog, or at least as far as I can tell, half of one. It still has its head and front legs, but with the charming addition of glued-on googly eyes, a zippered mouth, and a key chain coming out of its torso, as if it were meant to hang fashionably from a belt. This grotesque thing is Templeton's change purse. Part of me is totally freaked out with the idea someone could keep money inside a dead animal turned into a novelty key chain, while another part of me just finds it baffling that Templeton Rate would carry a change purse in the first place. I remember reading somewhere that sailors had sometimes killed Wandering Albatross's (*Diomedea exulans*) and made purses out of their webbed feet. I was reminded of that last night at The Strangest Feeling when I saw Templeton take this monstrosity out of his coat pocket and then oh-so-gentlemanly offered to pay for dessert. I was immediately disgusted then, but even more so now that I know it had been there all morning watching me sleep.

Waking up in an unfamiliar bed, being watched by a frog full of loose change, while another woman's panties lay on the floor is about as unsettling of a thing as I can imagine.

I notice there appears to be a cigarette hanging from the side of the frog's zippered lips. I move across the bed for a closer inspection, and realize it's simply rolled-up paper, torn from a page of lined foolscap.

Cautiously, I unroll it to find a note. It's obvious it's from Templeton due to the charcoal scribbling, all in uppercase, and the poor spacing with no punctuation:

GONE FOR
BREAKFAST SHOW
YOURSELF OUT AVOID ZIRK
AT ALL COSTS

My first thought is I wish I'd actually waited long enough to see Templeton take some notes in the library yesterday afternoon, if for no other reason than to see exactly what he's using as a writing instrument. I mean, charcoal again? Seriously?

And what the hoop is a zirk anyway?

No sooner do I ask myself this, does the door open. There's that sour milk smell again. A twenty-something man in what appears to be a spandex bodysuit enters the bedroom. The reason I'm wondering if I might still be dreaming, is that this white bodysuit is covered with fifteen or twenty familiar red, stylized Canadian maple leaves. If I am truly dreaming, I only hope I could be at home in my own bed right now.

"Zirk?" I ask, almost to myself. I try to cover up a little more with the bed sheet, even though I'm already dressed.

"Don't mind me, gorgeous. I'm just getting some more ammonia." The stranger pulls open a dresser drawer and begins digging through some old, rolled-up tube socks.

"What? Ammonia?" I rub my eyes hard with the balls of my hands, foolishly hoping he might be gone when my vision clears. Unfortunately, he's not. "Um, do you know where Templeton is?"

He turns to me with a peculiar look in his eye. He spots the red panties on the floor and then focuses back on me, as if trying to make a connection between the two. On his bodysuit, there's a maple leaf situated right between his legs, in true Adam and Eve fig leaf style. I pull the covers a little bit tighter around myself. He asks me, "Templeton?"

"Templeton Rate. Is he still—around?"

"Templeton went out for breakfast." He gestures toward the change purse at the end of the bed, as though he had put it there himself. "Didn't you get the note?"

I wave the note timidly in my hand, and he goes back to work searching through the sock drawer. Above me, the precarious ceiling fan gives me hope there might be a quick end coming to this awkward situation. I'm almost afraid to ask, but I go for it anyway. "If you don't mind me asking, what's with the get-up?"

He slides the dresser drawer closed and opens the next one down. "The get-up? If you hadn't realized yet, it's Halloween."

"Not for another two-and-a-half weeks, it isn't."

"Sure, if that's how you want to look at it." He continues to speak with his back turned to me, more focused on his search than anything. "But some things don't have to be celebrated for only one day out of the year, correct? Why do you put your Christmas tree up a month in advance?" I don't want to tell him that my landlord doesn't allow Christmas trees in the apartment at *any* time of the year, but he's not waiting for a response from me anyway. He feverishly continues to root through the contents of the open dresser drawer.

I'm trying not to stare, yet I can't help but notice one of the maple leaves on his suit is wedged uncomfortably between the crack of his fanny. Is he supposed to be a luge pilot or some kind of superhero? I try my best to block out the entire image rather than continue to be perplexed by it.

I'm not certain I received an actual answer the first time, so I ask him again: "Is your name Zirk?" For emphasis, I even point to the unrolled paper in my hand.

"You haven't seen a bottle of ammonia around here, have you?" he asks instead of answering. Closing the middle drawer and sliding open the bottom one, he continues his harried search.

With a quick look around me, the first thing I take note of is a grocery bag filled with t-shirts on the floor beside the bed. They must be from old music concerts, as I can make out faded tour dates from ten years ago and rock-and-roll mullets through the translucency of the plastic.

For some reason, there's a pink lawn-flamingo stuck in the carpet. Plastic flamingos are commonly thought to be imitations of the Lesser Flamingo (*Phoenicopterus minor*), since that is the bird they most resemble. However, in ornithology circles it is believed they are actually their own species. This theory is supported by phonetics, as a plastic flamingo is properly pronounced with a long 'a' sound (*"flay*-mingo"), unlike their real-life counterparts. Interestingly, the number of plastic lawn flamingos drastically outnumbers real flamingos in all of North America by a count of nearly fifty-to-one.

Hanging from the ceiling in the corner of the room is a plastic mobile with five birds. They appear to be Mallards (*Anas platyrhynchos*), but due to the juvenile nature of the designs, I can't tell if these are male drakes or females. The real key of course, would be the drake's unmistakable green head and yellow bill (females have light brown heads and dark brown bills), but since it appears the heads have all been shot off with a pellet gun, it's impossible to tell. And truthfully, not very important at the moment.

I don't see a bottle of ammonia anywhere.

The bottom drawer doesn't appear to have what this costumed intruder is looking for either. I ask him, "Does Templeton know you're rummaging through his bedroom looking for ammonia?"

"This isn't Templeton's room, gorgeous. It's *my* room. And before you ask: yes. You're in *my* bed."

I'm instantly too disgusted to respond, so he's allowed to continue freely without retort. "This is *my* dresser. And I'm looking for *my* bottle of ammonia, which I'll be using to wash *my* money. Your ass in my bed notwithstanding, I seriously cannot stand other people's dirt. Do you know how many people have handled a common twenty-dollar bill?" Even if I had an answer for him, he doesn't give me time to open my mouth. "One point two million. That adds up to over ten million fingers all over poor Andrew Jackson's face. Not to mention the twenty-two million all up in Abe Lincoln's grill. And nearly thirty million dirty digits have been in George Washington's curly locks. Those are some seriously filthy numbers. You don't even know who those hands belong to!"

I can't help but notice the poorly concealed bulge on his costume. This man really knows how to make a girl feel uncomfortable. "I guess I never thought about it that way before," I say to him, for lack of anything better to say.

"Of course you didn't."

I look back down at the plastic bag full of shirts. I think one of them says "Toad The Wet Sprocket" on it.

He catches me looking. "You're probably wondering why I've got that bag of shirts? You're wondering why I keep them there, aren't you? They're so old and faded I'd never wear them again. I don't even like looking at them. And I certainly don't want anyone to ever know I've been to a Crash Test Dummies concert before. You see that fan shaking above your head? If that fan should fly off in the middle of the night and slash my head open, I'm going to want something on hand to save my life. Some kind of bandage to stop the bleeding, you know? And what's better than an old Spin Doctors t-shirt, right?"

I look to the plastic flamingo in the floor and the shot-up mallard mobile, and I'm finding these birds are doing very little in the way of making me feel the slightest bit at ease here. I ask, "Why not just turn the fan off at night?"

"That is certainly not the point."

If Zirk had been telling this story, he'd make it incredibly hard to follow.

I notice a digital clock on the floor; it's blinking 9:23 AM. If the time is correct, then my Evolution class started almost half an hour ago. "I don't want to be rude," I say, throwing the covers off myself and jumping out of the bed. "But I've really got to go." I pick up my socks and shoes and head for the door.

He keeps talking, even as I leave the bedroom. And even as I'm out of the apartment and making a break for it — barefoot, down the stairs, and out to the street — I can still hear him yelling something to me about having a happy Halloween.

<div align="center">~~~</div>

I sit outside on the curb and put my socks back on, left foot first. Then my shoes. Yesterday's snow is already gone. Already a forgotten moment in history. I give myself a moment to catch my breath and focus. Where am I? Did Templeton even live at this apartment? I may not know where in the city I am, but at least I don't have to listen to anymore of Captain Canada's crazy ramblings.

I don't recognize anything around me at all.

There are rows of dingy apartment buildings, and across the street is a tiny park with a swing set. Only the chains are hanging where the seats used to be.

I see a poster on a nearby bus stop for some movie called "Dead Ducks." I honestly have no idea where that saying ever originated from.

The telephone pole beside me has a faded picture of a girl stapled to it; she can't be any older than twenty. There are piles of wilted flowers. A wooden cross lies flat on the sidewalk, fallen over from where it had once leaned.

There's a large chunk of the wooden telephone pole missing, at about knee-height. These are all tragic, telltale signs of an accident that must have killed this girl. Perhaps she was sitting on the curb, right where I'm sitting now. Maybe she was lost, just as I am. I pick up the cross and lean it back up against the telephone pole.

As I do, I notice the dead carcass of a bird laying in the gutter. The front of its head has been caved-in. I can tell it's a Domestic Pigeon (*Columba livia domestica*) and that it's probably been dead for over a week now. This girl, whoever she was, gets her own roadside memorial. But the bird? Nothing. A tear swells in my eye as I consider how maybe Templeton left me here for dead too. Will anyone leave a memorial behind for the memory of Isabelle Donhelle when I'm gone? Or will I be left in the gutter without a second thought?

Due to the broken skull, my best guess is this bird was likely killed by a glass collision, flying headfirst into a window. Astoundingly, hundreds of millions of birds are killed by glass collisions annually. Diurnal birds such as pigeons are attracted by the internal reflection of buildings with many windows. For all I know, this bird might have even flown right into Zirk's apartment window, two floors above me.

I know I should take care of this dead pigeon somehow, but I don't. The best I can do is shuffle down the curb to sit a little closer to it. I think back thirteen years to the bloody raven on my Power of Science textbook. I suppose some memories have a harder time than others when it comes to leaving for good.

I remember the light disappearing from the raven's eyes as its pupils dilated and it died right in front of me. It was the first time I had ever seen anything die. I remember the blood as it slowly trickled off the edge of the paper. The smell made my nose sting. It soaked right through the page numbers. I remember seeing the one feather that had snagged on the broken window, still alive as it blew ever so gently in the wind.

I remember kissing Templeton in the library last night. I remember Mr. Giacomin shaking his head at me disapprovingly as we exited. I wasn't embarrassed at the time, but I wish I was. I remember being outside in the parking lot and picking up where we left off. I remember how cold it was. I didn't care that there were other students mingling around the university grounds. I didn't care that Templeton had dirt on his face. I think maybe it was our heat that melted what little snow had remained.

I remember Templeton suggesting we get a bite to eat, as he was craving a piece of pie. *"I know a really great place,"* I remember him saying to me. He hailed a cab, and he paid for it himself, all in loose change. I remember the sound of the zipper as he opened the frog's mouth and dug his dirty fingers inside for the money. I was completely horrified by the sight of it. I remember Templeton telling me his fantasy of a world in some far future inhabited by giants who use humans as change purses. I laughed a little as he told me all about it. I remember seeing the cab driver's license; his name was Wilbur, which we both found funny for some reason. Even funnier and more amusing than Templeton's peculiar imaginings. I remember Templeton didn't help me out of the cab when it stopped.

We were back at The Strangest Feeling, and I remember thinking this would be the once-promised second date I had wished for a week ago. Kitty remembered Templeton, but I'm not sure if she recognized me. She informed us that the kitchen was out of pie, so we opted for a deep-fried chocolate bar and some coffee instead. He didn't say anything at all about my ditching him here last time. I remember looking at Templeton, and although we didn't have many words for one another, I came to the conclusion that I genuinely liked him. I thought Templeton Rate could actually make me happy. He made me smile, even though I'm not entirely sure why.

I remember Templeton suggesting we go back to his place. I asked him if he lived nearby, and I remember him telling me it was too far to walk so we'd better get another taxi. Templeton didn't open the door for me on our way out of the diner. I don't remember what directions he gave to the driver, but it felt like we were going in circles for a half hour. I remember our hands exploring one another for the first time in the back of the taxi. I remember everywhere his hand had touched me. I remember wanting it to never end.

For some reason, I wonder which of these memories will still be in my head years from now. Which ones will make the cut?

I turn away from the pigeon just in time to hear familiar footsteps approach behind me. Templeton Rate sits down on the curb beside me, the dead pigeon between our feet.

"Say, that would make a great handbag, wouldn't it?" He nudges the bird with the toe of his shoe.

And then I remember just how rude he can be.

"Where have you been, Templeton? I'm late for my class, and I don't even know where I am."

Templeton turns to me, confused. "I went out for breakfast. Didn't you get the note I left you?"

I stashed the note into my pocket on my way out of the apartment. I take it out and wave it in his face. "You mean *this*, right? Thanks a lot. It was very kind of you to leave it behind."

"You're welcome." He removes a cigarette from his coat pocket and strikes a matchstick on the sidewalk. He takes a quick drag, and then he holds the smoke out to offer me a puff.

"No thank you. Haven't I told you I don't smoke?"

"Well, thankfully, I think we skipped that whole boring first-date interview process last night." He flicks some ashes onto the dead pigeon.

"Don't do that! That's disrespectful." I push his hand away in the other direction. I take another look at the note, just to make sure I didn't miss any details that might help to clear things up for me.

Nothing.

He glances over, and taps on the AVOID ZIRK AT ALL COSTS part of the message. "So, did you heed my warnings?"

"That's a difficult thing to do considering how you left me in his bed."

"Well, I don't have a bed of my own yet. It makes for an awkward living situation."

"Tell me about it."

"Seriously though," Templeton continues. "Zirk is crazy. Mentally, he's just totally out to lunch. Completely, one-hundred-percent fucked-up. I honestly have no idea how he manages to hold down a full-time job. You should have just avoided him entirely."

"Now you tell me."

"He works with me at the hotel you know? He's a doorman too."

I have to ask, "What's the deal with the costume?"

"Costume?"

I can't tell if he's joking with me, or simply has no idea what I'm talking about. Either way, I decide not to dwell on it; it's probably best to just keep things moving along. "Never mind," I say.

He takes another long drag of his cigarette and looks off into the distance, watching the morning clouds roll into place. I've never seen anyone so peaceful. I wish I could calm myself down a little, but I'm still upset about everything that's transpired. "If you went out for breakfast, why did you leave your wallet behind? Just to keep an eye on me?"

"He doesn't have eyes anymore," he says calmly.

Finally, I turn my attention away from him. "I'm really mad at you right now, Templeton. Do you know that? This isn't how you're supposed to treat people. I'm mad, and it doesn't even seem like you notice."

"Don't worry about it. I notice *everything*." Templeton takes one long, last drag of the cigarette, and then extinguishes it at his feet. He motions to the girl's picture on the telephone pole beside us. "Did you know her?"

"Hmm? No. Why would I know her?"

"She was in your class, wasn't she?"

I take a good, long look at the picture, but it's not ringing any bells. Curly brown hair. Toothy smile. Her whole life ahead of her. She looks just like any of the girls at the school, or anywhere else for that matter. Students are students. They're all the same, aren't they? If this dead girl actually did attend Hawthorne University, then she went completely unnoticed by me. "Are you sure?" I'm already starting to put this morning's events behind me. "What was her name?"

Templeton looks at the picture at little more closely now too, as though he's searching it for hidden answers. "I don't know. I didn't know her."

Tied to one of the flowers is a note that reads:

We'll always love you, Autumn.

Again, I find myself wondering about my own memorial.

He tries changing the subject while I'm not paying attention. "I think it's funny."

"What's that?" I ask.

"It's funny how the ideas of life and death are so separate, but at the same time they're so closely connected to one another, aren't they?"

I don't have an answer for him, since I don't really know what his point is. He doesn't embellish either. After another minute though, I get tired of waiting for an explanation. "I'm not sure what you mean," I confess.

"What is it you see when you look around you?"

I scan everything with my eyes: the dead pigeon, the dead girl and the dead flowers. I even envision the dead frog back upstairs.

Strangely, he knows exactly what it is I'm seeing. Another Xerox copy of my thoughts. "All you see is death, don't you? But all I see are the traces of life that still surround it all."

He's right. Aside from the sound of traffic in the distance and a plastic bag blowing by us on a breeze in true *American Beauty*-style, I don't see anything in the way of life here. There's so much loss and sadness on this sidewalk. I want to tell him I know he's right. I want to tell him I can't help from seeing the worst in everything, because of my own inability to see the best in myself. And I want to ask him to elaborate — to share his own feelings on the subject — but thankfully Templeton continues before I can say anything too stupid.

"Do you see that?" He directs my attention to an old rusted car parked about ten feet from where we sit, and he points out a long scrape on the trunk. "You see where the paint has been scratched right off? There's a story about what happened there. Somebody somewhere knows that story, and they experienced it first-hand. That seemingly insignificant little scrape has its own complicated story for why it exists."

He reaches his hand out to feel something on the telephone pole beside us. "Somebody carved their initials into this telephone pole. Do you see? They stood right here in this very spot and scratched a W and a C into the wood with who knows what. Maybe a pocketknife? Maybe a rock? I don't know why they did it, but there's got to be a reason."

He picks up the wilted flowers, and inspects them delicately. Some ants crawl out onto his hand, but he doesn't bother flicking them away. "These flowers were left here by someone. Someone who went to some shitty corner store and overpaid for them. And somebody somewhere grew these flowers and cut them and sold them for the sole purpose of taking advantage of that one person's mourning." He tosses the flowers back down at the base of the telephone pole as though they don't mean anything at all now.

"I don't know," is what I tell him, which is certainly an understatement for how I feel. I don't know why on Earth he's considering the origins of a scrape on a car, carvings in a telephone pole, or even where the flowers must have come from.

"Don't you see?" he pushes. "All around us are casualties of life. Things that still exist, but at the same time are also non-existent. And yet the signs are still there. Within all the dead shit, the signs of life remain. Imagine we were sitting in the middle of a graveyard; what would you see? All you would see is death, wouldn't you? Most people would. But what's really more important to you? Life? Or death?"

I don't know the answer to that. I don't know *what's* more important. I only know I'm lonely. I know all I desperately want is for someone to finally love me, and not expect to receive cheapened birthday greetings; not cheat on their wife; not leave me scared and alone in their creepy roommate's smelly pink bed sheets.

"You know, Isabella—"

"Isabelle," I correct him.

"Right. You know, I was thinking that I like you. It's not particularly easy for me to be so open and honest. I know I'm not perfect. I probably say shit you don't like and do fucked-up things that piss you off. But I think that I do. I think that I really do like you."

I can't believe it, but those three words I've been waiting forever to hear? This was actually the closest anyone's come so far. It's kind of pathetic in a way. I'm still mad at him, but instead of telling him everything, instead of being as honest as he's being with me, I simply decide to say, "I think I like you too, Templeton."

"What do you say I get you back to school then? I'm missing class too, you know."

It occurs to me my car is still sitting in the school parking lot. We get up from the curb and walk to catch a bus to the University. In an unexpected move, he even pays for my bus ride with some more change from his pocket.

I instantly recognize the familiar orange plastic seats of bus #3031. This was my birthday present to myself last Thursday. This was the same bus I had gotten off of to avoid Templeton Rate a week ago. The same one in which he'd found me, all alone and miserable. Where he'd spotted some sign of life I was previously unaware of.

I sit in the same seat, and notice the same screw twisted into the pole in front of me. I was searching for answers within its X-shaped void just a week ago, but there's nothing hidden from me that's worth looking for now. There's nowhere I'm trying to run from. Nothing I'm trying to ignore. Templeton even puts his arm around my shoulder.

As I turn to him and smile, I notice something on the other side of the window.

Right around the corner from Templeton's apartment building, nestled between the same triple-x porn shops, is The Strangest Feeling café.

Strangely, we were only about half a block away.

Contemplating Curses

SO THAT'S WHERE this all started. Thinking back on it now, I wonder why I didn't get out of the whole darn situation that morning when I had the chance? I could have gotten up from the sidewalk and figured out what to do on my own, instead of following Templeton's lead. I could have made my own choices, instead of simply allowing things to happen to me. I could have stayed miserably single, instead of becoming so fatally involved.

But I wouldn't have sat on the bus with Templeton that morning if I hadn't slept with him the night before; if I hadn't had that argument with Professor Nickwelter in the back of his car; if I hadn't waited all those nights at The Strangest Feeling; if I hadn't left Ville Constance to come to Boston; if I hadn't met Cindey Fellowes; if I hadn't been rejected from the Doneau High basketball team.

Now that I think about it, I probably should have learned my lesson after running through the hedge that one afternoon before even thinking of joining the basketball team in the first place.

It's starting to make a little more sense now, isn't it? And I've only just scratched the surface of explaining how I got here. In this box without light. This cage without air. This life without hope. That's not too dramatic, is it?

I was doubtful at first, but now I'm sure my left arm must be broken. It hurts to touch, but I can't stop myself from feeling the bones under my skin moving in ways they shouldn't be moving. I've never had a broken bone in my life. It feels cold on the inside, but it burns to the touch.

I start thinking of my parents, back home in Ville Constance. The last time I'd seen my mother, I told her all about my feelings toward Templeton Rate.

Well, at least Templeton as he had seemed at the time, from my own delusional standpoint. I know that through standard and practical parental advice, she had just wanted to make sure I was safe out on my own in the big world; that the decisions I was making could never hurt me. I know that now, but a whole lot of good that advice does at this point. I wonder if my parents ever regret giving advice as much as I regret having to listen to it? I wonder if they're even the least bit worried about me right now? I suppose they could find some solace in the fact I'm currently laying in the safest possible place in Boston. According to Templeton Rate, anyway.

After all, he did tell me I'd be safest in here.

That this was the one place in the city I could be if I wanted to stay the way I was.

My only hope for a last chance.

My last chance at death.

I pull myself up off the floor again. Then I take a deep breath in and ready myself for my next big attempt at getting out of here. I charge across the floor, like a crazed Emu (*Dromaius novaehollandiae*). Because of the darkness, I'm not the least bit certain when I'll impact with the other side, but I trip over my own feet before I even get there. I hit the wall awkwardly with my forearm, rather than connecting with my shoulder as I had intended. But that isn't what really hurts; it's the fall back to floor where I land on my broken left arm that really hurts.

The real truth is all the lies I've been told up to now are what hurt the most. It's harsh the reality that one single person can be so cruel. Not just to me, but to an entire city.

I need to deal with this throbbing pain in my arm. It's radiating a smelly, wet heat now. I touch it and I'm horrified to discover my broken ulna has now pierced right through the skin. The sight of blood is one of a number of things that really makes me uneasy. The smell of blood is another. Thankfully though, the lack of light is currently negating one of those fears. I begin to feel light-headed; it's getting harder to think. I console myself with the thought that at least my bones aren't hollow, like that of a bird, or else I might have shattered the arm completely.

I want to come up with the most sensible way out of this horrible predicament, yet I find myself contemplating curses instead. I'm trying to think of which precise word I'll be yelling out loud in my one great final moment.

Awkwardly, I pull my right arm out of my Christmas Island Frigatebird (*Fregata andrewsi*) t-shirt, and then I slide the shirt over my left shoulder and carefully down my arm, making sure to not snag it on the exposed bone. The blood-soaked shirt will have to do its best to absorb a little more of my insides. Hopefully I won't need any more makeshift bandages tonight, because I'm quickly running out of clothes. And I'm finding no humor or comfort in the irony that an endangered species t-shirt is saving my own life right now.

I hug the metal floor once again. Just what is going on outside right now, I wonder? Are things really as bad as I suspect they are? Maybe I would have been better off out there. I mean, in all my life to date, I've never liked being the odd one out. Who does? But now that I consider it, embracing change has to be the way to go, isn't it? If you're the last to change, you're automatically the odd one out.

No. I'm not seriously trying to convince myself that being on the other side of these walls is the better option, am I? This lack of oxygen is really starting to take its toll.

Focus Isabelle. Where was I?

That image of Zirk in his costume suddenly pops into my head. It triggers memories of spending Halloween with Templeton. The answers were all right there in front of me that night, weren't they?

If only I'd paid closer attention to the details.

How could I have been so blind?

I used to believe in witches. I suppose the fortune teller I had visited in my youth with Cindey Fellowes was a witch, wasn't she? Over time, I had convinced myself that witches were simply characters created to be antagonists in movies and to scare children in October. The same applies to ghosts and haunted houses.

I used to believe in angels. I used to believe in Santa Claus too. I used to believe in doing the right thing. I used to believe in Templeton Rate. And I used to believe I'd find a way out of here. Now I'm not so sure.

Right now, I'm not sure what it will take to believe in something else again.

To really dream again.

Or to truly live again.

Should I ever get the chance.

The Molt

MONDAY, OCTOBER TWENTY-SEVENTH. I leave some food in Claude's dish before I go. I grab my bag and exit out onto Newbury Street. It's a sunny morning, but the freezing cold of October has definitely set in. There hasn't been any sign of snow in Boston since that first day two weeks ago. There's no trace at all of the snow that had blanketed the city on that one day, but the events which unfolded the same afternoon are still extraordinarily frozen solid in my memory.

My daily migration has begun. As I leave my apartment, I notice the wedding dresses in the window of the shop to my right. It's no surprise though; I notice them every morning. These dresses used to make me feel lost, as though they were representing something much too far out of my reach. I thought the portraits behind the glass were all frauds; the false brides and grooms were laughing at me from some made-up fantasy world. Of course, I'd always felt they still had more than I did. Until Templeton came along, that is.

I dodge a couple of yuppie moms pushing over-sized baby carriages and I find the same feelings of pre-Templeton loneliness racing through my head all over again. But just the thought of him helps me to smile again.

The popular orange Boston Duck Tours bus motors slowly along Newbury Street; its cartoon duck painted on the side splashing in a puddle, and its passengers inside pressed against the windows with cameras ready. The duck reminds me of the fact that drakes are among the few birds with a penis. The male organ of the Argentine Lake Duck (*Oxyura vittata*), a bird which only weighs about a pound, is a corkscrew-like appendage that becomes a foot long when fully erect. The female has a long corkscrew vagina, spiraling in the opposite direction. This bird is a riotously promiscuous species, and the drake's extraordinary organ has evolved in such a way to displace the sperm of the female's earlier mates. This cartoon duck reminds me Templeton and I have made love a dozen times in the last two-and-a-half weeks. The feeling is exhilarating, when I think about how lucky I am to have him.

I smile for the flashing cameras, whether I'm the intended subject for their photos or not.

If these tourists had been telling this story, they would assume I've always been this happy.

To my left is the Starbucks, and I go inside to grab my morning coffee. Most of the staff knows me by name now, but not one of them looks the least bit familiar to me. Much like students, baristas are simply baristas. On the counter, I spot a birthday card. It's standing upright, propped open enough so I can read what's been written inside:

> *To Sarah,*
> *Happy birthday! Hope you like the bracelet, please wear it.*

I note the lack of haiku in the greeting. Once I reach the front counter, the barista greets me with a good morning. Her nametag reads "Sarah," and I notice the absence of a bracelet around her wrist. I can't help it, but I instantly do not wish to deal with this person. I let the man behind me go ahead while I wait for the next register over to open up. I've been in a good mood for over two weeks now, and I don't need it spoiled by someone so ungrateful.

With a Grande Guatemala Magdalena in hand (an elegant and intriguing blend of gentle spice flavors), I head around to the back of the building where my car is parked. I can see Claude in the third-story window, watching me from his cage. "Bye-bye Bella," he calls out through the partially open window.

I almost respond, but stop myself before I do. He's looking directly at me, but there's something that seems off in both his motions and emotions. I don't know, it's almost as if his head is leaning a little too far to one side. I know Claude well enough to pick up on the subtleties. I wonder if he ever longs to fly, like all of the other birds he can see out that window. Sometimes I catch him staring at the Rock Pigeons (*Columba livia*) perched on the telephone wires across from him. Sometimes the pigeons are chased off and replaced by American Crows (*Corvus brachyrhynchos*). All of those birds with two wings that can simply come and go as they please. I don't believe the thought has ever crossed my mind before now, but it seems like it would be an obvious assumption: does Claude have the ability to yearn?

I open the car door and toss my bag in before responding, "Bye-bye Claude." I get in and I drive out of Public Alley 434, trying my best to not worry about him any longer.

I haven't been back to Templeton's apartment since that first awkward morning, but he's spent the night at my place a few times since then. He had seemed very interested in Claude, but I felt as though it was forced; as though he understood how important Claude was to me, and he felt he had to act accordingly. I've really only known Templeton for a very short time now, but I already know that's not in his character.

He wouldn't display false emotion.

He wears his heart on his sleeve.

Templeton Rate doesn't pretend to be someone he's not.

At the intersection of Exeter and Newbury Street, I sit in the shadow of the John Hancock Tower to my left. The Tower makes me uncomfortable, and it always has. I think it's all of the reflections off its sheer glass façade that make me dizzy. To my right, I can see the fifty-two floors of the Prudential Tower, and I think back to my conversation with Templeton when I told him my dreams of flying. I get lost for a moment when I see a pair of Ring-Billed Gulls (*Larus delawarensis*) take off from the rooftop and hover within that piece of sky before they flap their wings and disappear from sight behind another building. I just know they were sitting there, waiting for me.

Because that's the moment I'm most jealous of.

I'm still dreaming as the car behind me honks its horn.

I make a right turn onto the busy Huntington Avenue, and fight with the rest of the Monday morning commuters. From there, it's a right onto Parker Street and then a couple of short turns more before I'm once again parked in my own reserved spot within the Hawthorne University staff parking lot.

In terms of migratory routes, it's a pretty short distance; twenty minutes to work in the morning, and usually fifteen minutes to get home in the evening, traffic permitting. Although, where birds will make their migratory trips only a couple of times a year over large distances of thousands of miles — the longest of which is the Sooty Shearwater (*Puffinus griseus*), which makes an annual round-trip of roughly forty-thousand miles — my migration happens daily, nearly every day of the year. Still, sometimes I wonder who's got it tougher: me or the sooty shearwater.

I pull into the parking lot, upset my coffee is already lukewarm. But when everyday follows the same routine, it's always going to be lukewarm. Thankfully though, my life has felt much less nauseatingly monotonous since Templeton Rate along.

I guess you could say Templeton and I have been dating for the last two weeks. As odd as our pairing might seem, I still can't put my finger on what it is that makes me feel the way I do about him. Maybe it's something akin to a pheromone-type of effect. I don't consider myself to know much about the details of pheromone attraction. Although rampant in the animal kingdom, pheromones are mostly non-existent in birds, since in general, birds have a very poor olfactory sense. Corkscrew penises aside, their mating is done primarily through song and dance.

The only conclusions I've drawn so far is still that first one I made: that in my mind, there exists some absurd emotional connection with Templeton's smoldering dark brown eyes, that fantastic mop of hair and the cigarette breath. Because they're the very same traits Claude had. But Templeton is not the same person Claude was. He's not about the happy birthdays or the scheduled make-outs. He makes me feel special. He makes me a better person. He encourages me to embrace change rather than resist it.

If he hadn't made me feel special.

Templeton is not Professor Nickwelter; he's not trying to keep our relationship hidden and he doesn't buy me wristwatches and other such frivolities in order to keep me interested. He's not about the charitable birthday dinners or any secret rendezvous. I feel at ease around him. I no longer have to look for comfort in the images of birds. He sees things around him — and he sees things in *me* — that even some birds with their incredible visual acuity would have trouble spotting. There's a reason he found me on the bus that night and it's the very same reason I need him in my life.

If he hadn't found me on the bus that night.

Templeton's academic advancements are also amazing. He's a natural genius, and the vast amount he's learned in such little time makes me proud to have him as a student in my classes. His current papers are a major improvement over the original report that had appeared mysteriously on my desk just weeks ago. Whether he's written about wing and skeletal structure, flight function, muscle growth, or the respiratory system, they've all been meticulously detailed, and they've all received Professor Donhelle's famous blue checkmark. His work had been nothing short of flawless and immaculate. His understandings seem far beyond that of any other student who has ever sat in my class. I have yet to question him about those first random scribblings he'd given me, though I've convinced myself those reports were merely terrible on purpose. A cheap joke to pique my interest. Surely the intimate knowledge he's recently shown suggests Templeton Rate has a well-educated background. There's no possibility that a comprehensive familiarity such as his could be faked.

He's certainly not the man I had originally assumed him to be. His decision to switch from sticks of charcoal to ballpoint pens is almost evidence enough.

I lock my car and head for the ornithology department faculty entrance. I envision Templeton at the door smoking a cigarette as he waits for me. But instead, all I get is Jerry Humphries. His ugly brown car is parked right in front, its trunk open wide and one of the rear wheels up over the curb, buried in the grass. It looks like there's another shipment arriving I was unaware of. I think for a moment about talking to whoever's in charge of scheduling, but then it occurs to me that's actually Humphries himself. While he should have notified me in the first place, I'll gladly avoid making an issue out of it, if that means not having to speak to the dirty little man face to face. But unfortunately, there'll be no avoiding him this morning.

He's wearing his famous weathered, brown leather trench coat, and fumbling with a large cardboard box, sloppily sealed with an overabundance of orange electrical tape. His fingers are gnarled; the nails chomped down to the cuticles. His face is all patches of hair, some thick and some thin. Nose hairs spring forth in every direction. And his head is a really odd shape; like a rejected potato at the supermarket that you'll always find lingering on its own in the bottom of the bin after all the others have been taken. The one that will eventually get thrown out because it's been sitting by itself for far too long.

If Jerry Humphries had been telling this story, I'm certain it wouldn't find a very wide audience.

"Good morning, Bella. How was your weekend?"

I hear his wretched morning greeting, and I wish I could slug him in the stomach. Could I do it? Would it really be so bad to just hit someone I dislike so intensely? It certainly wouldn't be something I'd ever thought of doing two weeks ago. I hear Templeton's voice in my head insisting I embrace change.

I can change, can't I?

"My weekend was fine, Jerry." Maybe I'll hit him tomorrow. "And you?"

"Great! Went up to Portsmouth. Did some hunting. I've got enough meat for a month now! You know, you should really come with me one of these weekends."

Oh my goodness, no. "I really don't think so. Hunting's not exactly my thing." I hope that will be enough to end the conversation, but I know it won't be.

"How about church then? Why don't you tag along with me next Sunday?" For reasons unknown, Humphries has asked me to come to church with him a number of times. It surprises me that someone so vile can actually be putting his faith in something.

A glimmer of light catches my eye, from the bent cross dangling from his rearview mirror. It doesn't surprise him at all when I decline his offer yet again. "I didn't know hunting in Portsmouth was legal?" I ask him. I hope it's enough to soon find an end to our conversation, since I feel sick to my stomach just continuing this exchange.

"Well, it's like anything: you've just got to know where to look for it." He is such a creep.

But then, like divine intervention, Templeton comes out through the doors. He seems to walk outside with a purpose, and is a little surprised when he sees me. I'm not sure why exactly, as I show up at the same time every morning. Punctual like the Common Cuckoo (*Cuculus canorus*, striking every hour on the cuckoo clock.

"Greetings, Professor Donhelle," he says.

Humphries thinks he's doing a kindly favor by introducing us; "Bella, you know Templeton Rate, don't you? He's a student here." But I know there's nothing kind about the rat. "Templeton was just helping me unload some of these boxes."

"Oh, we're quite familiar, Templeton says. "Isn't that right, Isabella?"

I don't correct him anymore when he calls me Isabella. I'm not sure what he's expecting me to say in response here, but I show him a sign of approbation. "Well, that's very nice of you, Templeton. I'm sure Mr. Humphries appreciates the helping hand." As though I was his mother and he was five years old and helping unload the groceries.

"I just like to do my part." He turns back to Humphries, who's eyeballing us as though sensing something else might be going on between Templeton and I. But Jerry Humphries has never picked up on subtleties very easily. "Is this the last one then?" Templeton asks him.

"That's right." Humphries hands him the box. I hear something rattling around inside. It sounds like nails and broken glass.

"What have you got in these boxes anyway?" I ask warily. "I hope there aren't any birds taped up in there." I might sound as though I'm joking casually, but I really just want to make sure.

Humphries closes the trunk of his car, and his Jesus fish falls off, clattering off the curb and onto the pavement. "Just some lab equipment. You know, stuff of that ilk."

Templeton has already gone back inside the school with the last box. I decide it's best to follow him immediately, and not leave any parting words for Humphries. So, when Humphries turns away, bending down to pick up his metal fish, I use that precise moment to exit without another word.

I didn't expect Templeton to hold the door open for me; I would never mistake him for being such a gentleman. But at the very least, I thought he would have waited long enough for me to catch up. I have to run after him through the faculty halls, careful to not spill my coffee on the way. I ask him, "Whatever made you help Humphries with these boxes anyway?"

"I was just walking by and he asked for my help. That's all." He doesn't stop walking, and I'm at his heels following along behind him, like a dog looking for scraps. "I get the feeling you don't like that guy very much," he calls back to me.

"That's an understatement."

"You didn't fuck him too, did you?"

I stop in my tracks. "Jerry Humphries? Templeton, please! That man is disgusting."

Templeton stops now too, and he turns to face me. "Well, you already slept with Nickwelter. How am I supposed to know?"

"I had a life before you came along, Templeton."

"Really?"

"Well, what do you think?"

"I think you had an affair with one of your professors and your only other relationship has been with a one-armed bird. You can't be satisfied with just coming to this school every damn day and teaching these morons the same inane bullshit semester after semester after semester, can you? Don't you want anything more than that? Don't you want to leave something important behind when you're dead and gone?"

He looks at me, holding the box in his arms and waiting for some kind of response. I keep any answers from him though, and stand in awe of the things he's just said. What's come over him? And why is he talking about my demise so soon into our relationship?

Templeton's arms slouch, realizing he's overstepped his boundaries. "I'm sorry," he says to me for the first time ever. The contents of the box seem to apologize too, rolling in unison to one end. "I don't know what makes me fly off the handle like that sometimes."

"It's okay," I tell him. As hard as it is to hear it said, I think it's harder to actually admit to myself his words are mostly true. "Maybe you just need some coffee. I find it helps to calm my nerves."

He sets the box down on the linoleum floor of the hall, right outside the south laboratory. "I think I just have a hard time believing you slept with that guy, is all."

"I shouldn't have told you the details about my past relationship in the first place," I say to him. "It's just that, well, we all have things we've done in our past that we later regret, don't we? It's hard to simply wipe the slate clean."

"It's called change, Bella. It's what we *all* do. And it's inevitable, so you'd better get used to it." Templeton has a way of really making me think about every last word he says. And he's prone to following it up with a changing of the subject. "But don't dwell on it right now, okay? Let me walk you to your office."

I agree, and I think about his one-armed bird comment from a minute ago. "I hope you know birds have wings, and not arms, right?"

Templeton smirks. Had he purposefully set himself up to be proven wrong? He looks down at the box on the floor, and suggests leaving it there for Humphries to deal with. Taking the coffee from my hand, he gulps some down and squirms a little. I thought by now he'd be used to how much sugar I like. "You know, the only reason I was even helping that guy with his boxes in the first place was because I was waiting for you to show up this morning."

"What? Really?"

"Really."

"You were just waiting right there at the door?"

"It's true."

So far, my relationship with Templeton has not been much more than sex and homework, so it's satisfying to engage in what feels like an ordinary boyfriend/girlfriend squabble. He was right when he said it though; the only real relationships I've had so far in my life have been my affair with Professor Nickwelter and the feeding of my invalid parrot. I'm just glad I never mentioned the sad tale of kissing Claude in high school to Templeton. Admittedly, I don't have much to show for in the last twenty-nine years, but would my life really have been so different if Mrs. Wyatt had not made that single, heartless decision?

If I hadn't been rejected from the Doneau High basketball team.

I was still lost in Templeton's eyes when Professor Nickwelter came around the corner. As usual, he wins the contest for the worst possible timing. He stops in his tracks, no doubt in stupefied wonder as to what Isabelle Donhelle was doing longing after this student of hers while she had just put the moves on Nickwelter in the back of his car only a couple of weeks ago. He fidgets, adjusting his collar nervously, unsure of his next move.

Templeton turns to see where my eyes are fixed. He and Nickwelter stare each other down for a moment. I visualize a California Condor (*Gymnogyps californianus*) and a Golden Eagle (*Aquila chrysaetos*) challenging one another over who gets first dibs on a mountain goat carcass. Of course, I imagine Templeton as the golden eagle, but I'm now rethinking my role as the mountain goat carcass in this scenario.

Before any such bloodbath can occur, however, I break the silence by accidentally dropping my coffee on the floor. At least I think it was an accident. "Oh! Good morning, Professor Nickwelter."

I can tell he has no idea what he could possibly say to me right now that would make things any less awkward. "Good morning, Isabelle." My only hope is he's at least thinking of his wife. "Do you think I could speak with you at some point today? I have important matters to discuss."

"Of course, Professor," I say, making sure I'm not getting any coffee on my shoes. "I'll come see you when I can."

Nickwelter takes one last glance toward Templeton, eyeing him up for just the briefest of moments, before turning back to me. "Very good. Thank you." Then he turns and walks away. It's a sad exit, one which leaves a hurtful, burning sensation in my heart.

Nickwelter disappears from sight, and I look down at the mess of coffee on the floor. The plastic lid had popped off upon impact, and the creamy brown liquid slowly spreads out before me. I see my reflection, as well as the reflection of the ceiling lights above me. Templeton's dark silhouette is in there too. Like staring up at clouds in an effort find imaginative shapes, the coffee seems to take on an entirely new form; it begins to resemble a dense flock of birds. Flying across the cold hall floor, migrating toward Templeton Rate.

It reminds me of a birding expedition I was on a few years ago. We were in the marshes of some backwater Massachusetts town, studying the habits of the American Bittern (*Botaurus lentiginosus*). The sun was just rising, creating a beautiful orange and pink pastel sky. From across the marsh came the sudden and explosive sound of a gunshot, probably from duck hunters who had been waiting there all morning. The sound of the shot seemed louder than the booming cry of the bitterns, which flew off immediately. What I remember the most was the sight of the siege of bitterns; the idyllic sky had been overcome by this murky outline of the birds. They had lost all individual shape, and became one single, black sheet against the sunrise. It was, and still is, surprising to me how these birds could possibly find the room to flap their own wings in and amongst one another.

Templeton's own recent report on the very same bitterns I had once studied was impeccably thorough and insightful, from detailing its distinctive bellowing call to the bird's extraordinarily instinctive ability to camouflage itself amongst marsh reeds.

I look up from the floor to Templeton, who seems to have been watching me closely the whole time. "I can't believe you fucked that guy," he reiterates with wonder. As intelligent as he is, sometimes he's still in need of help when it comes to social interaction.

"I'd better let the janitor know about this mess," I say.

"Don't worry about it," he tells me. "I'll get Humphries to clean it up." Templeton has a knack for always finding the best possible solution. I don't want to know how that request might be initiated, so I don't ask.

Templeton convinces me I need to get my things together in order to prepare for class this morning. I ask if I'll see him again before the day is through, but he tells me he doesn't have class today. He's got a shift at the hotel, as well as some personal errands to attend to. He'll be by later, he says, and maybe we can meet up for lunch.

"That's fine," I say as I turn around to leave.

"Hold on, Bella. Can I ask you something?"

Memories of The Question instantly take over any thoughts I already had inside my head. "Of course. What is it?"

"What are you doing for Halloween?"

"I don't usually do anything for Halloween other than throw candy out my window to kids in the alley. Except for the mini Three Musketeers. I keep all of those for myself."

He stares at me with a blank look in his eyes.

"What?" I ask.

"I'm sorry," he says again for the second time now. "But that's pretty sad."

"Well, I'm not going to sit at the front door all night and get depressed when no kids come by." Which is exactly what I did my first three Halloweens in Boston. "Why do you ask? Do you have something better on your mind?"

"I usually go up to Salem for the Haunted Happenings festival. I was wondering if I could borrow your car."

That certainly wasn't where I thought this conversation was headed. "Did I hear you right? You want to borrow my car?"

"That's right." He looks at me with another blank expression, this time wondering why this wasn't what I had expected to hear. "Did I say something wrong?"

I reiterate, and speak slowly, hoping he'll be able to understand what I'm trying to get at. "You want to borrow my car so you can go to Salem for Halloween?"

"That's correct."

"By yourself?"

"It's what I do every year."

"And you didn't think of asking me to come *with* you?" Could I possibly ever date someone who isn't either twice my age or half my IQ?

"I'm sorry," he says again. "I suppose I'm still getting used to this whole situation."

"Situation? You mean our relationship?"

"Let me start over. Would you like to come with me to Salem for Halloween?"

"Thanks for the invite. But Salem? For Halloween? That seems pretty intense."

"Are you coming or not? You can bring your parrot and your Three Musketeers with you if you want, but I'm not going to ask a second time."

"Do I need a costume?"

"Have you ever celebrated Halloween before?"

"To be honest, it's never been one of my favorite holidays. I don't think I get it."

"It's kids dressing up as things they're scared of and it's complete strangers giving them candy. What's not to get?"

The strangers with candy part is the part my parents tried to keep far away from me when I was growing up. It didn't make any sense to me then, but I can see their point now.

"I know what really scares you about Halloween," he says. "It's the costumes, isn't it?"

"Costumes don't scare me."

"No, I know. But it's the change they represent."

He was right, wasn't he? It always comes down to my fear of change.

If I hadn't run through the hedge at Saint Francis Elementary.

"Can't I just be myself?" I ask.

"If you're coming with me, you'll need a costume."

"All right," I decide. "I'll come. But the whole idea really creeps me out, you know? Salem seems like the scariest place you could go on Halloween."

"That's the point, isn't it?" He turns around to leave me without so much as a kiss or one of his infamously unromantic high-fives. "I'll see you later then."

I look back down at the coffee on the floor which now seems to be taking on a much more sinister shape. I convince myself it's just my mind playing tricks on me. The puddle creeps to the edge of the box, and quickly begins turning the cardboard a dark, wet color. I decide I'd better move the box myself before anything of value is ruined. The south lab is sure to have some paper towels, so I decide to clean up the entire mess myself rather than trust someone else to do it. I unlock the door and flick the lights on.

The overhead lights come on, one by one. They illuminate the front of the laboratory all the way to the back. The center of the room has been cleared out, and there are boxes and crates piled up along the walls and on top of the tables. There are some unidentifiable bits and pieces of equipment strewn about, but I don't see much else of interest.

Until I spot the wooden planks at the back of the room, that is. Some strange framework of boards is being constructed.

It's probably been six months since I've stepped foot in the south laboratory, but this is certainly not how I remember it being maintained. It seems larger than I recall, but it's most likely just the empty space playing a trick on me. I'm beginning to question the extent of the fire in here that closed the school down for one weekend a month ago.

The back of the room smells like a lumberyard. This wooden frame must be as tall as it is wide; I'd say fifteen to twenty feet, almost a perfect cube. Tools and wooden boards are scattered around the floor. There's a table saw surrounded by mounds of sawdust that nobody seemed concerned about sweeping up. My mother would have a heart attack.

I don't find any paper towels anywhere, so I pick up the box from the hallway, and add it to the mountainous pile forming on the lab's tables. Something is going on in here I wasn't told about. I'll question Humphries about it later.

On my way out of the room though, I spot a single feather blowing around in the corner of the lab. It reflects the lights from above, giving it a kind of glow. There's an air vent on the wall that has caught the feather in a gentle, spinning pattern. It seems so lonely, as though it's lost its way. With the south lab's close proximity to the school's bird sanctuary, it's not uncommon for feathers to find their way around these parts, but this one has caught my unyielding attention. At first, it doesn't appear overly special, but I still feel compelled to investigate. I take the feather into my hand; it's soft like an ordinary down feather, but when I rub it between my fingers, the tip disintegrates into a dusty powder, indicating it must be a pulviplume. Between its size and the chestnut coloration, I surmise it must have come from a Goliath Heron (*Ardea goliath*). Herons don't have the common preen glands from which most birds obtain oil to condition and waterproof their feathers. Pulviplumes such as this have evolved in certain birds like the heron to create this cleansing powder, and they will comb it through their feathers with their toes. But goliath herons are only found in Africa and parts of Asia, and we don't have any in the bird sanctuary that I'm aware of. I let the feather float back to the floor and as I do, I hear its croaking call. But muffled, as if it was coming from somewhere in my mind. I dismiss it, assuming I'm mistaken, since I have to get going to my first class this morning.

~~~

It's a few hours later now and I still haven't seen any further sign of Templeton today. I'm sitting in my office alone, eating my terribly simple tuna sandwich. Every day, and with every bite, I feel more and more like the endangered Hawaiian Shearwater (*Puffinus newelli*), living on a steady diet of tuna. The ironic part is that the shearwater will travel in flocks when they hunt for their lunch, while I eat dreadfully alone in my office. Somehow at this moment I feel more endangered than the Hawaiian shearwater, if that's at all possible.

When I arrived at my office this morning, there was another "MOM" note from the desk of Steffen James taped to my door, no doubt torn once again from Jerry Humphries' notepad. I'd never called my mother back three weeks ago. Now the note is staring at me from my desktop, reminding me that I'm not quite the thoughtful daughter she wished she'd raised. Why on Earth would she call me at the school again when I was home alone last night?

There's something within Steffen's handwriting that reminds me of the self-inflicted mess I'd made of myself in the university library two weeks ago. Some of the staff has no doubt heard all about it; there's an awkward quality to Steffen's *M's* that seem to want to avoid bringing up the subject with me. I would think he'd know me better by now, and that there's no stinking chance I would want to be discussing my sexual exploits with anyone I see on a regular basis.

I consider heading down to Professor Nickwelter's office as I'd promised earlier, but then thoughts begin to race through my head. I start to wonder what it was that was on Nickwelter's mind earlier this morning. I wonder what we might discuss should I sit down across from him. I imagine he's probably heard about the library fiasco as well. I imagine him belittling me. I can hear
~~~

him mocking me. I can see his eyes tearing up and I wonder how this man can say these things to me when it's so obvious he actually cares so much for me still. Is this how I deserve to be treated? Even if it's only in my imagination?

I used to worry about the kinds of things that people thought of me, especially when I was questioning my own actions. Did Cindey Fellowes ever wish it was *her* kissing Claude instead of me? Did Antonia the ostrich ever think I'd abandoned her when I left Ville Constance? I assumed once I was older I would stop caring about how others judged me, or didn't, but isn't this when it really matters? When I'm a professional adult with a respectable career?

Am I second-guessing my relationship with Templeton Rate? Am I making a mistake or just being foolish? Maybe I shouldn't let him try to change me. Then again, maybe I'm not wrong about anything; maybe I'm reading too much into everything. Maybe there was nothing ominous about the way Claude was holding his head this morning. Maybe Nickwelter just wanted to ask me if I could switch a class with him. Maybe Templeton just really enjoys Halloween. Perhaps nobody really thinks too much about me or whether I'm happy or not. Maybe nobody cares the slightest bit about what happens to Isabelle Donhelle.

Is that worse, I wonder?

I crumple the second half of my sandwich inside the note, and toss the whole thing into the trash.

I don't want to talk to Professor Nickwelter today, so I don't. I don't want to give my mother a call back yet, so I won't. I didn't plan on going home early today, but I do anyway. I try to occupy my mind with thoughts of what I'll wear when I accompany Templeton to Salem on Halloween night.

Sadly, I can't help but worry about what he'll think of my decision.

~~~

I'm not in the habit of checking my answering machine the moment I get in, since it's never blinking anyway. The first thing I do when I come home from work is say hello to Claude. Ever since my apartment was broken into, I can't help but say hi to him as I open the door, before he can see me; I don't want him to ever think there might be another stranger in our home. He always answers me back. Today he doesn't.

From my coat closet, I step into the kitchen. I scoop out a third of a cup of mix to bring to Claude. That is what I do every day, and this is exactly what I do today.

But when I walk into my living room, I'm shocked to find there is no bird to feed. My heart stops beating.

Claude's cage is empty.

The metal latch on the cage door is broken, and lays on the floor in two pieces. The window is open, just as I had left it this morning. Just as I always leave it.

I have to catch my breath. I don't want to fear the worst, as there's no way Claude could fly out the window on one wing, and so I search the apartment. I keep cool. I stay rational. It's possible that Claude could have snapped the metal latch with his powerful beak. It's possible that the cold weather made the latch that much more brittle. Anything is possible, but the fact remains: he's not here anywhere.

With my head out the window, I search the back alley.

Nothing.

My car is the only vehicle behind the building. In my mind, I play out the scenario: Claude breaks the latch in two with his beak and he hops onto the window ledge. Maybe birds *do* dream. Maybe he has yearned to fly with the
~~~

other birds. Maybe Claude has even greater aspirations than I do. I wouldn't be surprised. I envision him reminiscing about the last jump he ever took, the one that would eventually lead to the amputation of his left wing. All he wants is that life of his back again. He never asked for this change in the first place; he never wanted it. And he jumps off the window ledge. Is he trying to remember how his old life used to be? Or is he trying to put an end to it all? What would it matter though, since the only resolution would be his poor body crushing against the pavement behind the Starbucks in Public Alley 434. Exactly where my car is parked now.

Was he still lying there when I pulled in five minutes ago, completely oblivious?

I dart out of my apartment. I run down the three flights of stairs and out the back door into the alley. I gather the courage to look under my car.

Nothing.

I look in the gutter. I look in and around the dumpsters.

Still nothing. Claude is nowhere to be found.

I look back up at my open window and I wonder how this could have happened. It just doesn't make any sense. I assumed out of *everything* in my life, Claude would be the one that loved me the most. He wasn't just biding his time, waiting to leave me, was he?

I look up to the telephone wires and see the same rock pigeons that were there when I left this morning. Maybe they know exactly what happened. The only witnesses to this crime.

When I start to think Claude might be gone forever, tears well up inside of me. I don't want to cry outside where passing vagrants can witness my embarrassing breakdown as they dig through dumpsters. I don't want them, of all people, feeling sorry for me. I can smell the bags of coffee grounds piled high in the trash, and the aroma helps me to regain my senses.

When I get back inside my apartment, I still don't cry; I take one last look for Claude instead.

Still nothing.

And still no tears.

Should I call Templeton? Is that the next logical step? This is what he's supposed to be in my life for, isn't it? I never did get too much in the way of comfort from Professor Nickwelter, and lord knows the infamous Claude of Doneau High was certainly not an expert in the fine art of compassion, but maybe Templeton can be what I need.

He had given me the number for his cell phone, but I've so far resisted the use of it, not wanting to seem too needy too early in this new relationship. I pick up my phone and dial, except it doesn't ring.

I hang up and try again, but I soon realize there's no dial tone. I check the cable to find it's been unplugged. I can't recall the last time I used my phone, or even the last time I'd heard it ring. The answering machine is unplugged too. I think of the note from Steffen James, and how my mother has been waiting three weeks for me to return her phone call.

If only I'd called my mother back.

With the phone plugged back into the wall I give Templeton's number another try, but all I get is his voice mail:

"You've reached Templeton Rate. This had better be good."

I leave a frazzled message, urging him to call me back. I tell him Claude is missing, and I suggest he come by my place as soon as he's free.

I wonder how my phone ever became unplugged in the first place. But I brush it off, since I'm more concerned with the fact Claude is still gone, and that I'm still not crying about it.

His cage is so empty. The metal door still hangs open, swaying a little back and forth. There's a slight breeze coming in through the window, but the air is freezing cold. It's colder in here without Claude. After one last look out into the alley, I close the window, and I lay down on my bed.

The phone doesn't ring all evening. And there are still no tears.

~~~

It's dark when I wake up. I'm in a haze, but I'm certain I hear a rapping on my window. I sit up to listen closely, but the sound has stopped. Immediately, I remember everything that had happened since I'd come home from work. The memories are soon interrupted when I hear it again. Is it Claude outside? Or is somebody trying to break in again? Well go ahead already, there's nothing left here that could be taken from me that I would miss.

Cautiously, I move off the bed and peek around the corner into my living room. A cold sweat comes over me as I see a shadowy figure outside on my fire escape. I duck back around the corner and I'm frozen in fear. If this person outside my window saw me, I have no idea.

As scared as I am, I still can't muster any tears.

There's another knock on the window, followed by a muffled voice. "Isabella? I know you're in there. I can see you hiding around the corner, dummy."

It's Templeton's voice for sure; no one else would constantly mispronounce my name like he does. But why is he going out of his way to
~~~

scare the beef out of me? I take a cautious look around the corner; he's crouched over, peering into my nest.

"Come on, open the window. It's fucking freezing out here."

With legs shaking, I slowly wobble toward him. I'm right beside the silent birdcage.

"What are you doing here?" I ask, sliding the window open.

"Uh, you called me remember? Something about a missing bird, I believe." he climbs inside my living room and thoughtlessly rattles the empty cage beside him. "Is it this one?"

"His name is Claude." I slap his hand off of the cage. "And I'm really worried, so be nice to me, okay?"

Ignoring the request, Templeton looks into the cage. It's demeaning to think he might be searching inside because he assumes I've maybe missed something. "Claude's kind of a silly name for bird, don't you think? Macaws aren't even French."

"I said be *nice*, Templeton. He's missing. Claude is gone, and I don't know if he jumped out that window and killed himself, or if he's still alive somewhere and suffering. I feel horrible. I'm sick to my stomach with worry, and you don't even care."

He dusts some snow off his coat, and shakes his wet hair like a dog. Then he puts a hand on my shoulder in an attempt at compassion. "Hey, I'm here, aren't I?"

"And then you scare me by coming through my window in the middle of the night? How did you even get up on the fire escape anyway?"

"There's a pipe. I just shimmied up the pipe, and grabbed on. You don't exactly have the best security system back there, you know?"

Still without any tears, I collapse into Templeton, and he wraps his arms around me. I don't ask him where he was this afternoon. I don't ask him why he didn't call me back. I don't know why he didn't buzz my door instead of scaling the side of the building like some crazy cat burglar, and I don't care. All I ask is for him to come to bed with me, and he obliges.

We kiss all the way into the bedroom, and once there, Templeton breaks apart from me and he lies down on the bed. I'm standing in the middle of the room. He asks me to undress, and I do. I'm still wearing my work clothes. Reaching up under my skirt, I remove my pantyhose, tossing them silently to the floor in a heap of black nylon. I unbutton my shirt and unzip my skirt; they fall together at my feet as well. I'm standing before him in my bra and underwear. Templeton remains motionless. He lies on my bed watching me, waiting for me to finish. Slowly, I remove the rest of my clothes. They seem to float down to the floor like a feather on the wind. Like the blowing down feather I'd spotted in the laboratory this morning. The look on his face remains unchanged, like he's feeling nothing. I'm naked before him and he doesn't feel a thing.

We get under the covers, and I kiss him as passionately as I can, but he's not giving me anything in return. He seems preoccupied. I sit on top of him. His hands feel my back, as though looking for something, maybe imagining something that isn't there. Pretending I'm someone I'm not. Only then does he really kiss me.

He doesn't waste any time inside of me. Again, romance is substituted for more of a cloacal kiss-type of experience. Still, I've never felt as wonderfully vulnerable as I do right now.

His hands never leave my back.

After he finishes, Templeton removes his hands from my shoulder blades, and holds my face in his palms. Then he says it. Those three words: "I love you."

If only I hadn't believed him.

For a moment, I completely forget that Claude is missing. That's the moment I finally cry. Templeton holds me, and he doesn't let go until I fall asleep.

~~~

I have no idea what time it is when I wake up. It's still dark. I don't look for the clock because the first thing that crosses my mind is the fact that Claude is still gone. Scanning the flattened sheets beside me, I can tell Templeton is missing now also. But he isn't far. He hasn't left me alone this time.

He's still here, standing across the room. He's naked, and looking out my window. The glow from the streetlight outside illuminates him. He's staring up into the night. What he's looking at, I have no idea. But it seems more like he's looking for something, rather than at something.

I don't think he heard me moving, but he turns back to me now. I don't move an inch; pretending I'm still asleep as he watches me. Staring at me, but not knowing I'm watching him too. The light catches his face, and I notice the dull wet shine of tears in his eyes. What is he thinking? What's going through his mind? I can't make sense of it. It's like I'm still asleep and dreaming. I don't know if he's sad or scared or something else I wouldn't even be able to understand. I don't dare ask him though. I simply wait. I wait to see what he might do next.

And then he turns and leaves. He takes his clothes, and he leaves my apartment without another word. Without even so much as another scribbled note stuffed inside a dead frog's mouth.

I don't sleep the rest of the night, so I don't know if I ever would've woken from a dream or if I'm still stuck in some horrible nightmare.
~~~

Fourteen Seconds for a Chicken

TUESDAY, OCTOBER TWENTY-EIGHTH. I don't have any classes today, which is a good thing since I would probably only be embarrassing myself. This cup of cold cafeteria coffee is the one lifeline keeping me awake at this point.

I'd left my window open all night, and I'd spent most of my sleepless morning continuing to search inside my apartment and outside in the alley. But there was still no sign of Claude anywhere. Oddly, those pigeons on the telephone wires were also absent this morning.

I haven't seen or heard from Templeton so far today, which is aggravating to no end. But it's also somewhat reassuring at the same time.

I'm thinking I should call it a day, I should go home and try to get some sleep, but I decide to bite the bullet and have that prearranged talk with Professor Nickwelter I'd reneged on yesterday.

I find Nickwelter in his office, reading a magazine and eating a sandwich from the university cafeteria. I knock on the doorframe, and he invites me inside. He sets the magazine facedown on the desk. On the back, there's an advertisement for contact lenses, and there's a picture of a Golden Eagle (*Aquila chrysaetos*). I can only assume this is due to the golden eagle's extra eyelid, or what is scientifically known as a nictitating membrane. This transparent eyelid closes to protect the bird's eye from wind shear, or when staring at the sun. Not quite the same as a contact lens, but I'm certain the advertising wiz must have thought it was a stroke of genius.

"Hello, Isabelle," he says calmly. "Thank you for coming to see me."

"I'm sorry I didn't come by yesterday, Professor. I wasn't feeling well, so I went home early."

"Hmm? Oh yes. Some of us were wondering where it was you'd disappeared to. I hope it wasn't spaghetti again."

"Pardon?" I'm unsure why it is, but my mind has already begun to forget about the birthday dinner that took place weeks ago, and the transparent excuses I must have used to escape from it.

Nickwelter sits back a little, almost in defense. "It's nothing. I'm sorry." He still knows when not to push my buttons. Even if some of my buttons are new ones he's now unfamiliar with.

"This isn't a bad time, is it?" I ask, for no other reason than the fact he might want to finish his article.

"Of course not. Have a seat."

I close the door behind me. Nickwelter's office chairs are much nicer than mine, with plush cushions and armrests. Perhaps it's because he likes having guests more than I do. This room is full of history, most of it ancient. It's the very same office in which Nelson Hatch, the founder of Hawthorne University, used to work out of. There's a painted portrait of the man hanging on the wall to my right. I imagine this is the way Professor Nickwelter would have looked if he had never smoked a day in his life. A little smoother. A little cleaner. A little more polished around the ornithological edges.

Nelson Hatch was a brilliant man. I admit I don't know as much about him as others around here do, Professor Nickwelter being our resident specialist on the subject. I know he was born somewhere in New York, and that he died somewhere here in Massachusetts. From the stories I've heard and read, he was not only incredibly intelligent, but he was also a gentle and caring man. He had devoted his whole life to the study of ornithology, and the only thing he seemed to care about more was the education of his students.

He was also known to be a bit of an eccentric, and the thing about him that most people still talk about are his famous sayings. He had many phrases that he'd created himself, seemingly for his own amusement, and it was not uncommon to hear his words spoken throughout the halls of the university. Even still to this day, you can hear students quoting him in passing. Such as:

"Looks like the flamingo has gotten the better of you." Meaning: you're blushing. The Flamingo's striking red, pink, and coral feathers, as well as its bright yellow legs, are colored by the carotenoids in their food. If deprived of the required canthaxanthin, the flamingo's feathers will fade to white.

"That's like fourteen seconds for a chicken." Meaning: that's impossible; due to the longest recorded flight for a chicken being thirteen seconds.

And my personal favorite:
"If pigs really could fly, would everyone finally be satisfied?" Meaning: this was more of a question, a musing on the popular saying "when pigs fly," which seems to only be uttered when somebody is already prepared to be disappointed by something.

If Nelson Hatch had been telling this story, it would certainly contain far more riddled bird analogies.
There are a few paintings of birds lining the walls also, one of them, a Hooded Merganser (*Lophodytes cucullatus*), being an original piece by John James Audubon himself. When Audubon would paint birds, he would first carefully shoot them with a fine bullet in order to prevent the birds from being

unnecessarily torn apart. He would then use wires to prop them up, back into life-like positions. Finally, he would return the birds to their natural habitat where he would use them as the subjects for his work.

I remember being in awe of this picture since my very first day at Hawthorne. It was the first time I'd ever met Professor Nickwelter, and it was one of the last times I thought somebody knew more about ornithology than I did.

The merganser and I are both eyeing the sad-looking, half-eaten sandwich on Nickwelter's desk. I don't think I've consumed anything but coffee today. An organic Harari blend this morning (a complex, medium-bodied roast with notes of fruity flavor), followed by four or five cups of not-so-fresh Hawthorne cafeteria mud.

Nickwelter removes his reading glasses, places them in his jacket pocket, and then slowly folds his hands in front of him on the desk. He seems unsure of where he wants to start, which is sort of relieving.

I try my best to simply get this meeting over with. "What did you want to see me about, Professor?"

"I've made a decision, Isabelle." When he's nervous, he always seems to speak slowly, as though he's reading from a textbook. "I'm not entirely sure what your reaction will be, however I sincerely hope this is something that will work for the both of us."

I get the sinking feeling that this probably has less to do with our respective positions at Hawthorne University, and far more to do with the position we found ourselves in two weeks ago in the back of his car.

His eyes lock onto mine. "I've done it. I've decided to leave Beth. I want to be with you, and you alone. I realize that now."

I instantly turn away from him, trying to avoid eye contact. Those eyes of his used to be able to convince me to do just about anything. I look to the hooded merganser for some kind of sign. Something that will get me through this conversation without me losing my highly caffeinated temper. The bird seems to shrug its wings, letting me know I'm on my own here.

"Bella?" he continues. "Did you hear me? I said I realize now that I want to be with *you*. I told Beth the very same thing last night."

"How on earth could you do that? Don't you remember what you told me last time?" He shrugs his shoulders in response, just like the merganser. "You told me to forget about everything that's ever gone on between the two of us, didn't you?"

"Did I say that? That doesn't sound like me."

"Of course it sounds like you. The back-and-forth decisions and up-and-down lies you tell everyone? It was all you ever were when we were together."

"You can't tell me that what we had meant nothing to you. You told me I was the only good thing in your life."

Maybe at the time, I think. I want to tell him I've evolved since then. I've changed. I've met Templeton Rate. But I don't say anything.

Nickwelter's eyes tear up. He rubs them with his hands, as though he's got dust in his eyes, but I can tell this isn't dust; this is a product of actual, human emotion. And he's never been very good at expressing actual, human emotion.

I figure I need to say something before this man falls apart here in front of me. Before he embarrasses that painting of Nelson Hatch. "I'm not comfortable talking about this right now, Professor. And especially not here."

"Isabelle," he begins, still rubbing his eyes. "There's absolutely no reason why we shouldn't discuss this now."

I want to say the words immediately, but it takes a good ten seconds before my brain can force my mouth open. "Claude is gone, Professor."

I don't know what response I'd hoped to receive from him, but he chooses to remain motionless; his face still buried within his hands.

"Did you hear what I said, Professor? Claude is *gone*! I came home yesterday and he'd simply vanished. I don't want to think he leapt out the window to his death, but there's no other possible explanation."

Nickwelter adjusts himself, yet his movement is almost imperceptible. He's not sure what he wants to say next; he knows how much that bird means to me. When he finally speaks though, his words are not what I expect. "Why do you always do that? You might think I haven't noticed, but I have. Why can't you just say my name, Isabelle?"

I want to say it's because I don't know it anymore, but I realize how stupid that would sound.

What better way to forget a memory then to start with a name? I quickly conclude that, not only had Nickwelter seen me in the hall with Templeton yesterday, but that he had probably seen me with him on other occasions as well. It's also very likely this is the only reason he's made the decision he has: Nickwelter has never seen me with another man before. Not once have I presented myself as being unavailable for him. I've never seemed unattainable.

I've never changed since the day we met.

But just like with the Greater Prairie-Chicken (*Tympanuchus cupido*), it's the female that will choose her mate. It is not the male that gets to choose to be with Isabelle Donhelle in this scenario. Not Professor Nickwelter. Not Templeton. I tell myself this is entirely my decision alone.

If Templeton hadn't followed me into The Strangest Feeling that night. Nickwelter doesn't wait for a response from me though; he's still just hanging onto his own last words. "You think I haven't noticed. But I've noticed."

"Listen to me, Professor. All this time, I'd always thought it was supposed to be *you* who needed to change. I thought that if *you'd* only left your wife, I could be happy with what we had. If only *you'd* actually taken me out somewhere in public, I could start to feel like I was special. But I've realized now after all this time it was *me* who needed to change. It was up to me to evolve. Your leaving Beth won't make any difference at all."

"But I've already left her. I slept in my car again last night! What are you saying, Bella? That I've made a mistake?"

"Isn't it obvious?"

"No, it's not. I love you."

"No!" I can't help but rise from my seat. The chair falls over behind me, and I raise my finger to him, cutting him off. "You do not get to say those words to me! Not now. Not after this long. Not after this much history has already been thrown behind us, Professor!" Not after Templeton Rate beat you to it and said the very same words to me just last night.

"Please keep your voice down, Isabelle. Someone's likely to hear you."

I lift the chair with both hands and stand it back up. Taking a quick peek out the window into the hall, I also hope no one's passed by to hear me raise my voice.

"Isabelle—I'm sorry for your bird, but do you really think I deserve to be treated this way?"

If Professor Nickwelter had been telling this story, it would be really, really sad.

"I think you do, Professor. I really, truly do. And you know what else? I know what it is that's gotten you to act this way. I know you're not comfortable with me being involved with someone else now."

"Involved. Yes, I heard all about your antics in the library a couple of weeks ago. Tell me, what do you really know about this Templeton Rate fellow?"

"I know enough to make me happy."

"More than that, though. Where did he *come* from?"

"Schenectady. New York."

"Does he have a job?"

"He's a doorman."

"A doorman?"

"Yes. He works at a hotel somewhere in this city."

"Well, that certainly sounds believable. But is he really any more your type than I am?"

I give him a moment, to let him think I'm actually considering what my answer will be. To let him assume I care more right now than I actually do. "People change, Professor," I say, folding my arms in front of me. "And none of this is really any of your business anymore."

Nickwelter ponders our conversation a bit longer. It's almost as though he's adding up all of the questions he could ask me right now, and calculating all of the possible answers I could give him in return, figuring out the best course of action. He's smart like that. And he's proud too, he always has been. He's not one to admit defeat so quickly. "Do you remember what happened when someone found out you and I had been involved with one another, Isabelle?"

Of course I do. I remember the whole chain of embarrassing events. One of Professor Nickwelter's students had found out about our clandestine relationship, and anonymously reported it to Anton Frye, the Dean of Hawthorne University. Nickwelter was given a temporary leave of absence while the school's board sorted out the details of exactly what the repercussions should be. It wouldn't have been such a big deal if it weren't for the fact I was far and away the top student in the program at the time. This didn't seem to reflect well on Professor Nickwelter's grading system, since he was the head of the department at the time, but it also didn't reflect well upon the rest of the school and its faculty.

Even though our relationship had continued, Beth Nickwelter had forgiven her husband's adultery, he was admitted back into the university, albeit in a less-prestigious role, and I had graduated at the top of my class.

Now it's me who holds the coveted position as head of the ornithology department. I know exactly where he's trying to go with this, but I still need to hear it. "What are you saying, Professor?"

"I'm saying that was the worst year of my life, Isabelle." He takes a good hard look at the walls around him. "That was the year I didn't have all of this. This school means everything to me. And it means everything to you too. I would hate to think you might make a mistake and lose it all like I did."

From his office window, I catch a streaking glimpse of what appears to be an American Oystercatcher (*Haematopus palliatus*) sprinting across the lawn. But that can't be right; oystercatchers aren't territorial to this area at this time of the year. It quickly disappears into some bushes, and I wonder if I just saw what I thought I saw. Its large, bright red bill is unmistakable, but I can only assume it was something else. Although the way my emotions are going right now, it could have just been a dog off its leash for all I know.

Nickwelter motions to the portrait on the wall to my right. "Don't you know how embarrassed this picture of Nelson Hatch makes me feel? I can feel him watching me every day. And I know he would be disappointed by the things I've done to his school. I would give anything for the opportunity to have my proper place in Hawthorne back. Anything."

Running across the lawn now is Jerry Humphries, and I know he must be chasing after the bird that plunged into the shrubbery. It definitely wasn't a dog, but there should also be no reason for Humphries to be holding any American oystercatchers in the bird sanctuary.

"Are you listening to what I'm saying, Isabelle?" he continues, seemingly unaware that I was focused on something other than him. "Don't you realize the price you might pay for getting involved with Templeton Rate?"

I open the door to leave. "You and I are finished here, Professor. You need to go back to your wife. You're not going to survive many more cold nights sleeping in the back of your car and living on cafeteria food." I take a step out into the hall, but I turn back to him before leaving for good. "And I really hope you weren't threatening me. You can't afford to fall any further than you already have."

Defiantly, I slam his office door behind me. I can hear the hooded merganser rattling against the wall. I also hear what can only be Nickwelter's fist slamming onto his desk, and then pushing his lamp onto the floor. The ceramic base smashes. The bulb breaks. And I keep walking away.

I can't help but wonder what it is Nickwelter will tell his wife, should he return home tonight. I wonder what I'll be able to say to him the next time we talk, and how long I'll be able to avoid that future encounter.

The Weeping Angel

FRIDAY, OCTOBER THIRTY-FIRST. A thick screen of milky white fog covers the "Welcome To Salem" sign, but I knew the instant we had arrived in Salem, as it was marked by a bat flying straight into the windshield. The only way it could have felt more like Halloween at this moment would be if the Headless Horseman were following along behind us. He just might be too, if the fake cobwebs which Templeton decorated the entirety of my car with weren't preventing me from seeing the road behind us.

With Templeton behind the wheel, it had only been a thirty-five-minute drive from Boston to Salem, but it seemed as long as the boat trip to Hades must feel like. Through the gate at Lake Avernus. Although I was hoping our destination wouldn't be nearly as final.

The buildings in Salem have what is often referred to as "charm," but they only seem old and run-down to me. And yet, all of the boxy, First Period and Gothic Revival architecture seems to take on an absolute feeling, as though something horrible had happened in each and every one of these houses at some point in their history. Were there really ghosts behind every door in Salem? Or does this place simply have the knack for playing tricks on one's mind?

The city of Salem is an odd one. Many people still associate it with the Salem Witch Trials of 1692; and that's the first thing I thought of too when Templeton suggested this trip. But even if that's not all the city has to offer, they do a good job at making it appear otherwise. Salem police cars have witch logos on their doors. We drive by a public school and I notice the name: Witchcraft Heights Elementary. There's a "GO WITCHES!" sign hanging beside the high school football field.

I take another Three Musketeers from the warm dashboard and gobble it down as I try to confirm with Templeton just what exactly it is we're doing here tonight. "Tell me again why I agreed to come here?" My Sunda Varanus blend — an unanticipated earthy complexity of smooth-bodied flavor — had been emptied five minutes into the drive.

"You know you didn't have to come along," he replies, with his usual absence of romance. Why is it that the incantation of the words Templeton speaks makes it sound as though he had not only planned to come to Salem alone, but that having me here with him bothers him to no end? I try and find reasons why I shouldn't want to be here with him, but I'm finding it more and more difficult to feel as though I don't need Templeton anymore. It's funny to think about how quickly people can change.

We follow Lafayette Street all the way to Salem Common, where we find ourselves right in the middle of what Templeton had referred to as the "Haunted Happenings" festival. It's a steaming cauldron full of parading candlelit walking tours, kids dressed as ghouls, pirates, and Harry Potters, vendor tables full of charms, voodoo dolls, kettle corn, pies, and candy apples, and the odd booth set up by local psychic readers. I shiver as the eerie music and wicked laughter streaming through the air scratches along my skin.

There's a row of zombies beside us, stumbling along the sidewalk. Their makeup is grotesque, with open wounds and faces covered with blood. One appears to have taken a gunshot to the skull, and it reminds me a little of the male Hairy Woodpecker (*Picoides villosus*), which is easily spotted because of the red patch of feathers on the back of his head. Unlike zombies though, the woodpecker has probably the strongest brain in all the animal kingdom. They lack cerebrospinal fluid, so their brains are packed tightly, preventing it from bouncing against the skull and causing damage when it pecks wood at twenty blows per second.

Although far less advanced, I imagine the brains of these zombies are probably about the same size as a woodpecker's. They try to entertain us by swarming around my car, slowing us down. Templeton lays his elbow on the horn and speeds up a little, almost running over their sticky, blood-covered legs. A few of the zombies break character, and curse at us as the car peels around the corner.

Templeton parks in a small, empty lot. I direct his attention to one of the signs clearly indicating that parking is not permitted here due to the festivities. He quickly dismisses the warning, telling me, "Don't worry about it. We're not bothering anyone."

I realize then that all of his *Don't-worry-about-its* are starting to add up, and they're really beginning to grate my nerves.

He turns the engine off, pockets my keys, and gets out of the car. He seems to take in everything around us, as if for the first time. With all of my upper-body strength, I push the frozen passenger door open and step out into the cold night.

"Let's get a look at you then," Templeton says, turning in my direction. These are the first words he's spoken in the last three days that show any interest in me at all. I flatten my costume down with my palms, still warm from holding them against the heater for the last half hour.

There's a costume shop on Newbury Street that opens up for six weeks of the year around Halloween, and I stopped in for the first time on Wednesday after work to pick something out. Spotting an intricate pair of sparkling, feathered wings on one of the mannequins, I decided to start there. Angels intrigue me, as they seem like nothing more than the perfect marriage of humans and birds. The inclusion of the attached glittering sequins aside, these wings would certainly never be adequate for an angel's flight. The elliptical wing shape is completely inaccurate, as the low aspect ratio of elliptical wings on birds allows for tight maneuvering in confined spaces, such as dense vegetation.

But I put my mastery of the science aside and bought the angel wings. The rest didn't matter much to me at the time, so I finished the costume off with a green, knee-length velour dress with sleeves so long they cover my hands, and some black fishnet stockings. Of course, now that I'm standing in a Salem parking lot on this cold October night, I'm beginning to wonder why I've never seen pictures of angels wearing insulated pants and ski jackets.

"It's a good look for you, Bella," he says. It might be unintentional, but Templeton sometimes says the sweetest things to me at oddest times. And for once, he isn't following it up with something rude.

If my costume had been telling this story, it would be awfully close to the truth.

I try to straighten my secondary covert feathers, brushing them downwards. "I think the wings got bent on the ride up here."

Templeton studies them for a moment. "You do realize that the mechanics of those wings wouldn't help you achieve flight, don't you?" Maybe this is the insult I was expecting, but if it is, then it's an extremely educated one with very little threat behind it. Wing shape aside, an angel could never become airborne, since they lack the powerful muscles attached to a deep-keeled breastbone. And angels don't have the hollow bones and toothless jaws as birds do, an evolutionary development which cuts down on body mass.

Blue checkmark.

"Yeah," I say to him. "Obviously."

"Come on, let's get moving." Templeton takes my sleeve-covered hand, and we walk into the crazed streets of Salem. "It wouldn't have killed you to show a little more leg, you know."

"Unfortunately for your libido, I'm not *that* kind of angel. I'm the *good* kind."

"Says you."

I should point out the fact that Templeton isn't wearing a costume tonight. It seemed so important to him that *I* dress up for Halloween, but when he showed up at my apartment earlier wearing nothing but his usual attire, I had to ask him:

ME: "You said if I was going to come with you, I would need a costume. Correct?"

HIM: "That's right."

ME: "Well, what about *you* then? What are you supposed to be?"

HIM: "I'm nothing."

ME: "If I'm going to be something, you can't be nothing. It doesn't work that way."

HIM: "Fine. If it makes you happy, I'm a pedestrian."

ME: "A *pedestrian*? You can't be a pedestrian for Halloween if I'm going to walk around dressed like this. That's a total cop out Templeton."

HIM: "Maybe so, but was it ever agreed upon that I would be wearing a costume tonight?"

ME: "Well—no. But that's not the point. As far as I'm concerned, you're dressed as a hypocrite."

HIM: "Fine then. I'm a hypocrite. Can we just get going already?"

Templeton holds onto my hand as he navigates us through the streets, winding his way seemingly unnoticed through the costumed crowd in true pedestrian fashion.

The colors, smells, and sounds are overwhelming my senses. The people of Salem live for this moment; as though they've planned all year for this festival, and as soon as it's over they'll begin plans for the next one. Their costumes range from the frightening to the playful, and everything in between. I see witches with noses shaped like those of the Long-Billed Curlew (*Numenius americanus*). I see a can-can dancer with the train of an Indian Peafowl (*Pavo cristatus*) on her head. I see a child dressed as a bat, but with large, leathery wings on his back like a bird, rather than under his arms like a bat's would be. All of them make my angel costume appear so meager by comparison.

There are firecrackers exploding everywhere. Dogs are barking. Werewolves are howling. Crazed denizens of the night run right up into my face and shake their tongues, hoping for a scare. Smoke machines are generating so much thick smoke I can't even see where we parked the car anymore. Scents of sulfur, incense, and kids smoking pot all mix together and irritate my nostrils. Children bump me. People push me. There's broken glass on the road and it crackles between the snow and my footsteps.

I take in a long, deep breath as soon as we emerge from the dense crowds. Templeton leads me to a cemetery, just one of many in Salem. The rusted gate is locked up, seemingly since the turn of the century. Last century, that is. Templeton hops over the gate, waving for me to follow.

"There's no way I'm going in there," I say.

"Come on." He urges me from the other side. "Why not?"

"Because it's not right. That's a graveyard, Templeton."

"So what?"

I don't want to tell him that being here right now only reminds me of one thing; and that's Claude, and the fact he's still missing. Already twice now tonight, Templeton has asked me to stop brooding over my loss. "I just don't want to be thinking about death at a time like this," is what I tell him. "That's all."

"Are you kidding me? There's no better time than this. Come on."

I still haven't spoken to Templeton yet about his strange behavior at my place on Monday night, nor did I make a deal out of the fact that he got up and left me without a saying a word. I've gotten used to the fact this man operates a little differently than most people. And if I asked him, he certainly wouldn't give me a straight answer anyway.

As Templeton helps me over the gate I tear my stockings on one of the protruding metal spikes. It's so cold though, that I can't immediately tell if the skin is also torn.

This cemetery must be one of the oldest in the city, and I can tell there must not be a groundskeeper here anymore since the weeds are growing every which way from everywhere. Many of the tombstones are all but covered in a splattering of overgrown dandelions, ivy, and Virginia creeper. What really strikes me is the richness and elegance of these old gravestones: highly decorated and elaborately carved sandstone, marble, and limestone markers, all ranging in size. The cemetery is not just filled with uninteresting run-of-the-mill tablet-style headstones; there's a wide assortment of scattered, beautiful stone-carved markers.

Many of these are embellished with avian figures, popular amongst cemetery symbolism. Sitting birds on a headstone generally signify eternal life, while birds in flight commonly symbolize resurrection. Specific types of birds can represent different ideas altogether. The large tombstone I'm standing next to right now has a dove with an olive branch, a symbol for peace.

Templeton's already forty feet ahead of me. "Where are you going, anyway?" I call out to him. He doesn't acknowledge my question though. He keeps walking away from me, slowly disappearing into the fog.

I run to catch up, dodging gravestones as best I can. I pass a tombstone with a Rooster (*Gallus gallus*) on it, which represents awakening or resurrection. I see a Bank Swallow (*Riparia riparia*) and I instantly recall its purpose as a sign for hope, fertility, and the renewal of life. There is another headstone embellished with a Bald Eagle (*Haliaeetus leucocephalus*) wrapped in stars and stripes, signifying liberty and eternal vigilance.

After a few minutes of cautious footsteps, I find Templeton waiting for me. He's smoking a cigarette and sitting on another forgotten grave off in the back of the lot. This one is a large sandstone block, on top of which is a four-foot tall sculpture of an angel weeping. Her wings are spread high above her head, with one of them only half the size, having crumbled apart after years of neglect. Her tears of poison ivy wind all the way from her hands to her mossy feet. It's beautiful though, and one of the most striking statues in the entire graveyard.

The plaque on the stone block reads:

WILLIAM S. ENDICOTT
MAY 29, 1799
OCT. 31, 1841.
ROSE M. ENDICOTT
JUN. 1, 1810
OCT. 31, 1841.

Above each name is an etching of a winged face, which represents an effigy of the deceased souls, also known as the "Flight of the Soul." I'm intrigued by what sort of event transpired in which William and Rose Endicott would both die on the same date, and today's date no less. I'm also wondering why I ever agreed to come to this horrible place.

The sounds of a thousand firecrackers pop and crackle in the distance. Bursts of light seep through the mist and reflect off of Templeton's face. He blows out a puff of smoke, and the nicotine wisp blends seamlessly into the fog.

A cold shiver shoots up my spine when I imagine the hundreds of dead bodies lying six feet below me.

"You seem uneasy, Bella." As much as I dislike hearing him call me Isabella, I think I'm even more bothered by Bella. There's something about the way he says it that seems to scare me a little bit more. Especially tonight, given the setting.

"It's this graveyard. You know I'm not comfortable being here."

Templeton holds his cigarette out toward me. "You should have a smoke. It helps."

"No thanks. I've never been one for peer pressure."

"Come on," he presses. "Just one puff is perfectly harmless. It'll help calm your nerves."

I take the lit cigarette from his steady hand, and examine it for a second before plugging it into my mouth. I inhale. I let the smoke wrap around my tongue. I can feel it winding down my throat. I almost feel like I'm choking, and I uncontrollably cough it back up. The exhaled smoke from my mouth mixes seamlessly with the fog surrounding us. The cigarette falls from my hand into a patch of snow at my feet, extinguishing it immediately. I imagine this is no different from anyone's first attempt at smoking, but the taste in my mouth has a comfortable familiarity to it.

"You feel better now, don't you?" Templeton asks, still perched on the grave marker.

"Not really," I cough the words out. Now I'm thinking about a whole mess of new problems, like cancer, heart disease, emphysema, and possible birth defects for my hypothetical children.

"You'll get used to it." He takes another cigarette from his pocket and lights it up. I'm staring again; I don't know why I'm so compelled to watch his face whenever it's illuminated.

"How long have you smoked, anyway?"

He leans against the weeping angel now, thinking back to the point of time in question. "I don't remember." And just when I think he's planning on leaving the subject there, giving me one more of his usual, non-informative answers, he continues. "I used to have a girlfriend in Schenectady. She was the one who first convinced me to start smoking. She said she liked the taste of cigarettes on guys' tongues when she kissed them."

"That's gross," I say, finding a disturbing familiarity in what this unnamed girlfriend had practiced.

"She had long, blonde hair and green eyes, just like you. But her fingernails were always painted brown. I remember thinking how unusual it was for a girl to have these muddy brown nails. Then one day she painted them orange, and that was the day I dumped her."

"You broke up with a girl because she painted her fingernails a different color?"

"I broke up with her because she made out with practically every other guy in school."

"When I was in high school, I had a boyfriend who smoked. I actually started to get used to that taste in his mouth when we kissed."

"Oh yeah? What was his name?"

"That's not really important," I say meekly, thinking I would likely die of embarrassment should Templeton find out Claude's name. For the first time, I start to wonder what Templeton's childhood must have been like. How many girlfriends did he have? How many had he slept with? How long had he lived in Schenectady? Did he have any siblings? Surely his home life could not have been any stranger than mine was. What did I have? Three hundred brothers and sisters? I've never discussed the finer details of my past with Templeton. Like I said before, our relationship was mostly just sex and homework anyway.

"Did your parents approve of this guy?" he asks me.

I wonder why he's showing this sudden interest, but I can't afford to miss out on what might pass as a meaningful conversation. "They only met him once," I say. All I can envision is my parents in the halls of Doneau High, surprising me at my locker on Valentine's Day. "It was awkward, to say the least."

He takes another long drag on his cigarette. "Those kinds of things usually are."

I think about my parents a little more, and I try my best to see things from their perspective for once. "Honestly though, I never really understood my mother and father very well. I couldn't figure out how they could ever be happy with the lives they had chosen. But I think I was like any other kid: I only ever wanted to be something special. Someone completely unlike my parents."

"And now?" he asks, as though sensing a change of attitude.

"Now?" I want to tell Templeton I think it was inevitable I would feel the way I do now; that sooner or later everyone decides their parents really did have it all figured out. Now I'm yearning for the simplicity, for the normalcy of everything they had. I opt to leave out the more complicated details though. "Now I think I need to re-evaluate those ideas. Now I think I'm simply ready for a change."

"I think you are, too." Templeton blows four or five smoke rings from his mouth. Aside from cartoon characters, I don't think I've ever seen anyone do that before.

"What about your parents, Templeton? What are they like?"

His answer is short and delivered quickly. "My mother is dead." He doesn't seem fazed at all by the thought of it. "And I have no idea who my father was."

"I'm sorry," is the best I can do. In a way, I guess Templeton is kind of an orphan himself. Just one more from the litter of angels.

"Don't worry about it," he says, as though he's been telling people the same thing for years. "It's not your fault."

I'm at a loss for words. Maybe I shouldn't have tried to be so inquisitive about his past. I should have left our relationship where it was. I'm sure Templeton's probably dealt with it for a long time now, and has already gotten over any negative feelings about his childhood.

Still, I can't stop myself from saying it again, "I'm sorry."

"What do you think ever happened to Claude?" He asks me. Even though I didn't tell Templeton the name of the boy from my past with the cigarette tongue, his is the first image that comes to mind. It doesn't help that he and Templeton are so remarkably similar. Just replace the sandstone block he's sitting on with the yellow electrical box behind the gymnasium. Voila.

But I come to my senses before answering him, and I recall the tragic disappearance of my bird on Monday night. "I have no idea what happened to him. I don't really want to think about it."

Templeton removes the infamous googly-eyed frog from his pocket, and suggestively rattles the change around inside of it. I still find it hard to believe how cruel he can be sometimes. Sadly though, I'm starting to get used to it.

"How can you even imply something so awful?" I ask him.

"Too soon?"

"Can't we discuss something else?" I rub my arms, trying my best to not feel the cold.

But Templeton won't change the subject for me. "He was locked in a cage and down to his last wing. Don't you think that bird was ready to die? What's the reason for living if all you're doing is waiting for it to come to an end?"

"Well, I'm not ready to die! Is it so wrong for someone to try and find something in life to enjoy?"

"People don't deal with death well enough. They're all bound to it, but they just try and ignore it."

"People like *me*, you mean?"

"It's *everyone*, Bella."

I think back to our conversation on the sidewalk a few weeks ago. When he told me that I would only see the negativity surrounding death, whereas he would look for the signs of life instead. Now he seems to be contradicting his earlier beliefs. Templeton stuffs the frog back into his coat pocket.

The noise from the streets of Salem is so loud I'm finding it hard to focus. I can still hear the firecrackers and the children laughing and the witches cackling and the werewolves howling, all in celebration of the most haunted holiday of all.

I almost make another worthless point, but I let Templeton continue instead.

"The Dick Van Dyke Show. Have you ever heard of it?"

"What?" Sometimes I find it hard to keep up with his wild, random thoughts. "Dick Van Dyke?"

"Did you get that program up in Canada? You must have." He kicks the heel of his shoe against the grave marker, and some ash from his cigarette flutters to the ground. "I remember watching a rerun when I was about eight years old. My mother used to think it was funny." Templeton leans back, and tilts his head up, blowing smoke at the unseen stars. "There was one episode that was taped right after everyone had found out Kennedy was assassinated. They had all heard the news during rehearsals, and the episode was filmed a few days later. The actors still delivered their lines, but to an empty audience. I guess because nobody felt like laughing. It didn't matter though; the laugh track was added after all of the jokes anyway, whether they were funny or not. But you could see tears just behind their eyes. They all tried to hide it, but they couldn't. There's this unseen black cloud hanging above them all when you watch that episode. Even if you saw it today and didn't know what the reasons were, you would still feel it." Templeton spits a wad of phlegm into the ground. A tree above him is dripping melted snow, and he shakes the cold drops out of his hair. "All of the camera angles were slightly askew too. My mother didn't pick up on any of it, but I did." I wonder what the point of this story is, and he stops for a moment to try and understand my reaction. "Don't you see? They were all trying to ignore death. Whether they knew it or not, they were all just waiting for their own end to come. But at the same time, they weren't about to let anything allow them to acknowledge it."

I shuffle my feet around in the snow, half in an attempt to warm them up and half due to this nervous feeling inside me. Templeton is talking strangely, stranger than usual. His peculiar fascination with death is beginning to scare me a little. The fog seems to be getting thicker. The fireworks continue to flash off his face, but they're fainter now. "Is this why you brought me here?" I ask him. "To tell me about The Dick Van Dyke Show?"

"We're just talking, Bella. It was only a memory that came to mind. Besides, I didn't bring you anywhere tonight. You followed *me*, remember?"

I don't answer him. Instead, I search his eyes with mine. I see if I can go longer than him without blinking.

I lose in less than ten seconds.

"Why are you fidgeting? What are you scared of, Bella?"

"I already told you. It's this graveyard."

There's an uncomfortable silence between the two of us for a few moments. He continues to smoke, while I remain shivering in the cold. Templeton is picking at the statue beside him. He's digging his fingernails into the cracks of the angel's wing, collecting the built-up moss and dirt onto his fingertip.

"I don't let death bother me so much. I have better things to be doing with my time here."

"Really. Unlike me, right?"

"Exactly. Unlike you. And unlike all of these people around us, who have already begun to walk the path of angels."

"Angels?" The sparkling wings on my back catch my peripheral vision. "Well, I'm *already* an angel, so I don't need to wait for death, do I?"

"You're only *dressed* as an angel, babe. You're not the real deal."

"So, you believe in angels?"

He keeps picking away at the rock with his fingers, answering me most matter-of-factly. "Of course I do."

"Really? Are you serious?"

"Of course I am." I think this must be the first time Templeton has ever convinced me he believes in anything at all. "Maybe not in the way you might think, but I do."

"Well, have you ever seen an angel before?"

"You mean a real one, right? Not just a costume?"

"Right."

"Not yet. You?"

"No. But I don't believe in angels."

"Well then—" Templeton finally removes himself from his perch. He jumps down onto the ground with a thump so solid, the bones of William and Rose Endicott probably rattle beneath him. "That's a pretty strange costume choice you've made."

"At least I *made* a choice."

"Do you know what an angel is?"

This is the same question I asked my father when I was a little girl. *"Angels are just like you and me and your mother,"* is what he told me.

"I have no idea," I say.

"And what is their purpose?"

"They're regular people who just want to help one another out," is what my father said.

"I don't know."

"Some people will tell you they're guardians. Some will say that angels are messengers. You might even hear they're supposed to be warning signs for the Apocalypse, if you could ever believe in shit like that."

"I don't," I tell him.

"Neither do I, Bella. But that's what people will tell you. Because that's what people will believe."

"So, what is it you believe in, Templeton? If you refuse to believe what you've been told?"

He takes one last drag of his cigarette before tossing it over the fence. "To molt is to change, correct? To change is to evolve. Let's just say it all comes down to evolution."

I look him over, and I watch as the lights continue to bounce from his face to my wings, and back again. This was the same thing he had said to me in my class a month ago. *"To molt is to change, whether psychologically or physically. Temporarily or permanently."* I still don't fully understand what he means.

"Listen, Bella. Don't think me any less intelligent than you because my beliefs differ from yours."

"That's ridiculous. You're the most brilliant student I have. You know that."

Templeton turns his eyes to look beyond the graveyard. There's a small cluster of old heritage homes in the distance. There aren't any lights on, but even from here, I can see the shadowy outlines of a few people wandering around out there. One appears to be walking awkwardly, as though hopping on one leg. Probably just some kids looking for somewhere quiet to drink and get high.

Templeton notices them too, but he turns back to look at me. "Don't condemn me for having different feelings than you do, Bella." I'm not certain if he's still referring to the angels, or if he's moved on to our relationship. "I can't force you to wholly believe in the same things I believe, but at the very least, I can make you accept it."

Was Templeton even there at all, or was he just one more from the litter of angels?

Templeton just stands there, his hands in his pockets. I have no reply for him. No answer for any question still hanging unasked. I don't know if I want to move closer to him, or farther away. All of the angels and winged sculptures surrounding us seem to be on the edge of their gravestones, just waiting for me to make my next move. This man has always made me unsure of myself. He's never left my side without leaving me questioning something gone unmentioned. Was it right for me to feel this way? He stands there looking me over. I don't want to, but I feel as though he's trying to push me away.

He walks back over to the weeping angel. I imagine it's still warm from him sitting there for the last fifteen minutes. He brushes some more dirt off with his sleeve. "Do you see this grave? This is the reason I come to Salem every Halloween. William and Rose are distant relatives of mine. Seven generations removed. William was a fisherman here, and he fished for Atlantic cod. Rose gave birth to John Endicott, who was my great-great-great-great Grandfather."

I feel foolish. I feel as though I'd forced myself to come along to Salem with Templeton tonight when it's clear now he was only coming here for personal reasons. I still don't know what I want to tell him, but it's okay because it was inevitable that he would once again beat me to the punch anyway.

"Would you mind leaving me alone for a moment? Maybe you should wait for me back at the car."

"Can't I just wait for you by the gate? You know this place gives me the creeps."

"Wait for me at the car. I think I'd like to spend a few minutes alone here." He stands beside the grave, just waiting for me to leave him.

"It's freezing out here," I plead with him. But I don't receive any further response. He's unmoving. Unwavering. The kids in the distance have disappeared from sight. "Will you take me home after this?"

"Of course I will. I'll see you in a few minutes."

I don't have anything else to say. I turn around and wind my way back out of the cemetery. I lift myself over the gate, and tear my stockings again on the metal spike. Eerily, the fog seems to clear as soon as I return to the sidewalk.

~ ~ ~

I'm waiting for over an hour before Templeton shows up. He still had my car keys in his pocket, so I've been huddled up on the ground beside the passenger door trying to keep myself as warm as I can with what little I'm wearing. I try to wrap my angel wings around myself, but they keep springing back open, as if they want to lift me away from here, to carry me from the gravel parking lot and take me somewhere better.

I was relieved to not find a parking ticket folded under the windshield wipers, so Templeton was right when he told me not to worry about it. However, there is a scratch on the hood that wasn't there before. Somebody carved "PUFFIN" on my car with a knife by the looks of it. Whatever it was the unknown vandal had meant by it, I find it hard to imagine it has something to do with the auk of the same name. I have no idea how much it's going to cost me to get it fixed, but I'm not terribly concerned at the moment. I just want to get out of Salem.

I try to ignore Templeton when he does shows up; partly because I'm ashamed I gave him such a difficult time in the graveyard, but mostly because he left me trapped outside of my car, unable to warm my hands up against the dashboard heater. Conveniently, he ignores me too, and simply opens the trunk and then slams it shut again.

He comes back around to the front where I'm crouched in a ball and clutching my wings in my icy fingers. He slides a knit cap over his head. "It's fucking cold out here tonight, isn't it?"

I roll my eyes in total agreement.

"You know, you'd have been warmer if you kept walking around, instead of just sitting there."

"Probably. Or you could have given me my keys before sending me off. Where'd you get that cap anyway?"

"I had it in your trunk."

"Since when did you start keeping things in my trunk?"

"I've got a shitload of stuff back there." It's misdirection; he doesn't answer the question, but rather, he amuses me by creating a slew of new ones. And just like a magician, he makes a pack of cigarettes appear from up his sleeve. "I've got smokes in there too." He takes one out and lights it up.

"Some nitwit carved the word *PUFFIN* on my hood while we were gone."

He looks at the scratches, correctly identifying the genus. "Ah, *Fratercula*." He mumbles something else to himself, but I can't make out the words. He turns and looks off nowhere in particular, speaking as though whoever committed the act might still be listening. "That's not a very nice thing to do, Fuckhead."

My wings spring open again, and I stand up now, rubbing myself in another failing attempt to warm up. "Do you really have to use language like that all of the time?"

He laughs a little. "Is me calling someone a *Fuckhead* any different from you using such charmingly derogatory names like *Nitwit*? Or *Cheese Monkey*? Or *Dilly Bar*?"

"There *is* a difference, yes. I was raised better than that."

"Come on. Just give me a *Fuckhead*. One little *Fuckhead*. I left you out here in the freezing cold. It's the least you could do in return. Really lay it on me."

"I don't think so."

"*Shit-For-Brains*?"

"No."

"How about *Cunt Flap*?"

"Oh my—! Templeton, that's horrible."

"Well, how about this then: how about you promise me you'll make your last words the most appalling words you can think of?"

"My last words?"

"You know, right before you die. Just yell them out loud for everyone to hear."

"I'll try to remember that when it happens," I tell him. "Can we just get going now?"

"But of course, m'lady." Templeton graciously opens the passenger door for me, and I climb inside. I'm already pre-adjusting the heater settings in preparation for when he turns the engine on. But he insists on finishing his cigarette outside before fulfilling any of my needs.

My anger might be enough to warm me up anyway.

As we find our way back out of Salem, a couple of firetrucks blast by us, sirens blaring. Of course, Templeton doesn't pull off to the side of the road to ensure them easy passage. I can't help but notice there's a house on fire in the distance. It appears to be one of the old heritage homes that I'd spotted earlier this evening from the graveyard.

I point out the house to Templeton, who replies with a very disinterested, "Well, well. Now that's a fucking shame, isn't it?"

The One with the Big, Bold MURDERED on It

MONDAY, NOVEMBER THIRD. I haven't seen or heard from Templeton for three days now. He drove me back home from Salem, just as I'd requested, but he didn't stay the night. And he didn't take the bus home, claiming he'd rather walk across Boston than ride the filth that is public transit. I chose not to remind him of where we were the first time we'd met. He said he still had some trick and treating to do before the night was over. That was how he said it too: trick *and* treating. Templeton told me he'd be working at the hotel all weekend, but he said the least he could do was give me a call on a smoke break. Turns out, he could still manage to do even less than that. I have yet to find out which hotel he works at.

He also should have been in my Field Identification class this morning, but his seat was noticeably empty. Noticeable by me, at least. I'm not sure if the other students are aware that Templeton Rate is even supposed to be in the class.

It's been a week now since Claude went missing. I still wake up every morning at 3 AM to crack open the mouthwash, but now I include another desperate search along the way. When I looked out my window this morning, all I noticed was the foot of snow that had fallen overnight. I stare at my buried car, dreading the commute. There's no worse time to see a foot of snow when it's a Monday morning and you already had no desire to leave your apartment.

I recall the first day of snow as being the day I made a fool of myself in the university library. That was four weeks ago now.

If I hadn't slept with Templeton Rate.

My class has just ended and I catch myself daydreaming. I'm staring out the window of my Taxonomy classroom, watching a murder of American

Crows (*Corvus brachyrhynchos*) adjust their flight patterns in accordance with the afternoon's falling snow.

A knock at the door behind me snaps me back to attention. I'm expecting to see him standing there. I've already envisioned the dirty hands and piercing eyes under an icy-wet head of hair.

But it's not Templeton who has come to see me this afternoon, but rather Anton Frye, the rarely seen Dean of Faculty at Hawthorne University. With him is one officer of the Boston Police Department.

"Isabelle, may we have words?" Anton Frye doesn't have many friends within the school that I'm aware of, which is likely due to his instinctive nature of speaking to intimidate. That being said, our relationship allows me to know him as Anton, whereas most of the other faculty simply refer to him as Dean. Or *The* Dean, as he has routinely preferred.

If The Dean had been telling this story, nobody would dare argue the facts.

"Of course, Anton. Good afternoon, officer."

"It's detective, actually." He responds in a completely expected thick Boston accent. He surveys the room quickly before suggesting, "Would you mind if we sat somewhere a little more private?"

I turn back to the window to see the crows have disappeared completely.

~~~

I close the door to my office as Anton Frye and Detective Dunphey take their seats. Dean Frye is a wiry little man, with round glasses that seem much too big for his head. Dunphey is his exact opposite: a large bear of a man, but his years on the force have seen what muscle I imagine he used to have overtaken by fat. Of particular distraction are the wattles of his throat. The two of them
~~~

bring an image to my mind of the Looney Tunes characters Foghorn Leghorn, a Kentucky rooster, and Egghead Jr., a baby chick. Both are of the same species, *Gallus gallus.*

"What can I do for you gentlemen?" I feel a slight pain in the back of my throat as I swallow.

"I'm sure you saw the news last night?" Anton hints aggressively.

"Uhm, no. What news was that?"

The two of them glance at each other, as though suspicious of my naïve response. "Do you read the paper?" the detective asks.

"No. I'm sorry. What's happened?"

Detective Dunphey pulls a rolled-up Boston Globe from the inside pocket of his uniform. He tosses it face-up in front of me. The date is this morning's and the headline reads:

SOUTH BOSTON WOMAN MURDERED

I look back up to both The Dean and the detective, still uncertain of what this is all about, and how it might have anything to do with me. "I'm sorry. I don't understand." I'm quick to assume this is a clue to the whereabouts of a certain parrot.

"Neighbors reported gunshots last night, but there were no signs of bullets," Detective Dunphey starts, coldly delivering the facts. "This woman was found dead in her apartment. She was keeled over with her head in the kitchen sink. The lights were left on, and a neighbor across the way could see the body from her window. There was a hunting knife dug into her skull."

I shiver a little, and turn back to the paper. The front-page story gives no names; no details at all have been revealed to the public yet. I look up again, my eyes questioning the both of them.

The detective says, "Her name was Rebecca Chandler."

I shrug my shoulders. "Should I know her?"

Anton Frye fills in the blanks for me. "Isabelle. Becky was one of your students."

"*What?*"

"And, *apparently*," Anton starts with a gulp in his throat, "she and this Nickwelter fella were engaged in some sort of—*extra-curricular* relationship."

"Professor Nickwelter?" I ask, as though there could be more than one.

"That's right. The police spoke with his wife, but no one has any idea where he might be."

The picture on the paper is not clear, and all I can make out is a body bag on a gurney being wheeled into the back of an ambulance. "Oh my God." Sickened, I push the paper back to the detective and then sit back in my chair.

He takes the newspaper back and rolls it up in his large hands. "Obviously, we want to find this man and ask him a few questions. We don't have any motives, but for now we have to consider him our prime suspect."

"Professor Nickwelter?" I think back to last Tuesday, to my last conversation with him. He told me he had left his wife. He said he'd do anything to have his position at the school restored. But he wouldn't be dumb enough to do something like this, would he? "This—this is *horrible*. There's no way he could have done this."

Anton pushes, "You seemed to know him much better than anyone else, Isabelle. You two were, *friendly*, yes?"

Friendly? He does an absolutely horrid job at dodging the details, especially since he knows the truth anyway. Anton Frye was the man who suspended Professor Nickwelter from the school for a year. Detective Dunphey cocks his head at The Dean's statement, as though hearing this information for the first time. He leans his body in over the desk, closer to me. "Did you and the suspect have a relationship, Miss Donhelle?" He points the rolled-up newspaper toward me menacingly.

"Do you have to refer to him as 'the suspect'? I can't imagine Professor Nickwelter could ever murder someone."

Anton Frye does the detective's work for him. "Answer the question, please."

"Yes. We dated for a while. But that was *two years* ago."

The detective writes my answers down on a notepad. "Was he married at the time?"

"Yes. He was married. How is that relevant to what's happened here? Like I said, that was two years ago."

My question goes ignored, in favor of one more from the detective. "When was the last time you spoke with the sus—with this Nickwelter?"

"Last week. Tuesday, I think."

"How would you explain his behavior? Can you describe it to me?" His pen is ready and waiting for anything I've got to say. His other hand is big enough to hold both the newspaper and a notepad.

"He, uh. He told me, um—he told me that he still loved me." I blew it off at the time, but maybe now I'm starting to piece together the significance of that statement. The two men are simultaneously putting the same pieces together. "But I have a boyfriend. I told him that. And I told him it wasn't going to work between us."

"Between you and your boyfriend?"

"No." I stop as soon as I register the detective's misunderstood words. Whether he'd meant to be or not, he was already one step ahead of me. Things really aren't going to work between Templeton and me, are they? There's nothing about him that's right for me, is there? I must have known it all along too, but I've waited until now to tell myself the truth. "My relationship with Professor Nickwelter was over. I told him as much."

"How did he react?"

"Well, he was angry. I know he was still bitter over the fact I had taken over his position at the school. And he told me I was risking my *own* career, and that he would do anything to get his job back."

"Risking your own career? How exactly?"

If Detective Dunphey had been telling this story, he wouldn't have started until he had all the facts.

"My boyfriend. He's one of my students."

Anton perks up again. "A student?"

"His name is Templeton Rate."

"Templeton Rate?" he asks. "I've never heard of him. Who is he?"

"Well, he's a new student. I think."

"You think?"

"I don't really know any of these kids. Students are just students. They're completely interchangeable. They're all generic to me. Just names on reports."

Detective Dunphey gets back to his reason for being here. "Can I ask where you were this weekend? Did you go anywhere at all?"

"I was out Friday night. With Templeton. We went up to Salem for Halloween. But I was home the rest of the weekend. I didn't go anywhere."

Anton throws another suspicious look my way. "Did you hear about the fire in Salem on Friday night?" I instantly recall seeing the fire trucks speed by us as Templeton and I were leaving the city, and I remember the burning house past the graveyard. But I don't say anything. I let him continue. "Five houses in Salem burned to the ground on Halloween night. Five old, abandoned houses that have been empty for decades. One of those houses was where Nelson Hatch once lived." Detective Dunphey turns to Dean Frye, wondering what the point is. The Dean obliges his unspoken query, and turns directly to the detective to explain. "Nelson Hatch founded this school in 1932. He was born in Brooklyn in 1895, and he died in Salem in 1974."

The detective fails to see the relevance in this bit of disconnected information, and returns instead to the subject at hand. "One last question, Miss Donhelle: do you have any idea where Nickwelter might be? Any idea at all?"

"I don't. I'm sorry."

Dunphey tosses the newspaper into my trash, and hands me a card with his name and number on it. I didn't know police carried their own business cards. "Thank you for your time." He gets up from his seat, letting Dean Frye know there are still a few more questions that need to be asked. Anton glares at me once more before they leave my office together.

The bold **MURDERED** hangs over the edge of my wastepaper basket, and I can't help but think that of all the wrong things Templeton is for me, the worst might possibly be the death of my career.

If Becky Chandler had been telling this story, it would have a dreadfully horrible ending.

~~~

I stay in my office for another fifteen minutes, attempting to figure out everything that's fallen apart in so short of a time. As unbelievable as it sounds, a student of mine is dead. Professor Nickwelter is missing and accused of this girl's murder. Claude is still gone too, probably buried under
~~~

the snow somewhere and wondering why I haven't come looking for him. Templeton still hasn't called me. I'm trying to figure out which of these has me more unnerved.

The falling snow outside makes me realize this is definitely not the change I was looking for.

If Templeton hadn't avoided me for the last three days; if he hadn't taken me to Salem and scared me like he did; if he hadn't climbed up my fire escape and told me that he loved me; if he hadn't made go back looking for him at The Strangest Feeling; if he hadn't followed me onto the bus.

What am I doing here? I never would have made such poor judgment calls a year ago, back when I had my act together. Sure, I'd slept with Professor Nickwelter, but I knew from the very start that was the wrong thing to be doing. I wasn't fooling myself then like I am now.

Or was I?

Maybe this is *every* relationship. Maybe this is normal. Maybe there could be someone somewhere who might be jealous of what I have for once. Maybe it was Antonia the ostrich. Maybe Becky Chandler. Maybe it was the dead girl named Autumn.

No. I can't accept that *any* of this my fault. I'm better than that. I won't put everything I've worked toward in jeopardy.

I need to find Templeton.

I need to talk to him.

I need to tell him everything about him is completely wrong for me.

And I need to tell him it's over between us.

But as I get up from my seat, the first thing I do is throw up in my wastepaper basket. Everything has literally come to the surface. It's all over the morning paper, the one with the big, bold **MURDERED** on it. I crouch over the trash, completely light-headed. I don't want to smell this, but it can't be helped. I don't want to look, but I do. What I've coughed up is startlingly black, like wet coffee grounds. Shining like the sheen of the dead raven on my textbook.

~~~

Five minutes later, I'm slipping on my coat and taking the trash out with me. I lock my office door behind me and slowly make my way outside, bracing myself against the wall with one arm the entire way. A couple of students approach me, laughing as they pass by, and I'm careful to not to appear as awful as I feel.

Opening the door into the courtyard, it's actually a relief to be out in the cold and to feel the snow fall on my face again. It helps me feel less nauseous. There's a dumpster just ahead of me, and I toss the wastepaper basket and all of its contents into it: the empty coffee cups, the scribbled phone messages, the half-eaten tuna fish sandwiches, the newspaper, and the throw up.

I follow the path to the parking lot. I see the same crows I'd spotted earlier from the classroom window. They're hopping around, bumping into one another and pecking at the fresh snow in an attempt to find buried treasures. The word "murder" comes to mind again, but I try not to think about it.

I stop for a moment to watch them, marveling at their intelligence. It's incredible, the systems they use in order to know exactly how to find what they're looking for. Suddenly they stop, all six of them, and look up at me. Their beaks point in unison toward the school. I realize if I'm going to find Templeton, I'm going to have to start in the south laboratory.

~~~

I'm only a footstep away from the lab door when I begin to feel woozy again. My equilibrium is off, and my vision blurs. I reach out for the door handle, but I crumple to the floor instead. It takes me a few seconds before I can regain my senses. Thankfully, no one is around to see me like this.

I try my key in the lock, but it doesn't turn. Checking the key, I make sure it's labeled "South Lab." I bang on the door a few times, with no answer.

Hearing footsteps coming toward me, I straighten myself out, hoping I don't look too horrible. But it's only Jerry Humphries approaching, in the same grubby trench coat and with his usual revoltingly cheerful greeting.

"Good afternoon, Bella," he starts, completely unaware I'm really not myself today. "I saw some thug with a badge wandering the halls with The Dean. Someone in trouble?"

"It's really not a matter that's of any concern to you, Jerry." The inside of my mouth is so dry, it's almost a challenge to speak. There's a water fountain on the opposite wall, so I step across the floor and drink some quickly. Humphries stares at me, watching every gulp I take.

"It doesn't have anything to do with Professor Nickwelter, does it? I haven't seen him around today."

"Please," I urge him, trying not to visualize the front page of the Globe. "I really don't have the time for this conversation right now. When I say something is none of your business, you need to take me for my word and leave it at that." He jumps out of my way as I move back toward the laboratory door. "Who changed the lock on this door?"

"I did," he says nonchalantly.

"Why would you do *that*?"

"Hey, I just do what I'm told. That's all I'm good for around here." Humphries tries to brush some fresh snow from my shoulder, but I swat his hand away before he can touch me.

"Well, can you open it for me?"

"Do you mind me asking what it is that you're looking for?"

"Just open the door, Jerry."

Humphries pauses for a moment, as though taking orders from me is below him. He unlocks the door and flicks the light switch. The overhead lights slowly illuminate the large room from where we're standing and all the way to the other end. The wooden frame is still here, a little more progress has been made on it. The piles of sawdust have gotten bigger, and the boxes seem to be stacked closer to the ceiling now. Tools and incomprehensible equipment are still scattered everywhere; stuff like metal cylinders, sealed canisters, coils, and wires. But there's no sign of Templeton Rate.

I can hear birds chirping from somewhere nearby. I think I hear the call of an Amazonian Antshrike (*Thamnophilus amazonicus*), but I'm not certain.

"Do you know where Templeton is?" I ask Humphries. But all I get for an answer are shrugged shoulders. "Do you know who's been using this space?"

"Some student. Mitch? Mitchell? Mitchie, I think his name was."

"Who's giving students access to this lab?"

"I am."

"You? Why would you do that? These labs aren't here to be the students' personal storage lockers."

Jerry Humphries looks around suspiciously and then leans in, a little too close for my liking. "Well, let's just say that the two of us came to an agreement." He rubs his index finger and middle finger against his thumb, hinting at some sort of financial arrangement.

I think I hear the musical chirps of a Resplendent Quetzal (*Pharomachrus mocinno*) from somewhere unknown.

I'm about to turn the lights back off, but then something else catches my eye. Inside the wooden box, there are some sheets of metal being laid across the walls. Within the reflective surface, I see something concealed in the corner of the room, hiding out of sight. Six giant, fiberglass, swan-shaped somethings covered with a tarp. Immediately, I think of the missing swan boats from the Lagoon, but I'm certain I don't want to ask Jerry Humphries about it. I thumb the detective's card in my pocket. Maybe I'll call the police and let them know about this, but right now I've got far too much on my mind.

Deep inside me, I know Humphries has to be aware of more than what he's giving me. "Do you know where Templeton is?" I ask him, accusingly.

"You already asked me that."

I guess I did, but my mind is totally scattered right now.

"But if I see him," Humphries says, "I'll be sure to let him know you've been snooping around here."

"This is ridiculous," I say, shutting the lights off and closing the door behind us. "Listen. I can't believe something like this could even begin to happen, but I want you to fix this situation, Jerry. Find that kid. Get those keys from him. And get your head straight."

"Does this mean you'll be breaking up with your boyfriend?"

"If I can find him."

"One can't change sides once they've been placed by God, Bella" I hear him call out behind my back, ominously. I'm not sure what it is he means by it. I don't want to ask him, and he doesn't tell me either.

~~~

When I get back outside to my car, I brush off the snow that's accumulated all morning. With the very first swipe, I uncover the "PUFFIN" on my hood. As I
~~~

sit behind the wheel with the engine running and waiting for the heat to kick in, I begin to feel light-headed again. My head is pounding. The muscles in my right arm begin twitching; my pronator teres pulsates beneath the skin. I realize I haven't had a single cup of coffee today, and I wonder just how much my body would notice if the vast amount I've ingested over the last month suddenly dropped to zero.

I'm sweating, so I turn the heater dial from red to blue and roll down the window. Leaning back, I allow the winter chill to envelop me once again, and that's when I spot a pack of Templeton's cigarettes wedged between the driver's seat and the hand brake. I don't know what's come over me, if it's the news about that poor girl's murder or if it's the realization my relationship with Claude What's-His-Name will have lasted longer than my relationship with Templeton Rate, but I need something to calm myself down.

I pick up the cigarette package and study it carefully for a minute. I read the message on the front, straight from the desk of this mysterious Surgeon General:

WARNING: Smoking Causes Lung Cancer, Heart Disease, Emphysema, and May Complicate Pregnancy.

It was just as I'd feared.

If the Surgeon General had been telling this story, the cover would have warnings all over it.

Popping the lid open, I smell the nicotine and recall my first feeble attempt at smoking a few nights ago in the Salem graveyard. I know I can give it a better effort than that.

Pumping the cigarette lighter a few times, I acknowledge this is probably the only feature of my car that's never seen any use. Pulling it out of its warm dashboard nest, I hold it up to the cigarette in my mouth for a few seconds before the paper lights up.

Instantly, I find truth in what I've heard smokers say when they talk about the calming effect a cigarette can have. The smoke seems to lick its way all over my insides: in my mouth, down my throat, through my arms, soothing my twitching muscles, and enveloping my brain.

In fact, I'm so calm that I'm totally oblivious to the sound of crunching snow underneath very familiar shoes. Templeton sticks his head into my car, and scares me a little with his discovery. "Well, well, well. If it isn't the girl with no vices?" I jump back, and drop the hot metallic lighter into my lap. It burns on my leg, and I kick it to the floor quickly.

"Templeton?" I say, and I accidentally swallow the smoke in my mouth, almost choking. He doesn't flinch at all. "What are you doing here?"

"Just wondering where you're off to. Don't you have another class this afternoon?"

"Don't start getting on my case about proper attendance. Where were you this morning? Field Identification? Do you remember that one?"

He reaches in and takes the cigarette from my hand. "These things will kill you, you know that?" He takes one long drag off of it before flicking it away over his shoulder. The cold air extinguishes the cigarette before it even touches the snow. "That identification class of yours is bullshit, you know? None of that stuff is of any use to me. Or anyone else there, for that matter."

He always does this. He always tries to get me riled up about something he knows I won't be able to change his opinion on, whether he actually believes what he says or not. Templeton always wants to win. And he always does.

But not this time. This time I won't let him.

I shut the engine off and push the door open. Templeton has to jump back to avoid being hit. I step outside of my car defiantly. I haven't yet rehearsed the words in my head, aside from thumbing through thoughts in my office thirty minutes ago. So I cut to the chase.

"Templeton—it's not working."

"Of course not. You took your keys out, dummy."

"Not the car. *Us.* This relationship isn't good. It's not doing *either* of us any good."

Templeton stares at me, unblinking with his hands in his coat pockets. He's staring at me almost as though he'd seen this coming. As though he knew it from the first moment: that moment on the bus, or the moment he sat beside me in The Strangest Feeling and we stared at each other's reflections in the mirrored mini fridge. What I'm saying to him seems completely expected, like the moment the ball drops on the television and everybody in the room yells "Happy New Year!" Like the first fireworks shot into the sky on the Fourth of July. Like when the phone rings on your birthday, and you know it's your mother on the other end and the first thing she'll say is "Happy Birthday, sweetheart." Like any celebration that loses all of its exhilaration because nobody is the least bit surprised. Because they've anticipated it all year long, since it happened the last time.

I notice Templeton is again wearing the shirt with the little brown-headed nuthatch on it. I wonder if it's been washed since that first night a month ago.

"It's over," I say with finality.

And an uninterested "Uh huh," is what I get from him.

"Is that all you've got to say to me?"

"Well, what do you *want* me to say? It sounds to me like you've already made whatever decision you think you need to make."

I guess I have. It was inevitable though, wasn't it? He wasn't exactly taking this relationship seriously, was he? Was I?

"Does this mean you'll be getting back together with Nickwelter?"

"Of course not." Again, I try my best to not think about the newspaper, and the words written in bold across the front page. "I need to focus on what's really important to me."

"And that is?"

"My job. This whole school. I can't afford to lose *any* of this."

Templeton studies my response for a moment. I'm telling the truth, but I don't think he's completely buying what I have to say. Or maybe it's just that he doesn't care. If he ever did.

"Templeton, please. This just isn't working. I realize that now."

"Is that what you *really* believe, Bella?"

"Yes. I'm sorry." It's me who's apologizing, but I know it shouldn't be. That's how it always works with people. "Maybe I was hoping something would be right between us. That this change would be good for me. But that was just wishful thinking. Just a moment of weakness on my part."

Templeton keeps looking at me, knowing there's more to this story than what I'm telling him. How does he always seem to know these things?

He walks around to the front of my car, and sits down on the hood. I expect him to reach into his coat and light up a cigarette, but he doesn't. Instead, he shares another memory with me. "I used to go to church all the time when I was a boy. Every Sunday."

"I didn't know that," is all I can say to him. And really, why *should* I know that? It's not as though he's shared much in the way of his past with me before now. Why does he always have to act like this? Why does he always have to be so puzzling in the moments I need him to be straight with me? I think I would ask him that right now, if I wasn't trying so hard to simply put an end to everything.

If I hadn't stayed in the parking lot, wanting to listen to him.

"One particular Sunday we left the church, my mother and sister and I. It was a morning just like any other morning. But it was not going to be the same as any before. It felt sort of—*unusually usual,* if that makes any sense to you. As soon as we'd walked back to the car I realized I'd lost my chain. The holy cross my mother had given to me. The one I'd worn around my neck for as long as I could remember. So, my mother suggested I go back in and see if I could find it. She said something absurd like, *'Jesus would leave it in plain sight.'* I can't believe how religion can bring out the most idiotic ideas, even in somewhat intelligent people."

He hasn't even made a point yet, but his story is already sending shivers down my spine. It's already making me regret things I have no right to be regretting.

If I hadn't gone to Salem that night, wanting to be with him.

"I went back inside to look for it, but I didn't find anything. That church floor had always seemed impossibly clean to me, as though God himself had personally cleaned it." He stops for a moment, hanging onto his last words. "You see what I mean about religion making intelligent people say the most fucked up things?"

If I hadn't made that phone call the night Claude went missing, so badly needing him.

"Anyway, I asked a few of the religious stragglers if they might have seen it. Some of the grazing sheep, still standing around and marking themselves with the sign of the cross. But no one could help me. I went to the pews and took one last look. There was a man sitting right where we had sat for the morning service. I was too young to remember what he looked like, but I can recall what he said as I approached him. He said, '*Hello, Matthew.*' I didn't know what to say, but that man held it up in his hand. He had found my necklace for me. I reached out for it, but he pulled his hand back in. Then he went on to tell me things like there was no God. He told me there was no such thing as angels." Templeton leans back on the palms of his hands. He turns his face to the sky. I watch his fingers as they dig into the hood of my car like talons. "He told me we were all wasting our time waiting for Jesus. He told me there was no truth to Heaven or Hell. And he told me that churches held no purpose other than to give ignorant and misguided people a false sense of hope."

If I hadn't sat outside on the curb that morning, waiting for him.

"And I told him I'd heard of people like him before. People who wouldn't ever believe in the things I was taught to believe in. And that my mother told me I should never listen to the things these people would tell me. And I asked him who he was. He tossed the chain back to me and he told me he was my father. But I didn't believe him."

If I hadn't waited in the library that afternoon, wanting to help him.

"Do you know what I did then? I put that necklace in my pocket. Without another word, I turned around and left the church. When my mother asked me if I had found it, I told her I didn't. I told her Jesus must not be such a helpful guy after all."

If I hadn't returned to The Strangest Feeling so many nights, wanting to see him again.

"I never wore that chain around my neck again. I think I tossed it in a ditch or something. I'm not sure. And I refused to go to church with my mother and sister from that day on. They couldn't understand the things that I was now starting to believe, but it didn't bother me."

If only that night, exactly one month ago, hadn't been my birthday.

"A few months later, my mother and sister died when our house burned to the ground."

If I hadn't been rejected from the Doneau High basketball team, none of this would have happened.

His story is sad, but there's only one thing I can ask him. "Why did that man call you Matthew?"

"Because he was *crazy*. That's my point."

"I couldn't tell there was a point to that story."

"Of course, Bella. I realized then, people are only good for telling you what *they* believe in. They don't care what you really want, or what the truth really is; they simply want to force *their* beliefs on *you*. To convert more sheep."

"But you believed what that man told you, didn't you? Isn't that why you never went to church again?"

"No. I realized my beliefs sat somewhere in the middle of what my mother preached to me, and what that stranger had said. But don't condemn me for having different beliefs than you do, Bella."

The same words he spoke in the graveyard three nights ago.

"Don't think me any less intelligent than you," he'd said that night.

"I can't force you to wholly believe in the same things I believe," he had said.

"But I can make you accept it," he had said.

From somewhere, I think I hear the unmistakable wooden *bonk* of the male Three-Wattled Bellbird (*Procnias tricarunculata*).

"I think I'd better get going," I say to him.

I don't know why it hurts so much, but it does. How can it be wrong for me to do exactly what my heart is urging me to do? I climb back inside my car and close the door. As it slams shut, it seems to force more tears out of my eyes. I want to throw up again, but this time for completely different reasons. Templeton is outside the windshield, still sitting on the hood of my car.

I turn the key. The engine fails to start.

Templeton stands up and turns around. There's a look in his eyes that tells me he knows far more than I thought he did. And that all of this is far from being over.

From wherever comes the distinctive call of a Sulawesi Thrush (*Cataponera turdoides*).

I turn the key again, and I don't let go of it until the engine roars back to life. I shift the car into Drive.

"Everyone will believe in something different, Isabella," he says, almost as a warning. "And if you're lucky enough, some of them will believe everything *you* tell them."

He steps out of my way, and he lets me leave him. With the window still rolled down, I can hear his words as I pass by. But he's through with his preacher's warnings, and he's moved along to simply being cryptic. "That's why Nickwelter killed that girl."

I don't get the connection, but I'm also trying my best not to make one.

I don't know how he knows the things he thinks he does, but I tell myself it doesn't matter anymore.

I keep driving. I look into the rearview mirror, and he's standing there in the patch of rectangle where my car was just parked. It's the only empty spot I see. Even the crows have moved on. Templeton Rate is the only sign of life I leave behind in the snow-covered parking lot.

If I had stopped telling this story, now would probably be a good time.

The Constant City

SATURDAY, NOVEMBER EIGHTH. I had to fly all the way from Boston to the Pierre Elliot Trudeau International Airport in Montréal, and then connect to the Sept-Îles airport before I remembered why I hate coming home. Well, aside from the obvious reasons. From Sept-Îles, it's still an hour-and-a-half-long bus ride to Ville Constance. I'm sitting on a Greyhound with a cold cup of airport coffee, behind a sweaty window, and staring at the familiar winter skies. I imagine my parents inside the warm Donhelle home right now: my father sitting in his chair watching the hockey game while my mother prepares dinner. Same as it always is in the Constant City.

I decided on Wednesday night I would make the trip home this weekend. A few days away from everything that's been falling apart in Boston would certainly be good for me right now. I haven't been home since last Christmas, but even that was three years removed from the time before. I remember coming back to my apartment last year and telling Claude my parents would be coming to see *me* the next time. He didn't care though, he was just happy to be home too, after spending a week at the Nickwelters' house.

This time around I don't have to worry about who'll be looking after him while I'm gone.

From the Greyhound station in Ville Constance, I place the pre-arranged phone call, letting my parents know I've finally arrived. The conversation is short, and my father tells me he'll come pick me up, just as soon as the first period of the hockey game is over.

Across the street from the bus station is Saint Francis Elementary School. That old familiar hedge may be iced over, but it still taunts me. I wonder how many kids have cut their faces and scraped their knees and torn their coats since I've been through there? I think about carrying my bags over to the school right now and giving it another run, but then I remember just how good change has been for me lately.

There'd been no sign of Templeton Rate or Professor Nickwelter for the rest of the week. No further visits from Anton Frye or Detective Dunphey. I hadn't followed up with Jerry Humphries about the suspicious goings-on in the south lab. And I completely forgot about those six swans covered with the tarp until now.

The death of Becky Chandler had been made public on Wednesday morning, and I had a long talk about everything that afternoon with Steffen James. At first, he didn't want to discuss it, but I think he could tell I needed to talk to somebody. Uncomfortably, he listened to me drone on about my relationship with Templeton, from start to finish. He sat through everything I had to say. And after it all, Steffen was the one who convinced me to take some time off.

Now I'm standing alone in the dark, cold, and empty bus depot. Even the Greyhound has left by the time my father pulls up in the familiar family car. The same car since I was twelve.

Same as it always is in the Constant City.

He pops the trunk open and steps out as I toss my bags in the back. "'Allo, Bella! So good to see you again." He gives me a hug, which I have to admit, is a nice feeling, and one that I haven't experienced too often outside of Ville Constance. But he is quick to let go. "Hop in. We can still make it back for the second period." A part of me was hoping Dad would have grown his beard back by now, but he still keeps his face shaved clean to this day.

We're home in another seven minutes, which included, at most, a minute more of conversation. My father is happy to tell me that the Boston Bruins are playing in Montréal tonight, and they play each other again tomorrow in

Boston. He calls it a "home-and-home" series, which strikes a strange parallel in my mind: I think this weekend will be my own personal home-and-home series.

"What's the score, Dad?" I ask, but no possible answer could really make me care either way.

"Zero-zero," he says, stepping on the gas.

Touching the freezing window with the tips of my fingers, I peer through the glass. As much grief as I give this town, I'm honestly still surprised that nothing appears to have changed at all. I'll give it the benefit of the doubt however, since it is dark outside, and it doesn't seem as though they've ever put in more than the same six streetlights along this road.

As soon as I enter the house the smells hit me. It's pine trees. It's lemons. It's roses. It's a roast beef cooking in the oven. It's the hardwood floors that have just been washed and waxed. The carpets that were recently vacuumed. The footprints that were sure to have been on the carpeted stairs have all been carefully brushed away; all of the fibers no doubt meticulously combed forward. I want to run my finger along the top of the picture frame, but I know exactly what I'll find: nothing. The cork coasters are already pre-set and waiting for me on the coffee table.

And then Mom comes out of the kitchen, in her famous pink "MOM" apron, arms spread wide as a Wandering Albatross (*Diomedea exulans*). As dismayed as I sound, I look forward to the oncoming embrace, and hope I can get a bit more from my mother than what my father had graciously provided earlier.

"Bella! It's so good to have you home, sweetheart!"

"Hi mom. I guess it's about time, isn't it?"

"At the very least, you could start returning your mother's phone calls."

"I know. I'm sorry about that."

"Why don't you get your father to take those bags upstairs for you?"

We both notice Dad has already sunk back into his chair and all attention has been diverted back to the television. "That's okay. I'll bring them up myself."

"Okay. Make sure you wash up, too." She turns back to the timer on the oven, although I'm sure her internal clock is far more accurate. "Dinner will be ready in six-and-a-half minutes."

"Of course it will."

"Oh, did you see how nice the table looks?" My mother proudly directs my attention toward the dining room. It's the same table setting they've used since I was nine.

Same as it always is in the Constant City.

"Very nice. It's good to see you, Mom."

~~~

Opening my bedroom door, I'm not the least bit surprised to discover the sheets on my bed are the same ones that were there when I'd left twelve years ago. Nothing that used to be in this room seems to have been taken out, and nothing new has been added. At first glance, it appears as though my old bedroom has been unaffected by time, yet I can tell something is, well, off.

My reading lamp sits in the same position, angled just so I could read my Power of Science textbooks and the Audubon Society Encyclopedia before bed.

My stuffed pig remains on the top of my dresser, eyes to the door, exactly where he has always sat.

The same cutout paper stars dangle from the same ceiling light.
~~~

The same old tape player sits on the ledge beneath my window, the ledge where I would sit and wonder what kind of a world was really outside; out beyond Ville Constance. One night I saw the neighbors across from us making out in their kitchen, which I considered to be pretty exciting when I was twelve. I see their kitchen lit up now, and all I can visualize is Becky Chandler with her head in the sink. I close the same old curtains to try and block out the horrible visual in my head.

A few colored drawings I scribbled in school when I was eight remain pinned to the same spot of the same corkboard above the same small desk where I would sit and do all of my homework. There's a drawing of our house, with me standing outside by myself. There's a pond of ducks, even though I can tell now they're horribly inaccurate and extremely off model. There's even a drawing Antonia herself had scribbled during one of the dozens of times she stayed with us. I think it was supposed to be an elephant, but it's hard to tell since it has far more spider-like qualities. I remember telling her how I would pin it to this very desk, so she'd never lose it. But Antonia's not here anymore and her purple pachyderm/arachnid is.

There are some notches carved into the doorframe that marked my growth spurts when I was young. Tiny dates are scribbled beside each notch in pencil, in my father's printing. I can visualize myself getting younger and younger as I follow them down with my fingertip. There's a few more here; added by some of the children who stayed with us, but they never returned to see how much they'd grown. They would find new homes, where they would probably pick up in their new rooms where they left off in mine. Those marks are scattered all around in the middle, but mine dominate the highest points.

There's one mark that's slightly above where the top of my head is now, and I remember adding that one the last time I was here. I don't know why I did it, but I smile a little when I think about it now. Of course, the reason as to why I appear to have shrunk since then is a mystery. I try to remember what shoes I was wearing a year ago, not that my mother would let any shoes go beyond the front entrance.

Everything is as it was. And yet there's still something in this room that feels oddly out of place. Something unusually usual, and I don't know what it could possibly be.

~~~

I turn off the light and walk back out into the hall. There's a boy, maybe seven or eight years old, coming out of the other bedroom. I guess I'll be sharing the bathroom with him for the next few days.

"Hi there," I say to him, realizing I don't really know how to talk to kids anymore.

"Hello!" he says with unexpected jubilation. "Are you my sister?"

"Well, I am for this weekend. My name is Isabelle. What's your name?"

"Claude." Of course it is, I think to myself. Why wouldn't it be? "And it's dinner time!" he yelps, and he runs down the stairs like he's been waiting his whole life to be fed. He's about as excited for dinner as Dad is about the hockey game, as Mom is about her table setting, and as I am about taking these next three days to avoid my life back home in Boston.

~~~

The four of us sit around the table passing plates of roast beef, mashed potatoes, and corn. Mom scoops servings onto Claude's plate, and he gobbles it all up at practically the same speed. Dad continues to watch the game from the table, which my mother would never have allowed when I lived here. The conversation is typical, and I have to put on a brave face when they ask me about work and Claude.

"Who's Claude?" asks the boy of the same name. The name that's almost making me sick at this point. The name that's got me craving yet another cigarette. I actually bought my first pack last week, and I brought another with me for this trip. It's lying inside my bag upstairs, just waiting for my first moment of weakness. The familiar pink plastic lighter sits in there too, having returned to its hometown now as well.

My mother explains that Claude is the name of my parrot, and the kid is curiously amazed by the coincidence. Even if coincidences are almost entirely beyond his understanding at this point in his life.

Picking at my corn, I somberly say, "Claude is dead, Mom." At that exact instant, the Montréal Canadiens score a goal. Dad cheers and accidentally flings a piece of roast across the room. My mother loses a bit of potato from her mouth as her jaw drops open in reaction to both my comment and the food on her floor.

"Did you see *that*?" my father asks anyone willing to listen. "What a goal!"

"That's—*awful*," my mother says, resurrecting the conversation. "I'm sorry. When did that happen?"

"You know, I don't really want to talk about it, Mom."

"Oh. Okay then, sweetheart."

"A parrot is a bird." Claude says, as bits of chewed-up corn spew from his mouth. As oblivious as this kid is to my feelings on the subject, I have to give my father some credit for being even more oblivious.

"That's right," Mom tells him, reaching over and wiping his face with her napkin. "Isabelle teaches people all about birds. That's her job."

"I know *everything* about birds," he says to me.

I'm almost impressed by his enthusiasm. "Well, you probably know more than some of my students do." I try my best to not think of any one student in particular.

With his fork, Claude spears what's left of the roast beef on his plate and holds it up to me inquisitively. "What kind of bird is this?" he asks.

~~~

After my parents have gone to bed, I sneak outside to the front porch and have a cigarette. Smoking has been the only thing that's kept me relatively calm all week. Steffen James was considerate enough to pretend he didn't even notice. I take a long drag, leaning defeatedly upon the porch railing.

Coffee hasn't been working. My parents don't drink coffee, and I've gone almost all day so far without a cup. I had a cup at the Tim Horton's in Sept-Îles, but that's a far cry from the Starbucks I've grown used to in Boston. At least at Starbucks you can control your own cream and sugar ratios; the girl at the Tim Horton's insisted I decide between ordering it *"Black, single-single, double-double, or triple-triple."* Or any of the combined variations. As if the commoners could not be trusted with their own cream and sugar. Canada seems so strange to me now. My muscles have been twitching all evening, so I'm hoping a cigarette will help put everything at ease for just a tiny bit longer.

It's not long before my mother comes outside and catches me. It shouldn't be a surprise though, she probably heard me coughing from her bedroom. I hide the cigarette behind my back, worried about getting busted, and being sent back up to my room.

"What are you doing out here, sweetheart? It's freezing outside!"

"I'm just doing some thinking, Mom." It's the most generic answer I can
~~~

give, and I pray it's enough to satisfy her curiosity. But I should know nothing much gets by my mother, ever since she told me she'd always known it was a hickey she found on my neck that one Valentine's Day so many years ago. "What are *you* doing up?" I ask her.

"I was just washing the floors," she responds, and follows that by sniffing at the air outside on the porch. "Is that smoke?" she asks. "Were you smoking?"

Embarrassingly, I swing the cigarette back around to show her the evidence. God, I don't miss being a kid at all anymore. "Yeah, Mom. I've picked up a few bad habits here and there along the way."

"Are there any good habits?" my mother asks, as though she's long since come to terms with the fact her daughter is inherently flawed. Or maybe as an indication she's acknowledged her own bad habits over the years.

Either way, I take another puff, hoping the smoke will be enough to take the blame for these tears in my eyes. It's not though.

"Are you okay, Isabelle?"

"That's a tough one to answer, Mom." It's hard to admit anything to my mother. And especially hard to admit I've finally changed after all these years, since I left this small town behind me. "I guess I'm just hitting a rough patch." Not that she can relate.

"Everybody hits those patches, sweetheart." She sits down on one of the two cold, frosted plastic porch chairs. A feeling comes over me: the strangest feeling that I should've already had this conversation with my mother. Like we were supposed to have had this talk years ago, but just accidentally missed out on it.

"I think this is a bit more than that," I confess. As I stand before her, I go on to tell my mother all about the foolish affair with Professor Nickwelter.

How it all started, and even how it ended. I tell her about my birthday a month ago, and when I met Templeton Rate, and how I thought a change would do me some good. I tell her how wrong I was. I tell her about the awful night in the Salem graveyard on Halloween, and that a student of mine was murdered. *Murdered!* I can barely even believe it myself as I say the words. I tell my mother how I ended things with Templeton because I was afraid of losing my job. There was far too much at stake. A relationship shouldn't feel so costly, should it? I listen to myself ramble on, and I think maybe I'm being selfish. I'm hoping for nothing more than a relationship, when there are people in this world without anything at all. A woman has been killed. Professor Nickwelter — a good friend of mine, like it or not — is accused and missing. There's a litter of angels in Ville Constance, just hoping for a family.

"Sometimes things change," is what I get from my mother. "Whether you want them to — whether you *think* they should — or not." But I don't want to hear that. Especially not in this town. She stares beyond me, out into the street which is lit only by the dimming lights of the neighborhood. From somewhere, there's a warm breeze that sweeps up onto the porch. It carries a leaf, which whirls around the corner of the house. I'm convinced I'd seen that very same leaf fifteen years ago. Same as it always is in the Constant City.

I toss the cigarette into the neighbor's yard. When I turn back to my mother, I'm surprised to find her now holding one too, and trying to light it up behind the shield of her hands.

"Mom? What are you doing?"

"Everyone's got habits," she says with the cigarette hanging out of her mouth. Finally, she lights the thing, and leans back in the porch chair with a smile. "But not all of them are *this* good."

"When did you start smoking?"

"I always have. Sometimes things don't need to change in order to appear different. Sometimes things remain the same, but go unnoticed."

I don't know what to say to her. I find myself trying to imagine my mother and I sitting together on this very same porch fifteen years ago sharing a cigarette. But I can't. It's just too implausible. I don't have to come up with anything more to say though, because she's not through yet.

"Your father and I are getting a divorce."

"What?" Thanks, Mom. Thanks for the all-too-perfect capper to my week. "What are you talking about?"

"Things haven't been working for a long time, Isabelle. We finally decided we'd both be better off if we were apart."

If my mother had been telling this story, it would be bursting with the unexpected.

"Like I said," she continues. "Some things always remain the same, but simply go unnoticed."

"I don't know what to say. When were you planning on telling me?"

She takes a long drag and exhales it like a seasoned pro. "Maybe you should call your mother back every once in a while."

Thanks for not holding a grudge, Mom. That's sweet of you. "The night Claude went missing, I also noticed my phone had been unplugged," I tell her. "The more I've thought about it though, the more I've considered maybe it was Templeton who had done it. Even if I can't figure out why."

"Honestly, Isabelle. It doesn't sound like this man was a very good choice for you." She's right of course, and the more I think about Templeton Rate, the more I realize he scares me more than anything. "What are you going to do when you get back to Boston?" she asks.

Finally, I sit down in the empty chair next to her. What *am* I going to do? I think back to the last conversation I had with Templeton, in the university parking lot. He told me everyone would always believe in something different. And he knew about Professor Nickwelter, even before the whole horrible story had been made public. In the cemetery, he told me he believed in angels. He told me he couldn't force me to believe in the same things he did, but he could make me accept them. I remember the night he told me he loved me. I remember waking up to find him by the window with tears in his eyes. The morning we sat on the sidewalk outside his apartment, he told me he could see traces of life everywhere, when I could only see death. The dead pigeon. The wilted flowers left for the dead girl. The frog purse. *Casualties of life*, is what he called them. He asked me what was more important: life or death? But I didn't have an answer, and he never gave me one. We were only a block away from The Strangest Feeling. From the place where he told me there wasn't any right answers for anything in this world. He told me the number of things we don't know outnumbers the amount of things we do. He told me if I was going to spread my wings I'd better have a safe place to land. He told me he was better than stale cheese bread and watery pea soup. He made his first appearance in my classroom and told my entire class that molting can be psychological. A temporary change, or a permanent one. He once asked me if I'd ever dreamt of flying.

And I told him everything he wanted to know. I told him all my dreams. I opened myself up and told him everything I believed in. And in return, I believed every word he said to me.

I try to narrow down the exact moment where I really went wrong. That one critical event I can blame for getting me to where I am right now. It wasn't when I tried out for the Doneau High basketball team. It was much, much later.

I'm certain now that it has something to do with all of the blue checkmarks. Templeton Rate knew far more than he should have known, and I blame myself for that.

My mother's question still rings in my head. What am I going to do when I get back to Boston? "I'm going to figure out the truth behind Templeton Rate," is what I tell her.

Before I head back upstairs to bed, I recall the sense of something in my bedroom feeling out of place. But I couldn't put my finger on it until now. I ask my mother, "You've been sleeping in my bedroom, haven't you?"

"Yes. Ever since you left here twelve years ago."

If I hadn't left Ville Constance.

"Good night, Mom." I kiss her on the cheek, and I go back inside the house.

Blackbird's Grill

SUNDAY, NOVEMBER NINTH. It's 10:00 AM by the time I roll out of bed and take a shower. The shower had seemed smaller when I was younger, and I once again consider the absurd possibility that I'm twenty-nine and shrinking. As I walk downstairs, I can hear my mother talking to Claude in the kitchen, probably explaining just how much of a mess his sister's gotten herself into. Most likely, my father is still sleeping; his usual Sunday routine has never changed. I honestly don't know if I can look my parents in the eyes this morning, so I leave through the back door without a word.

There was rain last night, and Ville Constance is nothing but wet, slushy snow. remember mornings exactly like this so clearly. I don't even realize where it is I'm walking to until I'm already approaching Doneau High. I'd done this walk so many times before from the nondescript front door of the Donhelle home to the big, red double doors of the high school, I suppose it's just become instinctual. The sidewalks are all the same. The same old cracks I remember hopping over are still there. The last stretch of sidewalk wraps around a small hill, which I and every other kid would always cut across. There's still a dirt path cutting through the middle of the grassy hill from all of the foot traffic. The walk from my parents' house is only five blocks, but it seemed like such a chore when I was younger. It was probably the hardest thing I had to do when I was a kid, paling in comparison to the problems I'm dealing with these days.

Then I see the familiar red doors and the flagpole. Embarrassingly, the first thing I think of when I see the waving red maple leaf is Zirk's ill-fitting costume. There's a scattering of cigarette butts at the base of the flagpole, and

I imagine there must be kids today playing the parts Claude and I once played. It's the way life seems to circle around again and again. Same as it always is in the Constant City.

I walk right up to the front doors, and I peer inside the window. It's like I've never been away from here. In a microsecond, my memory runs through all the problems and worries and heartbreak and tears and laughter I endured within these halls; I recollect it all in an instant. I step back a little to regain my place in this world. I think of the entire landslide of problems I'm running away from right now, and I wonder: If we actually had the power to relive our lives, to erase regrets, would things really be all that different? We'd just generate entirely new problems for ourselves, wouldn't we? If one truly had the ability to make life-altering decisions, I would imagine those decisions would be much harder to make.

I try the door, but thankfully it's locked up tight for the weekend. I don't think I'd really want to step inside, anyway. Studying the details on the other side of the window, I see clouds of dust motes floating under a shaft of hopeful light. It's as though all of those particles and atoms have been sealed away since the moment I left. Like it's now an airtight museum preserving the childhood of Isabelle Donhelle: the floors she walked across; the doorknobs she handled; the water fountains she drank from. Would anyone care to see that? I can make out the rows of framed student pictures on the walls, and I'm sure my graduating class is up there amongst them all. I wonder if anybody passes by my photo and wonders what her story is. Where is she now? Is she happier than she looks in this picture? Has she ever allowed someone into her life and then regretted it when he completely ruined everything?

I think I see a familiar Raven (*Corvus corax*) roaming the halls alone, but when it suddenly disappears from my sight, I'm convinced it's just my memory playing dirty tricks.

I decide to do my nostalgia a favor and I walk around behind the school. There's the empty lot where some of the students would park their cars; those were the students who never had any problems fitting in. Over there, the bike racks where kids would kick the bikes that weren't theirs; or they would slash the seats and let the air out of the tires. I remember balancing on the middle bar of the bike racks, and how we would try to walk from one end to the other without falling. It felt like my first attempt at flying, as I tried to keep my feet off the ground for as long as I possibly could. There's the track we would run around at least once a week. Just walking across the crunchy, orangey-brown gravel of the track makes me want to skip class again.

There are some basketball hoops sticking out from mounds of shifted, crumbling concrete. I recall the first time I ever sunk a shot; the first time the basketball swished through the unraveled netting hanging limp off the metal hoop. It filled me with so much delight and confidence I decided to try out for the girls' basketball team the next day. And we all know how that turned out. I partly blame this crooked hoop for the predicament I'm in now, possibly in some lame attempt to find something else to pin it all on.

I look up, and there are the two windows of Room 210. One of them is noticeably out of place, a little off-color. A yellow-tinted window replacing the old one which had shattered when the raven flew through it. When he crash-landed on my textbook, and opened my eyes.

And of course, just like bad poetry, there's the yellow electrical box behind the gymnasium. More cigarette butts mark the spot where I'd spent two months of my life making out with a boy who didn't deserve my attention in the first place. I sit down for a few minutes. Staring at the back of the school, I imagine the embarrassing dances which took part behind that wall, inside the gymnasium. I recall going to only one of them, being dragged along by Cindey Fellowes. I've sometimes wondered what I'd missed out on by having never gone to the rest.

A skein of honking Canadian Geese (*Branta canadensis*) flies overhead, and there's a man jogging around the track with his dog. I don't know why, but a feeling comes over me that I shouldn't be here. What if I should bump into someone who recognizes me? I can't imagine what that conversation would turn into; what I might confess to people who don't need to know anything about the person I've become. What if I convinced them there was something else out there? Some reason to leave this place like I once did. I feel like I need to disappear before this man notices me. I'm a ghost here. I used to believe Ville Constance was all I'd ever be, but now all it does is hurt my heart.

It's about time I find somewhere in this town to get some breakfast and a cup of coffee. From Doneau High, it's a short walk into the town center, which isn't much more than a crumbling strip mall book-ended by opposing gas stations. Everything appears closed, but a little farther along, directly across the street from the paper mill, I find the Blackbird's Grill. There are semi-trucks parked outside of the restaurant, and judging by the snow, a few of them have been here for some time now.

I'm not in the restaurant long before that ghost-like feeling eerily creeps its way up my arms again. It's in this moment I realize what Templeton had told me is actually true. He told me I was changing. He called it molting, which might have been scientifically inaccurate, but there was truth to his words. And the truth is that I have changed. I'm not the same girl who grew up in this town; I don't belong here anymore. I've become obsolete in the Constant City. And I need to go home.

Even if it kills me.

There's a hand-stitched picture on the wall beside me; framed and set behind glass. Just as the name of this restaurant is the Blackbird's Grill, the picture depicts a Common Blackbird (*Turdus merula*), surrounded by lyrics from the Beatles' song of the same name. A few of the lyrics seem so foreboding to me as my eyes scuttle across them. As though I've never really known the words before now:

Blackbird singing in the dead of night
Take these sunken eyes and learn to see
All your life, you were only waiting for this moment to be free
Take these broken wings and learn to fly
All your life, you were only waiting for this moment to arise

The waitress finally comes to my booth, and places an empty ceramic mug with faded, sepia-toned image of a Blue Jay (*Cyanocitta cristata*) onto the table. Without a word, she begins filling the mug with coffee. I watch closely as it pours into my cup, and it makes me uncomfortable to realize how much I've come to rely on things I'm not used to. The stream of rich, brown liquid is hypnotic. So much so, I don't even flinch when it rises up over the brim of the cup, extending its murky reach across the table and dripping onto the floor.

"Isabelle?" the waitress says. "Is that you?"

I look up to the waitress, who has now ceased pouring the coffee so indiscriminately. She's about my age. I wouldn't say she's attractive, at least not as attractive as I remember. A little overweight now. A little fuller in the face. Her frizzled hair is pulled back into a messy bun, exuding that small-town feel. But I know for certain it can only be her.

"Cindey Fellowes?"

"That's right. Although it's Cindey *Devereaux* now." I'm trying to spell that out in my head, adding up the E's along the way. "What the hell are you doing back in Ville Constance?"

"Just seeing what's new."

"New? *Here?* Jeez-us, you should know better than that." Cindey takes a rag from her apron, and starts mopping the coffee up from the tabletop. She tells me she's got a break in two minutes and she'll come sit with me for a while. I ask her if she can bring me a scone on her way back, but when she's unclear of what a scone is, I settle on a bran muffin instead.

I haven't seen this girl since high school, so five minutes later when I realize I'm sitting across from Cindey Fellowes at a dirty diner in Ville Constance, it seems a little surreal, to say the least. She's drinking her coffee black, and I can't imagine what would possess someone to do so. Neither of us knew the first thing about coffee in high school, but I suppose it's only fair to assume she must have changed at least a little bit too. Her cup's almost empty by the time I stop pouring sugar into mine.

"It's funny," she says as she looks around the little restaurant. "I didn't know this place existed when we were in high school, even though our fathers worked right across the road. We were so oblivious to everything when we were growing up."

I can't help but agree with her.

"So, what have you been doing since you left? Weren't you going to school in Austin?"

"It's Boston, actually. But close."

"Well, that's still down there near Florida somewhere, right?"

I don't have the heart to correct her. "That's right."

She asks what it was I had studied, and I realize the whole raven-through-the-window event never really held any significance to Cindey. In fact, I think we barely spoke to one another after that moment. "Ornithology," I tell her. "I'm an ornithologist now."

"What is that, rocks?"

"Birds, actually." I point at the image on the side of my coffee cup. I've been staring at it the entire time, because it seemed to be making me comfortable again. "You see that? That's a blue jay. Its scientific name is *Cyanocitta cristata*."

She reaches across the table and turns the mug around, staring at the colorless image painted on the ceramic. "How can you tell it's blue?"

I don't want to bore her, but I could point out at least ten clues from that tiny, faded drawing as to why it's a blue jay and not something else. It's obvious. "I just know these things," is all I say.

Cindey goes on about how she married two years out of high school and that she has an eight-year-old son. Her husband, Rory, worked at the paper mill too before being laid-off a year ago. She took this waitressing job to help them make ends meet. She pulls a photograph from her apron pocket and shows it to me. "I always carry this with me. This is my son, Sylvester."

I look at the picture, and I can't even begin to imagine what this kind of life must be like. Sylvester is beautiful, and I worry a little bit about the hearts he might break once he's older. Once he's making out with some girl on the electrical box behind the high school.

There's something else about this boy's photo. Something that makes me question every decision I've made in the last twelve years. I don't know what it could possibly be. A glint in his eye? The angle of his smile? The cheesy, country lane backdrop behind him? Whatever it is, I wonder now for the first time if I had made the right choice in going to Boston. I wouldn't have gotten mixed up in my relationships with Professor Nickwelter and Templeton Rate. Should I have stayed here nestled within the safety of this town I hated, never knowing anything else outside of it? What have I really gotten from getting where I am? Was there a reason for any of it?

I recall the conversation I had with my mother last night: all those questions about Templeton I told myself I would find answers for as soon as I returned to Boston.

But do I even want to go back there now?

If Sylvester Devereaux had been telling this story, would he make you question everything you've ever done?

I hand the picture back to Cindey, and finish the last bite of my bran muffin without another word.

"Do you remember when we were back in high school?" she asks me, as if just recalling we'd known each other then. I don't say a word, hoping there's another thought coming. "You had a crush on some boy, and the two of you made out behind the gym like every day for a year. Remember?"

"Vaguely," I tell her. I don't want to admit it was ten months shorter than she can recall.

"Did you ever find out what it was he wanted to ask you?"

"You mean *The Question*, right?"

"Yeah! That's right. The Question. What was *that* all about?"

"I have no idea."

"Don't you ever wonder what it must have been? Wouldn't it eat you up inside to never know something you always wanted to? I think something like that would just kill me."

"You know, I never really gave it much thought, Cindey." I wonder how convincing I actually sound.

I thank Cindey for the coffee and muffin, and she graciously informs me that my two-dollar meal is on the house. But she does make me promise to come back to Ville Constance one day, so we can have more time to talk. I get the feeling she must have some amount of pity for her unmarried and childless old friend.

I do promise her, and I leave the Blackbird's Grill hoping I can be true to my word.

All my life, I was only waiting for this moment to arise.

~~~

When I return to my parents' house, my mother is on the front porch with Claude. He's got his bag with him, which means he's probably on his way back to the orphanage. Mom's going to walk him there. She asks me where I've been all morning, and I tell her I was merely reminiscing.

There's a large finch, a Pine Grosbeak (*Pinicola enucleator*), foraging in the neighbors' bushes. The same bushes I tossed my cigarette into last night. I nudge Claude with my elbow, and ask him if he knows what kind of bird it is. He tells me it's not a bird, it's a bunny. I tell him it was nice to meet him, and Mom says she'll be back in a half hour.

I hear the sound of the television, turned up far louder than it needs to be, indicating my father has already sat himself down for the afternoon. "Hockey again?" I ask him.

If my father had been telling this story, it would be very predictable.

"It's a matinee game," he tells me. The second part of the home-and-home series between Montréal and Boston. I sit down for a moment to watch with him. So far, the Bruins are up one goal to none.

It's not until a commercial break that my father acknowledges me again. "Your mother misses you, Bella," he tells me. "You should really call home more often."
~~~

There's a Long-Eared Owl (*Asio otus*) on the television screen. I think it's a commercial for life insurance, but I'm not really paying attention to it.

"I know, Dad," I tell him. "But sometimes I really don't have anything to say. My life is so—well, it's not very interesting."

He takes a look around the living room, moving just his head like a bird would do. "But it's got to be better than this, no?"

I think about what my mother told me last night. Something about things going unnoticed. "Mom told me you guys are getting a divorce. What did you do, Dad?"

"Me? Why does it have to be *my* fault?" His eyes become glossy, and he stares at me accusingly. "Sometimes things just don't work out, Bella. Life is full of change you can't predict or control. You just have to accept things for what they are."

Do they rehearse these lines just so I'll have no idea what they're talking about? So I won't know who I can blame for anything? "Yeah, Dad. I know."

Just then, Boston adds another goal. Two-to-nothing. I find it ironic that it's a French-Canadian doing the scoring for them, but no one else in the crowd seems to make a deal out of it. There's a loud noise, like a train's horn as the home team scores. Dad is not nearly as excited as the fans on the screen.

Before I can think another thought, the horn goes off again. Dad is furious now, although there appears to be some confusion on the ice. The horn sounds yet again, but nobody has scored. The arena is having some sort of technical difficulty with its sound system.

The players on the ice stop skating, and they look up into the stands, pointing.

The horn blows once more, and this time the cameras pan up into the crowd. Some of the fans are yelling, panicking. Some are running from their seats. Beer and popcorn are flying. Before I know it, the hockey game quickly cuts to an unscheduled commercial break.

But I know what it was that I saw. There was just enough time between the screaming crowd and the commercial for Glade Plug-Ins to notice them. The Boston Garden was full to the rafters with Australian Superb Lyrebirds (*Menura novaehollandiae*).

Instantly, I recall Templeton's tale of wasted potential. His story about the birds that flew through New York City, speaking Mandarin.

And I know immediately that I need to get back to Boston.

The Glorious Age of Templeton Rate

MONDAY, NOVEMBER TENTH. Last night, I wasted no time in packing my bags and taking the first Greyhound I could from Ville Constance to Sept-Îles. The first flight I could get to Montréal was at seven o'clock, and I didn't get back into Boston until one in the morning.

Which was right about the time I realized the magnitude of the whole situation.

I could see it as the plane neared the tarmac of Logan International: the murky, black cloud hanging over and within the city in the near distance.

I could feel it from the taxi, as the cab emerged from Boston's massive system of tunnels and onto Storrow Drive: the war-zone-like explosions reverberating off the back of the Charles River.

I could hear it on the radio: callers and talk-show hosts trying to understand how all of this was happening, and why it was happening to them.

The cab driver explained to me that last night the Boston police had encouraged everyone in the city to stay indoors if they could. He says I was lucky to have flown in when I did because apparently the airport is expecting to be shutting down all services. It seems the birds have, at least temporarily, won the competition for air space. And they've been battling for years. Black-Bellied Plovers (*Pluvialis squatarola*), Horned Larks (*Eremophila alpestris*), Mourning Doves (*Zenaida macroura*), and Upland Sandpipers (*Bartramia longicauda*) make up the biggest aircraft-bird collision threats in North America. The most tragic reported accident in US history occurred right here at the Logan International Airport in 1960, when a plane struck a murmuration of Common Starlings (*Sturnus vulgaris vulgaris*), clogging the engines and killing sixty-two of the seventy-two aboard when it crashed.

Nobody knew if these birds were dangerous, or if they might attack people at random. I, of course, know differently. I know Templeton Rate has to be involved in this somehow; his story about the wasted potential of Mandarin-speaking myna birds was all the evidence I needed when I first spotted the lyrebirds on my father's television.

And yet, I can hardly comprehend it myself as I return to my apartment and look out my window to see four Myna Birds (*Acridotheres tristis*) now perched on the telephone wires, their common screeches oddly replaced with blaring sirens. They've no doubt scared off the regular crowd of rock pigeons and American crows. I'm three stories off the ground, and it seems like there's a fire truck right outside my window.

I look down into the alley to see a Northern Mockingbird (*Mimus polyglottos*) calling out with the fury of a jackhammer. The call only intensifies, bouncing off the shallow cavern of Public Alley 434.

From the rooftop across the way, a lyrebird (*Menura novaehollandiae*) mimics a gunshot. And another. And another. Like an impatient sniper trying to rub me out.

I turn on the news, but I can barely hear it over the city's newborn din.

It's absolute chaos.

It's utterly overwhelming.

It *has* to be Templeton Rate.

I leave my suitcase on the living room couch and I quickly exit my apartment. With only one destination in mind: Templeton's apartment, where I'm hoping I'll be able to find some kind of answer.

~~~

I have to brush a foot of snow off my car; it must have been coming down ever since I left for Ville Constance on Saturday morning. It takes about ten minutes to warm the car up, and as I sit with my doors locked, all I can hear are the jackhammers, the fire trucks, and the gunfire surrounding me.

As I pull out of the alley, there is another myna bird in front of me, cleverly mimicking a car alarm. A part of me wants to run the thing over, just to make it shut up, but I swerve to avoid it instead.

I pass a group of Barred Parakeets (*Bolborhynchus lineola*), sitting together on the hood of a parked car and beeping like microwave ovens. Outside the Prudential Center sits a solitary Hill Myna (*Gracula religiosa*), and I do a double take as it strangely and unmistakably cries like an abandoned baby. Outside The Strangest Feeling, European Starlings (*Sturnus vulgaris*) mimic grinding metal, like a train coming to a hard stop. I hear a Sun Conure (*Aratinga solstitialis*) keeping the neighborhood awake as it mimics five blaring fire alarms at once. And from somewhere, there's the infuriating soundtrack from "Super Mario Brothers" letting me know that an Olivaceous Cormorant (*Phalacrocorax olivaceus*) has just leveled-up.

The faintest hint of sun is rising from the east when I park my car outside Templeton's apartment. There's nobody around. Nothing but out-of-place birds making the most maddening and inappropriate sounds imaginable. I don't blame people for staying inside, but what is anyone going to do about this?

I walk up the front stoop of the building, where an African Grey Parrot (*Psittacus erithacus*) is perched on the railing. I give him an odd look, partly because there's no way an African grey parrot should be sitting alone in a
~~~

Boston suburb, but partly because this is probably the first bird I've seen this morning that hasn't been making an obscene racket.

But just before I turn away to look for Templeton's buzzer number, the bird opens its beak and swears at me. And in a British accent, no less. "The fuck you lookin' at?" it barks at me.

"Pardon me?" I say, already regretting my response.

"Fuck you," it replies.

I can't believe I'm having this conversation. The intercom has a number for "ZIRK," so I press it. I can't hear anything from the speaker because of the clamor, but after a few moments, I'm buzzed in. Maybe he doesn't care at all about who might be outside his apartment at three in the morning. As the door buzzer goes off, the parrot beside me mimics the sound. Except at maybe three times the volume. I'm careful to make sure it doesn't follow me as I enter.

I arrive at apartment 3G and knock on the door. I haven't rehearsed in my head yet what I'm about to say, but I don't care. I just want to know what's going on in Boston.

Zirk opens the door. At least I think it's him; it's mostly the lack of any brightly-colored bodysuit that makes recognizing him difficult. His jet-black hair is slicked back and there are dark red rings under his eyes. He's now wearing a long, black, tattered housecoat and there's a bandage across the bridge of his nose, making him look something like a prizefighter. I consider the possibility he's simply switched from one costume to another.

"Do you know what time it is, gorgeous?" he emits a deep growl, almost like a rumbling chainsaw, after he speaks. I'm certain he didn't sound like this before.

"No idea, actually. Where's Templeton?"

"*Where's Templeton? Have you seen Templeton?*" he says, mocking me. "Is that all you ever want to know?" He stops talking, but his growling continues for a little longer.

I try to look past him, into the apartment. I don't see anything to indicate Templeton's presence here. There's a very distinct fish-like smell though, like Zirk had just opened a can of sardines before I got here. I know I don't want to be going any farther across the threshold. Zirk is waving his face close to mine, a little too close for my comfort. His nose almost touches mine. He's swaying a little from side to side too, waiting for some kind of response from me.

"Have you seen what's going on outside?" I ask him, challenging him to reveal any bit of information to me.

He doesn't answer; he just keeps swaying back and forth and creeping me out.

"Do you know where Templeton is right now? Is he working?"

"Working? Templeton?" Underneath the bandage, I can see some sort of crusty formation on his nose. It looks like it might be infected.

"Yeah. Is he still doing the doorman thing?"

"This entire city is in lockdown," he starts with some more rumbling under his breath. "If Templeton was smart, he'd be at your school right now. He told me that's where I could find him if I needed to."

Without another word, I turn around to leave. As I walk away, Zirk asks me if I want to come inside for a while, just to be safe. I ignore him, and keep on going.

~~~
~~~

The grey parrot is gone when I get back outside, replaced by some Cockatiels (*Nymphicus hollandicus*), which are wading through the snow around my car, ringing like old-fashioned telephones. I shoo them away, and head for the university in search of Templeton. I feel around the seats for any lost or forgotten cigarettes, disappointed when I find nothing.

Along the way, I try to piece together exactly what has gone wrong here: the birds drowning out this city with their horrifying calls; the murder of Becky Chandler, and the subsequent disappearance of Professor Nickwelter; Nelson Hatch's Salem house burning to the ground; Claude's disappearance; Templeton's paper mysteriously showing up on my desk. Are these events all related somehow? Does Templeton have the answers, like I'm starting to think he does? Or is it all still Mrs. Wyatt's fault?

Maybe it's *my* fault?

If I hadn't left Ville Constance when I was seventeen.

If I hadn't left Ville Constance when I was twenty-nine.

It's 3:30 in the morning when I arrive at the university. There's only one car in the parking lot: only Jerry Humphries' ugly little beater of a vehicle.

From somewhere, some feathered aberration is setting off fireworks, but there are no bright flashes of light to accompany the devastating sounds of explosions.

I park in my regular spot, even though I could probably pull up right in front of the ornithology entrance. I guess habits are much easier to pick up than they are to break.

Just as I reach for the door, I notice something fantastic: there's a lone male King of Saxony Bird of Paradise (*Pteridophora alberti*) sitting to the right of the faculty entrance. I know it's a male immediately, it's simple, since it is the only bird in existence that sports such unique ornamental plumes: more than twice the length of its actual body, these two blue and brown scalloped brow plumes are extraordinary. He watches me, just as I watch him, but he doesn't make any sound at all. It's so breathtaking I almost forget how crazy things have become, and how mad I am at Templeton right now. But then the bird scurries off around the corner, probably without thinking of me quite as fondly.

The door is unlocked, and the security system has been left unarmed. The halls are dark, but I know my way around by instinct so I leave the lights off. Like the echolocation of the Barn Owl (*Tyto alba*), I could probably guide myself through these halls using sound alone. Even with all of the noise outside, I can still hear my heels as they clack along the linoleum floor. I've never walked through this school when it's been so empty, although I know it's not quite as empty as it seems.

I know Templeton is around here somewhere.

Doors creak. Windows shatter. It sounds like boiling water and witches cackling; something like a Halloween recording of frightening sounds. But this is no recording. Within the breaking glass, I can hear a Bull-Bellied Monarch (*Neolalage banksiana*). The witch's laughter contains the call of the Eared Grebe (*Podiceps nigricollis*). Amazingly, through it all, I pick out a hammering sound not too far away, and I know it must be coming from the south laboratory.

I haven't been to the lab since last Monday, when Jerry Humphries had been courteous enough to let me inside. That wooden structure was in there, as were the city's beloved swan boats. It's locked tight, but with my ear to the cold iron door, I can hear the undeniable sound of a hammer banging on metal. Maybe more than one.

I knock on the lab door, but the noise behind it doesn't seem to take notice. I knock again, this time with all of my strength. "Templeton!" I call out. The hammering continues. "Templeton? Are you in here?"

Silence. I take a step back from the door in anticipation.

"Who is that?" asks a voice from inside.

"It's Isabelle. Let me in."

And whoever it is asks me to hold on a moment, which turns into another minute or so of nothing. I kick at the bottom of the door with my foot a few times before I hear the locks turning.

Some kid I'm sure I don't recognize opens the lab door. "Oh, hey," he starts, obviously knowing who I am. "What are *you* doing here?" This kid, he's a tubby little kid, standing close to my height, and maybe twice as wide. There's something odd about the shape of his head, but I can't place it. And he's got dark bags under his eyes, as though he hasn't slept for days. I shouldn't judge though, as I probably don't look much better. I didn't sleep on the plane, and I've been awake for nearly twenty-four hours now.

"This is my school," I tell him. "What's *your* excuse?"

He doesn't say anything more, but steps back as I push the door open far enough to let myself in. From what I can see, there are two other people in here: another couple of kids I can't identify are staring at me from the back of the lab. They're both holding hammers and standing where that wooden frame was two weeks ago. The wooden structure that has now been replaced with a big metal box. Like a bank vault. Or a bomb shelter.

Like a hiding place.

Like a death trap.

This tubby kid is still waiting for me to say something else.

"What's going on in here? How did you get into the school at this time of night?"

"Mitchie let us in."

"Mitchie? Who's Mitchie?"

One of the guys from the back of the room makes his way over. He's on crutches and his right leg is in a cast. He's wearing a faded red t-shirt and black shorts, even though it's freezing in here. His nose is very pronounced, long and droopy, and his hair is cut to a short buzzcut. "Jonah Mitcherson. But everyone calls me Mitchie. Don't you recognize me, Professor Donhelle?"

I'm trying, but his face isn't ringing any bells. "You're a student here?"

"Shit, I've been in your class for like five months now."

"Humphries gave you access to this space, didn't he? You know this lab is strictly off-limits." Now the third kid comes over, and the three of them all look at one another for an answer, but no one's going to come up with one. "And what about you two? You're students here too?"

"No," says the fat one. "We go to Harvard."

I tell the three of them to get out of the school before I call the police. They don't even pack up their mess before leaving; they simply vanish without another word. Mitchie Mitcherson hobbles out on his crutches. Exactly one minute later, I'm wondering why I didn't call the police anyway.

The back of the room is much cleaner now than it was the last time I was in here. No more table saw or wooden planks or mounds of sawdust. The tarp and giant bird shapes underneath it are all gone too. It's just this big, cold, gleaming box.

I inspect one side of the room, where there are cardboard boxes full of random bits and components of equipment I don't understand. Sealed crates that are either waiting to be opened, or on their way out of here. There are a few boxes of books piled up on the table. Some books are obviously from

Hawthorne's library, while some are unmarked or missing their covers altogether.

There's one box containing what appears to be a collection of old, leather-bound notebooks from who-knows-when-or-where exactly. I pick one off the top of the pile; it's a dusty hand-written journal of some kind, and rather small, only a few inches wide. The handwriting is atrocious, even worse than Templeton's. But at least it's not all dirt and charcoal. Flipping through, it seems to contain a lot of formulas I can't begin to make sense of. A few scattered sketches on every other page. I check the front page to see if there's some kind of identification, but before I can find any answers, I hear footsteps from the hallway coming toward the lab.

I barely have enough time to conceal the journal in my coat pocket before turning to see Templeton in the open doorway.

"Bella?"

The last time I saw him, I told him it was over between us. And he told me something about why Professor Nickwelter had killed that student of mine. The last time I saw him, he was in my rearview mirror. That was one week ago. And since then, the city of Boston has been turned into a bizarre kind of avian variety show.

Some bird somewhere makes the same sound my heart would make if it fell on the floor.

"What's going on here, Templeton? I come back here to find this city overrun with birds, and there's some Harvard students building a big, metal barn in my lab."

He takes a look to the back of the room, toward the structure, without uttering a word.

"What is it?" I ask him, terrified.

"Well, for one thing, it's not a barn. This is nothing more than a tool."

"A tool? A tool for what?"

He wanders over to the giant, metal box across the lab. He watches his own reflection in the gleaming surface. I'm reminded of an avian territorial behavior known as window-fighting, where a bird will feel threatened by the reflection of itself in a window, or some other similarly reflective surface. I've read a study in which an American Robin (*Turdus migratorius*) fought its own reflection in the hubcap of a car for three straight days without knowing any different. The robin lost much of its own blood in those three days, and only conceded the fight when the car eventually drove away. But where fear and combativeness are hatched in birds, Templeton receives the exact opposite from his reflection. If anything, it calms him. Whatever this thing's purpose is, Templeton seems satisfied with it.

He runs his right hand along the shining, flat metal. There are thin trails of sooty charcoal left behind from where his fingers touch. Patting the box gently, he turns back to me. "It was designed for chemical testing. It's completely airtight, so we can analyze volatile gases and other such constituents. And it's done its job. But everything can be multipurpose, Bella. We can still get some more use out of it."

I'm afraid to ask, but I do anyway. "Like what, exactly?"

"Well, for *one* thing," he begins slowly. "The forty-five hundred cubic feet would allow for about five-and-a-half hours of air." I can only assume his math is correct. Finding the handle for the door, he pulls on it, making sure it's sealed tight. He turns back and looks me right in the eyes. "You would be very safe in here. Probably safer than anywhere else in this city." There's a glimmer in his dark eyes. A couple of weeks ago, I might have found this very same glimmer to be part of his charm, but now I can only describe it as a portent of evil.

"Me?"

"Or anyone," he says, hoping I'll believe his words. "It would be the one place where you could stay the way you are. If you wanted to resist change, or if someone wanted to deny you of it." His brow furrows, as though the words he speaks might be making him as uncomfortable as they make me. "If you wished to continue living out this dismal life you've been living, this would be your only hope." It's as though he couldn't possibly understand what it must feel like to be someone other than himself. As though he would frown upon anything or anyone that might ever resist his ideas. "Your last chance at death. Death as *you* know it, that is." As though he's happy thinking about how he'd never really loved me in the first place.

"Right," I say. I try not to show how much his words shake me to my core. "Who were those kids that were in here?"

"Mitchie and the others are helping me. But you don't have to worry about them," he says. "We've already established our pecking order." He turns back to me with the same cocky grin I saw on his face that first night inside The Strangest Feeling. "How was your trip back home?"

"Not good. But certainly better than *this*. Templeton, there was an Eastern whipbird outside in the parking lot making noises like breaking bones. Birds like that shouldn't be in North America."

He pulls on the door again, but it still won't budge. The muscles on his forearm tighten and relax with each tug. I wonder if there might be something inside already; something Templeton means to keep trapped within the cold metal walls.

"There was a group of budgerigars waiting beside me at a traffic light. They sounded just like that big spinning wheel from 'The Price Is Right.'"

My earlier feeling before about this room being bigger than I remembered was correct. I notice now there's the empty outline on the floor of where a wall used to be. About three feet from the back of the room. Three feet of once-enclosed space is just small enough that nobody would ever suspect it was even hidden from sight in the first place.

"I saw a scarlet macaw chasing a cat, and barking like a dog. That's not right. Someone has done something horribly rotten to this city."

He turns back to me, as though I had been pointing an accusing finger directly at him. "Someone?"

I stare into my own reflection on the metal surface now. I can clearly see I'm tired and lonely, and I just want some answers. So why isn't it clear to him? I turn to his reflection now, just as we did in the mirrored mini fridge. Just like the first night we met in The Strangest Feeling. "Templeton, what have you done?"

"I have a gift for you, Bella. Do you want it?"

"You know I can't answer without knowing what it is first."

"Come with me."

He turns away from my reflection and opens a door at the back of the lab. A door I'd never noticed until now. A door which had likely been hidden behind a fake wall for as long as I've known. I take a look, and there are steps leading down to a basement I was also previously unaware of.

I'm hesitant to move even an inch, but Templeton turns back to me with an abundance of enthusiasm. "Come on. Don't be scared."

We walk down into the darkness, and I can hear the ordinary tweeting and squawking of birds below us. A nice change from all of the non-stop hysterical gunfire, electronic beeping, and repetitive video game soundtracks outside. He still refuses to answer any questions I have, as I inquire about the existence of that extra three feet of floor space above us. He doesn't show the slightest acknowledgement when I ask about this basement we're walking into, and why I had never known about it. Templeton simply flicks the lights on. This basement is at least as large as the laboratory above us. The walls are lined with cages of varying sizes, but most of them are empty; hanging open as if there was a jailbreak. From the chirping, I'd guess there are only five or six birds left down here.

Templeton leads me to the far end, toward a long table full with even more random machinery and equipment. I spot some syringes and vials of mystery chemicals too. Hints of a mad scientist's laboratory.

"Now, don't get all freaked out like you usually do," he warns me. But there's no way I can promise any kind of reaction at this point. He opens the very last cage along the wall, reaches in and pulls out a Blue-and-Gold Macaw (*Ara ararauna*). The bird jumps from Templeton's arms and onto the table. There's a familiarity in its eyes as it turns to look at me.

"See?" Templeton asks.

Obviously, the first thing this bird reminds me of is Claude, but I try my best to not make it seem obvious. I've never been good at that though, and especially not with Templeton. "Can you tell me why this basement I never knew existed is crammed full with bird cages for birds that probably should never have even been here?"

He continues to ignore my questions, still focused on trying to impress me. "Don't you see what I've done, Bella? This is your bird." The parrot spreads both of his wings apart, and flaps them quickly, excited to be free from his confinement. He squawks a little, and his white face turns pinkish, due to his excitement.

"That's impossible," I tell him bluntly. "For obvious reasons."

"Is it? I know you're more observant than that."

I refuse to be impressed at this point, but I take a closer look at this bird, no more than three feet away from me. The bird has a butterscotch-colored belly, just like Claude had. The green-feathered forehead comes back just slightly farther than its white face, at the same point as Claude's once did. I've spent enough time with Claude to know the black speckles on his face were just as this bird's are. Its jet-black beak has the same tiny, grey, fork-shaped line along the lower jaw. But this macaw has two wings, which is a dead giveaway. All the proof I need, to know for sure that I'm still missing my best friend.

"Hello, Bella!" he squawks, probably wondering why I haven't shown any love for him yet.

"Claude?" Timidly, I touch his left wing with my hand, and the bird jumps about with glee. Forget proof; there can be no mistake now.

For a moment, I turn back to Templeton, questioning him with my eyes. "That's your bird," he boasts, proudly. "Good as new."

Claude jumps up into my arms. Suddenly, my disdain over everything I'd seen and heard since I returned to Boston two hours ago has dissipated. I'm overcome by gratitude, and relieved things aren't even half as horrible as I had thought them to be.

Even though they were twice as bad.

If I hadn't gone down into the laboratory basement.

Through tears in my eyes, I look back at Templeton. "I don't understand."

"I grew its wing back," he tells me matter-of-factly.

The wing is flawless. The bones are strong, the blue feathers perfect. "But that's *impossible*. How in the world did you ever do this?"

"There's always a possibility for everything. That's what science is all about. I used amphibian DNA. A salamander, to be exact. Salamanders generate what's known as a blastema, a mass of cells which are capable of growing into tissue, organs, or bones."

Claude flaps his re-grown wing with enthusiasm.

"Or in this case," he continues, "a bird's wing."

I have to hand it to him; he's got a way of making everything seem possible. As ridiculous as that explanation sounds, somehow Templeton does make it seem plausible. And the evidence is right here in front of me.

If I had never believed a single word he'd said to me, I wouldn't have believed that.

But I did.

If only Claude had stayed missing.

"But, how? How did you even know where to start?"

"By now, Bella, you should realize you don't know everything there is to know about Templeton Rate."

I hold Claude up with both hands, as high as I can. "So, can he fly then?"

"That wing only grew back two days ago. There are still a few tests that should be run, so I'd let it rest for a while if I were you."

"Do you hear that, Claude? You're back to normal again! One hundred percent!"

"Yeah, it can even count to eight now too."

"What?" This story just keeps getting better and better.

Or is it getting worse and worse?

"That's right. Just watch." Templeton reaches into his coat pocket and takes out a pack of cigarettes. Opening the package, he counts some cigarettes, and holds them out before Claude in the palm of his hand. "How many?" he asks.

And Claude says it. "Eight." It's true. "One two three four five six seven eight." Claude counts them all, and he doesn't skip any numbers at all.

I look back at Templeton, a smirk on that smug face of his. "I'd give it one for a treat, but as you know, these things can be quite addictive." He puts seven back in his pocket, and lights up the remaining one. He doesn't care at all whether we're indoors, or if these birds will be breathing in secondhand smoke. "I did this for *you*, you know?"

"I don't know what to say." What I want to say is that I love him for doing something like this, even if the entire idea scares the pancakes out of me. But I know better than to fall into that trap again, don't I? "So, he never jumped from my window?"

"No."

"But, how did—"

"Humphries took the bird, and brought it here." I don't know what bothers me more: the fact that Jerry Humphries was actually in my apartment, or that Templeton keeps referring to Claude as an "it."

I remember seeing the ugly brown car outside in the parking lot when I came in here this morning. "Is Humphries here right now?"

"No."

"But he *was* here, wasn't he? I saw his car outside."

"Don't you see, Isabella? There's more to this than all of that. Humphries is only doing what he thinks is best. But he doesn't really understand." Templeton reiterates what he said a few minutes ago, in regards to the structure upstairs: "He's nothing more than a tool. A tool for this new age we're entering."

The glorious age of Templeton Rate.

My mind flashes back to our talk in the Salem cemetery. I can't bring myself to question his intentions, but he knows exactly what I'm thinking anyway.

"There's more at stake here than you realize, Bella. Finding Jerry Humphries is not going to solve any of your problems. Finding who killed that girl is not going to make things any easier during what's about to come."

"I thought you said Professor Nickwelter killed her?"

"None of that matters. We're all just a means to an end. That's all any of us ever were."

I hate it when he talks like this.

"I told you before; there's a difference between having the right answer and knowing the truth."

"Well, tell me the *truth* then. Just *once*. I think I deserve that much."

Templeton takes one long drag of his cigarette, and hands it to me. I take it from him, and watch the paper shaft as it burns between my fingers. I want it so badly, but I know I shouldn't.

"You'll find the truth in that book you've got."

"What book?"

"The journal you stole. The one in your pocket."

I run my hand across the outside of my coat pocket, and I can feel the journal underneath. He doesn't make any indication that he wants me to hand it back to him. He doesn't tell me it's not mine. It's as though he wants me to keep it. As if he's challenging me to take another look inside of it. And I want to look inside, but I know I shouldn't.

"But don't tell me you deserve anything, Isabella. After all, you're the one who dumped *me*, remember?"

I can't help wanting Templeton still, even though I know I shouldn't.

He turns away from me and walks back up the stairs. "Stay here," he tells me. "I'll be right back." I watch as his feet disappear from sight.

And I wait. Claude and I both wait. That first night, at The Strangest Feeling, I thought it would be best to not wait for Templeton Rate. I made the decision then to walk away before things got worse.

And yet. Here I am.

Things are much, much worse and I don't even know how it got this bad so fast or why I've now found myself standing here waiting for him. I smoke the rest of the cigarette, now ignorant of the second-hand smoke myself.

Ten minutes later, I bring Claude upstairs with me. But Templeton's nowhere to be found. He's gone. And the box of old journals is not here anymore either.

I begin to wonder if my lack of sleep has led me to imagine any of this.

Was Templeton even there at all, or was he just one more from the litter of angels?

I turn off all of the lights and close the laboratory. With Claude under my arm, I make my way back outside. Jerry Humphries' car is gone now, too. In the entire lot, only my car remains. All alone under the only burnt out light.

I hear what sounds like a Black Vulture (*Coragyps atratus*) throwing up, but it could just be the memory of when I tossed my wastepaper basket in the parking lot dumpster. I hear a frog croaking, and I'm not sure whether it's actually a frog, or a perfect imitation from a Peach-Faced Lovebird (*Agapornis roseicollis*). It might just be the thought of Templeton's change purse coming to life at the end of the bed.

The sun is rising now, but all I want to do is sleep. I could either lay in the back of my car or just fall down into a snowbank right here in the parking lot. But I hear the exact sound my alarm clock makes, coming from some nearby bushes. It's the one sound that won't let me fall asleep.

I get into my car, and place Claude beside me on the passenger's seat. He counts the number of European Magpies (*Pica pica*) that land on the hood of my car. "Eight," he says. "One two three four five six seven eight."

An old folk rhyme comes to mind, as I recall the supernatural powers magpies have been considered to possess. Depending on the number which one encounters, it was suggested that magpies could predict the future, and bring either good or bad luck:

One for sorrow, two for mirth,
Three for a funeral, four for a birth,
Five for silver, six for gold,
Seven for a secret not to be told,
Eight for heaven, nine for hell,
And ten for the devil's own sel'

I feel a tiny sense of relief from the eight magpies, but there's a pretty good chance I'm simply finding any excuse I can to remain calm at this point.

"One two three four five six seven eight," he repeats again. A part of me wonders just how Templeton Rate ever managed to teach Claude how to count the number eight when I never could, while another part of me simply worries that the novelty has already worn off.

I take the journal out of my pocket and inspect it a little closer now. A couple of pages in, I find one of the answers I was looking for. There's a name scribbled at the bottom of the page:

N. HATCH

Nelson Hatch? It seems impossible. Like fourteen seconds for a chicken.

Nelson Hatch. Founder of Hawthorne University. Died in 1974. His house in Salem burned to the ground ten days ago. And now I find a whole box full of his journals in one of the school's laboratories. The very same laboratory in which students are preparing for what, exactly? The end of the world? The glorious age of Templeton Rate?

Did Templeton steal these books the night we were in Salem? I remember seeing a group of kids prowling around those old heritage homes as we sat in the cemetery. He told me he took a knit cap out from my trunk, but he could just as easily have been putting something else inside of it.

Claude and I both turn to one another for a moment.

I flip through the book in an effort to find the truth, as Templeton promised I would. But there really isn't anything that makes much sense here. There are pages and pages of scribbles. It's mostly about bird anatomy, and from the parts I can make out, it all seems pretty standard and accurate.

But some of the science goes beyond anything I've studied. There are formulas, after calculations, after charts, after detailed diagrams. I start to wonder if this was merely one journal from an entire box-full, what would the totality of them add up to?

A quarter of the way through, the sketches of birds become sketches of different animals altogether. Mice. Rabbits. Frogs. Salamanders. There are more complicated calculations, but they don't make any more sense than the rest before them did, if they're even supposed to.

I skip past much of it, and when I turn a page about three-quarters of the way through, it hits me. There's a drawing of a pig with large, feathered wings protruding from its shoulder blades. It's extremely meticulous. This isn't just some child's imaginative fancy. This isn't a doodle Nelson Hatch drew while sitting on the toilet or talking on the phone to his mother. There is an exact science to this drawing and the accompanying calculations. But it's still incomplete.

He was actually going to make it work, wasn't he?

If pigs really *could* fly, would everyone finally be satisfied?

If Nelson Hatch's calculations were correct, would the world be content?

The magpies take off as soon as I start the engine, and Claude counts them again, not distracted at all by the air horn sounds they make in the growing distance.

~~~

There isn't so much as a police car on the road along the way back to my apartment. These Bostonians are really taking things seriously, aren't they? Aside from being incredibly annoying, I know these creatures outside don't pose any real danger to anybody, but I suppose everyone's seen *The Birds* one too many times.

I spot ten or twelve Great Wandering Albatrosses (*Diomedea exulans*) flying high above the city. They glide like magic, rarely having to flap their long, slender wings. They look almost like crosses sailing through the sky. If I was a religious person, I might think of them as a good sign.

I have to slow down as four Capercaillies (*Tetrao urogallus*) cross my path along Parker Street. The capercaillie is the world's largest grouse, hailing from Scotland, and it feeds on a diet consisting mostly of pine needles. My stomach grumbles, letting me know I haven't eaten anything for some time now. Although I wouldn't dream of eating these birds, my education reminds me its diet will sometimes make its flesh taste like turpentine anyway.

There are two giant Ostriches (*Struthio camelus*) in a state of confusion along the subway tracks which run down the middle of Huntington Avenue. I'm not sure how they got behind that metal fence separating the tracks from the road, but the ostrich has never been known for being the smartest of species; even its eye is bigger than its brain. They stare at me as I drive by, looking for help. But I have neither the time nor the patience to help these unfortunate animals out at this moment. I can still hear their frightened hissing and drumming sounds behind me as I continue east toward Back Bay.
~~~

Just before I turn north on Exeter, I notice a Brown Kiwi (*Apteryx mantelli*) rummaging through a small garden along the sidewalk. The kiwi's nostrils are positioned at the very tip of their long bills, and they hunt by smell. It moves like a blind man, tapping its bill along the ground as it searches for food.

At this time of the morning on any other day, the alley behind my building would smell almost entirely like coffee. Just thinking about it now makes me want a cup. But the coffee shop is closed, just like everything else in this city.

Ring-Billed Gulls (*Larus delawarensis*) litter the entirety of Public Alley 434, scuttling around in the snow, and hiding under cars and dumpsters. They aren't making any noise other than their familiar shrills. No fire trucks blaring. No nails scratching on chalkboards. No farting. I have to drive so slow my car crunches through the snow and crawls along at an emu's pace in order to avoid them. I wonder if these are the same gulls I normally see at the top of the Prudential Tower every morning? Has their accustomed home been taken over by some invading species? Or maybe they've simply come here to check up on me? I'd like to think *somebody* around here still cares.

I hope there are still some cigarettes left inside my suitcase upstairs because I'm going to need them to calm my nerves.

I take Claude from the car, and we go upstairs. I place him back in his cage and I make sure the window is closed tight. The lock on the cage is still broken, so I try my best to secure it with a garbage bag tie. I know he could chomp through the plastic-covered wire in seconds, but it'll have to do for now. At least he seems happy to be home.

The lyrebird on the opposing rooftop is still taking shots at my window. That mockingbird remains somewhere nearby, still at it with the jackhammer. The same myna bird car alarms continue to resound outside.

The suitcase on my couch does hold one more cigarette, tucked into one of my right socks, and I light it up with the pink plastic lighter which was tucked into the left one. If the smoke detectors in my place were actually working, they would probably go unnoticed at this point anyway due to the ruckus. I toss the journal onto the coffee table and I change out of my two-day-old clothes. From my suitcase, I remove a clean tank top, one t-shirt from my endangered species series — this one featuring the Christmas Island Frigatebird (*Fregata andrewsi*) on it — my Hawthorne University sweatshirt, my favorite pair of oversized, flannel sleep pants, and my fuzzy King Penguin (*Aptenodytes patagonicus*) socks. I know I must look like a homeless person at this point, but I'm too frazzled out to care.

Collapsing onto the couch and staring at the ceiling, I watch as the smoke from the cigarette slowly begins to take form. My eyes water from being awake for so long now, and it's becoming harder to sustain any focus on reality. I want to close my eyes, maybe for good this time, but I'm too afraid. The swirling smoke warns me that as much as I'm reeling from these nightmares of the past few days, they probably pale in comparison to whatever I might find waiting for me in my dreams.

But I'm so tired. Since I woke up in my bed in Ville Constance Sunday morning, I've been back to Doneau High, and I've sat on the yellow electrical box that I've tried so hard to forget. I've spoken with Cindey Fellowes, and lied to her about how much she ever meant to me. I've denied the fact I had ever once thought about The Question. I've stared into the glossy, photographed eyes of her son and felt sorry for everyone that boy would ever meet. I've seen a Laughing Kookaburra (*Dacelo novaeguineae*) bleating like a sheep. I've seen a Chestnut-Vented Nuthatch (*Sitta nagaensis*) braying like a donkey. I've seen an African Grey Parrot (*Psittacus erithacus*) cussing at me in Chinese and another one cursing at me with a British accent. I've held a journal in my hands that was handwritten by Nelson Hatch. I've discovered his secrets. I've seen my best friend come back to life. I've seen Templeton Rate, and he's scared me more than any nightmare ever could.

All I wanted to do was go to sleep, and now I can't wake up. My dreams are as horrible as I imagined they would be, maybe even worse. Templeton laughs at me in my dreams. He gives the world a gift, but denies me of it. Men are turning into birds. Women are doing the same. They're sitting at the counter at The Strangest Feeling, as Kitty refills their coffee. They dip their beaks into the coffee cups like those glass drinking birds with the top hats. They're running behind the hedge of St. Francis Elementary School. They're making the high school basketball team and winning championships. They're saying "Happy birthday!" to one another. They're jumping off the Prudential Tower and flying between the snowflakes. They're molting, both physically and psychologically, and they're becoming something more than they ever were. Something better. Something worse. And now they're all laughing at me.

But their laughing slowly becomes something else. Something that sounds an awful lot like, snoring? I'm so sleep-deprived I can't even differentiate the ringing phones outside my window from the conspicuous, nasally sounds I can hear coming from my bedroom. It takes me a few more rings before I realize what's going on.

I stand up, a little less on edge than I should be thanks to the nicotine. The smoke still lingers around me, indicating I'd only lost consciousness for a minute at most. The cigarette had fallen from my hand, and is now burning on the floor. Sadly, it didn't even have enough time to put me out of my misery.

I pocket the lighter in my pants and walk cautiously through the miasmic haze of my apartment. Slowly, I peer around the door, and into the bedroom.

I don't know why, but I'm sure I was expecting to see Templeton Rate sleeping in my bed. I couldn't be more wrong.

"Professor Nickwelter?"

Frightmolt

"WHAT ARE YOU doing here Professor?" I ask him.

But the man doesn't have an immediate answer for me. He sits up on my bed, and wipes the sleep from his eyes. I'm a little bit jealous of his time spent sleeping, in spite of the racket outside.

"You know they're looking for you, don't you?"

"They? The police?" he asks, slowly regaining his senses. "Of course they are. God, they—they think I killed that poor girl."

"I know. I was questioned by some detective last week." The curtains are already shut, and I make sure they're just a bit tighter. Outside, I hear police sirens blare. But it's only a Nightingale (*Luscinia megarhynchos*) making me feel as though I've done something wrong.

"And what did you tell him?" he asks me.

In my heart I know this man isn't dangerous, but I can't help from shivering a little when I think of the last conversation we had. When we were in his office, and he told me he would do anything to have his old job back. My job. At the time, his words scared me a little; as though it was some kind of threat. But there's no way Professor Nickwelter could ever be capable of committing the crime the police say he's guilty of, is there? So I tell him exactly what I told Detective Dunphey. "I told him you couldn't have possibly done it." I sit down next to him on my bed, but then I get the feeling that maybe I shouldn't have. "Wait. You didn't do it, did you?" I ask, moving a little closer toward the end of the bed. My clammy hands are clutching the bedpost as tightly as they can.

"Christ, how long have you known me, Isabelle? *Of course* there's no way I could perpetrate something so awful."

Outside, I hear a violin. But it's only a Piping Plover (*Charadrius melodus*), forcing my pity upon him.

"No, of course not." I can hardly believe I asked him a question like that. "I'm sorry."

"I could never do something that horrible," he reiterates.

I try my best to change the subject, but changing subjects has never been one of my strong suits. "I always had a feeling you were fooling around with more of your students. I knew I could never be more to you than just a way to kill some free time." I know I shouldn't have uttered the word "kill" but I suppose it was the most appropriate word. Nickwelter doesn't seem to have noticed though; he continues to sit on my bed with his face in his hands.

"How long have you been here?" I ask him. "And how did you get in?"

"There's a pipe outside. I just shimmied up, and grabbed on to your fire escape. You really should get a better security system back there, you know?"

Tell me about it.

"I don't know how long I've been here though," he continues. "Two days, maybe? Three? I can't seem to keep track of my time very well anymore." His focus is fading. This man seems totally consumed by something right now. Something big enough, and something important enough, that even such mundane details as calendar dates are now completely insignificant to him.

"You probably shouldn't tell the police that, should they ever ask you." I can't help it, but tears begin to well up in my eyes. I wipe my cheek with the palm of my hand. "How did all of this happen, Professor? How did everything go so wrong, so fast? We were all out for dinner a month ago, and I was sitting there agonizing about why my life had seemed so boringly stagnant. But now? That one night out seems like a lifetime ago. Everything has changed since then."

Outside, I hear a bell chiming ominously. But it's only a Moluccan Cockatoo (*Cacatua moluccensis*), making me wonder how I could've wrecked my life so badly in just one month.

"I'll tell you what happened," he says quietly, turning back toward me now. "It was Templeton Rate who changed everything."

It really is that obvious, isn't it?

If only I hadn't left the restaurant on my own that night.

I confess to him, "That was the night I first met him, you know? It was on my birthday."

"I know, Bella. He followed you from Café d'Averno onto the bus."

I never told anyone what had happened that night. The night I'd finally decided to change. The night my own molt had begun. "How do you know that?"

"He told me so himself."

"You spoke with Templeton? When?"

"A couple of times. But listen to me, Isabelle. You need to stop all of this. Stop interfering and just leave it alone."

"Interfering? Interfering with what?" Suddenly from outside, I hear the deafening crash of a train derailment. There's the unmistakable sound of shattering glass and twisting metal that can't possibly be more than a block away. But I'm pretty sure it's only more lyrebirds driving me ever closer to my breaking point. I have to speak up over the reverberation off the alley walls. "Do you have any idea what's going on in this city right now?" I ask, even though it's more than obvious.

"Of course I do," he tells me. "How could anyone ignore all of this madness?"

"Well, you seemed to be sleeping fairly well up until five minutes ago."

"I suppose I just got used to it. I imagine everyone will eventually."

We sit on my bed together, probably another minute without any words between us. Nickwelter seems to know something more about what's going on here. I want to ask him about Templeton. I want some kind of explanation for all of this. I want him to tell me the truth. But I worry all I'll hear him say is that he still loves me. I think there just might be a limit to the amount of truths I can handle at this point.

"Listen to me, Isabelle. I discovered some things about Templeton Rate that I wasn't supposed to. Okay, I admit I disliked him from the start. I was jealous of your relationship with him. I wanted to find his secrets, whatever I thought they might have been at the time, in order to make you hate him as much as I did."

"Professor, I'm so *tired*. I don't think—"

"No. You need to listen to me. I discovered the *truth* about him, Isabelle. And it was the truth that killed that poor girl."

I try to speak again, "I don't know if I can—" I'm not even certain what it is I'm trying to tell him, but I only get so far anyway.

"Isabelle, he was never enrolled at the university. That's why nobody at Hawthorne knew who he was. That's why he seemed to just appear out of nowhere."

If I hadn't agreed to go to Salem on Halloween with him.

"He doesn't work as a doorman. There's no hotel in Boston that's ever heard of him!"

If I hadn't woken up in his apartment that morning.

"And he wasn't born in Schenectady. All those things you'd told me about him aren't even true. He's lied to you and everyone else."

If I hadn't waited for him in the library.

"Isabelle, he's not who he claims to be."

"What are you saying?"

"There is no Templeton Rate. There *never* was."

What better way to forget a memory then to start with a name?

"I know it sounds made up," Templeton had told me that first night. *"But that's really my name."*

If I hadn't gone into The Strangest Feeling.

"Then who is he? I know I'm not imagining things. I may feel like it, but I know I haven't lost my mind."

"I don't know who he is. But the day after I asked him that very question was the day Becky Chandler was found dead."

"Are you serious? I've been dating a murderer? Is that what you're telling me? Professor, how am I supposed to believe any of this? This is crazy!"

"I know it sounds extreme, but I'm only telling you this because I'm worried about you, Bella. Because I don't want to see you get hurt. Is that so awful?" I can feel the words coming that I know I don't want to hear. I can sense them on the tip of his tongue and within his quivering hands. "Is it really so horrible to still be in love with you, Isabelle?" And there they are.

If only I'd ended this conversation two minutes ago; if I'd never kissed him that first time in Cape Cod, none of these feelings would even exist. And we could be sitting here now trying to help each other, rather than feeling awkward about the whole mess.

If I hadn't been rejected from the high school basketball team.

"Don't do this, Professor. I can't go through this again."

He sniffs at the air, smelling the smoke that still lingers in my apartment. "What's that smell?" The thought of another cigarette may just be the only thing keeping me from saying something much too awful to him right now. I cough a little just imagining it. "Were you smoking, Bella?"

"I guess I've got habits just as bad as yours now, Professor."

"Christ," he says, with a beleaguered look in his eye. "I feel like I know everything there is to know about you, Bella. And then sometimes I feel like you're someone else entirely."

I remove the lighter from my pocket. Reaching across him, I take a cigarette from my bedside table. Like a Blue Jay (*Cyanocitta cristata*) will bury its acorns in the ground many months in advance, I suppose I've been hiding these all over my apartment. I don't know what else to say to him, so I share the nightmare I was having only a few minutes ago. "I was having a dream just now." I light up the cigarette, and take a puff. "The whole world had changed without me: everybody was everything I ever wanted to be. But I was still just me, and I was all alone." I cough again, and the smoke mocks me, as it seems to take a bird-like form. "But I *have* changed. And I've always *needed* to change, but now that it's actually happened, it scares me more than any nightmare ever could. I have no idea what this thing is that I've become."

There's a silence between us that is at once comforting but also completely uncertain. I know Nickwelter well enough to know he's stumbling to find the right words to say to me. He opens the drawer and removes a cigarette for himself. I pass him the lighter; the lighter only Claude and I had shared until now.

"It does feel good," he says to me, tasting the cigarette in his mouth, "reverting back to something we once were."

The two of us sit on my bed, blowing smoke in lonely unison.

"I want to show you something," I say to him, slowly peeling myself off the bed and walking into the living room. I return to the bedroom with the journal in my hand. Passing it to him, I say that according to Templeton, the book is supposed to contain all the answers I would need. But I have my suspicions that nothing could ever be so absolute.

Paging slowly through the journal however, it seems as though Nickwelter may already be familiar with some of its contents. He turns to me, and through the translucency of the smoke, I see bewilderment in his eyes. "This book belonged to Nelson Hatch, didn't it? Where did you find this?"

"Templeton gave it to me," I tell him. "Well, actually it's more like I stole it. But I think *he* stole it first, from the house in Salem before burning it to the ground."

He extinguishes his cigarette into the wood of my bedside table, and flips fervently through more of the journal. He stops when he comes to the very same drawing I had stopped at. The pig with the eagle's wings.

And then he speaks, although mostly to himself it seems, as I have no idea what he's talking about. "*As Gregor Samsa woke one morning from uneasy dreams he found himself in his bed, transformed into a monstrous insect.*"

"What's that?"

"It's from *The Metamorphosis*. Kafka. I thought it seemed appropriate. But maybe I was wrong."

He usually is. I hear Claude in my living room, rattling his beak across the cage bars. "Templeton fixed Claude's wing," I say to him. "Did you know that? The wing you amputated years ago has grown back."

Nickwelter turns away from the journal, looking at me exclusively now. "What? But then that would mean—"

It means this is the glorious age of Templeton Rate.

"It's a miracle." I tell him. "It means Templeton's a genius. And he's capable of even more than that."

"Yes. It's all in here," he says, redirecting his attention back to the book in his lap, and flipping through more of the pages. "I've heard stories before about the journals of Nelson Hatch. Since before your time, professors at Hawthorne University have been discussing them in secrecy, and contemplating what his science might've meant for the world."

He turns to one of the last pages in the old, dusty journal, and his jaw drops at whatever it is he sees.

I only catch a glimpse of it before he closes the book for good.

Maybe I'm not understanding the impact of everything. Maybe there's still some small detail I'm overlooking. It probably would be completely over my head anyway. "It's like I'm standing in the middle of a place I've never been before," I tell him, this man I used to love. I'm doing the best I can to try and explain these thoughts and feelings that are flying through my head at four hundred miles-an-hour. "How do I just go back to where I was before all of this madness began?"

But of course, he doesn't understand my feelings. "Do you mean with me?" He never understood the feelings of Isabelle Donhelle.

"Not with *you*. We tried that before and that didn't work either."

Rejected again, he turns back to the closed journal in his lap. "I suppose I've never really understood what it was you wanted, Isabelle."

I ignore him completely, and continue along the path my thoughts were taking me. "What I mean is, in an effort to make the right choices for myself, have I made one too many mistakes?" I hate Templeton Rate. A part of me wants nothing more than to slap him across the face for lying to me all this time, and yet another part of me still wants to defend him from my own selfish thoughts. To preserve his genius. Even after all of this. Because maybe this part of me still loves him too.

Claude's rattling becomes more furious, but I know he's just excited to be back home. This is his way of readjusting to familiar territory.

"Isabelle, Templeton is dangerous. But as much as I despise the man, this is all much bigger than him. I didn't know it before now, but there's so much more at stake here than your bird's wing or the university. It's so much more than that racket outside. Or even my being here right now."

"What's all of that supposed to mean?"

"My point is that, well, we all make mistakes in our lives. And usually there's never anything you can do to fix all the mistakes you've made along the way. But if you have that chance, you take it. I should have left Beth when the decision was an obvious one, but now it's so much more complicated. I didn't understand all of it myself at the time, but now I know what Templeton Rate is capable of."

I know Templeton much better than he does — at least I think I do anyway — but even I don't know everything he's capable of.

It looks like maybe the flamingo has gotten the better of me.

"It was Nelson Hatch," he says, shaking the book with one hand, indicating the truth really was within those pages after all. "He was the key to all of this."

I reach out, and take the journal from his hand. I flip through the pages again, looking for answers within scribbled text that seems to contain nothing more than more questions.

Page by page, new images unfold before me. I read some of what I'd only skimmed through before now. And I only need to see the one diagram on the last page before I really do know the truth. Before I truly realize this molt may not be finished quite yet.

If Nelson Hatch's journal had been telling this story, it would be giving away the ending.

It seems impossible. Like fourteen seconds for a chicken.

Outside, I hear a woman screaming. But it's only a rooster, beating me to the punch. From my living room, Claude's beak continues to rattle along the metal bars. But the rattling echo becomes deeper, louder. It's not Claude doing all of the work anymore.

I stand up, and grip the book in my hands a little bit tighter. The first thing that comes to mind is the fire escape outside my window. The same way Templeton came into my apartment. The way Nickwelter came inside. The way Jerry Humphries probably got in too. The sweat on my palm makes the book feel slippery. I want to peek around the corner, but I don't know if I have anything left in me to endure being scared anymore. I tell myself that it could just as easily be another superb lyrebird making the racket instead.

It doesn't seem as though Nickwelter is hearing the clatter outside; he's far too engrossed in the discoveries he's made. "Isabelle, Nelson Hatch was on to something unimaginable, and it looks as though Templeton knew about it. Maybe he is a genius?"

"Professor?" I ask, without really asking a question. He doesn't hear me. He doesn't sense my concern. But he does say possibly the only thing that could scare me even more at this moment.

"Templeton Rate could very well save us all!"

I don't even let the words sink into my head before I interrupt his thoughts for good. "Professor! I think someone is here."

"What? Where?"

"I think they're coming up the fire escape." The rattling continues for a bit, and then stops suddenly with a loud, metallic clank. Like somebody has landed heavily on the balcony outside my window.

"We've got to get out of here, Bella."

It's quiet now. If I clenched this book any tighter, surely it would break apart in the vice-like grip of my sweaty hand.

Peering around the corner and into my living room, I see them. Two shadowy, black silhouettes outside on my fire escape, gazing back at me. I want to take Claude from his cage, but there's not enough time. Something tells me it's not Templeton, but whoever these men are — and for whatever reason they're here exactly — all I know is I need to get out of my apartment before I become the next Becky Chandler.

Nickwelter is already at my front door, urging me to follow. "I have to get Claude," I yell at him.

"There's no time for that, Isabelle," he says. "We need to leave. Now!"

One of the men outside taps on the window with something hard and heavy. I get a chill when I see the dull glint of a gun in his hand. But I don't want to leave my bird behind. Hasn't he gone through enough already? "I'll come back for you, Claude," I say, and I hope he believes me. But birds don't know promises, and they'll never hold you to them.

I turn back to Nickwelter, standing in the open doorway, and there must be some kind of look in my eyes powerful enough to make him change his mind, because he turns and runs across the living room, toward the birdcage. I think it's maybe because he really does love me. And who knows, maybe he always had but I couldn't see it until now?

One of the men says something, but I can't make out the muffled words through the glass.

They try to slide the window open, but it won't budge, probably due to the icy cold. They don't waste another second before kicking it in. I hear the breaking glass, but I'm already running out the door.

Nickwelter tells me to keep running. I don't even look back at him, and I hate myself for it. With the journal and a cigarette still in my hands, I run out into the hallway in my socks.

I'm already down the first flight of stairs when I hear a gunshot. It's definitely not coming from the lyrebird.

And then I hear another one, followed by what sounds like a body hitting the floor of my living room. I can't imagine any bird could replicate such a particular combination of sounds.

Once in the lobby, I figure I can either exit through the front onto Newbury Street, or I can head out the back door and into the alley where my car is parked. I consider getting into the car and simply leaving everything behind. I could forget about all of this and drive back up north to Ville Constance. I could get a job at the Blackbird's Grill. I'm sure Cindey would recommend me, even if I *haven't* had a baby. But the best idea I have is to drive directly to the police station; surely there would be someone there who could help me. Someone who might help this entire city. I can't do this on my own anymore.

And I realize I've changed even more than I'd thought; I used to be able to — and insisted upon — dealing with any problems I had on my own. But apparently, I've molted into something much weaker. This new me simply isn't strong enough. Maybe I should tell Detective Dunphey about the missing swan boats I saw in the university lab too.

I hear footsteps coming down the stairs, indicating I definitely don't have the time to be standing here any longer. I throw the back door open with such vigor, the colony of ring-billed gulls that had been loitering in the alley all morning fly off all at once, but still without making a sound. The wall of wings and feathers that springs forth before me is enough to stop me in my tracks.

And when my vision clears, I see someone sitting on the hood of my car. It's Zirk. He's still wearing that dirty black housecoat, and he's carving something into my car with a knife. He doesn't even turn when he speaks to me; he remains focused on whatever it is he's doing.

"Hello, gorgeous," he says, his vocal chords still rumbling peculiarly.

Before I can respond, the two men who broke my window, and who most assuredly shot Professor Nickwelter, arrive. I don't turn around, but I can feel the gun behind me. I'm trapped; they've got me cornered. I curse to myself, realizing I didn't have my car keys with me anyway, and that I should have just run out onto Newbury Street when I had the chance ten seconds ago. I think I called myself a "goober," but it could just as easily have been some other charmingly derogative nickname.

"There's nowhere left to run, Professor," Zirk says. "I think you'd better come with us." He pockets his knife and jumps off the hood of my car, into the snow. He lands awkwardly, and stumbles forward a bit, as though his legs were shorter than he's used to.

The flannel sleep pants I'm wearing have large pockets, big enough for me to slide the journal into. I think I'm being incredibly sneaky, but I'm sure these guys simply don't care what I'm doing with it. "What are you doing here?" I ask them all simultaneously, hoping between the three of them, they can come up with an answer that will satisfy me. "And where's Templeton?" I try my best to not let my emotions get the better of me. I could easily just give up, especially with the thought that Nickwelter is no doubt bleeding on my carpet right now.

"There's that question again," Zirk comments. "Is Templeton Rate really the only thing you care about? Because it sure seems like it to me." I notice the word "PUFFIN" has once again been carved into my hood, right next to the last one. And this time it's much larger, and much rougher. Messy, like how a five-year-old might try and spell.

"Puffin?" I ask out loud, but really just to myself.

"That's me," he boasts proudly. "Everyone needs a nickname." He scratches at himself through the housecoat, trying to track down an itch somewhere under there. Motioning to the men behind me, Zirk asks, "Have you met Rob and Bob yet?"

I turn around and get a good look at these two. These were the same two kids I saw in the south laboratory earlier this morning; the two who claimed to be Harvard students. Bob is holding the gun. He's the tubby one I spoke to earlier, and I notice now he's wearing a t-shirt that simply says "Virginia" across the front. I thought there was something strange about the shape of his head before, and now I can tell it seems dispropor-tionately small in comparison to the rest of his body. Rob is much livelier than his friend; his movements are erratic. Twitching, and shifting his weight from one foot to the other and darting his head back and forth like a bird.

"What's going on here? What do you want from me?"

"Templeton wants to see you," Zirk tells me. He's still got the same bandage over the bridge of his nose, but the crusty, bruised infection I'd noticed earlier seems worse than it was before. Perhaps it's just an incredibly bizarre coincidence, but it reminds me a little of the colorful orange, yellow and blue plates of an Atlantic Puffin (*Fratercula arctica*). As does the rumbling under his breath after every sentence, now that I think of it. He scratches at himself some more underneath his black housecoat.

I take a look up at my broken window, and I'm relieved to see Claude is unharmed, and watching us all from his cage. The earlier gunshots must have scared off all of the other birds in the area though. The alley seems emptier, and quieter, than it's been all morning.

"I think I'm fine without him," I finally respond. Motioning toward my car, I hope they might have the courtesy to let me go. Maybe these guys have what it takes to respect a girl's decision. And I'm praying they have absolutely no idea just how scared I am right now.

But Zirk grabs my arm, preventing me from going anywhere. His grip feels tight, even through my heavy sweatshirt. I struggle to break free, but his hand tightens even more. I plead for him to let go. "Come on now, Professor," he says to me, his fishy breath making me sick to my stomach. "There's no point in struggling anymore."

"Hey, Puffin," one of the guys behind me says. "You ever seen a movie where the prisoner begs for freedom, and they actually let her go?"

Zirk doesn't have an answer for him, he remains as calm as can be. I want to scream, but instead, I defy my captor by wriggling my arm out of the sleeve of my sweatshirt. From my peripheral, I notice Bob and Rob moving closer. So, I give it everything I've got. In my free hand, I'm still holding onto my smoking cigarette. I stab it into Zirk's face; it sizzles a little on the bandage between his eyes before bouncing off the bridge of his nose and into the snow. Twisting away from him, and using the free arm underneath my shirt, I pull the sweater over my head and slide my other arm out of the sleeve. Zirk falls back: the bold, proud, yellow Hawthorne University font covering his face.

I don't even know how I do it, but I kick backwards and hit Bob, knocking him into Rob and against the side of my car. The handgun hits the ground, and spins on the icy cement. I pick it up and head west down Public Alley 434. I hear the familiar "Bye-bye, Bella" calling out from behind me as I leave Claude again, and I try my best to ignore it.

As I near Exeter Street, and just as I'm feeling as though I'll get out of this mess once and for all, Jonah Mitcherson appears, hobbling into the middle of the alley on his crutches. He still has shorts on too, but he's now wearing a ski cap to at least keep his head warm.

"What do you guys want from me?" I ask him, hoping for a different answer than I received from the other three.

Of course, I don't get one. "It's not us, Professor Donhelle. It's him." He licks his lips with his large tongue. It appears abnormally thick and oily, frighteningly similar to that of a flamingo. "Templeton Rate just wants everyone to be happy."

As selfish as Templeton's always been, I find this more than a little hard to swallow. I point the gun toward Jonah, but I know I wouldn't have the guts to actually use it. "I'm going to the police. And you can tell Templeton that they won't be happy."

I hear footsteps in the snow behind me, and I know that the three men I've already eluded are fast approaching. Maybe it's the adrenaline pumping through me. Maybe it's the realization I've finally run out of options tonight. Or maybe it's the fact I'm not the same person I was a month ago, but something inside me makes me kick this man's crutch out from under him. Mitchie Mitcherson falls face-first into the snow, and I turn the gun back toward the other three.

I order them to let me walk away from this, and they all step back at my command. It feels good to have this kind of power, although I know I really don't have any idea how to work this cold metal thing in my quivering hands. But it doesn't matter. With fuzzy penguin socks in flight, I run out onto Exeter Street.

I sprint by a deceit of Blacksmith Lapwings (*Vanellus armatus*), sounding something like popcorn popping. I pass an unkindness of Ravens (*Corvus corax*), sounding remarkably like television static. I'm not paying attention to the street signs, but I must have run four city blocks already. The morning sunrise not only beams off the glass veneer of the Hancock Tower to my left, and the Prudential Tower to my right, but also off the cold, metal gun in my hand.

I think I hear birds chirping. Actual chirping. Not making noises like electrical generators or screeching tires, but actual peeping, cheeping, tweeting and twittering. It's extraordinary.

Then in my most glorious moment, I slip on some black ice, and I slide right into an oncoming car. My body soars across the street. I barely even have enough time to register the irony of how much I've yearned to fly over the years. I hit the curb, and bounce into a snowbank. My head thumps hard on the bottom step of a brownstone's brick staircase.

My body hurts. I'm frozen still on my back and staring straight up into the sky. I hear the car door creak open, and I raise my head just enough to see Humphries walking toward me. Jerry Humphries, in his old weather-beaten trench coat. My head drops back down, cushioned a little by the fresh snow. I taste blood. My left arm is in an astonishing amount of pain.

He picks up the handgun I dropped, and then crouches down beside me, leaning in close. "Funny running into you here," he says. I'd almost like to give him credit, as this is probably the wittiest thing I've ever heard Humphries say, but I really cannot justify it at the moment. God, my back hurts too, but I think I'm more bothered by the smell of this man's breath.

I can't move. I can't speak. My body is in shock. I can only dart my eyes back and forth between Humphries' ugly visage and the sky above us. The clouds have darkened already, and have taken on a new, somewhat bruised colorization.

Without the benefit of anyone interrupting him, Humphries continues. "Look at you Bella. Lying there all helpless. Like a poor, little bird with clipped wings." His eyes scuttle across my body, making me feel even more defenseless. "You know I've always imagined you this vulnerable. What I would do with you. And what you might do for me." He leans in closer, studying my lips as close as he can. He takes his finger, his wretched, hairy, little, chewed-up finger, and touches my bottom lip, then wipes the blood from the corner of my mouth. "Can you stand?" he asks me.

I try to, but I can't.

He asks, "Can you lift your head?"

Again, I try, even though success would mean bringing my face that much closer to this despicable man who I've spent the last eight years or so trying to avoid. But I can't move my neck either. I can hear his ugly car still running. I can smell the exhaust polluting the air and my nostrils.

"No? Is that it then? Is this all the fight you've got to give?" He seems upset, as though expecting so much more from me. "Surely you've got more of a fire inside you than this?" He stands up, puts his hands on his hips and looks around. He looks around as if trying to figure out what to do next. "So, all you can do is just stare up to the heavens? Is that it?" I don't know if he's really looking for an answer from me, or if he's simply content with having this conversation by himself. "Well, there's nothing up there for you, Bella. There's nothing up there that's any good for any of us down here. I don't know if there ever was."

I don't want to try and make sense of his ramblings, even if I possibly could. But he's not overly concerned about receiving a response anyway. He looks at the handgun, nesting within his filthy grip. "Maybe I should just end it all for you right now then? Would you like that, Bella?" I give him no answer, although I almost wish I could say "Yes" at this point. Next, he points the gun directly at me. "Do you want to share the same fate as Nickwelter? Or that girl? Do you want me to do the same for you as I did for her?"

I try to get the words out of my mouth. "You—?" And due to the numbness and pain, it's only now I realize my mouth has been full of icy snow. "You killed Becky?"

"Well, we wouldn't want Templeton to get his hands dirty, would we? I mean, dirtier than they usually are, that is. Have you ever noticed how mucky his hands are? And you just let him do whatever he wanted with them, didn't you? You let him put those hands wherever the hell he wanted to." I've never heard Jerry Humphries go on like this before. There's an inferno inside him that's fueling his emotions; consuming him. "I do *all* of his dirty work for him. I have been for months now."

I never would have believed Humphries' connection to Templeton ran as deep as it apparently does. I knew there was something strange about their relationship. But this? To have the audacity to actually commit a murder? The feeling is returning to my mouth, and I almost wish it wasn't, since the pain is unbearable. "But what's in it for *you*, Jerry? Why have you done these horrific things for him?"

"He's a brilliant man, Templeton Rate. He was smart enough to figure out how to have *you*, Bella. I've been trying for years, if you haven't noticed." There's jealousy in his green eyes; nothing I haven't sensed before from the man. But now there's an underlying calmness about Jerry Humphries. Some kind of acceptance for whatever has already been done. Or possibly for what's still yet to come.

"But what is he really planning to do?"

"He's already done everything. And he's letting me be a part of it all."

"All of what?"

"Things are about to change around here, Bella. All of the misery and sadness. The depression, hopelessness, desolation, and all of the shittiest, most fucked-up, unfair feelings everyone has to go through in this life. They're all coming to an end."

"What are you talking about?"

"Some call it Armageddon. Some call it the Apocalypse. But no matter who you are, you believe that the end of the world is always signaled by the arrival of angels." Humphries looks at me. His eyes are urging me to agree with him, to acknowledge what he's saying as fact, even though I now realize he's utterly mad. "Look around you!" he screams, his arms spread wide. "Do you see any angels here? Obviously, the end of the world has already come, or else things wouldn't be as fucked as they are. But there was no warning. There was no messenger from Heaven."

I still can't move. If I could, I'd physically try to knock some sense into this man. Instead, I try my best to do it verbally. "Maybe that's because it hasn't happened yet," I suggest. "Or better yet, maybe all of that religious mumbo jumbo is just made up? Wouldn't that actually make more sense?"

"That's bullshit. The truth is obvious: no angel is ever going to want to come back to all of this. Would you want to? Would you come back here if you had it so fucking good up there?" Humphries has always been a religious man, I know because of all of the times I've rejected his invitations to go to church with him. But this is bordering on psychotic behavior. Much more than a Jesus fish could ever hint at.

"So, humanity is doomed then?" I ask him, wondering what it will take to make him stop. "You're saying we should just give up since there won't be anyone to save us anyway?"

"Haven't you been paying attention? Of course someone will save us." I can tell from his eyes that this man really has lost his mind. "Someone is *already* saving us, and his name is Templeton Rate."

It's just as Templeton once told me: *"I can't believe how religion can bring out the most idiotic ideas in people."* Is this really what Templeton wished for? Is this really what he believed?

And there was something else he said to me in the university parking lot, the day I broke up with him. The words still ring in my head: *"Everyone will believe in something different,"* he told me. *"And if you're lucky enough, some of them will believe everything* you *tell them."*

Is Humphries just believing whatever Templeton had told him? Or is this really the end of the world? Above me, I notice a Black-Capped Chickadee (*Poecile atricapillus*) is trapped inside the brownstone. It tries to fly out through the closed window, repeatedly hitting his beak against the glass in fits of fury. In some American superstitions, if a bird flew into your house, it was the bearer of important news, but if it couldn't get out again, some believed it was a sign of death.

I spot a Downy Woodpecker (*Picoides pubescens*) pecking at the wooden door at the top of the steps. In Alaska, it's believed that if a woodpecker tapped on your door, it brought bad news, possibly even the death of someone in the family.

I've also heard that the call of a Whip-poor-will (*Caprimulgus vociferus*) or the hoot of the Great Horned Owl (*Bubo virginianus*) was sometimes a sign of death or bad luck. Beyond the already all-too familiar sounds of train whistles, machine guns, and wood chippers, I can hear them both: a whip-poor-will to the east and a hoot to the south.

Jerry Humphries moves toward me again, reaching his hand out to grab me. But I find the strength to resist. My body hurts so much, but I won't have this man lay another finger on me. I pull my legs in, and kick out with both of them. My feet connect with his rib cage, and he falls back.

I kick him farther than I expected I might, as if I'm stronger than I thought, or as though he weighs far less than he should. He lands with such a weightlessness in fact, that it actually seems to aid him in quickly getting back on his feet. Immediately, he turns his attention back toward me. "A change is coming, Bella. There's nothing you can do to stop it." He's right in my face again already; his speed is hard to believe. "And everyone, except you, is going to have Templeton to thank for it."

"Why not me? Don't I get a choice in all of this?"

"Maybe you did, but I'm taking that choice away from you. Because you don't deserve it. You don't deserve any of it, you ungrateful bitch."

The wind catches his coat, blowing it away from his body momentarily. And I think I understand him now. I don't believe what I'm seeing, but I think I am accepting it: I'm certain I see a pair of white, feathery wings underneath his coat.

And that's right about when he pulls the gun back and strikes me in the head.

That's the moment I fall unconscious.

And that's when this story actually begins.

Full Circle

I THINK THIS is about where we started, isn't it? This is when I attempt to feel my way out of here. This is when I charge into the wall, and when I trip over my own feet. This is when my ulna tears through my skin, and when I wrap my shirt around my arm to stop the bleeding.

And this is when I blame Mrs. Wyatt for putting me where I am right now.

I wonder if I'll ever be able to find a way out of here.

If I hadn't been hit by that car; if I hadn't come back to Boston; if I hadn't been teaching at Hawthorne University; if I hadn't joined the high school science club; if I hadn't been rejected from the Doneau High basketball team.

Yes, this is exactly where we started; we've come full circle inside this square box. But it feels kind of like those misshapen pegs. Like trying to stick the square peg into the round hole.

I wonder when I'll ever find the courage to blame myself?

But Professor Nickwelter had tried to stop me, hadn't he? At the very least, he tried to convince me I had it all wrong. He wanted me to stop interfering with things I didn't understand. He told me he'd found the truth, or was getting much closer to it. He told me, should I ever get a chance to undo the mistakes I've made, I should take it. He told me maybe Templeton Rate could be the one to save us all. Nickwelter called Templeton a genius. Just as Humphries had. And just as I had before them. We couldn't all be so blind, could we? But is it not also possible that we've been seeing the same thing, just completely differently?

And I think that Professor Nickwelter was only hoping I'd stop mucking about in all of these awful things because he actually wanted them to happen.

And I think that the things I saw in Nelson Hatch's journal were possibly the very same things I'd seen beneath Jerry Humphries' coat.

And I think that this really might be the age of Templeton Rate, whether glorious or not.

As Isabelle Donhelle woke one morning from uneasy dreams, she finally discovered she had changed.

I plant my socked-feet firmly on the metal floor, brace my right arm on the wall, and stand up again. But this time with the feeling it might be for the last time. I touch my left arm wrapped in my blood-soaked t-shirt. I recall tripping as I ran across the floor. Did I trip over something other than my own feet though? I reach out my one good arm to make sure. I try to fool myself into imagining that if I can find what it was, it will be the one thing that can help me. Honestly, I'm not entirely sure how I could have missed something in this vault in the first place, but the probability is made indisputable when I grab hold of what feels to be a leg.

My heart skips a beat or two when I realize there's someone in here with me.

I question the degree of this person's existence, whether alive or dead, or perhaps somewhere in between, but my uncertainty is answered when the leg shakes my hand off of it.

"Do you mind?" a deep voice asks me from the darkness.

"I—I'm sorry," I say. "I didn't know there was anyone else in here."

"I was wondering how long it would take you." This man's voice is strong and rumbling, reminding me of Zirk and his buzzing vocal chords. But due to the nature of this metallic vault, the voice I hear now is an unsettling sort of reverberation. "Couldn't you hear my breathing?"

"Honestly, no." I tell him. "But I don't think my head's been working properly of late."

Now that I'm aware of it though, this man's breathing really is quite evident. My head must have been ringing this whole time from when Humphries knocked me unconscious. "It's Isabelle, right?"

"Uh, yes," I say in slightly bewildered wonderment. "Do I know you?"

"Just making sure."

"How did you get in here?"

"The same way *you* did, I suppose."

I pause for a moment before asking the next question my mouth wants to rattle off, but only because I'm fearful of what the next answer might be. "Do you know Templeton Rate?"

"Doesn't everyone?" His breathing continues to make me uneasy. "Do you hate him as much as I do?"

I think it takes me longer than it should to answer this. "I want to. I really want to hate him, but I don't. Even after everything he's done to me."

"That's nothing," he grinds. "You should see what he did to *me*."

"What's happened to you? What has Templeton done?"

"All of us just wanted to be a part of it. Me and Mitchie. Rob and Bob and Zirk. Jerry too. We just wanted somewhere to belong when this was all over. There were others too. But some people are willing to change, and some people aren't. It's as simple as that."

"It's not always that simple," I answer. "Change is harder for some of us. Not everyone evolves at the same time."

"They do in Templeton's world. Or at least, they *will*."

The ambiguousness of this conversation makes me feel like I'm listening to Templeton himself. "What's your name?" I ask.

"Tony," he says tentatively. But then he corrects himself. "My name was Tony. But not anymore."

"Not anymore?"

"*'Everyone is supposed to have a codename,'* is what he told us. Mitchie chose Flamingo. Zirk chose Puffin. Naturally, Robin and Bob chose Robin and Bobwhite. Bob's last name is White too, if you can imagine such a stupid coincidence. They all thought they were so clever, but look at them now."

I think of Zirk and those colorful, crusty scabs forming on the bridge of his nose. Rob and Bob. Even Mitchie Mitcherson, standing on crutches and balancing on his one good leg just like a flamingo.

"And there were *more* of us. There was even a Bird of Paradise and a Goatsucker, but I don't know what happened to everybody. Some of them just disappeared. One of them — *Crossbill* I think his name was — was on top of the State House the last time I saw him. He was trying to tear the copper pinecone off the roof with his teeth. Well, the teeth he still had left anyway."

In my head, I see the pictures from Nelson Hatch's journal of pigs and rats and frogs with wings. And the very last picture in the book. The one that made Professor Nickwelter stop when he saw it.

All of the terrible pieces were falling into place.

"Everyone was supposed to have a codename," he reiterates. "I chose Ostrich, and before I knew it, Templeton Rate was introducing Ostrich DNA into my body. Bird hormones. And now my toes have fused together and these stupid long eyelashes keep getting in my mouth. It's horrible."

I can't help but think of Antonia from back home in Ville Constance. Cruelly, the kids at the orphanage nicknamed her Ostrich simply to make fun of her weight. She was always looking for somewhere to belong too.

"Templeton told us it was all part of a bigger plan," he continues, not holding back anymore. I suppose he was finding some sort of freedom now in being able to talk to somebody. Or maybe it was more like finding redemption for whatever he might have done. "But now I'm stuck in here." He begins to sob a little. I don't know whether to be afraid of this man I can't see in front of me, or to have pity for him. "It's horrible," he repeats. "I helped him build this thing, you know that? This stupid metal box. Me and the other guys, we did *everything* for him. But it's hard to imagine he was just using us in the end."

"Humphries told me Templeton was going to give me a choice," I say, remembering the last words I heard before waking up in here. "But then he took that choice away from me, because he said I didn't deserve it. And that's when I saw the feathers under his coat."

"Humphries was the first one," he says. As distorted as this man's voice is, I can still sense some jealousy in his words. "He was the first one to receive Templeton's gift. And we were all supposed to get it, but just like you, I've had that choice taken away from me. Templeton called it a gift, but it would have been so much better than that."

"But why would he deny you of it, Tony? And why would Humphries deny me?"

"Because you always hated Humphries, and this was the only thing he could think of that would hurt you as much as you'd hurt him."

"That man is absolutely crazy."

"But that's why you're here. And the only reason *I'm* in here is because I tried to save you."

"I don't understand," I say, wondering why a total stranger would want to help me. But then I consider everything. And because of the fact that everything in the last month or so hasn't made any sense at all, it makes this one absurd detail that much easier to believe. There's just enough familiarity to this conversation that helps me make the connection. Sadly though, I think it's all the sobbing that really gives it away.

This isn't a man at all.

I turn unseen to this invisible person on the floor in front of me, and I ask her, "Antonia?"

"It's *Ostrich*, Isabelle," she growls. "They've always called me Ostrich."

Just as the *Fratercula arctica* DNA mutated Zirk's larynx and vocals, those of the *Struthio camelus* must have affected Antonia's.

"Did you ever get that letter I sent you?" she asks me.

"I did. I still have it. It's still on my bookshelf. You said you'd write me again, just as soon as you were adopted. But I never received another letter."

"That's because I was never adopted. Eventually, I ran away from the orphanage with a boy I met. I thought he was my boyfriend, but he dumped me less than a week later. He said he only needed me to help him get out of there. One day, just a couple of months ago, I came to Boston to look for you, because I realized you were the only friend I'd ever had. But I found Templeton Rate first, and I fell for him and all of his fantastic dreams. Did you know that he's an orphan too?"

He told me his mother was dead and that he'd never met his father. Just one more from the litter of angels. Now that I think of it though, I'm sure I never really believed him when he had told me William and Rose Endicott of Salem, Massachusetts were distant relatives of his. I'm sure he was only trying to get rid of me that night so he could steal the journals from Nelson Hatch's home.

"I helped him, just like the others helped him. We stole the swan boats from the lagoon. We built this vault. We released all of those birds into the city. We did everything he asked us to do."

"But, why would you do all of that?"

"To belong. To actually matter in this world. All my life, I've only ever wanted to matter. My parents weren't dead; they abandoned me. Which I'm sure is much worse. All I knew was that orphanage, and all of the kids in there who hated me. The only time I felt like I mattered was when I lived with *you*. Everyone there felt exactly the same way. All of us loved you for what you had. You had no idea how lucky you were."

I guess I never stopped to think about what it must have meant to leave the orphanage for the warm nest of the Donhelle home. Even if for only one day. "Maybe I *was* lucky," I tell her. "But I still had my *own* dreams. I still wanted *more*. It's the same for everybody."

"What did *you* dream?" she asks, almost in disbelief that it could even be possible.

I recall the time when Templeton had asked me about my dreams; when I told him I only ever wanted to fly with the gulls from the top of the Prudential Tower. To be caught in the wind and hang for the briefest of moments, stuck in that one tiny piece of sky. But then I think back to my entire relationship with Professor Nickwelter, and when I sat there feeling worthless in the backseat of his car. In my mind, I relive my one month with Templeton, and the two months with Claude. It should be no contest, but I can't decide who hurt me the most. I remember the last talk I had with my mother, sitting together on the porch and sharing a cigarette. And I recall the photograph of Cindey's son, Sylvester Devereaux, that I held in my hands. And when Templeton said those three specific words to me, the night he had his hands on my shoulder blades. I can't imagine now how I'd ever believed him. "I only ever wanted to be in love," is what I confess to Antonia. "And for someone to love *me*. That's the moment I'm most jealous of."

"I only ever wanted to fly, Isabelle. To fly as high as you had always seemed to me."

"I'm sorry." I wish I could have given her a gift like that, but I'm apologizing for the impossible. Though I'm sure if you asked anyone what they would want if they possessed the power to have anything at all, ninety percent of those telling the truth would tell you they wished they could fly. "I'm sorry I could never give you that."

"But Templeton *can* give me that," Antonia says. "And he wanted to give it to *everybody*. Everybody except you."

"Why not me?"

"Because you never believed in anything he wanted you to believe in. The stuff that really mattered, anyway. And he realized he couldn't force you to either."

In a microsecond, I think about every word Templeton Rate had ever said to me. From the diner to the library to the sidewalk. From the cemetery to the parking lot to the university laboratory. When both of us were staring into the glimmering walls of this menacing metal box, he told me I'd be safe in here. He said this would be the one place in the city I could be, if I wanted to stay the way I was. This would be my only hope for a last chance. My last chance at death.

"He was going to put you inside this thing. To deny you of everything," Antonia continues. "But I begged him to put me in here instead."

"But why would you do that for me?" I ask her.

"It's just like Michel Bourdon told me years ago," she answers, but I don't remember what that was. "Because the ostrich is the fattest of all birds. That's why it will never fly." She tries to sniff back the tears, but it's too late to stop any of it at this point. "It was *my* turn to save *you*. But then Jerry Humphries put you in here anyway, because he hated you even more than Templeton did."

I reach out to touch her face, to wipe her tears for the first time since we were children. And that's when I feel them: the feathers, wet from crying. It's chilling; quite possibly the most disturbing thing I've ever experienced. I'm actually relieved now that it's too dark in here to see anything.

I apologize to her for all the pain she's ever known. But she says, "Don't worry about it. It's not your fault." Exactly how Templeton would have answered me.

The two of us embrace the silence for a moment. This is how most of our conversations would go anyway. After I would fool her into believing everything would be okay, we would sit in silence together before moving on. Of course, now I'm finding it hard to convince myself things really will be okay. I don't know if either us can simply move on at this point.

My breathing has slowed down considerably, and I fear the lack of oxygen may have finally caught up with us. I wonder if I should give up, and start welcoming an end to it all. Death over life. Like I said earlier, it's a much harder decision to make when you're actually given the ability to make it.

But I give my life one more chance. I ask her, "You said you helped him build this thing we're in?"

"That's right," she sniffs.

"And there's no way out of here?" I feel like I'm grasping at straws. "Think, Antonia."

I can tell she's thinking about it. She'd probably already given up herself, but now she considers the details. "There's an emergency lock," she says finally. "If there was a fire in here, the door would open."

The lighter I'd slipped into my pocket earlier has shifted a little, and it's only now when I realize I've been sitting on it this whole time. Taking it out, I roll it in my hand, and consider how fantastic it was to have ever had that relationship with the Claude from my youth. Because if I hadn't known him, if he hadn't ever broken my heart as casually as he did, I would never be here now. And I wouldn't be holding this in my hand now either.

"But how would we start a fire?" she asks me. "Unless you happened to bring some sticks to rub together?" I didn't know sarcasm was part of Antonia's repertoire.

I tell her about the lighter in my hand. But I leave out the details concerning its origins.

"Are you serious?" she asks. I want to thumb a tiny flame just to prove it to her, but I'm fearful I might catch a glimpse of this girl I once knew so well, and that I wouldn't recognize her at all now.

Taking the journal out of my pocket, I mull over my options. The amount of raw, scientific data inside this journal and the number of original thoughts from the mind of our school's legendary founder is astounding to think about, but choosing death over life is a ridiculous notion at a time like this. I place the book into my left hand, and my broken arm does all it can to hold the tome steady.

With my thumb, I flick the lighter's metal wheel a couple of times, but with no result. I'm about to try again, when Antonia stops me. Her hand tickles my arm a little; the coarseness of her palm indicating something other than flesh. "Please don't look at me when you light it," she says. There's a fear in her voice I never knew possible. "Please, Bella. Promise me?" Even throughout the whole, horrible ordeal she's been through, there's still something new that can scare her.

"I won't," I tell her. "I promise."

She lets go of my arm, and I try again. This time it works, and the flame creates an odd flicker across the six metallic panels encompassing the two of us. I'm trying not to look, but I can see in my peripheral Antonia crouched into a ball, covering herself up as best she can. I don't look at my broken arm either, though I can't help but catch a glimpse of the puddle of my own blood on the floor.

The yellowed paper within the leather journal catches fire easily, and I have to drop it quickly before it burns my hand or any of my makeshift bandages. There's a putrid smell, like a dead bird in a gutter, stinging my nostrils. The book is smoldering on the floor, and I'm completely conscious of how great a loss this will be. To have such information only to throw it away? It's inconceivable in an academic community such as mine. Especially factoring the importance of its author into the equation. I tell myself it was this book or my life, but I still have a hard time truly believing I've made the right choice.

"Do you know where Templeton will be?" I ask Antonia, still curled into an egg-shape on the floor.

"Just look up," she tells me, muffled under feathers. "Whether or not he's already done what he promised to do, he'll be up there."

I'm not entirely sure what she means, but I think I have an idea.

I hear the emergency locks click open, and I push the door with my one good arm. It's heavy, much heavier than I could have imagined, but it does slide open eventually. The flames are already beginning to subside, but the pile of black ash is far beyond saving. Without looking, I ask Antonia to come with me. There's still enough left of the old Isabelle Donhelle to want to help this poor girl. I haven't changed completely.

"No. Leave me here," she whimpers. "I don't want to go out there anymore. Not like this."

Still without looking at her, I step outside, back into the lab. But I wait for her, and again beg her to come with me.

"Just leave me," she keeps weeping. "Leave me."

I try to imagine just how many lies Antonia must have had to believe in order to get to where she is now. I wonder what else I could have done; how many more lies I should have told her just to keep her in that orphanage in Ville Constance. To keep her inside the safest possible nest.

But I don't have an answer for myself. I turn around and leave her for good.

~~~

The school seems so empty. And quiet. There are no more Parasitic Jaegers (*Stercorarius parasiticus*) screeching. No more Grey Shrikes (*Lanius excubitor*) shrieking. The horrible sounds I'd grown accustomed to hearing since coming back to Boston are gone. The dark of night lurks outside the windows, but I don't know if this is still Monday, or if I've been sealed away from the world for much longer than that.

I stop by my office to find it's been completely overturned. Somebody was looking for something in here. What exactly, I'm not certain. The textbooks and field journals from my bookshelf have all been tossed to the floor. My ornithology diploma still hangs on the wall, but the glass frame has been smashed. The bottle of wine remains unharmed, and I pop the cork with my one good arm and guzzle some of it down, hoping to numb the pain. As I do, I notice the once-sealed wooden box, the years-old gift from the Diaz family, lies open on the floor. The superstition was that if its contents were ever revealed to me, bad luck was destined to follow. What those contents might have been is a mystery though, since it appears empty. I don't know whether this curse still applies, or if my current situation is trumping whatever preordained bad luck was meant to befall me.
~~~

Across the hall from my office, I notice Mrs. Claus has already got her Christmas decorations up. She must have done this while I was away, since I don't remember the gaudy display being there before I left. Snowmen, impish Santas, smiling trees, and penguins. I don't know when the penguin ever became such a relevant icon for the holidays, but I put it out of my mind, and continue down the hall toward the exit. I bump the wall with my broken arm. The wine is already throwing me off balance.

Upon opening the door to the parking lot, I'm frozen in fear by what I see: the ground is littered with birds, but this time they're unmoving.

They're all dead.

I almost step on a muster of dead Wood Storks (*Mycteria americana*), piled on top of one another just outside the door. In fact, the majority of the birds seem to be along the exterior of the school, as though they'd all flown to their deaths against the cold, brick walls. I don't see any signs of life, and I think the silence is much scarier than when the air was filled with that now-absent clamor.

I crouch down to inspect some of the birds at my feet. Their beaks and skulls are crushed. There's blood everywhere. I convince myself that blocking out this massacre is really my only option.

On the university rooftop, at the northeast corner, something odd catches my attention: one of the six giant fiberglass swans is perched on the edge of the roof. The white of the bird stands out significantly against the night sky. The swan seems ominous, but its purpose will have to remain a mystery for the time being. I escaped from that vault in the lab for one reason alone: to find Templeton Rate.

I'm out on Parker Street now. The wine and the freezing air have combined to numb my left arm to the point where I barely feel the pain anymore. My bloodied, fuzzy penguin socks leave faint pink footprints in the snow. Strangely, the entire city is completely dark, with no lights on anywhere in sight.

As far as I can see, there is destruction everywhere. Apartments and storefronts have all had their windows smashed. The windshields of cars are caved-in, their hoods dented. And there are piles upon piles of dead birds. It's so uncomfortable, and so incredibly hard to stomach. There's a misty haze everywhere, like a dusty sort of chemical filling the air. It tickles my skin. It's scary, and it makes me think of Lake Avernus, the ancient lake the Romans once believed to be a gateway to Hell. The one with the toxic fumes that would kill any bird in its vicinity. Because Hell was a place without birds, and now I'm right in the middle of it.

I think back to the thick fog on Halloween night in Salem, but this is even more frightening since there's no one else around to reassure me things will be okay. Even if they were lying. I have to stop myself for a moment when I consider how much further outside of Boston this catastrophe might have struck. I try not to breathe any of the mist in, and I make my way northeast toward the intersection of Parker and Huntington.

I near the Museum of Fine Arts, and atop its neoclassical portico, I spot another giant swan. Again, there's no indication as to why it would be there, but when and if the city should ever care to start looking for their six precious lagoon swan boats again, I'll at least be able to tell them where to start.

There are still no lights anywhere. The only illumination cast upon me is from the glow of the moon. I look up, and recall what Antonia had said to me when I wondered how I might ever find Templeton again. *"Just look up,"* is what she instructed me to do. So I do, and the first thing that catches my attention is the tip of the Prudential Tower. The dreams I've shared with Templeton tell me to head in that direction.

Even along Huntington Avenue, there are still birds everywhere. I spot a pile of dead Short-Tailed Albatrosses (*Phoebastria albatrus*). I see the same two ostriches from earlier, their bodies now lying dead on the subway tracks. There's so many species out here, it's like an avian zoo. Or maybe more like a museum, considering how lifeless they are.

I try to come to a reasonable conclusion as to why and how all of this has happened. It's almost as though these birds simply fell from the sky. Some of them hit the streets or smashed into parked cars, others crashed through windows. My first thought is it must have been caused by whatever this chemical is in the air. Perhaps this really is some kind of deadly, toxic gas. But I've walked a mile already, and it hasn't slowed me down, giving no indication the gas might be poisonous.

Because birds fly by the use of navigation along the Earth's magnetic fields, I consider whether the answer might be related in this way. An electromagnetic pulse would not only temporarily damage the magnetic field, sending the birds into chaotic tailspins, but it would probably also knock out power to the city at the same time, which is a good indication as to why the streetlights are all dead too. It seems like something right out of a science fiction movie, but I'm finding more and more that my ability to believe in anything — and I mean absolutely *anything* at all — has become far less filtered over the past few weeks.

Still, all of these puzzle pieces are just that. And I'm afraid if they should all come together, things might make even less sense to me.

A little farther east on Huntington is the Prudential Tower. Its radio mast points like an arrow to Heaven. Or maybe acting as a marker for it. I run across the Prudential Center courtyard, but I stop cold when I see three dead

Southern Cassowaries (*Casuarius casuarius*) on the grass. These giant, Australian flightless birds are strikingly beautiful with their blue face and neck, but they are also fearsome with their sharp toe claws and horn-like casques. The loss of these creatures saddens me, but I also feel a little relief, as there may have been no way I could've come so close to the front entrance if it was still guarded by these dangerous animals.

Conveniently, the front door to the tower has been left wide open for me. The elevator doesn't seem to be working, but the stairwell is also open. Running up fifty-two floors has never seemed so inviting to me as it does right now.

But if every step I take is meant to bring me a little closer to Heaven, then why do I feel as though Hell is the more probable destination?

Broken Heaven

WITH ALL MY strength, I push the heavy door to the rooftop of the Prudential Tower open and step outside. It's cold up here, and the air seems thinner than it did when I was down on the streets below. I feel a bit disoriented. Dizzy. Light-headed. I assume this is only because I'd just run across the city and up fifty-two floors with a sore tailbone and a broken arm on half a bottle of red wine.

Once I finally catch my breath, I take a look over the rooftop's edge. If it was quiet back down on street level, then here above the city it's like deep space. The stars seem brighter now without the luminous effluence of the city lights below. The thin mist that had been hanging in the air does not exist up here. Everything is as quiet as death. "The calm before the storm" is the phrase that first comes to mind, but it feels as though the storm might have already happened.

With my eyes, I follow along Exeter Street and Newbury until I spot the rooftop of my own apartment building. I can barely see it through the cloudy vapors below. It appears so small and sad from up here. I wonder if this is what the gulls had seen every morning, and if they had imagined my loneliness before jumping from this exact spot. Before hanging in the air, as if suspended by magic. Before rubbing it in my face, that moment I'd been most jealous of.

I turn my head and look along the cold, icy rooftop to the southeast. And this is when I see the giant fiberglass swan, perched on the corner and overlooking all of downtown Boston. A shadowy figure sits behind it, exactly where the peddler of the Lagoon's swan boat would have sat. He's smoking a cigarette, and ignoring my arrival completely.

Hesitantly, I step closer to Templeton. I decided to come up here for a number of reasons, but what sickens me and saddens me the most, is the most selfish of reasons: that I might try and find some closure to our relationship.

If I hadn't gone to The Strangest Feeling that night, he'd have found me anyway.

Closer still. The ice and snow crunch under every cautious footstep I take. He must know there's someone here. I don't know why, but I start to feel a little bit sorry for him at this moment. He looks so lonely up here by himself, with only the moon and his thoughts. He stares out into the misty nothingness of the city below us. After all of the awful things he's already done, it seems as though he's regretting something; some decision he had made that he can't make sense of anymore. The first thing I think of is the night I'd seen him crying at my window. He said he loved me that night. It was the worst lie anyone has ever told me.

If I hadn't believed him that night, he'd have fooled me eventually.

I move even closer now, still without uttering a word. I want to ask him what's wrong. I want to ask him what it is he feels at this moment, and if there's something I can do to make things better. But that's exactly how I've treated this man ever since I've known him, and that is not the way to deal with a person like Templeton Rate. Besides, I have no idea what he could say to me right now that could possibly satisfy any of my feelings. He still scares me. As much sorrow as he's brought upon me, and as much tragedy as he's brought upon everyone else, I still can't seem to find the words that need to be said. Those laudable words that would make me the hero in my own sad, little world.

I'm standing right next to him now. The freezing air exhaling from within me intertwines with the smoke from his cigarette. Neither of us can speak.

Not me, because I'm too scared and still in too much stinging pain. And not him, because he always waits for me to go first. Even when he knows I don't want to. Especially when he knows I'm too scared to say the first words. He just sits there, sucking that cigarette. Even if there is something on his mind wanting to be set free, he still intends to ignore me completely until I can find the courage to speak first. He holds the once-amphibious change purse in his hand. He rolls it around in his palm. He squeezes it so the front legs kick out from his grip, and then fall limp as he lets go. Again and again.

I recall the first time I'd seen him. We were on the bus. I felt so awkward and uncomfortable, and I'd wished he would stop staring at me so I could continue my search into the void of the X-shaped screw in front of me. But this sensation I feel now is nearly the complete opposite of that moment. As if I might be the one making him anxious. I wish I could remember what it was he said to me that night on the bus that made me so scared of him, because I'd like to say the same words to him now. But what if I opened my mouth, and all I could ask him is whether or not he still loves me? Just as I had asked Professor Nickwelter in the backseat of his car in one of my most ridiculous moments of utter weakness.

And whether it's simply to break the silence, or if he's finally just given up on waiting for me, Templeton speaks. "All I wanted to do was change the world." He doesn't turn to me. His voice is laced with more than a hint of regret, failure, and personal dissatisfaction. I don't believe I've ever heard him speak this way. He's never been anything less than the most confident man I've known. He nonchalantly tosses the frog in his hand off the rooftop, deep into the misty emptiness below us. "That's all any of us wants out of life, isn't it? To change this fucking world?"

"That's impossible," I finally say, and I'm surprised to find I'm still a bit out of breath. "Nobody can actually change the world."

He stays fixed on what seems to be the tiniest of spots within the city. "You read the journal, didn't you? By now I'm sure you're aware of the plans Nelson Hatch had for us. You must know that nothing is too far from the impossible. I mean, how hard would it have been for that chicken to fly for fourteen seconds? We could have done it. But the human race got lazy, didn't they? It's always all talk, no action with these people. You did read that journal, right?"

Yes, I read the journal. I saw the winged pigs and frogs. Page by page, they slowly evolved into winged men. I read what Nelson Hatch had written. I read every word and saw every helix of DNA he'd scribbled onto those pages. I saw the blueprints for Claude's regenerated wing. I saw the white, feathery wings under Jerry Humphries' trench coat right before he knocked me unconscious and locked me away. Before he tried to deny me something I'm sure I wouldn't have wanted anyway.

Yes, I saw everything I needed to see in that journal. And all of the answers might have been right there in front of me, but still, all I want to know right now is: Why? Why hurt me like you did? Why tell me you loved me, when it's obvious you didn't? Why let me believe I was something special, when it's clear that I'm not? "Why, Templeton?"

"Why? Because this is the way things were meant to be, Isabella. Remember what I told you that night in the graveyard?"

"You mean the night you and your mercenaries burned that house down?"

Not surprisingly, he chooses to ignore my question completely. "I told you that to molt is to change."

Physically or psychologically.

"To change is to evolve," he says.

Temporarily or permanently.

"It all comes down to evolution." He takes a long drag of the cigarette. "That's all I was doing here." And he blows the smoke out the side of his mouth. "In a way."

"But this way—It always has to be *your* way, doesn't it?"

Of course, he ignores this question too. At least he turns to face me now. There are tears in his eyes, just like that night at my apartment. The night he said those three horrible words.

"This was everyone's big chance," he tells me. "And somehow it all got fucked up."

I have no idea what he means, because things seem about as bad as they could possibly be right now. What else could he have been trying to prove? What more could he have done to hurt me? As poor as his marks were in my class, I never believed Templeton Rate could possibly fail at anything.

"I thought I had worked out all of the details," he continues. "I did all of the tests I needed to do. You saw Jerry Humphries, didn't you? You saw what I did!" I still don't speak. Any of the stupid words that want to come out of my mouth are held back by the searing pain now returning to my broken arm. Templeton directs his own arm out across the city. "But take a look out there. Where are they all? Do you see any fucking angels?"

This is just what Humphries had asked me earlier. Although, where Humphries had been blaming the non-existence of angels on an interruption of faith, Templeton was blaming it on some failure of science.

He gets up from his seat behind the swan. I didn't notice before, but now I see that this gigantic bird has some sort of electronic device attached to its beak: a metallic cylinder with copper wire wrapped around it, and what appears to be a transformer connected to one end. I also see the familiar box of old, dusty journals sitting inside the hollow swan.

Templeton walks closer to the edge, and takes a look down the side of the tower. "There's *nobody* out there!" He flicks the cigarette out of his fingers, and it hovers in the air for moment before blowing fifty-two floors away from us. "I was giving them everything they would've needed. But I failed."

"Who are *you* to make these decisions anyway? You don't have the right to make people's minds up for them, to force your beliefs on them. You never did." His back is still turned to me, still looking out over the edge for something that was never there. "This world won't accept it."

He whips around, turning to me accusingly. Trying to connect pieces in his head. Forcing pieces that have no right fitting together. "You?" he says, with fire in his dark eyes. "You did it, didn't you? You threw the wrench into all of this. You wrecked it all for everyone!"

"What? Me?" A part of me worries I already know more than I should, while another part of me thinks this man is giving me far more credit than I deserve. This is another side of Templeton I've never seen before: he's mad at me. And he's mad altogether; crazed. I'm terrified, and I tighten my arms into myself forgetting how serious the injury to my left arm is. "I didn't do any of this. This is all *your* fault!" I try to convince him. "But if I had known how to stop any of this I would have."

Templeton studies my face for a moment. He studies my words too, as if trying to find some way to tell if I'm being honest or not. "You know more than you give yourself credit for, Bella. It's like you told me before: '*Change is one thing, but evolution dictates another thing entirely.*'"

"You've lost your mind, you know that? This isn't evolution."

"Sure it is. Evolution is what separated the continents. It raised the mountains, and wore them back down again. Climates shifted, plant life flourished, and habitats disappeared. Species died because they had to die, and then new ones took their places. Lifeforms evolved to suit their ever-changing environments. But evolution doesn't have to be something that just *happens* over time anymore. It's become something we can actually *control* now. Why wouldn't science be the right way to take us to where we're meant to be? What would the purpose of science be, if not to change us?"

In the university library, Templeton Rate waited until he saw the first changes within me.

He says, "Since the dodo was destroyed, seventy-eight other species of birds have become extinct. And more than half of those were due to mankind's corrosive ways. Before we know it, we're going to wipe ourselves out."

For Halloween, Templeton Rate wanted me to try being something new.

He says, "But just because we like to kill ourselves doesn't mean we can't better ourselves at the same time. If one man can enact change through science, then another can just as easily prevent it, correct?" His brown eyes flicker; they're now accusing me of changing more than I should have. "So, what did you do?" he asks me. "Did you tamper with the flux compression generators? Did you sabotage the chemicals I'd injected into the birds? What was it? How did you ruin everything for everyone?"

"I already told you. I didn't do anything! I've just been thrown into this whole mess, without any way of getting out. This is *your* fault, not mine."

"It's not like that at all, Bella. You weren't caught anywhere with your ornithological pants down. You were exactly where you were meant to be. Why do you think I went to all the trouble just to find you in the first place?"

"You mean on the bus that night?"

"No. This goes back much further than your silly birthday party. I've known about Hawthorne University's great Professor Donhelle for quite some time. That's why I came to the school. You're the only reason I ever came to Boston. You knew everything I needed to know. I only needed to learn from the best."

I can't imagine this is who Templeton has really been all along. Although the more I think about it, the more it actually makes sense.

"You disappoint me, Isabella. I thought you of all people would desire change."

"But I *have* changed. Maybe not in the way *you* wanted me to. Maybe not in the way you wanted *everybody* to change, but I can't deny it anymore. I'm not the same person I was a month ago. Before *you* came along. I was a completely different person before I met you."

"Everybody was," he proudly declares. "That's the point though. Everybody in this world needed a change, but they couldn't do it — or at least, they weren't willing to do it — on their own. They all got lazy, and just rested on their crooked beliefs. Fuck-ups like Nickwelter believed some sort of redemption could make up for all of the mistakes they'd made in their lives; some miracle to wipe the slate clean. Dipshits like Jerry Humphries all believed that Jesus was coming back, to bring to them whatever it was the world needed. A time of peace on Earth without war or poverty or dumbasses who are dumber than they are. But you know what I say? Let's just cut out all of this Messianic bullshit crap, and get to the fucking point already. It's all just talk and no action, right?"

I think about when he told me religion could bring out the strangest ideas, even in seemingly intelligent people. I remember the story he told me about when he was a boy and he met that stranger in church. The stranger who I believed was actually Templeton's own father. That was the day when Templeton — or Matthew, or whatever his name really was — had decided to form his own beliefs. "So, you brought it upon yourself to do something about it? Is that it? You thought mutating everyone would really solve all of the world's problems?"

"It couldn't hurt. Everybody dreams of flying. You told me so yourself when you tried to enlighten me with your *own* dreams. And you were right; those dreams were the same dreams that Tony had. They were the same dreams that Mitchie dreamed. Zirk and Humphries, too."

Ask anyone what they would want if they possessed the power to have anything at all; ninety percent of those telling the truth will tell you they wish they could fly.

"When I first came to this school to find you, I met another girl. She was a student of yours. I think her name was Summer, but I don't really remember. Maybe she just looked like a Summer. One night, she told me her dreams; she just blurted them out right then and there. Right when I had her bent over the bed. I never asked her to tell me. And guess what her dream was? She wanted to fly as well. She had tears in her eyes just thinking about the whole thing. She knew deep inside her this was how we were all supposed to be. So, I told her I could give that to her. I told her more, too. But I made the mistake of telling her everything. She freaked out. I told her that maybe I couldn't force her to believe in the same things I believed in, but at the very least, I could make her accept it."

These are same words he said to me in the parking lot. Ironically, that was the day when I had actually *stopped* believing in him.

"She threatened me. I couldn't believe it when she said she would actually call the police. We were having a good time up until then. I think it was probably the Ecstasy though, now that I think about it. But she never got the chance to make that phone call."

I think back to the morning I was sitting on the sidewalk outside Templeton's apartment. I remember the picture of the girl on the telephone pole. Her name was Autumn, not Summer.

"After that, I learned to keep my beliefs to myself. And between you and the journals of Nelson Hatch, I had all of the answers I needed. Because *he* had the same idea *I* did. It was Nickwelter himself who had told me stories of those books when he asked me for a way to help him. And that's where we are now."

"The glorious age of Templeton Rate," I say the words, and I shiver with fright. Templeton is even more dangerous than I thought. How many more Autumns and Becky Chandlers were there?

"If that's what you want to call it. But I wasn't doing this for myself."

He doesn't notice when I begin to back away from him. He's too caught up in his delusions.

"I was doing this for *everybody*."

I've backed right up to the giant swan now. I run my trembling fingers down its icy neck, and into the alcove between its shoulders.

"And I was waiting here for everyone to come up and thank me for what I'd done. But the only person who showed up was you."

Is it possible that Templeton Rate is really doing good for the world? Are the changes I dream of not as selfish as I first thought? Maybe I was fine, and it was the world that needed to change, just as Templeton has advocated all along? Maybe everybody does want the same thing?

If Templeton Rate had been telling this story, he'd almost make you believe it.

"How was I to know?" he asks, "How was I to know you were going to ruin everything?" I don't answer him, but he seems content with not receiving an answer from me anyway. He inches closer.

I reach inside the swan. I feel the thick spine of one of the journals. Did Nelson Hatch truly share the same ideas? Was he just as passionately fanatical as Templeton? Was he just as foolish? Maybe he was simply missing something. One small piece of the puzzle that Templeton found when he found me.

I take the journal into my right hand. My one good hand.

Templeton's eyes are on fire. I see a hatred inside him now that can only scratch the surface of what truly courses through his veins. He moves closer with the fullest intention of destroying me. "You ruined everything!"

His fist slams into my face, and there's the dreadful sound of wet skin against bone. Red blood spurts from my eye and onto the white of the swan. The pain equals all of the emotional hurt I've allowed to pile up inside me for the last twenty-nine years. I clutch the book tighter in my unseen hand.

He jabs me in the neck, and the pain reminds me of the night at the graveyard, when he left me freezing and locked out of my car.

He elbows me in the ribs, and it hurts as much as when I watched him standing there in the parking lot. When I drove away from him for the last time.

He kicks my left arm, and there's a pain that doubles what I felt when I snapped my ulna and it pierced the skin.

He kicks me again. I can't even tell where his foot lands because it hurts so much. It hurts as much as it did when I first met Templeton Rate.

I'm sitting on the bus again. His hand covers the screw. His bottomless eyes search inside my own. He has plans for me. I want him to turn away and let me go. But I also want him to keep looking, and to realize all of his ideas are wrong. I want him to get off that bus, so I don't have to.

I want him to leave me alone.

I want him to forget about me. Forget about Humphries and Nickwelter. Forget about Nelson Hatch and my students and the rest of this world.

I want him to forget about his broken Heaven.

And I want him to go to Hell.

It's in this precise moment when I remove my arm from the inside of the swan, and I use all of the pain he's given me. I focus that pain through the journal of Nelson Hatch, and I use it to knock out his front teeth. Templeton stumbles back a little, and I swing the book right into his jaw. I throw it at him, only missing by inches. The journal sails over the edge of the rooftop and hangs in the air for just a moment, before disappearing from sight.

I take another book from inside the bird, and toss it. I throw another. And another. And another, until the sky is full of bird-shaped books, their covers and pages flapping in the wind and descending deep into the city.

"Go to Hell!" I scream at him. There's only one book left in the box. I take it into my hand and with everything I have left, I throw it. The book doesn't miss. It hits Templeton hard enough in the mouth that he falls; he falls right over the edge of the rooftop.

I wish I could have seen the look on his face, but all I could see through my bloody tears was the final silhouette of Templeton Rate: the X-shape of his arms and legs spread wide. Just like the void I stared into on the bus.

He hangs in the sky for a moment before falling fifty-two stories to the courtyard below.

Swallowed by the mists of Lake Avernus.

Through the gateway that leads to Hell.

How poetic I thought, before throwing up one last time.

Epilogue

TRUTHFULLY, I DON'T know any more if that was where the story ended or if I had simply released everything I had left inside of me.

I didn't know whether it was day or night when I had finally pulled myself to the rooftop's edge and looked down.

I didn't know for sure if it was toxic gas I saw below me, or if I was floating above clouds like the fortune teller had once foretold. I remember her saying to me my death would be something important.

I didn't know if I was dead or if I was still alive. Had I woken from a dream, or was I still trapped in a nightmare? How does one know these things?

I didn't know the difference between what was real and what was imagined when all I saw below me was a sky filled with birds and men.

I didn't know if my arm was still broken.

I didn't know what it was my hand had discovered when I reached behind me to feel something on my back.

But I knew then that I had changed. And I smiled because I knew I'd finally deserved it.

END

From the Author

Molt is my baby. The first book I ended up writing, when I decided to try writing a book. It began as a challenge for myself; having gone through a disheartening rut of starting projects — mostly art, animation, and comic books — and never finishing them. It wasn't until I'd attempted a novella for a local 3-day novel writing contest (*what was I thinking?*) that I discovered this addiction to fiction, and realized the creative power behind the written word. I was happy with that short story, but immediately wanted to write something bigger. *A novel? Could I actually write a novel?* It seemed like something impossible. Something so far out of my reach or know-how. Still, I was lured by the challenge of it all. But what would I write about?

I was on the bus, crossing Vancouver's Granville Street Bridge, and staring up at one of the looming, innocuous towers along False Creek. There was a bunch (a *colony*, they're properly called, as I would later learn) of seagulls on the top of that building. And for some reason, I kept my eye on them. I watched as they suddenly jumped off the edge and into the sky, held in place for a moment by the wind, and then flapped off to wherever seagulls happen to go. With a freedom unknown to me; not in a seat on a bus moving northbound along a bridge. They were completely unhindered, unanchored by the world I knew.

And I was so jealous of that moment.

It sparked the very slow creation of a story about a girl resistant to change. This girl would meet a boy; a boy who wants nothing more than to change *everything*.

I passed on my jealousy of those seagulls to Isabelle Donhelle and eventually came out of it with a book called Molt.

This story changed me, too. And as soon as it was finished, I had to write more. So really, I owe everything to those seagulls.